The Candidate's Husband

Wendy Sacks Jones

SRL PUBLISHING

SRL Publishing Ltd
London

www.srlpublishing.co.uk

First published worldwide by SRL Publishing in 2025

SRL PUBLISHING
THINKING DIFFERENTLY, DELIVERING CHANGE

ISBN: 978-1-915073-55-6

3 5 7 9 10 8 6 4 2

A CIP catalogue record for this book is available from the British Library

SRL Publishing is a climate positive publisher offsetting more carbon emissions than it emits.

To the author's husband, whose support has been unwavering.

I remember something you once said. Men should be banned from politics, it would save a lot of trouble if they were. That's more or less how you put it. Keep men out of politics, leave it all to women. It was a joke of sorts, a late-night joke as I opened a second bottle of wine and you continued to unpick the world's problems. Men don't think things through, you said. They're impetuous, programmed by their hormones, prisoners of their sex. They make bad decisions, for themselves and for the other half of the population. First World War to Iraq, there's always a pattern – men screw up and the world would be a better place if they didn't run it. I laughed and refilled your glass. Here's to you, Kirsty. Another of your dazzling ideas.

That was years ago, of course, just the two of us at the kitchen table in our old flat, the hypothesis exhausted but you still blazing with righteousness. But it comes back to me now as we sit, still the two of us, in another, bigger kitchen, the press mob outside, baying for blood, your blood, intent on maximising your shame. It's early morning, barely light, and the house creaks, stretching its limbs at the end of a sleepless night. Your ebullience is gone, your confidence now paper-thin. Don't say I didn't warn you. Right at the beginning, I told you. Politics is a rough business. Malicious. Threatening. Dangerous. And there really are special tortures reserved for women. I told you and you took no notice.

But there's no point in dwelling on that. It's time to go. You put on your grey coat, unpin the rosette from the lapel and give me a watery smile. The front door bell rings. There's been a short lull. Now it's starting again, and the bell is followed by a knock on the window. They're out there in strength, interest in the story fortified by the absence of any firm rebuttal.

'Right,' I say. 'We go straight to the car. Don't look at the cameras. Don't say anything – "good morning", if you like, nothing else. And whatever you do, don't have a go at them. Ready?'

'Ready,' you reply.

I open the door and step out ahead of you. It's trying to rain. The press pack seems momentarily caught off its guard. Reporters and photographers are idling on the pavement, on our drive, talking to each other. Perhaps we'll make it to the car unnoticed. But a voice calls out 'Kirsty', there's a flash of cameras and microphones are thrust in your direction.

The worst day in your life is underway.

Part One

A Vacancy

It all started, obliquely, with sex. I guess everything in life starts with sex and some things end there, too. It was Tuesday evening, I was working late and someone had been hammering nails into my right temple most of the day. I wanted to go home, but a blank document sat open on my screen, demanding my attention. All I had to produce was a short editorial, five-hundred lawyer-proof words with which to hold to account an errant politician – male, naturally, one of those who in that ideal world of Kirsty's wouldn't exist.

A local MP stands accused… It was a start. *A local MP stands accused of sexual impropriety.* It should have been straightforward, except editorials like this never are. The real story has to be tucked between the lines. I pressed on, my fingers playing the keyboard, the thoughts working themselves into phrases, the phrases merging into sentences, an argument in there somewhere.

Earlier that evening, my boss had called me in to talk things through. His office was a large corner cell, two sides glass, looking out onto the newsroom. It was just the two of us: him, Clive Pascoe, managing editor of *The Humberside Citizen*, and me, Rick Dewhirst, his deputy, the underappreciated workhorse who made sure we produced a paper every day. All the others had left, but the door was firmly shut and the atmosphere close. It must have been nudging freezing point in the Hull night outside, but here, in Clive's greenhouse of an office, we were locked in our own micro-climate. He stood glaring at me, a single bead of sweat making its way down his forehead and disappearing under the rim of his glasses.

'For fuck's sake, the accusations are… well, who the hell are these women? No names. It's dodgy.'

I was leaning against the wall next to a framed, yellowing certificate, *Regional Newspaper of the Year, Highly Commended, 1987*. Once upon a time, this had been a paper going places. But that was long before I arrived, long before Kirsty forced us to move to Hull, long before life imploded. The frame was slightly askew. I resisted the urge to straighten it. Our conversation was about to change down into a lower, deeper, uglier gear.

'You know what this is, don't you?' A finger jabbed the air in my direction. 'It's a witch hunt. Except the witches aren't the ones being hunted.'

He nodded with satisfaction, as if the words exposed an evident truth.

'Another decent man doing an important job, and they go for him. It's a conspiracy. Poor sod doesn't stand a chance.'

He left a pause to allow this further batch of truths to sink in. Somewhere in the world outside a police siren whined.

'And what's he done? An appreciative pat on the backside, I bet you, a compliment whispered in the ear, nothing more. I mean, we've all done it, haven't we?'

No, Clive, we haven't. We don't all behave like that.

But it wasn't worth the breath. Let him simply run out of steam. Kirsty would get that. Don't dignify his rubbish with a response, she'd say, stick to the moral high ground. So I said nothing and stared through the glass at the empty desks in the newsroom as he bleated on. The place always looked dismal at night. There was something about it when it was unoccupied, when human activity no longer disguised its essential shabbiness. It badly needed redecoration and refurbishment, but redecoration and refurbishment weren't part of the management's business plan. The grimy cream walls were crying out for a lick of paint, the cheap nineties desks and chairs were hanging in, just, and the thin beige – or was it grey? – carpet had absorbed all manner of unguents over the years and long since given up hope of ever being cleaned.

I turned back. He was now pacing round his office.

'Don't get me wrong, I've got a lot of respect for women. But let's face it, what's happening now is crazy. One move they object to and you're on the sex offenders' register, your career in ruins, your life well and truly fucked.'

Like the newsroom, Clive sometimes struggled in the twenty-first century. He was a throwback to a former, grubbier age. I unfolded my arms, wiped my cheek – his last observation had been delivered with a light spray of spittle – and pushed myself away from the wall.

'Have you done, Clive?'

He wheeled around and looked fazed by my question.

'Two simple points,' I said. 'Unwanted touching is assault and no-one's above the law. That's all there is to it.'

'Pfft.'

The word, if it was a word, hung in the air like the final splutter of a broken engine. It was debatable how much Clive genuinely believed this crap and how much he just enjoyed trying to wind me up – not that I was easily wound. I came close to it once when Kirsty had been at the receiving end of his behaviour, but I wasn't going to think about that now.

'Can we get back to specifics?' I said. 'After all, what we're dealing with here looks like being more than patting a backside.'

The rumours about an unnamed 'senior politician' had been circulating for a week or so. They bobbed around on social media, fragments of innuendo, wisps of invention. The digital stratosphere is full of stuff like that, pathetic allegations, personal point-scoring. It comes from nowhere and fades into nothing. But these messages had refused to evaporate. They became more insistent, more explicit, less cryptic. It was obvious that someone prominent was in deep shit.

From the outset I'd had a hunch who it was. Martin Barraclough was the Shadow Home Secretary and MP for North Humberside. Our local man. Someone we all knew, someone who visited foodbanks and old people's homes, who presented prizes at Kirsty's school, someone who was in the paper all the time. And someone it was easy to dislike. Barraclough was an arrogant so-and-so, with an old-fashioned reputation as a ladies' man – the term now felt shot through with irony. Over the years, various tales had done the rounds, but no-one had taken them seriously, or perhaps had chosen not to. Not until now.

I started to dig. If I was right, this had the makings of a massive local story, even if its epicentre was Westminster. I didn't tell Clive – he and the MP were old cronies, bastards both, cut from the same crude template. Nor did I mention it to Kirsty. It seemed wiser not to. She was a party member and knew people locally. I didn't want her alerting them, just in case I was wrong. Anyway she would probably have tried to persuade me it had to be a Tory. I needed to be cautious in my enquiries.

In the end however, those enquiries got me precisely nowhere. The phone was slammed down on me, my calls weren't returned. I was drawing nothing but blanks. After two frustrating days I still had no more than that hunch to go on. I certainly didn't have a story. I should have been down there, at Westminster, putting myself about, in the Lobby, in the bars, picking up the gossip, finding out who knew what. Instead I was stuck in an obscure newspaper office nearly two hundred miles north. No-one was going to talk to *The Humberside Citizen*.

And so I had to just sit and watch it play out elsewhere – another paper's scoop, someone else's byline. That afternoon the website of a national tabloid with a large circulation – and enough in the coffers to take risks – had blazoned the headline, *Barraclough faces sex attack claims*. I was vindicated. I was also bitterly envious.

The MP's accusers were anonymous, two women he'd worked with at Westminster apparently, although the paper hinted there were others. On the face of it, the published story seemed insubstantial, but if it had got past their lawyers, then it must have been reasonably solid. Barraclough had been in Parliament since the early nineteen-nineties, part of the resurgence of Labour, once a figure of hope, a future leader, some had said. Now his career appeared to be not so much juddering to a halt as heading off a cliff. Mine in contrast was just idling along. I'd failed to get the story and all I could do was write a sanctimonious editorial.

But not even that, if Clive had his way.

'It's too risky, legally' he said.

'There's a bigger risk in ignoring it. It'll look as if we haven't got a clue what's going on, we're out of touch. Or…'

I slowed down. I was about to deliver the decisive blow.

'Or worse, we're in cahoots with Barraclough.'

I'd hit home and Clive's face showed it. In my mind, Kirsty was already congratulating me. You've done it, Rick, you've got him. He took his glasses off and looked into the middle distance. It was the moment to press my advantage.

'We've asked him to respond,' I said. 'He hasn't. So we ask again – publicly.'

Clive turned towards me.

'The *Citizen* calls on Martin Barraclough to break his silence and speak out on the allegations. He owes it to his constituents,' he said slowly. 'Is that it?'

'Exactly.'

'It'll be thoroughly lawyered.'

'Obviously.'

'And I want to see it before it goes.'

'Naturally.'

'Well in that case, fuck off and get on with it.'

All this had taken about fifteen minutes but it was worth it. A necessary process. I went back to my desk in the newsroom to savour my victory. And to bask in Kirsty's imminent approval. A small thing maybe, but she'd be proud of me for holding my ground. I spent a lot of time second-guessing my wife's judgement. What would she think of this or that? Would she cheer or be disappointed? I carried her around like a hidden barometer, although the mercury could rocket off the scale and sometimes I miscalculated the readings entirely. But this time I was confident. Loyalty to her gender would surely trump loyalty to her party. And she always said hang in there when you're right.

I glanced over at Clive who was riffling through a pile of papers on his desk. He was clearly still annoyed – with me, with himself, with Barraclough for carelessly causing the problem in the first place and almost certainly with the whole of womankind. After a moment, he jumped up, grabbed his coat and scarf and slammed his office door.

'We need to do something about the heating in this place,' he said and was gone.

An hour later, I was giving the editorial a final read-through. I was alone in the newsroom, apart from the cleaner who was making unenthusiastic efforts to remove the day's detritus, collecting mugs, emptying bins and occasionally flicking a feather duster over a keyboard. I smiled at her across the room and she nodded back without altering the slow rhythm of her work. It was doubtful whether the feather duster served any purpose at all.

The place felt a little cooler. Perhaps the heating thermostat had fixed itself. I checked the time – almost nine – and my mind wandered back to Kirsty. She'd be more than half-way through her meeting by now. That night, as usual on the third Tuesday of the month, she was hard at it with her governors, dealing with politics of a different sort. I'd never been in one of her meetings of course, but I could picture them. She and a dozen other people would be seated around trestle tables sandwiched together at the warmer end of the school hall. In front of them were agenda papers stained with coffee mug rings, littered with biscuit crumbs and decorated with doodles. Eyes strayed towards the big wall clock as the evening drew on, voices cut across each other in irritation and every now and then someone stifled a yawn. And there she was, my heroic wife, the one to whom they all looked for explanations and justifications, a headteacher under siege, phone switched off, isolated from the outside world in a dark place of drifting GCSE results, struggling recruitment, declining funds, social deprivation, and hopelessness.

Of course, she didn't see it as hopeless. She loved her relentless job in a way that continued to astound me. Her work was a cause, while mine was merely an honest trade. I didn't have a mission – thank Christ – and I wasn't going to save the world. I certainly wasn't responsible for eighteen hundred kids in one of the poorer parts of Hull.

I looked again at the final paragraphs on my screen and wondered how she would read them.

> *Martin Barraclough has been found guilty of nothing. The accusations against him are as yet unsubstantiated. The allegations may be wholly fabricated. Martin Barraclough may be an innocent man, unjustly framed. But the public needs to know what he has to say. People have the right to hear from their MP. That is how democracy functions.*
>
> *It is up to the Labour Party to decide on Martin Barraclough's political future. But while those decisions are being taken, we appeal to him to end his silence. In the public interest, we offer him the columns of this newspaper to speak to his constituents.*

She'd poke at the piece and pronounce it too bland. Can't you just tell the truth, she'd say. Here's an establishment figure who's assaulted women, abused his power and betrayed the trust of those who voted for him. The big people screwing the little people and thinking they can get away with it. Yes, Kirsty, that's what I should have written. It would have made a pithy editorial.

But that wasn't how things worked. Barraclough was as yet innocent. There were no charges, not even a criminal investigation, it seemed. This was, out of necessity, limp journalism. The fluorescent light immediately above me hummed and flickered, as if objecting to what I'd written. I'd had enough of Martin Barraclough. If I hurried, I could still get home before she did.

As I packed up to go, my phone buzzed several times in quick succession. *Barraclough resigns from front bench…*

Labour leader accepts resignation 'with sadness'… Statement expected shortly… Police investigation underway.

'Shit.'

The word travelled unchecked across the empty newsroom. The cleaner, on her way out, caught my eye, then looked away. So much for the editorial. I opened a new document, ready to bang out a short news piece instead. I'd barely started when Barraclough's statement came in. His resignation as Shadow Home Secretary would take effect immediately. He denied any wrongdoing but would offer the police every assistance with their enquiries into the allegations against him.

There was a brief final sentence. In the circumstances, he was also standing down as MP for North Humberside.

I punched the air. A by-election. Hallelujah. We'd not had a decent political story since Hull's embrace of Brexit and this, with its added components of sex and shame, was even better. There was something deeply satisfying about observing someone's just humiliation. Schadenfreude – a perfect word, and an emotion crucial to journalism. I rarely wondered what it was like to be the man – it was always a man – in the eye of the storm. The feelings of panic, denial, self-loathing… who knew what people went through when they were caught out? They had only themselves to blame.

It was after eleven when I finally switched off the office lights. Clive had rung a couple of times, fussing about the wording of my news piece and threatening to write a political obituary himself tomorrow. A requiem for a dubious ex-friendship, more likely. I didn't care. I was going home.

My car was the only one left in the underground car park. I switched on the ignition and the headlights picked out the skid marks at the bottom of the ramp. I put my foot down. Barraclough was an idiot and I wanted to hear what Kirsty really had to say, something enlightening, something I hadn't thought of – about the principle, not the tawdry details, of course.

But she'd also have more pressing things to share – some new battle at school, no doubt. I was used to her priorities.

**

He's late tonight. And I've got so much to tell him. My God, what a meeting. I knew it was going to be difficult. But it was worse than that. Even Charlie turned up. The first time in ages. It's a mystery to me why that man ever wanted to be a school governor. No interest in kids, far as I can tell. I was rather hoping he'd get turfed off for poor attendance. But we made it into his diary tonight. And a fractious meeting it was too.

We started with the merger. Louise gave her chairperson's cough and made the announcement – she'd talked to the local authority and her opposite number at Humber High and it was off. Pity. We thought they'd welcome it, what with their intake dropping. And two heads in three years. We could have offered them such a lot. Executive head of a two-campus school – I was looking forward to that. But the Humber parents have started a petition. Small is beautiful and so forth. It just isn't going to happen.

Of course Charlie said we should press on, twist their arms, it was a big opportunity to spread the brand. The brand – I ask you. We're a school, not a coffee franchise. But Louise shut him up. We weren't a board of shareholders making a hostile takeover bid for another company, she told him. We were dealing with people's futures, children's and teachers'. Couldn't have put it better myself.

So that was settled, more or less, and we got onto the real business. Exclusions. I've worked so hard to keep the numbers low, to keep kids on the register – the ones who are really struggling. Of course if the police are involved – knives or drugs – well, it's difficult. But failing their mocks, playing up in class a bit, we shouldn't be chucking them out for that. We've got a duty of care to these kids and some of them get precious little of that at home. If we don't stick up for them, who will?

But Louise proposed that we change the policy. Not that it's ever been a formal policy, just usual practice to give kids another chance… and another if they need it. Other schools were being more rigorous, she said, and that was feeding through to results. We needed to think about the school's reputation – as if that was the principle to guide all others. If reputation means cherry-picking exam entrants and getting shot of those who aren't going to get the top grades, it's not one I'm interested in. I told her that and she said, noted Kirsty, but we do need to consider everything. Then Charlie piped up and said, what about pupil referral units? Couldn't we get more of the low-achieving kids with behavioural problems moved to places they're better suited to?

Except he didn't say low-achieving. He said thick.

Honestly, I could have wept. That someone can understand absolutely nothing about the children whose interests he's meant to be serving… Well, people cleared their throats and stared at their papers and I started to explain why thick wasn't a word we recognised at Phoenix Academy, but Louise cut across me and said she was sure everyone understood it was just a turn of phrase. A turn of phrase? God help us.

At times I feel so alone on that board and wonder if

it's all worthwhile. Maybe after eight years I'm getting restless. Taking on another school, an extra thousand students, would have been good. But not much I can do about that now, so I'll just keep going. And if I can make a difference to one kid's life, it has to be worth it. Keep one child off the streets, away from drugs, out of prison, get one child to turn up for their exams, start an apprenticeship or even go to university… help one child to do something useful with their life and not waste it.

Rick laughs when I talk like that. Tells me to get off my soapbox. It's just a job, he says. Once told me I couldn't save the whole world. I wasn't Jesus. Or even Mother Teresa.

Perhaps he's gone to the pub. A bit of bonding with his colleagues is no bad thing. In fact I wish he'd be more enthusiastic about the whole work situation. Being deputy editor of a regional daily paper isn't *bad*. And when that arsehole Clive goes – he's got to go before too long, he's well over sixty – well, then Rick's bound to step into his shoes and perhaps he can breathe some life into the *Citizen*. I'd feel better about having dragged him here in the first place if he'd got the top job. He says he's forgiven me for the move, but I know he hasn't. If I mention it, he shrugs it off, even eight years on.

I've got some papers to go through while I wait for him, some academic work on exclusions. Louise has asked me to look again at our policies and report back. But I'm not giving in. It's wrong and I'll fight. Phil's on my side. You couldn't hope for more in a deputy. Every head needs someone like Phil behind her. Rick doesn't get him. Rick doesn't get a lot of things about my job. Or me, for that matter. He thinks he does. But he doesn't.

**

Her ancient red Mini was in its usual place on the gravel drive. The downstairs lights were on, the sitting room blinds undrawn. I unlocked the front door, called out, 'Hello, anyone home?' and tripped over first a pile of education journals on their way to recycling and then her scuffed black pumps. She always kicked them off at the door and they caught me out every time. Leonard Cohen was wailing in the background – music to drown yourself in the bath to, but she claimed it was uplifting.

She was lying on the older and more comfortable of our two sitting-room sofas, knees bent, skirt scrunched up to her thighs, eyes closed, dozing, gently snoring. A litter of folders and papers lay scattered on the floor next to her, a pen still balanced between fingers resting on her stomach. I bent down to kiss her and was greeted by a semi-conscious groan. She opened her eyes and raised her head.

'You're late. It must be nearly midnight.'

'Sorry. I had–'

'Oh, Rick, what a meeting. I don't know where to start.'

Her usual steamrollering. The energy and the single-mindedness that always beat the tiredness. I was home. And Barraclough was going to have to wait.

'It was a full house. They all turned up.' She was now sitting upright, her knees under her chin, her face lit up at the prospect of her own story. I turned down the music, poured us both a whisky, small for Kirsty, large for me. She took it without missing a beat in her speech. Mergers and exclusions… policies and regulations… league tables and petitions… community politics – the stuff of her life. I nudged her feet out of the way to make space for my bum and perched next to her, one hand on her knee, continuing to follow the narrative torrent, letting it wash over me. My wife was a form of therapy, especially after a day of too much Clive Pascoe. As always, I let myself step over the professional divide between us and enter her world, stand in her place and immerse myself in her problems, blocking out my own. For a few minutes, I could imagine being a headteacher. But that's all it was, imagining. The following day it wasn't me who had to face dictatorial governors, bureaucratic officials, nit-picking inspectors, inadequate staff, lousy parents and beyond-hope kids. Problems at Kirsty's school were chronic and intractable, while matters at the *Citizen* got fixed speedily, decisively. Yes, Clive was a bastard, but at least you knew where you were with him. A quick and dirty row, and you moved on. Each day was a fresh start, a new edition. You had deadlines. There was no time to agonise. I poured myself another whisky, an even larger one.

And still she talked. Charlie… the mind-boggling ignorance. Louise… cowardice, looking for the easy way out. Phil… a rock. Kids who don't stand a chance, except Phoenix has to give them a chance. Poverty of aspiration, deprivation and desperation, systemic failure – Kirsty's lexicon. Most of it swirled over me. But I loved watching her. I always have. I loved the way she took deep breaths at the start of sentences. I loved the way she gesticulated with her hands, sometimes in unison, sometimes one hand taking the lead, the way she looked at me hard to check I was still – loosely – with her.

'Time for bed,' she said suddenly, the signal that she was done. She jumped up, drained her whisky and picked up my empty glass as well. It looked as though Barraclough was consigned to any other business. Perhaps that was all he was worth.

And then she stopped and turned towards me, her brow wrinkled.

'Oh, Rick, I haven't even asked. How was work?

What kept you?' She put down the glasses and rubbed my arm. A sort of apology. She always remembered to ask, eventually.

'Martin Barraclough,' I said. 'He's resigned. Haven't you heard?'

'What? No, I forgot to switch my phone back on. What d'you mean he's resigned? When?'

'Statement came through just before ten.'

'But – resigned – what, from the front bench or as MP?'

'Both.'

'That stuff on social media…'

'Yep.'

'Why didn't you tell me before?'

'Have you ever tried to interrupt you when you're in full flow?'

She ignored that and sat down again heavily, pulling her phone from her bag.

'Did you know this was coming?'

'I had my suspicions.'

'You didn't say anything.'

'Well…'

'What's he accused of?'

'Serious sexual assault. Two women so far.'

She scrolled up and down the screen, slowly twisting side strands of hair.

'Oh God… this is bad, isn't it? Really bad, I mean it's shocking that he's got away with it for so long. If it's true, that is. And it usually is. Women don't invent things like this, why would they? The women… are they okay?' She was still fixed on her phone and there was more hair twisting. 'No, that's a stupid question. How could they be okay?'

'Quite. The honourable member for North Humberside is a serial sex offender from the look of it.

Innocent until proven guilty and all that, but I'd say the bastard deserves whatever he's got coming to him. Lock him up and throw away the keys.'

She looked up from her phone sharply, her lips tightening, creases of irritation at the corners of her mouth. Come on, I could have said, there's no need to take me literally. Why do you never know when I'm joking, or at least half-joking? I get your jokes. Why can't you get mine? But her face suggested it was more than that. Was I appropriating women's exclusive right to condemn a male sex offender? Or was it something else? Once of course she'd been part of his world, research assistant to another MP, years ago, before she turned her back on all that and went into teaching, a proper job.

But she was heading in a direction I should have anticipated. Kirsty never missed an opportunity to enlighten me.

'Facile sentiments don't help anyone, Rick.'

I braced myself for the lecture.

'What you've got to realise is that men like Martin Barraclough are imprisoned in their own obsolescent values, their own distorted sense of male privilege. However much we criminalise their actions, some of them will simply never get it. In fact, there's a part of me that almost feels sorry for him.' She looked down at her phone again and shook her head. 'Almost.'

'I can't believe you're defending him.'

'Of course I'm not. Don't be ridiculous.'

'Just because he's from a different generation, it doesn't excuse—'

She slammed her phone down next to the empty glasses.

'I'm not excusing anyone. I'm simply pointing out that *MeToo* has changed everything – about time, too – and men of a certain persuasion have got left behind. I'm explaining not justifying. Barraclough's caught in an ugly time warp.'

'A time warp? Tell that to the women he's raped.'

'Oh, give it a rest, Rick. You really don't need to prove your credentials with me.' (But I did, I always did, even when they got chucked straight back in my face.) She shook her head as if the world were a disappointing rather than an immoral place. At times it was beyond me how my contrary wife could switch in a trice from despairing at the whole human race to being unfashionably forgiving, her levels of tolerance well above zero. MPs who couldn't keep their flies closed or kids with behaviour problems – to Kirsty they were all faulty humans who needed her sympathy. And apparently I wasn't profound enough to get that. Well we'd see what the courts had to say about Martin Barraclough.

'Come on, I've got to get up early,' she said.

I switched the light off and followed her out of the room. At the top of the stairs, I said, 'What about you? He never tried–'

She paused, her hand on the bedroom door.

'For Christ's sake Rick, I'm a headteacher.'

'But at Westminster, when–'

'We're not talking about me.'

The speculative question was squashed and rubbed into the ground, and I was made to feel foolish for starting to ask it. But what man wouldn't have asked it?

In the bedroom she opened her wardrobe, picked out a skirt and blouse, not dissimilar from what she was wearing, her usual non-descript headteacher's uniform, and placed the hangers on the bedroom door hook. She appraised the outfit with concentration for a moment and then discarded the blouse in favour of another seemingly identical one.

'So what now then?' She was picking specks of fluff

off the skirt on the hanger. 'This must mean a by-election. You're going to be busy.'

'Yep. Safe seat, perhaps, but anything can happen in circumstances like this.'

I slumped onto the bed, watching her as she started to undress. My head was rotating. I shouldn't have had that second double, or more likely triple.

'The party has to pick a woman,' I said.

'You don't say.'

'Any thoughts on who? Off the record, of course.'

She unzipped her skirt and it slipped to the floor.

'I haven't had chance to think.'

'What about Patsy Harvey?'

'Possible. She's done a good job on the council.'

'Or that woman who started the food bank,' I said. 'What's her name? Yasmin something. She's big in the party, isn't she?'

'Again possible. But the National Exec might want to ship in someone more experienced.'

'Or…'

She stood at the foot of the bed in her underwear, brushing her long and faintly greying hair, the outline of young Kirsty still there, if a little blurred round the edges. I took a breath.

'Or Kirsty Osmond.'

See, I could have added, you're not the only one who has dazzling ideas. I can come up with them, too.

'What?'

'You.'

'Yes, I know my name. But–'

'You could do it. You know you could.'

'Oh, come on, Rick. I've got a job to do. A school to run.'

'Exactly. You're a… an experienced headteacher, totally dedicated. And what if… what if you brought all that experience and dedication to bear on… well, on representing the good folk of this constituency?'

'I'm out of all that. Politics for a living? No thanks. I may still go to meetings and help with campaigning, but I've never been on any list. I've never even stood for the council.'

'All the better. Not one of the usual suspects. The voters will love you.'

I let my head sink into the pillow and looked up at the ceiling. A dizzying halo the colour of pale single malt radiated from the overhead light.

'You'd stand a strong chance, you really would. You should go for it.'

At least I think that's what I said, something like that. Kirsty switched off the light and a surprisingly white moon poured into the bedroom. Then she closed the blinds and climbed into bed. She turned away from me and said, 'You're mad.'

I'm late. And the traffic's bad. Not getting to bed till after midnight was a mistake. But the Barraclough business threw me. Why Rick didn't say something sooner, I don't know. And yet the whole thing is somehow unsurprising. Martin was famous for his wandering hands, at least among us assistants. He wasn't the only one, either. We all knew who they were. We knew and we didn't say anything. We were young and that's the way the world was. It was one of the perks of their job and one of the drawbacks of ours. We tried to keep out of their way as much as we could. And yes, Martin did try it on with me, just once, a rather unlovely squeeze of the breast when he'd dropped in looking for my MP and I was in the office by myself. I'd got up from my desk to find a correspondence file and somehow he managed to place himself between me and the shelf I was reaching for. The look on his face – I'm not sure how you'd describe it, a smirk of entitlement perhaps. He was an MP and I was nobody. I froze for an instant but then I kneed him in the groin. He whimpered and said, now what did I do to deserve that? I despised him for his presumptuousness, but I also felt bad. I didn't mean to hurt him.

I never told anyone. What would have been the point? He'd have denied it. My word against his. Not something I'd have wanted following me around Westminster. So I told myself it was just groping and tried to forget it. If I'd said anything to Rick last night, he'd have gone on at me to go to the police. The file's open, they're clearly looking for more victims, he'd have said. Well I'm sorry but I don't want to be a victim. The past is the past, embarrassing, but done. I've got other things to worry about now and I'm not going to resurrect something from years ago. It looks like there are stronger cases anyway, people ready to provide evidence of serious assault. They'll make a far better job of it than I would. I wish them luck, I really do. After that one incident, Martin Barraclough kept out of my way, and when I introduced myself to him at a local party meeting a few years ago, he didn't seem to make any connection between this middle-aged headteacher talking about curriculum change and the young woman who'd hurt his pride and his balls twenty years earlier. Some things really are best forgotten.

Still, one less self-serving male MP has to be good, even if the whole business is uncomfortable for the party. Baggage we should have got rid of long ago. What is it, twenty-five, twenty-six years? Too long for anyone to be an MP. And as Rick so obviously pointed out, Barraclough's replacement has to be a woman. A woman who'll let the people of North Humberside forget their previous bad choice, who'll do her utmost to help those at the bottom of the pile get the lives they deserve, who'll contribute in her own small way to making the world a better place.

Could I?

I mean, it's why I went to work in Parliament in the first place – it was where things got done, and I thought I'd learn how, serve an apprenticeship, evolve into a politician myself. Early on, it was all I ever wanted, the pinnacle of my ambitions. I knew I could do it. It was going to be my life's work to fight for others. But then disillusionment set in. There were too many egos lurking around Westminster. Too much dishonesty and bad behaviour. Too much back-stabbing. Too much risk. Teaching seemed a better way, a quieter way, to make myself useful to the world. For more than twenty years, it's felt the right decision.

Now it's all come back, that old yearning. Kirsty Osmond MP. I tossed and turned all night thinking about it, I got up thinking about it, I can't get it out of my head. What might have been. What still might be.

Perhaps I should talk to Rick again. Was he joking? You never know with Rick. He likes his imaginary games. How about we swap jobs for a day, he once suggested. Just to see who copes better. Like some reality TV show. I had to laugh. He wouldn't last five minutes at Phoenix and he knows it.

But Rick's not the problem. The idea is simply impossible. What am I even thinking of? I can't abandon the school now. Phil and I have got staffing matters to deal with, and there's the exclusions policy to work on – I'm going to win that one if it kills me. There are so many people dependent on me. And so many reasons why not, not just the guilt about the school, the kids, the parents – what would *they* say? – but the fear of failure, of humiliation, the media, the lack of privacy, the exposure, every imperfect decision getting combed over… all of it a heavy blanket, suffocating. I chose teaching for a reason. I preferred to be out of the spotlight, my head below the parapet, quietly making a difference to young people's lives.

I'm nearly at school. I wind down the car window to clear my mind. The cold air is shocking, but it does the trick. I've got a job to do and Rick's mad idea is going in the rejects file where it belongs.

**

I poured my second coffee of the morning. It tasted bitter and my eyeballs prickled. Defective tear ducts, lack of sleep or too much whisky? Kirsty – after doubting my sanity – had pulled the duvet over her head and I was left trying to unpeel an idea that had come from nowhere. I'd been drunk, tired, and playing games. My wife, an MP? Why had I let things even drift in that direction? Once of course, when she was young and part of the Westminster circus… once, perhaps. But now she was out of all that, like she'd said. Now she was wedded to the school. And to me, of course. There wasn't room for anything else in her life. Thank Christ she was a practical woman, practical enough to realise that. I'd run my hand along the length of her sleeping back and whispered, 'Ignore me.'

I took a final sip of the coffee, swilling away the memory of my drunken rambling, and put the mug in the sink, next to Kirsty's. She'd already left and I had to get going too. The frost was heavy outside and the kitchen a cocoon I was reluctant to leave. Winters have always been more raw up here than they were in London. There's something about the exposed flatness. Hull has no hills to divert the wind and the blasts of northern air come in uninterrupted all the way from Siberia.

My phone buzzed.

> *Hi Mum, Dad, hope you're well. Thinking of coming home next weekend. Hope that's ok. Adam. PS: What's going on with this MP? What a perve!!*

I couldn't help smiling as I tapped out a reply.

> *Always great to have you back. Look forward to dissecting MP story. How's Newcastle? Love, Dad.*

Newcastle's good. Just finishing some work before 0900 lecture. See you Friday night. A.

There'd been a ragged hole in our lives since we'd packed him off to university. Maybe it's always like that with only children, although I'm sure the eighteen hundred adolescents in Kirsty's charge must have eased the pain for her. My emotional needs as a parent tended to get overlooked. But it would be good to have him home for the weekend, to have him padding around the place, leaving his things everywhere and taking up more space than one person should.

I found my gloves and glanced at Adam's message again. Seven-twenty. I couldn't remember ever being up at seven-twenty in the morning when I was a student… at the end of a long Saturday night, yes, but not the beginning of a working day. Then again, he was a medic while I'd meandered through an English degree – he was bound to be more serious about work than I was. I was pretty sure I'd never made it to a nine o'clock lecture. Did we even have nine o'clock lectures? When I got onto the newspaper graduate training scheme in Newcastle, I discovered I was expected to turn up by nine every morning, even earlier if a story demanded it. Adulthood was full of shocks like that, not least among them Kirsty.

I met her when I was three years out of my traineeship, a fully-fledged journalist who'd just landed a job as a regional political correspondent at Westminster. I had a Lobby pass and my career was primed to take off. Kirsty was a parliamentary assistant to Janet McConnell, a prominent Opposition backbencher and education committee chair. Our first contact was by phone. It was the spring of 1994 and Labour was about to elect a new leader. I wanted to speak to McConnell, but Kirsty was the gatekeeper, a brusque Northerner, a barrier to my objective. I'd tried before and she was usually short with me, as if journalists were an impediment to the real business of the House. She was entirely confident in her assumptions about whether my enquiries were significant, whether Janet would want to talk to me and even what she might say.

'I'm telling you, she hasn't got time to speak to you.'

'But could you just ask her, please? A written quote would do. All I want to know is where she stands on the leadership contest.'

'She's not declared her support yet. She's obviously not going to give you a quote.'

'Just ask her. Please.'

'At the risk of repeating myself, she's busy. And so am I. So, if you don't mind…'

I forget who put the phone down first. Probably me. I clearly wasn't getting anywhere. This impossible woman was standing in my way and I had other people to try. Just as well not all MPs' assistants were as obstructive as Kirsty what's-her-name.

The following week, I was drinking in a Whitehall pub with some fellow hacks when I glimpsed a striking woman in a red shirt, standing in a mainly male group at the other end of the bar. It was a Friday evening and the place was crowded and smoky. I vaguely recognised some of the faces in the group, people I'd seen around, all young, parliamentary staff of one sort or another. It was a huge village, the Palace of Westminster, you couldn't hope to know everyone and almost certainly didn't want to, but after a couple of months my contacts book was filling up and I was getting to know several people well enough at least to nod at when I passed them in the corridors. I'd made some mistakes, saying 'hello' to – and being snubbed by – senior politicians I thought I knew but then realised I only recognised from TV.

There was one man in that group in the pub that I was certain of, the clerk to a select committee, Tom something-or-other. I'd collected an embargoed report from him a few days earlier and was sure I'd impressed him with my knowledge of local planning law. I slid away from the journalists and pushed my way through the throng.

'Hi. It's Tom, isn't it? Rick Dewhirst. We met last–'

'Yes, I remember. Any queries about the report, I'll be back in the office on Monday. Off duty tonight, mate.'

Another snub, and this time from a lowly official too. But the humiliation had served its purpose. I smiled at the red-shirted woman, who was standing next to him. I'd been right in my judgement from the other end of the bar. She really was striking, in a fragile sort of way. Pale, velvety skin, no make-up, a cascade of nearly-black hair and eyes like chestnuts.

'We've spoken before, too,' she said, without smiling back. 'On the phone.'

She coughed and I leant over to an ashtray to stub out my cigarette. When I turned back, she was looking at me with her head on one side and a challenging stare. There was a tiny half-moon scar above her left eye, a shiny exception in the otherwise matt expanse of her forehead. Her voice was familiar, Yorkshire vowels – like mine, but broader, more authentic, not prep-schooled out as mine had been.

'Kirsty Osmond. From Janet McConnell's office.'

She should have been older, plainer, grimmer. I felt the heat pool in my cheeks. The others in the group seemed to have decided that Rick Dewhirst was of no interest and probably a nuisance, and were closing their small circle to exclude me. Kirsty was half-in and half-out of the circle. I shifted my position, to make her face me more directly, with her back to the others.

'Well,' I said, 'this is a coincidence, isn't it?'

'Hardly, given that we both work up the road.'

'I'm sorry if, the other day, if I…'

'Oh, don't bother about that. It's just that I haven't got time for journalists faffing around when I'm busy and Janet clearly doesn't want to speak to them. Sometimes you have to take no for an answer.'

She was going to be hard bloody work, that was obvious. I wouldn't have bothered if she hadn't been… well, I couldn't take my eyes off her. To my surprise, she didn't make any attempt to return to the group.

'So then, tell me about yourself, Rick Dewhirst. How long have you been working in Westminster? You seem pretty new to it, if you don't mind me saying.'

Hold on, wasn't I the journalist, the one meant to be asking the questions? But Kirsty had this habit, even then, of taking charge, of running the conversation, of changing the subject when she saw fit. And of putting me in my place. It should have been a warning but I chose to ignore it.

Instead I jabbered on about my time in Newcastle, expecting her at any moment to stop me with a withering remark. She didn't. At one point she actually smiled, and I was mesmerised by the tiny almost invisible creases around her eyes and lost track of what I was saying. After ten minutes or so, she said sorry, but she had to go. I said I was going too and we could walk together the few minutes to the Tube. Along the way, she dropped a coin, a pound coin I noticed, in the tin of a rough sleeper sitting with his dog outside a government building. She smiled at him and said, 'How are things, Lee?' and he mouthed back, 'Not too bad, Miss, thanks.'

At the station she said, 'Nice talking. See you around.'

And we went our separate ways, she on the District line east, I west. She'd told me barely anything about herself. All I knew was that she worked for Janet McConnell and probably lived somewhere in east London. Oh, and that she talked to beggars. Perhaps I should have left it at that.

I wound an extra length of scarf around my neck and scraped away at the ice-crust on my windscreen. It was a sunny but breathtakingly chilly morning. I got into the car, sat for a moment watching the wipers smooth away the last smears of de-icer spray and then turned to take a quick final glance at the house, checking, out of habit, that I really had shut the front door. The house looked back, solid, serious, built by the Victorians with permanence in mind. At the beginning, Kirsty had fretted that the place was too big. With just one child, why did we want five bedrooms? What could we possibly do with all that square footage? With a national housing shortage, wasn't it simply irresponsible? No, she could have her own study, and we'd have space for visitors and Adam's sleepover friends. What's more, the place cost less than the flat we were selling in north London. Magnanimously I even suggested that if ever we found ourselves kicking around in all that space, we could let out a room at a peppercorn rent to one of her rough-sleeper mates. She gave me an excoriating look, but after that let the subject drop. It was one of the few battles with my wife that I'd ever won.

I pulled out of the drive and raised one hand to a neighbour standing patiently with a plastic bag in her hand while her dog squatted on the pavement. Maple Avenue was a place where people stuck to the rules, where they respected the need for order and privacy, a self-contained neighbourhood where nothing much happened.

On the main road, the houses were even larger, set further back, cold, self-important villas built for merchants who had made their money out of the Humber docks and wanted to put distance between themselves and the source of their riches. Most of the buildings had long since been converted into flats or offices, their grandeur wearing thin, as if they were waiting for a benefactor to rescue them. Benefactors, it turned out, had not been plentiful over the decades and transformation had been slow. In spite of last year's accolade as UK City of Culture, Hull retained its stern, wintry character. There was a reticence about the place, which I rather respected.

But it was going to have to come out of its shell for the by-election. I'd have to start planning straightaway. We'd need a small team to cover the speeches, hustings and campaign extravaganzas, not to mention the visits by assorted political celebrities who would suddenly see the constituency as the most exciting place in Britain. Mid-parliament by-elections are always an indicator of the national mood, and this one looked like having the added pzazz of taking place alongside preparations for a rape trial. Sex, violence, and politics – an irresistible combination.

After that chance meeting in the pub, I'd rung Kirsty the following Thursday.

'Janet's busy,' was the unsurprising response.

'No, I was ringing you, actually. I wondered whether you'd like to go for a drink tomorrow evening.'

There was a moment's pause.

'Yes. White Lion. Seven. See you there.'

She was the one to put the phone down first this time. I held the receiver to my ear for a few seconds, listening to the continuous tone. I couldn't believe my luck.

The luck held out, although that first date – if that's what it was – was like no other I'd been on. I must have passed some sort of initiation test because, quite differently from the previous week, she seemed set on doing most of the talking. And talking was clearly an area of expertise for Kirsty. She talked about her work, about party policies, about the need for radical change. She clearly rated Janet McConnell, thought she was doing a good job on the education committee and expected her to become a minister when Labour won the next election. No 'if', just 'when'.

'I mean, this government's tired. It's run out of steam – no new ideas, no sense of purpose. And it's eating its own innards over Europe. It's a dead administration. There's neither the will nor the imagination to improve things, to make life better for people, fairer.'

She stressed the final word – fairness was obviously a big thing for Kirsty – and took a sip of wine. A silver bangle slipped down her skinny wrist as she lifted the glass, and for the first time I noticed the gentle ridge of her knuckles and the white half-moons of her unvarnished fingernails. I wanted to take her hand and squeeze it between mine, but I didn't. I could have done with a fag, but I wasn't going to risk that, either. Instead I nodded and picked up my pint. She appeared to take that as assent.

'There's so much needs doing and the Tories are just fiddling while Rome burns. Schools, hospitals, they all need money spending on them. People deserve more – more than they're ever going to get with this lot. Sorry to be party political, but Labour just have to do a better job, whoever leads them. I really believe that.'

I nodded again. It was a common enough view in 1994, although it wasn't common in my circles for people to express it with such conviction. Politicians, of course, but that was their job. Among my friends – and not just the journalists – scepticism and even cynicism were the norm. It might have been different at university, but here, in the real world, ideology and commitment were suspect. Belief was no longer cool.

But this was a different way of looking at the world. It was certainly a different way of conducting a first date.

'I suppose it's not the same for you,' she said. 'I mean, being a journalist. You've got to talk to everyone, that's your job, and you can't always say what you think. You've got to keep your personal views under wraps.'

'Well yeah, that's more or less how it works.'

'But you must have personal views.'

'Yeah…'

'Well?'

'Well…'

'I know – you're a Lib Dem.' She gave me a triumphant look, as if she'd prised out a lifelong secret.

'I have voted Lib Dem once, if you must know. Tactical voting. And Labour once. And Tory in local elections.'

'Oh my God, Rick, you're a floating voter.' She hooted with laughter and rocked back on her chair. I'd never seen her laugh like that before. This political fanatic was also human.

'Nothing wrong with a bit of floating,' I said. 'It's what keeps the parties on their toes. Principles are fine, but if everyone stuck to their allegiances, well, there wouldn't be much point in replaying the democratic process every few years, would there? Elections would be like Groundhog Day.'

'You're funny.'

I took that as a compliment, as much of a compliment as I was going to get for the time being.

'And even if you are a political ignoramus,' she went on, 'at least you don't pretend to be what you're not. There's an awful lot of bullshitting in that place.'

She waved in what was roughly the direction of Parliament and knocked over her glass. White wine trickled over the edge of the table onto my trouser knee. Her cheeks flushed and she fumbled in her bag for a tissue.

'I'm sorry. That was careless of me.'

'Don't worry. It's nothing. Let me get you another.'

'No, my fault. I'll do it.'

She pulled out her wallet and got up to go to the bar. I watched her narrow shoulders squeeze past a group of men standing round a tall table and I reckon that was the moment I fell in love with Kirsty Osmond.

My head was still in the 1990s when I arrived at the *Citizen* offices. I ran into Clive in the lift going up to the newsroom. He was breathing heavily, his nose dripping, coat and bag slung over his shoulder. He had recently taken to parking a mile away and power-walking into the office – good for his cholesterol, he said. Not so good for the atmosphere in the lift. I breathed in cautiously.

'Thought you might take the stairs, Clive – you know, in line with your new fitness regime.'

'Fuck off,' he wheezed. 'You could do with some exercise yourself, if you ask me. Knocking fifty, aren't you? Not too young for a heart attack.'

He shot out of the lift into the gents. There was a small shower in there, partitioned off by a torn plastic curtain. With luck, he was going to make use of it. But no sooner had he gone in than he stuck his head out of the door again.

'And by the way, Rick, I hope you've got some ideas on how we're going to manage this fucking by-election disaster. Last fucking thing we need. Meeting at twelve. Want your thoughts.'

He'd get them. But there were things to do before then. I gave the Barraclough story to Shona Jefferson to check for further reactions. She was good at cultivating contacts and would be useful in the coming weeks, my right-hand woman. She reminded me of a young Kirsty – it was the eyes, deep wells that drew you in. Or maybe the cheekbones. Or maybe the take-no-nonsense working-class manner. Whatever it was, she was definitely one of the better things about *The Humberside Citizen*. We'd appointed her three years earlier, but she was bound to get snapped up by regional TV before too long – a sound reporter who knew the area well and would look good, really good, in front of camera. She was made for the screen. It could only be a matter of time.

But for now, she'd be keen to prove herself – her first by-election. Of course we couldn't get cracking properly until the parliamentary writ came through, but a date in late April looked a fair bet. I glanced at possible Thursdays in the calendar and started making notes in preparation for the meeting with Clive.

'Right, if we've got to do this, let's get on with it,' he said, as I walked into his office. 'Just you and me, twenty mins max.'

'I want to involve Shona – I reckon she's going to be on by-election duty full-time once we get going.'

'Forget the full-time. But get her in.'

I put my head out of Clive's office and called over to her. She came in, giving him a hesitant smile, which he ignored. Nurturing talent was not something he wasted time on. No point, he'd once said, the bright ones just move on anyway.

'Can we all get this straight?' He didn't wait for us to sit down. 'This is a *by*-election, a vacancy for a single seat. It affects just one of the Humberside constituencies and even there most people don't give a damn.'

I'd noticed before how he tended to moderate his language in front of Shona – 'damn' was hardly his usual swearword of choice. I'd been keener on her appointment than he had and he still seemed uncomfortable with her – the *Citizen*'s only black reporter – out of his depth, unsure. She must have been aware of it, but she'd never said anything.

I got out my notes and started to outline the current state of the parties locally, the results last time, the Brexit factor, the need to expect the unexpected. Clive waved his hand at me.

'Yeah, yeah, no need to lecture us. Let's just decide who's doing what and leave it at that.'

'Rick suggested I cover the formal kick-off of the campaign,' Shona said. 'The announcement of candidates, all that. We should–'

'Routine stuff, no need to go to town on it,' Clive said. 'We're not going to neglect real news to cover pointless meetings – half a dozen people on a wet night in some lousy church hall.'

'But this is a big story,' she said. 'A national story – the eyes of the country will be on us. We've got to do it justice, give it space.'

And she gave a long sigh, as if to say, I know what's what and I'm not going to be put down by the men I work with. Yes, definitely the young Kirsty. I didn't need to say anything. Clive grunted.

'We need a few even-handed pieces on the candidates,' she went on. 'And the issues – NHS, schools, jobs, Brexit of course. What people are talking about.'

Clive grunted again. 'Only if you keep them lively – human interest more than politics.'

I wasn't sure how we were going to keep politics out of a by-election. Shona raised her eyebrows in my direction. The *Citizen* didn't deserve her. Clive certainly didn't.

'We're also going to need to keep an eye on any developments on Barraclough of course,' I said, as we left.

'Nah, don't hold your breath. All that's going to go quiet for a while,' Clive said.

Well he was monumentally wrong about that, as it turned out. Barely an hour later I was at my desk scanning a Metropolitan Police statement. Investigations were underway into a *number* of sexual assault allegations against Martin Barraclough.

I wondered how big the number was. Three, four, a dozen? This story had substance. Again I remembered Kirsty's words from years ago. Maybe men *should* be banned from politics. But then that admission from the previous night came back to me. *There's a part of me that almost feels sorry for him.*

You can't have it both ways, Kirsty. Bad behaviour's bad behaviour. Don't muddy the water with pity.

When I first met her, Kirsty was the most uncompromising person I'd ever known, with clearcut opinions about everything. The water was deep, but never muddy, and if I was out of my depth, I didn't care.

I paddled endlessly to keep afloat.

In the spring of 1994, I had gone on a date with a glorious, headstrong woman and had unintentionally fallen in love with her. I was besotted and any niggling doubts that we were just too different didn't stand a chance. That first date had paved the way for others and soon we seemed to have a 'relationship', although for a few very long weeks an unconsummated one. There were moments when she was soft and funny and laughed at my jokes, but other times when she was impatient with the world and with me. She seemed to regard my political neutrality as a personal challenge and, although I would never have allowed anyone else to tell me what to think, I let her get on with it. Love conquers all, or at least it did in those early days.

What she didn't talk about much was herself. She said she was from Sheffield and I told her I grew up in Yorkshire too, north Yorkshire, Richmond, but she laughed and said, 'Posh Yorkshire, that's different.' No White Rose solidarity there then. When I asked about her family, all she said was, 'Not much to tell. Four of us. Mum, dead now, dad, sister, me. I left home to go to university in Leeds,' and abruptly shifted the conversation to the north-south divide and the need to get more regeneration in areas hit by the demise of the old heavy industries. After that, it was private education and how it perpetuated the class system and drained resources from the mainstream. I kept particularly quiet at that point.

It took a few more evenings in the pub – and a lot more of Kirsty's views on the state of the nation – before she agreed to come home with me. I'd been working towards this for a while – well, obviously from the beginning, but I'd persuaded myself not to force the pace. The rules of engagement with Kirsty were different from those with other girlfriends and I didn't know how long my probation would last. But then one week, she surprised me by saying, 'Maybe, next Friday.' She shared a flat in Whitechapel with two other women, both teachers. They were nearly always in. I rented a place in Notting Hill Gate with one other journalist who was nearly always out. That settled that.

I made time before I left for work on the Friday morning to tidy up the flat. I remembered what she'd said about not pretending to be what I was not, but I wasn't going to take chances. I got rid of a stash of empty beer cans and, most important of all, I rearranged books and magazines. *Loaded* and even *Rolling Stone* went out with the beer cans. A biography of Nelson Mandela and the previous weekend's *Observer* lay casually on the sofa, and back copies of the *New Statesman* were neatly piled in the bathroom. I wasn't sure about *Private Eye*. In the end I played safe and shoved it in the magazine rack where it was partly hidden.

We got to my place about nine, having stopped in the pub for a few birthday drinks with one of her friends. I unlocked the door and ushered her in. She looked around briefly, incuriously, and I wondered if I'd agonised too much over the tidying up. But then she picked up the Mandela book and said, 'Isn't it amazing how someone can turn such negative experience into something so positive?' and it was worth it after all.

I poured drinks – she said she'd had enough alcohol and asked for fruit juice – and she settled on a large floor cushion with Mandela while I flicked through CDs, looking for something that would set the right mood. She hadn't actually said, 'Let's go back to your place for sex,' and I hadn't said, 'I fancy you like mad and really can't wait to fuck you,' but when did that ever need articulating? I started to feel less sure. Had I got it wrong?

Our relationship had not yet progressed to discussing previous partners, but perhaps she was a virgin. Unlikely, but not impossible. Perhaps she'd had a bad time in the past. Perhaps she didn't trust men. Perhaps – much as I hated to contemplate it – she simply didn't want me enough. This could have been awkward. Nina Simone was doing her best to offer us encouragement from the stereo system, but it seemed we were in for an evening discussing revolutionary freedom movements.

Then she looked up from the book and said, 'Come here.'

I knelt down on the floor next to her and tentatively let my finger trace the contours of her cheek. I sensed the muscles of her face relaxing and my fears melting. I started to unfasten the buttons of her shirt and cupped one breast inside her bra, and she kissed me and undid my belt and slid her fingers down my belly. The Mandela book slipped to the floor.

Afterwards we lay there, still partly dressed, Nina Simone now silent, and Kirsty said, 'You're kind. I think I could love you for your kindness.'

An odd judgement. I surely had many appealing features and I'd never thought of kindness as chief among them. But I've always been willing to take compliments, however they land.

I asked if she was going to stay over – another thing we hadn't clarified – and she said yes, if that was all right. The sheets were clean – I had remembered that – and we fucked again, this time enjoying our nakedness against the crisp linen. I lay awake for a while, congratulating myself that now things could be normal but wondering what exactly normal meant with Kirsty.

Three months later, she moved into my flat. The journalist I'd been sharing with had moved out of London and Kirsty arrived with two suitcases and a collection of carrier bags. Now twenty-four years, several flat, house, and job moves later, here I was, still with her. We were truly grown up, she a headteacher and I a newspaper editor – well, soon-to-be, for sure, but a deputy for now. I looked again at the police statement on Barraclough and wondered what at that moment she was looking at and whether she ever thought about me when we were apart like I thought about her.

**

Adam's coming home for the weekend. There was a text message as I walked into school this morning, Friday night he says. A proper family again, the men and me. They'll no doubt spend the whole time going over the Barraclough business, outdoing each other in their condemnation of him. Not thinking about the women, just condemning the man. Adam's young, he's got a lot to learn. But Rick – well, Rick's never been a subtle thinker. Words, yes, he can work magic there, but thoughts, no, they're all plain black and white. Maybe that's part of his charm, or at least it was once. At the beginning I was bowled over by his manner, his public-school jokiness, those self-conscious good looks, that worried smile, trying so hard to impress, sometimes just to please. He was sweet. Sweet? My husband, sweet? Yes, he was, like a Hugh Grant character in some rom-com. And so non-threatening. I remember that first time in his flat, how gentle he was, how nervy, as if he expected me suddenly to do a flit. Sorry, Rick, I've changed my mind, I'll be off then. And him all the while trying so hard to be cool and casual. Nina Simone on the stereo. And the Mandela book. He'd got everything worked out. But that was so long ago.

People change.

But I can't think about any of that now. I barely have time to bang out a see-you-soon-love-Mum reply to Adam as I unlock my office, and then everything starts to kick off. Phone calls and problems and people wanting a word and a to-do list that never shrinks. A normal day at school.

Yet all the time, underneath the normal, there's something else. It wells up in the middle of taking a call from the council, of chatting to a group of senior prefects, of reading new guidance on the curriculum. I still can't get it out of my head. I thought I'd expunged it and somehow it's crept back. Kirsty Osmond MP? Could I? Could I? I don't know. There are things to consider, things that made me turn my back on Westminster all those years ago… But circumstances change. A decision made once doesn't need to define me forever.

So could I?

Should I?

But it's nearly eleven o'clock and I'm about to take a year 11 citizenship class. I've always insisted on carving out one period of teaching a week no matter what else is happening – I still love the buzz you get in the classroom. We're covering courts and the legal system, but all the students want to talk about today is 'that MP'. I've made it a rule that if there's something they're really interested in, we vote on it. If the majority go with it, then that's what we discuss for the last fifteen minutes. And so we do today.

Once the cracks and the sniggering have subsided, I ask them why they think Martin Barraclough has resigned. Because he broke the law and he's going to jail, says one boy, you can't be an MP if you've done a crime. Well we don't know that for sure yet, I say. But it wouldn't be in the news if he hadn't done something, would it? says the boy. It's like that film producer in

America, the one that raped all those actresses. He's in jail now. There's more laughter and the kids don't wait to put their hands up. It's worse him being an MP, someone points out. We're meant to respect them, treat them like they're important… yeah, people vote for them, they're meant to behave themselves… they're powerful… they make the laws, don't they?… decide what the rest of us have to do. I nod encouragement. Something has clearly sunk in during our earlier lessons on the workings of Parliament. Bet he's not the only one, says one girl, just shows what rubbish MPs are. You mean what rubbish men are, says another. And the giggling starts again.

The bell goes and the students are gathering up their things and jostling for the door, laughing and talking and looking more animated than they usually do after forty-five minutes of citizenship. I look round the empty classroom after they've gone and ask myself again, could I? The answer is starting to feel inescapable. If Martin Barraclough has been an MP for all these years with that on his moral record, then why should anything stop *me*? And it's not just one man, there are others like him still out there, the kids got that right. We've let him – them – get away with it for so long. Don't we have a moral duty to show that politics doesn't have to be tainted like that? That there's still goodness in the world?

Difficult class? It's Phil, his large frame filling most of the doorway. No, not at all, I say. We discussed Barraclough. Some interesting opinions. He laughs and says out of the mouths of babes, and turns to go. But I say, look, if you've got a minute or two, we need to chat, come in and close the door.

I want to talk about exclusions before the senior team meeting and also think about staffing for next year. There are going to be several vacancies to fill – retirements, parental leave, people moving to other jobs. He sits on a desk at the front of the classroom and we go over the main points and then, after a brief hesitation, I take a breath and say, there's one other thing I need to mention. I'm giving some thought to putting myself forward for selection as the Labour candidate in the by-election.

I've said it. Until I took that breath, I wasn't even certain that's what I'd decided. But now I know. My doubts have been pushed aside. Phil says nothing. This must sound absurd. One moment we're talking about finding a new head of IT and the next I'm telling him I might be gone, too. Is this where the whole idea comes tumbling down? But it doesn't. I've shared my thoughts with him. They're more than thoughts now. They're starting to feel real.

It's the longest shot imaginable, I say, it'll probably come to nothing, but it's only fair that I mention it. How would you feel if… well, if I wasn't here next term? He seems to take it in, slowly. It's hard to imagine Phoenix without you, he says eventually. I'm flattered, I say (and I am), but try, because no-one's irreplaceable. His eyebrows go down behind his glasses and his eyes seem to shrink. He has this knack of combining disappointment and mild panic in a single look – I remember once when he tried to calm down an aggressive parent who'd walked into school yelling that he was going to deal with us lot because his daughter had lost her place in one of the football teams. It was just a stupid threat, not thought through, but it was irrational behaviour that upset Phil's sense of order. The father came in the next day and apologised.

He's silent for a second or two more and then he says, if it's the right thing for you, then I suppose you have to do it. If you're sure. And I say, I think I am sure, almost. He slides off the desk and comes and stands next to me. What's Rick think? It was actually his idea, I say, well sort of his idea, he suggested it last night, very enthusiastically, though he had had a drink or two, you know Rick. It's been gnawing away at me since then. Perhaps a life in politics has always gnawed at me. But I worry about ditching the school. And he says, well it hasn't bothered others. You wouldn't be the first teacher to become an MP, though maybe headteachers are a bit more of a rarity. But you'd be better than any of them.

I'm not sure that amounts to outright approval. Is it daft of me to expect a ringing endorsement straight off? I'll have to work at it. I love Phil, I really do. He might not be the most dynamic, but who needs that? His feet are solidly on the ground, and he's the best, most conscientious colleague anyone could hope to have. I'd like him to get my job if I leave, though the board may want to appoint from outside. And I doubt he'll even go for it – he's never been overly ambitious, Phil.

We're both quiet for the moment and then he says, it'll be tough for us, Kirsty, but I suppose it won't do any harm to have someone like you fighting for education. The country's gain. Our loss. He touches my arm and says, let me know when it's definite.

I still don't know what he thinks, I mean really thinks.

But Rick… I need to tell him, too. He'll want to take credit for the idea, of course.

**

Phoenix Academy is on the east side of the city, beyond the docks, along the Humber estuary a mile or two and then north. Kirsty's work-home drives were always longer than mine, but she didn't seem to mind. On the increasing number of occasions when her car wouldn't start, she did the journey by bus – two buses, in fact. It took an hour and a half and she'd arrive home looking perished from the cold. She refused ever to take a taxi. Her staff couldn't afford taxis home and in solidarity she wouldn't either. I'd given up arguing with her on that.

She'd rung to say the Mini was being towed to the garage again.

'I've told you, you really should get rid of that old tin can,' I said.

'The garage will fix it. But in the meantime, any chance of a lift home? If not, I'll get the bus.'

And so that Wednesday evening I was on my way to pick her up. I flicked between radio channels and found a classical station playing *The Marriage of Figaro*. I turned up the volume and between gear changes my left hand became a baton. Life was good. Shona and I knew where we were going with the election and Clive was an obstacle we would manage. On days like this, I could almost persuade myself that being deputy editor of a fading regional paper was exactly where I wanted to be.

What's more, Adam would be home in a couple of days and the weekend was going to be great, just the three of us, like it used to be before he went off to university. He hadn't said why he was coming home. There'd been a girlfriend towards the end of his last year at school, Jess, if I remembered correctly, though it had seemed a bit on-off. But the three of us could surely scrape out some quality time together – perhaps Sunday lunch at our local Italian. Adam liked Italian. And if he wanted to bring a friend, that was fine.

I'd left the river behind, had turned off the main road and was approaching the school. It had been renovated and extended during the New Labour school-building boom of the noughties and converted into an academy when Kirsty took over. Mainly red brick, sympathetic angles and not too much glass, it was a low-key masterpiece that blended into the surrounding canvas of grey housing and nineteen seventies tower blocks without shouting out that it was different. Phoenix was a firm presence that offered a haven to hundreds of kids who sauntered into the building each day, at least that's what Kirsty claimed. Lots of them came in early for a free breakfast – porridge or eggs instead of a bag of crisps or nothing at all. She'd introduced that as soon as she arrived. And the same ones were often there until six-thirty in the after-school club. As she constantly reminded me, her job wasn't just education.

I drew up on the road outside, turned off *Figaro* and texted to say I'd arrived. I was parked next to the main school sign. The words 'Phoenix Academy' stood out on a dark blue background, with 'Rated good by Ofsted' at the top – she was desperate to make 'outstanding' next time – and at the bottom, in small letters, 'Principal: Ms K.R. Osmond OBE'. Those three letters were recognition for all her hard work in rescuing a sinking – no, completely sunk – comprehensive. She'd been reluctant to parade the honour on the sign. In fact, she'd had some doubts about accepting it – remnants of empire and all that. But she was told it was for the good of the school. At the side, in a different font, was the school motto: 'Be all you can be.' There'd been a dispute about that, too. The governors had decided the new academy needed an inspiring slogan, like all the best schools had. Kirsty wasn't convinced. It was pretentious. Phoenix wasn't Eton. But at least she persuaded them not to attempt it in Latin.

She'd been at the school for eight years. The move to Hull had been fraught and for me a defeat, or rather the confirmation of a suspicion – in our marriage my career came second. I was then editing a small but growing political magazine based in Westminster and Kirsty was deputy head at a large comprehensive in north London.

She was a leader-in-waiting, just looking for the right headship at the right school. Being Kirsty, she wanted to go where she could most make a difference.

'Honestly, Rick, things have got so much better in London,' she said one evening.

We were sitting in the kitchen. Supper was finished and Adam was absorbed in a video game at the end of the table. It was a cosy scene and Kirsty was about to wreck it.

'London schools have had so many advantages in recent years. Quite right, too. Things were a mess. But it's different in other parts of the country...'

I began to spot where this was going and a small knot of panic planted itself in the pit of my stomach.

'But we're pretty well settled in London, aren't we? And... and well, my job's here too...'

She blotted some drops of spilt salad dressing with the corner of a paper napkin.

'I'm just saying we need to look at the options. Perhaps we should think about going back north, back to Yorkshire. Going home.'

Adam looked up from his game, a small frown crinkling his face. 'Hey, are we going to move? What about my friends?'

'Woah. We're not doing anything yet. Your mum and I are just talking.'

'You'll be moving school next year, anyway,' she said. 'So it'll be a new school, new friends, wherever we are.'

I picked a single grape from the fruit bowl on the table and chewed it slowly, crunching the pips. She'd never referred to Yorkshire as 'home' before. I knew I'd lost the argument. In fact, there hadn't even been an argument. Nine months later Kirsty was appointed principal of a failing Hull comprehensive about to be converted into an academy, I was applying for a job as deputy editor of the local paper and Adam was saying goodbye to his friends at his London primary school.

The lights in the building went out, with just the external security lights left on, and Kirsty emerged, carrying a battered carrier bag packed with the usual folders. Phil was with her, his head towards her as she talked. He seemed breathless, as if he were having difficulty keeping up with her. I wound down the car window, bracing myself for a few moments' small talk and hoping he kept it short. All I wanted was to get home. It was cold out here, colder than in the city centre.

Phil bent down and rested his hands on the open window.

'Long time no see, Rick. Everything okay on the paper?'

'Yeah, busy, as you'd expect. The by-election… and all that.'

'A bit of a shocker, eh?' He paused as if to say something else, but then straightened up. 'Oh well, I better be off. See you in the morning, Kirsty. And don't worry.'

She patted his hand. 'Drive safely.'

He walked towards the school car park and Kirsty got into the passenger seat, hugging the bag of folders. I leant over to kiss her. Her cheek and lips were icy.

'Don't worry? About what?'

'What?'

'Phil said don't worry. What's up?'

She took off her woolly hat, tossed it on the back seat and shook her hair free. It looked like she'd had no time to wash it that morning. She would have hated me to point it out, but the recent streaks of grey always showed up more when they were a little greasy.

'I'll tell you as we drive.'

She had a story to tell and I would listen, as I always did. We passed a small gang of kids larking around in the bus shelter and Kirsty turned her head, no doubt checking whether they were her students. They almost certainly were. There was hardly anyone else on the streets. This part of Hull always seemed quiet at night, although there were lights on in nearly every window. People got home from work – if they did work – and stayed home. It wasn't just quiet. It was depressed and downtrodden and it provided more than its fair share of the crime stories the *Citizen* carried. But Kirsty treated it like home turf.

'One of the students was selling drugs today. In the lunchtime queue.'

'Really?'

I heard her breathe in sharply, forbiddingly. She was about to remind me of what she always reminded me and I lifted one hand from the wheel to stop her.

'Don't worry. I know the rules. In confidence.'

'I should hope so. Anyway, one of the lunch supervisors spotted it. Seems he was selling miniscule packets of cannabis for a fiver a piece. Where my students get spare fivers from, God only knows. But it all seemed so blatant, as if he wanted to get caught. We had no choice but to call the police and the social work liaison officer. I tried the boy's mother several times. No reply, I left a message. But I got through to Louise and, of course, she hit the roof, wants him excluded, permanently. So much for the policy note I was drawing up.'

She gave a short sigh and her thoughts disappeared into a place where I couldn't follow them. Her chair of governors surely had a point. Dealing drugs in school was a red line. You got caught and you were out and that was it. They couldn't have the boy staying on, an object of celebrity or notoriety for the other kids. Rules were rules and sometimes individuals had to be sacrificed for the greater good. We'd argued about things like that so often. You can't keep making excuses for people, I'd tell her. If they behave badly, they have to face the consequences. People are victims of their circumstances, she'd say. Of course they have to face up to their mistakes (mistakes? I always queried, and she always ignored me), but the important thing is rehabilitation. It was a waste of time protesting. I won arguments at work, but Kirsty wore me down. I glanced out of the side window at the warehouses we were passing and wished I was still listening to *Figaro*.

'It's such a crying shame,' she went on. 'Josh – that's the boy's name, Joshua Wenham, not that you need to know that – he just sat there, terrified, trying not to cry, and asked me whether he'd go to prison. I mean, it breaks your heart. He's just not one I'd expect to be caught up in this sort of thing. Attendance is good, works hard, should do well in his GCSEs next year. And I told him, of course, he wouldn't go to prison. He just had to tell the police the truth about who'd given him the drugs to sell. Honestly, I wanted to hold him and tell him it'd be okay, even though it probably won't be.'

Her voice had dipped. I looked across at her. Her eyes were closed and she was biting her lip. I allowed her a moment's silence. Then she took a deep breath and said, 'We've got a battle on our hands, Phil and me. Josh needs saving not just from whoever's criminally exploiting him, but from the system and from Louise and the rest of those who'd throw him on the scrapheap.'

Here we go again, I thought. A simple case of juvenile criminality is about to turn into a crusade. On the soapbox she goes.

'And it's not just one kid. There are kids like Josh everywhere. Kids the rest of the world would prefer not to know about. Everywhere – whole communities that need rescuing, not just one terrified teenager who's made a mistake. Funding, support services – the demands are overwhelming and what can I do from the principal's office at Phoenix? A little, but not enough.'

We were drawing to a halt at traffic lights. She turned to look at me and said, 'I'm going to do it.'

My brain stopped.

'Do what?'

'Labour candidate. I'm going to put my name forward. I've more or less decided.'

A car behind us hooted.

'Green, Rick, go.'

I tried to shift gear and stalled. The car behind hooted again.

'I just need to sound out a few people,' she said.

I was trying to control my breathing, and think, and find first gear.

'But it's… it's not… I mean, you've got a school to run, a proper job. Isn't that what you said last night?'

'Come on, you were the one who suggested it.'

'I was…'

'You were what? If you've changed your mind, say so and we can have a proper argument.'

'I'm… I'm thrown by your about-turn, that's all.'

'*My* about-turn?'

'D'you actually remember last night, Kirsty? Dismissing everything I said, like you usually do? Telling me I was mad?'

I could hear myself, the wronged party, turning up the volume, while her voice became provocatively softer.

'I just wanted you to shut up so I could think,' she said.

'And? What did you conclude?'

'I reckon I can do it.'

'What, with everything that's going on at the school?'

'That's exactly the point. I want to be able to say and do so much more. On a broader platform. The things I have to deal with happen everywhere. We need systemic change. And I honestly believe I can make a difference.'

'Make a difference? Please. Even Barraclough must have said something like that when he first stood.'

'Why do you always have to reduce everything to the lowest common denominator?' She thumped her own thigh, the nearest she was going to get to losing her cool. 'Anyway, I've mentioned it to Phil, and he thinks—'

'You've mentioned it to Phil? Before you thought to discuss it with me? That's brilliant, that is. Bloody brilliant.'

'It's not like that. We were talking about staffing and I had to say something. I trust him.'

'And you don't trust me?'

'Of course I trust you. It's just that I worry about the school.'

'Hm. Well there's a surprise.' I paused to let my sarcasm resonate. 'Would've been nice though if you'd spoken to your husband first. I wouldn't have thought that was too much to ask.'

'Rick, don't go all sulky on me now.'

We drove in silence for a minute or two and then I said, as quietly, as reasonably, as I could, 'Are you sure you're up to this?'

'I beg your pardon?' Her voice was cold.

'I mean, in terms of mental resilience. After all—'

'I can't believe you're throwing that in my face.'

'I just thought...' But I could almost hear her humming with indignation. 'Okay, I'm sorry. Forget I mentioned it.'

I knew I shouldn't have raised it — I'd not said anything for years — and at that moment I vowed not to do so again. Kirsty's psychological state was forbidden territory.

She said nothing for a few seconds and then put her hand on mine on the steering wheel, appeasingly. She was trying to tell me that, whatever I may have thought, she was most certainly up to it. And in that moment, I knew she was right. Bile rose in my throat. Defeat? Anxiety? Panic? All of those, but there was something else too. Envy. I envied my wife. In the hierarchy of sins, was that a greater transgression than envying a stranger? I had no idea. I just knew I envied her. Not because she might be about to become an MP — Christ, that's the last thing I'd ever want for myself. No, I envied her because her career was, once again, set to be in the ascendant and mine no longer seemed of any consequence at all. She was about to begin a political life that would lead who knew where and I was the deputy editor of a mediocre rag going nowhere. The ambition gap between us was getting even wider.

I pushed down on the accelerator.

'We better get home.'

She didn't hear me. She was already on her phone, looking through her contacts.

**

I'm in my study staring at a full diary — can I really cancel everything over the coming weeks to chase some sort of dream? I'm going to have to be utterly single-minded to make this work, ruthless with my time and energy. But it's much more than that. Once I leap off that cliff, there'll be no looking back, no rescue ropes to haul me up, just a freefall into space. Life is risky and you can't always play safe. I know that.

Rick's gone into the kitchen to make sandwiches. The journey home was terrible, I didn't mean the discussion to go like that, perhaps I should have brought it up differently, or waited till we got here. He doesn't shout very often and it was worse being stuck in the car with him. I wanted to walk away and leave him to calm down, and I couldn't. When he eventually did, there was this current between us, tension, suspicion, whatever. It was the same when we got in the house. Was cheese and tomato alright? That's all he said, and I just nodded. I'm not sure I feel like anything to eat. There's too much to think about and time is short. I made two calls from the car. Friends in the local party. People I want to get an opinion from, informally, before this goes any further. What did they think? Was it worth throwing my hat in the ring? I genuinely wanted to know their views before I make an idiot of myself. And they were positive. Surprised maybe, but definitely encouraging. An interesting idea, one of them said, why not? The field's open, you'd be a strong contender. I've been a foot-soldier often enough, turned out to help others get elected – councillors, MPs, even Barraclough once, though generally I preferred to join the canvassing in a neighbouring marginal constituency. So maybe now it really is my turn.

Rick comes in and places the sandwiches in front of me, and a glass of wine that I didn't ask for. A surly peace offering? He doesn't look at me. I take a sip of the wine then put it on a shelf, out of reach. I need to concentrate, to process what I'm about to do. The truth is, the idea was worming its way through my subconscious before Rick even raised it, the moment he mentioned Barraclough. He hasn't begun to understand how serious I am about this. And the way he twisted everything I said, that was the worst thing about his behaviour in the car. Last night he was egging me on, I thought he meant it. Yes, he'd had a drink, we both had, but even so – how could I misread him like that? And now he's suggesting I'm letting the school down – as if I've not thought of that, as if I'm not already agonising over that very thing.

But as long as he's not a distraction, a drag on my energy… perhaps that's the best I can hope for. And I'm going to have to put the Rick problem to one side for now. There are more pressing matters to deal with. What I really must do straightaway is talk to Jim. He'll have the best sense of who else is likely to stand. He'll tell me whether I'm wasting my time or whether there's an outside chance. I know he'll be frank with me. He was the first Labour person I met when I arrived here and I backed him when he stood for chair. I like him.

I wait for him to answer and it almost feels like there's someone, something, on the line, listening. No clicks or anything like that, just the ringing tone and the beats of silence in between, beats that seem in time with human breaths in and out. I'm imagining it. No-one's interested in my phone calls, I'm just a woman who… wants to be an MP. But it's as if someone's trying to listen in, prise open my head. They won't succeed. My head is tightly sealed, a box nailed shut. My thoughts are out of bounds to intruders. There are some things in there, small things, that no-one else needs to know. And that includes my husband.

**

I could hear the mumble of one side of a conversation from her study. I was sitting on the bed in our room next door, trying to occupy myself on my laptop, idling on social media, scanning my emails, pretending to be busy.

There was an ache in my throat, like the start of a cold. After a while I got up and went in to collect her plate. The sandwiches were untouched. But it seemed we were talking again.

'That was Jim Prodham, the constituency Labour chair,' she said.

'I know who he is.'

'Well, he doesn't think it's as crazy as I thought he might. I'm seeing him on Saturday. He says I should start canvassing wider support straightaway if I'm serious. So if you don't mind…'

She picked up her phone again and I left her to it. What had happened to my wife in less than twenty-four hours? After more than two decades of teaching – not just teaching, but being the most committed teacher on the planet – she wanted to return to what she had once very decisively rejected. I remembered that precise moment in 1996 when she'd announced she was going to quit her parliamentary job and train as a teacher. It was shortly before we got married and we were having a rare lunch together, queuing with our trays at a self-service restaurant in the Palace of Westminster.

'A PG-what?' I picked up a cellophaned baguette.

'Post-graduate certificate in education. You know.'

'Why?'

'I want to teach of course.'

I felt a thud of disappointment. I liked the fact that my girlfriend, my about-to-be-wife, worked for a prominent MP. It reflected well on my credentials as a serious journalist. At the time I thought she might eventually go for a seat herself. We'd have made quite a power couple, her a politician and me a rising star of the political commentariat. But teaching? Teachers were two a penny.

'I've been mulling it over for a while. I mean, I still

believe in what people like Janet do. It's probably the most important job you can do. But there's something… something about this whole world. This place…'

She looked around her. The restaurant was crowded with familiar and unfamiliar faces. A hundred conversations, important and trivial, were in train.

'… it's full of ruthless ambition, people nurturing their egos… and I don't think it's for me after all. I want to do something worthwhile with my life, and maybe the best thing I can do is teach, go into a tough comprehensive, work with challenging kids.'

Two men were getting up from a table nearby. She nodded at one in recognition and we sat down in the vacant seats.

'Well, say something, Rick. What do you think?'

'I don't know. Surprised, I guess. Has something… happened to make you change your mind?'

'No, of course not. I've just had enough and I want to go. Can we leave it at that?'

I pushed my plate aside. I wasn't that hungry after all.

'Well, if it's what you really want… and you're sure…'

I soon came to realise that she was sure, that it was truly what she wanted. Almost as soon as she started the course, and certainly by the time of her first teaching practice, she became more relaxed, more comfortable with herself, less prickly, less critical of me. She was still driven by her incorrigible ideals, but they were softened by pragmatism. Above all, our professional lives no longer had any intersection and that made living together easier. It was the best decision she'd ever made, even if we weren't going to be quite the power couple I had envisaged.

But now things had come full circle and she wanted to head back into that world of egos and ruthless ambition where ordinary decency didn't count for much. Politics was not the honourable profession it had once been, if ever such a golden age existed. Politicians had long been down there with estate agents – okay, and journalists – but in recent years things had got even worse. Expenses scandals, cash for influence, access, honours – too many of them were in it for themselves. It was a murky world they inhabited and I no longer liked the idea of her – us – becoming part of it. Our lives were good as they were. Kirsty gave to the world. Adam was going to. Head teacher and doctor, high-flyers, virtuous people, serving others.

And me, well I got by, sanctioning other people's ideas, writing inflated headlines and pompous editorials that no one read. But it was my job, the only one I had for the time being, and it was beginning to feel under threat. How could I continue as deputy editor of *The Humberside Citizen* if Kirsty became a local MP? In all her flights of fancy, she clearly hadn't given any thought to the impact on me.

Still, it might never happen. Jim Prodham, the party chair – perhaps I should give him a call too, exert a little influence of my own.

The following morning Kirsty left for work without mentioning the by-election. Promising, I decided. She insisted on going by bus and, for once, that seemed a good idea. The slow rhythm of a bus journey would offer plenty of cold thinking time. She'd come to her senses, reflect on the disadvantages of a political career, arrive at the obvious conclusion. After all, she was (usually) a reasonable woman. All was not yet lost.

The *Citizen* meanwhile provided a welcome distraction from my domestic difficulties. I had worried that the Barraclough story might derail regular business on the paper, that Hull would shrink into itself and other news would be thin. But as ever, human folly and human wickedness saved us. There'd been a bad accident overnight on the dual carriageway. Black ice. Two fatalities. A Humberside police sergeant and his girlfriend were charged with murdering the sergeant's wife. The city's biggest care home was facing closure. (Its residents included Hull's oldest citizen, one-hundred-and-seven-year-old Gladys, whose birthday the *Citizen* had celebrated the previous week and who recommended a daily half-pint of stout and never having 'bothered with men' as her recipe for a long life. She's got a point, Kirsty had said.)

We were hard pressed to decide what to lead on. But then our chief reporter Mike Hufford said he was almost ready to run with his bad housing exposé. A large commercial landlord was letting out places that were unfit for human habitation and among the tenants was a number of families with children. Mike was getting it lawyered. He was certain it would stand up.

'It had better be really bad to beat the love triangle cop,' Clive said. 'We don't want the odd bit of rising damp. We need filthy conditions, swarms of cockroaches, kids with asthma, that sort of thing.'

'It's better than that,' Mike said. 'Rats. Running round a flat occupied by a woman and her three children. Loads of them, big brown ones, the woman says, long as your arm.'

This promised to be a great exclusive. Just what we needed. My only concern was that another paper also seemed to be onto the story. There was a danger we'd lose it if we didn't move quickly. But I wasn't going to let that happen. After my failure with Barraclough, I was determined we wouldn't be pipped to the post again. I looked at the photos on Mike's screen.

'If you're sure they're rat droppings… I mean, couldn't they just be mice?'

'Size, lad, size. And the shape. Look at them. Big fat pellets.' Mike prodded his screen with a pen. 'They're bound to come from rats. Bloody medieval, it is. The kids are having nightmares, they're terrified they'll get bitten, catch some terrible disease.'

It was a gut-wrenching story, too good to lose. A stark example of the national housing crisis, Kirsty would say – I couldn't wait to tell her. But the story had to be watertight and I insisted Mike moved quickly to get confirmation from a pest control company.

After lunch, Clive set off for a board meeting and, as always, his departure raised the oxygen levels in the office. It was proving to be a very good day. The pest control people confirmed that the droppings did indeed come from large rodents, and my headline was merciless: *Children Terrorised by Rats*. The allegedly murderous police sergeant and his girlfriend awaited an appearance before magistrates. The two dead in the road crash had been named. The care home company was prevaricating on the closure. I even found time to have a pep talk with Dan Stapleton, the laziest reporter in the north of England but nominally our education correspondent. I suggested he write a feature on school exclusions.

Kirsty rang mid-afternoon. I saw the number and braced myself. She rarely called during the day. What now? But she just wanted to tell me she'd be working late and could I pick up some food for the weekend. With Adam coming home, we'd need to cook. Fish perhaps. It was a good sign she was managing to find headspace for a few domestic details. And she didn't say a word about the Labour nomination. Again, promising.

'By the way, we've got a very strong lead for tomorrow,' I said. 'A shocking housing story. Worth watching out for.'

'Oh, yes? Anyway must go. Don't forget the fish.'

If only she could occasionally show some appreciation for what I did. The fourth estate and all that, Kirsty. Don't underestimate us.

I put the phone down to find Shona standing next to me. All day I'd tried to avoid talking to her about the by-election. It was awkward… Kirsty… I couldn't say anything for the time being. With luck, and some effort from me, the whole idea was going to peter out and nobody on the paper need know anything. But Shona kept nudging.

'How about doing an initial piece on likely runners? You know, talk to people in the parties, see where the early money is, whip up a bit of election excitement.'

I started going through my emails, trying to ignore her. She ignored my ignoring her.

'I'd say Patsy Harvey's going to be the hot favourite for Labour, though there could be quite a contest, who knows? And I bet all the parties will be thinking about female candidates.'

The ache had started up in my throat again. I was definitely going down with a cold.

'Look, Shona, why don't we just sit on it for now? Clive's probably right, there won't be that much interest yet. Let's wait till we've got names confirmed.'

'But Rick, I thought…'

She shook her head. Another woman disappointed in me. Of course it was a good idea for a piece. Under other circumstances… But at that moment I just wanted to put the world on hold. I didn't want people to have bright ideas. I wanted them to write about car crashes and housing crises, to lose their phones, to stifle their curiosity, to drink themselves into oblivion, whatever it took.

'See what you can find from the Tories,' I said. 'We'll decide on Monday.'

I really did need to put in that call to Prodham. Just a precaution, to ensure commonsense reasserted itself.

I sat in my car in the station car park, with a good view of the exit from the station. No Adam yet. I checked my phone. Most of the trains seemed to be running late. I sat and waited and felt shivery. To kill time, I pulled a rolled-up copy of that morning's *Citizen* from my bag and scanned it, objectively, as an ordinary reader might. The housing story took up most of the front page and yes it was shocking, with the family staring bleakly at the camera and a close-up of rat turds. Human interest writ large – not to be ignored, Kirsty. This should have sold a few more copies than we usually managed. I read it again, from start to finish. The property company who owned the flat had chosen not to comment – their decision, but a foolish one. I wondered now whether we should have pressed them further, got something in writing, just to be completely certain. But Mike was confident it was all spot-on and our lawyer had raised no particular concerns. Good journalism sometimes meant taking risks.

I'd just turned to the back-page sport when Adam tapped on the passenger window, an enormous grin stretching across his face. I unlocked the doors and he got into the front, his rucksack on his lap, his legs filling all the space in the footwell. Could he still be growing? Not at eighteen, surely. He leant over the handbrake to give me a hug, as well as he could in the confined space. I responded awkwardly, unsure which part of my son to take hold of – I'd never got the hang of man hugs.

'It's freezing out there.' He pressed his fingers against his stubbly cheeks. 'The heating broke half-way down. And the coffee machine thing in the buffet wasn't working. Totally rubbish service.'

'Time to renationalise the railways, your mum would say.'

Adam rolled his eyes and laughed.

I turned on the ignition and took another glance at my son before moving off. How like Kirsty he looked. That always struck me when I hadn't seen him for a few weeks: the same mobile expression that could switch from smile to frown in a flash.

'What's brought you home, then? Missing your parents by any chance?'

'Of course. And, well, thought I'd come back for Jess's party tomorrow. It's her birthday.'

'Jess? Didn't you go out with her for a while? She's the pretty one with the red hair and the long legs, right?'

'Dad! Sexual objectification. Lay off.'

Objectification? Not a word I could remember spitting out when I was eighteen. And unfair, all considered. She *was* the pretty one with red hair, though maybe I shouldn't have mentioned the legs. At times there was something quite puritanical about Adam. His mother's son. I raised my eyebrows in mild complaint.

'But since you ask,' he went on, 'no, we're not really seeing each other anymore. We're good mates.'

Oh yes? I'd never understood how a girlfriend could suddenly turn into a good mate. Exes were always exes, as far as I could remember. My son was far more versatile than I'd ever been.

'She's applied to Newcastle,' he said. 'Don't know why she didn't do it last year. But she took a year off to work, says she needs the money. Seems a waste of time to me. Once you know what you want to do, just crack on with it.'

Definitely Kirsty's son. Decide what you're aiming for and shoot. Don't let anyone dissuade you, just do it. I felt a fresh twinge of anxiety, the first for twenty-four hours.

'So how's the course?' I asked. 'Hard work?'

'Yeah, but it's great. I love it.'

That, it seemed, was as much as I was going to get. He fiddled with the radio and found a station that wasn't one of my pre-sets. The insistent rhythm of whatever was playing hurt my ribcage. But I was prepared to indulge him. We were nearly home.

'How's work?' he said. 'Humberside's very own sex scandal keeping you busy?'

I turned the radio volume down a little.

'We're just waiting for the charges now.'

'Always thought he was a bit off, that MP. And Mum? How's she?'

We were pulling up in the drive. Her car was there. The garage had managed to patch it up again.

'She's good. Still completely immersed in the school, of course.'

**

I knew they'd be late. Those Newcastle trains are never reliable. Public transport, lack of investment in the rail network – huh, so much for the Northern Powerhouse. But this government's neglect has, indirectly, given me time to cook. It's the least I can do when Adam comes home – take an hour off emailing and phoning to prepare a meal. Fish pie. His favourite. There's a tempo to chopping and stirring that oils my thoughts.

I can hear Rick's car on the drive. I wipe my hands and open the front door and walk down the porch steps and embrace my son. How are you? How was the journey? I take his hands and hold him at arm's length and look at him, and he laughs. Mum, honestly, I've only been gone a few weeks. You need a better coat in this weather, I tell him. It's fine, he says, I've got a thick sweater. But anyway how are things with you? Dad says you're busy–

I look across at Rick. He's locking the car and checking the doors, his back to me. We've barely spoken in twenty-four hours. Let's get inside, I say to Adam. I've got something to tell you. We'll chat over supper. He bounds upstairs to his room, but Rick follows me into the kitchen. After the crisp air outside, the fish smells in here are pungent. I switch on the extractor fan and resume stirring the pan on the hob and Rick says, well? I take a deep breath and my head fills with the cooking fumes. We need to talk again, I say. I turn to a cupboard, pull out a deep pie dish and start to transfer the fish mixture. This evening I want us to have a frank discussion, you and me and Adam. I've got my back to him and I can't see his face. He doesn't say anything immediately but lifts my hair and kisses the nape of my neck and then says he hopes I don't get his cold. He's not well and I hadn't even noticed, but I can hear it now in his groggy voice. Perhaps I've been hard on him. He needs time to process things. He'll come round, he always does. I twist my head to kiss him on the mouth and the spoon drips juices back into the pan.

The kitchen door opens. Smells good, Adam says, I'm hungry. Oh… excuse me, didn't mean to interrupt. I look at him over Rick's shoulder and he grins in that way he's done since he was a little boy, his lips tight as if he's trying to keep in a giggle, and once again I realise how much I've missed him. Don't be daft, I say. Your dad was just showing me a little bit of affection. We've both had quite a week.

Half an hour later we're seated around the big table in the kitchen. I've served the fish pie and Rick's opened a bottle of wine. I pick up my glass but then put it down again and look at Adam, not Rick. I'm considering putting my name forward for the Labour nomination in the by-election, I say. We thought – your dad and I – we thought we should talk it over with you. Rick clears his throat. He's objecting to the 'we', but I'm sure he'll behave in front of his son. He knows it's good parenting to involve Adam in our serious conversations, in any big decisions. There was a period in his early teens when he wasn't interested, just didn't want to talk, at least not to us. I should have known how to deal with it, I'm pretty expert at teenage hormones. But with your own it's different. He'd been such a loving child and I was worried stiff I was losing him. Rick dismissed it as normal adolescence. He'd spent five years not talking to his parents, he assured me. Adam would grow out of it, just as he had. For once Rick was right.

But now, at the kitchen table, Adam's eyes narrow and he stops eating, his fork mid-air. Am I overburdening him? An only child has a lot to bear, finding their way through a maze of confusing adult behaviour without any sibling support. After a moment he sucks in air through his teeth and breathes out loudly. Wow, well – wow. And he shakes his head. Not sure what to say. I mean, I know you go to Labour things and you used to… ages ago, before you became a teacher… you used to work in Parliament, didn't you? But wow, bit of a surprise really. And I explain that putting my name forward doesn't necessarily mean I'll get it. It's a long shot, a very long shot. There'll be some strong people in the running. But the opportunity's there and this weekend is decision time. Why, though? he asks. Are you fed up with being a headteacher? No, of course not, and I smile. But perhaps teaching and politics have something in common. Year 11 on a Wednesday morning could be good preparation for what goes on in the House of Commons. And after twenty years in teaching, I reckon I'm smart at handling people. Adam still looks bewildered. But didn't you once say you'd had enough of all that political stuff? A long time ago I had, I say. I was young and very idealistic. Politics seemed a messy business. People didn't always behave well.

They still don't, to state the obvious, Rick chips in – the first thing he's said since we've sat down and not a particularly helpful contribution. It's best ignored.

**

So it hadn't gone away – why on earth would I think it had? Jim Prodham hadn't revealed much when I'd eventually called him. Just told me there'd be some strong contenders for the nomination and he hoped Kirsty would be among them and I must be thrilled she was considering it. Hmm. I was her husband, he could have engaged rather more. And now she wanted this ludicrous discussion with our son. But maybe Adam would have more influence than I had so far. It wasn't as if these ping-pong exchanges between the two of them were going entirely her way. Adam was asking all the right questions and didn't seem convinced by the over-stretched analogy between year 11 and the House of Commons. I finished my first glass of wine and let him get on with it.

After a few minutes the mood changed. Kirsty and Adam were both quiet, as if she was purposefully standing back and giving him space to think, and then he said, 'You know what, Mum? You're ambitious, aren't you? You always have been.'

I felt a sliver of a memory, sharp, familiar, reverberant. I'd been ambitious once, too. I remembered

70

what it was like, having goals, believing anything was possible. Early on I had been the one with the career, the one going places, the one to watch, and she was merely someone's assistant, then lots of people's teacher. Somewhere along the way, all that had changed. My job now just contributed to the family income.

Kirsty's face twisted in a mock grimace.

'Oh, I don't know about ambition.' (My wife could be wickedly disingenuous when she chose to be.) 'I just feel I should be doing something on behalf of a lot more people. But there are pros… and cons. In fact, Rick, I've been thinking' – she turned to me – 'what would be really helpful is if you could play devil's advocate. You know, be negative, you're good at that, you're a journalist. Just come up with all the reasons why I shouldn't do it and I'll answer them.'

It seemed I had my uses after all.

'You mean like a hostile media interview? That's easy. So Ms Osmond, can you explain to our viewers why a level-headed professional woman such as yourself would want to go into one of the least respected jobs in the world?'

'Very funny, I'm sure.' She gave Adam what appeared to be a nervous smile. 'But no, I mean more like a court hearing. Point by point, measured, forensic.'

'Novel.'

And, come to think of it, rather brilliant. Yes, I liked this approach. I'd be quietly reasonable, expose the obvious weaknesses of her plan, Adam would side with me and she'd have no choice but to acknowledge the majority opinion. There'd be no shouting, like in the car.

She unfolded her napkin – she had made no move to eat so far – and picked up her fork. Both she and Adam looked at me expectantly. I cleared my aching throat. Point by point then, starting with the smallest.

'Okay, first then, the effect on our family life. Your mother will be down in London during the week' – I addressed Adam as the arbiter in this game – 'and when she is here, she'll be on duty most of the time. Sorting out people's housing and benefit problems. Visiting old people's homes, making speeches, opening fetes – we'll hardly see her.'

'No worse than what I have to deal with on weekends now,' she said and pointed to a pile of paperwork sitting on the worktop. 'Obviously I'll be busy. You don't go into politics for a rest. But come on, you can do better than this. Let's get down to the real issues.'

'I'm being methodical. And my next point is key – the nature of public service.' I looked straight at our judge again. 'Your mum's a brilliant headteacher, and she's already serving the community in the best way anyone could.'

The judge (and jury) nodded.

'Politics will be a leap in the dark. Voters are a fickle lot and you gain or lose a job overnight. There's no notice period. Phoenix Academy will discover whether or not they've still got a headteacher at about two o'clock in the morning. That'll be it. Goodbye school. I'm off for good.' I was twisting the knife as much as I could. 'You can't just clear off on a whim. What about your students? They need you.'

She slammed down her fork and Adam flinched.

'Emotional twaddle,' she said. 'I have a very able deputy. I'll be in touch with him throughout the campaign and then if I win, a proper process will be put in place to appoint my successor. No-one's irreplaceable.'

'Keep calm. I'm just doing what you asked.'

And doing it rather well. I turned to Adam again.

'It's a fierce business, politics. Messy, like your mum said. Everything you say gets filleted, every action judged.

Put one foot wrong and you're front-page news. And believe me, the right-wing tabloids will look for anything they can use against you. Your right to a private life goes. Everything is exposed. Any embarrassing little indiscretions from your past come back to haunt you.'

Adam shifted in his chair – parents didn't have embarrassing pasts – and Kirsty said nothing. I was getting into my stride.

'I mean, for women especially, the exposure can get really rough. Social media can be barbaric. The misogyny, the abusive language you see on Twitter, on Instagram. And not just abusive. Malicious. Threatening. Dangerous.'

Kirsty glared at me. 'So I should think twice about going into politics because I'm a woman? Rather than stop the abuse, you stop the women? Is that honestly what you're saying?'

'I'm just pointing out the reality. Politics isn't a bed of roses. And there are special tortures reserved for women.'

'You don't run a tough secondary school without getting some very personal attacks. Public ones too, Ofsted, the whole inspection business.' She took a slow sip of wine to demonstrate her coolness under fire. 'When anything goes wrong at the school, you get it in the neck. And you learn to deal with it. I know when to take notice and when to ignore things – particularly when to ignore social media.'

Adam nodded and looked from Kirsty to me and back again. She went on.

'And remember, we often have to deal with physical violence as well. From kids, and sometimes parents.'

'It's not the same. MPs have been murdered.'

'Dad!'

I was merely pointing out the facts. Kirsty reached

out to touch Adam's arm.

'So have headteachers,' she said. 'And journalists. Thankfully all quite rare in this country. There's no need to scaremonger.'

'Politics is a whole new ballgame,' I said.

'And one I think I'm ready for. I wasn't when I was young. I am now.'

The cases for the prosecution and the defence were set out. But the other side's barrister now seemed more on top of her brief. I was losing momentum. It was time for something even further below the belt.

'And there's the effect on me… on my job.'

Adam was chewing his food intently, firmly fixed on his plate. But Kirsty looked straight at me with something in her eyes that I couldn't quite place. I pressed on.

'I'm not sure how easily I'll be able to continue doing what I do now. If you're an MP in our patch, I can't get involved in covering what you do. I certainly can't have any say in reporting the election.'

'Well I don't see exactly why—'

'Oh, Kirsty, come on. The first sniff of a conflict of interest and your opponents will yell foul. There's just no precedent for the deputy editor being married to a local MP. And when Clive goes, well, I'm not going to get his job with this on my personal CV.'

'Couldn't it be an advantage? You always said Clive was close to Barraclough. No-one objected to that.'

'Being chums with an MP is different from being married to one. Just think about it. Writing about you, deciding where to place a story about you… it'll be impossible. My career here will be over.'

I was no longer the lawyer, the wig and gown had gone. This was too close to the bone, the bone of my existence. What did she expect me to do? Quit journalism, write a book about the demise of local papers? Sell my soul and go into PR?

She blotted her lips with her napkin and said, 'Rick, I'm sorry.'

The game was over, but she wasn't caving in. She was just saying she was sorry that her ambition was going to cause me problems. It was as simple as that, and I realised what that look in her eyes had been. Pity.

Adam stood up and leant across the table to refill our glasses.

'Dad, I think Mum's got to do this. She'll be great. She just has to be. When you look at some of the weirdos who get to be MPs, well, she'll be brilliant. I'd vote for her any time.'

I looked at the full glasses. They were ready to be lifted in a toast, to wish Kirsty the best of luck on the exciting road ahead. Counsel on each side had had its say and the family court had reached a decision. I had lost. Were there grounds for an appeal? Maybe.

Or maybe I should change tack completely.

I picked up my glass and rested it across my bottom lip. Then I raised it further and said, 'Here's to the future MP for North Humberside. I guess we're all in this together then.'

My voice sounded listless. Maybe it was the gestating cold. She looked at me keenly and her lips parted a little, but she said nothing. Her eyes were serious, unsmiling, her body tense. The burden of public office was already hovering over her shoulders.

I'm sitting in an empty Starbucks at nine o'clock in the morning, looking through my messages, stretching out one overpriced flat white. But my mind keeps going back to that debate last night. Rick certainly played his part with gusto. There were points when, oh so easily, I could have agreed with him – you're right, Rick, I can't do it. But no, I'm not giving in, absolutely not. Women are too readily persuaded to give up, see reason, do the sensible thing. And we have to hold out and say, I won't be reasonable, I'll do what I have to do.

Adam is the surprise, though. He seems dead keen on me standing and last night after Rick had gone to bed, he even asked about joining the party. Wants to come canvassing with me. My son, the activist? I don't quite see it. But the world opens up to you in your late teens. New ideas knock on the door and they're amazing and you wonder why you never realised any of this before. I just don't want to distract him from his studies too much.

Yet Rick… What is it with Rick? He looked peaky when I left this morning, as if the role-playing had taken it out of him. Just a cold, he said. But there's a dense seam of self-pity running through my husband, he's like some mardy kid. I'm going to have to be patient – not my forté. I suppose he did eventually manage to say we're in this together. Those were his words – they're stamped on my brain. In this together. He's always been a political fence-sitter, his job he says, but I know it's more than that. So what's going to happen over the next few weeks? His work to start with? Surely they can't banish him from the newsroom entirely. They'll still get him to edit the rest of the news, won't they? Court cases, housing stories, the stuff of local papers. I certainly don't want him moping around on the sidelines, interpreting the polls in his usual smart-alec way, telling me where we're going wrong. And afterwards, if I make it to Parliament, what then? In this together, what does he even mean?

But there's no certainty about any of this yet, just loads of work. And I've got a lot to get through today, more soundings to take, more people lined up for a chat. I'm meeting a couple of them here, then I'm doing a stint on the Saturday stall, catching the weekend shoppers. Elections are relentless. Jim's been in touch a few times since I first called him, wanting to make sure I'm going to do it, not getting cold feet. The first time he rang I was with Louise and Phil and the social worker, discussing Josh. We didn't need Louise interfering, but she'd insisted on coming in. She's digging her heels in on getting the lad excluded, and Phil may have to handle that without me. All in all, not the best time to have the constituency chair phoning to nag me about applying. I said I'd call him back later.

And when I did, I was stunned. His initial open-mindedness had turned into positive enthusiasm. But what about Patsy? I said. She's got such an impressive political CV, served on the council, stood for selection in other constituencies. Lots of people will see her as the natural successor. But he wouldn't have it. There's no such thing, he said. And she's a lawyer, too many of them in politics if you ask me. You've got real-world experience, you're a proper activist, with people skills and serious leadership qualities. What you don't know, you'll learn. And you've kept your nose clean. You've stayed out of the more idiotic rows. You'll be good at taking all the factions with you.

I take another sip of the coffee – it's gone cold – and

my phone buzzes. Jim *again*. Just thought I'd remind you about the application deadline, he says. I laugh. I've not forgotten. I'm doing it. Good, he says. But there's one other thing I feel I should mention. Your husband. My husband? What about him? Well, he says, how supportive is he? Campaigning is tough, it's best if you've got real family support. Yes, of course Rick supports me, I tell him. He was only saying last night how we're all in this together. Why do you ask? Well, I had this call from him, he says. General political chit-chat, but then he started going on about how difficult things are for you at the moment with the school and all that. I got the distinct impression he's none too keen on you standing.

Rick… calling Jim… talking about me. I feel my jaw stiffening and try hard to relax it. Oh no, that's just Rick's natural caution, I say, he's a bit of a worrier, but he's always supported everything I do. Okay, Jim says, I guess you know him better than I do. And you know what, Kirsty? You're going to be a fine MP. Just what we need in this constituency. I'll have the application in by the end of the day, I promise him, and then it's in the lap of the party gods. He seems satisfied with that.

I, however, want to know what Rick's up to. General political chit-chat I don't think.

But there's one other thing I can't help mulling over and that's what Adam said about ambition. I know what he means and yet it was uncomfortable, hearing my son tell me I've always been ambitious. Maybe Rick was right when he talked about special tortures set aside for women and a special place in hell for ambitious women. The press will look for things. Rick said that, too. Well, let them. I have nothing to be ashamed of. I've got here on my own merits, perhaps even against the odds. It's what you achieve – and go on achieving – that counts, not the starting point. Let people judge me on that.

But here's my nine o'clock appointment. About time, too. Smile, offer to get them a coffee, listen. On your persuasive best, Kirsty. You can do it.

**

The cold emerged fully fledged that morning. My head was hollowed out from persistent nose-blowing and my throat raw from coughing. An elderly man stared at me from the bathroom mirror, the tip of his nose red and bulbous, dark circles under his eyes and a leprous-looking sore on his upper lip. Kirsty had ordered me to rest. I swallowed a couple of aspirins, then went back to bed. Mangled parts of last night's conversation – the Great Dinner Debate Fiasco – kept coming back to me. I'd lost, that was certain. But had I at some point actually suggested that politics was no place for a woman? Was there a renegade part of me that hunkered down there with Clive in a macho underworld, longing for some stone-age life where women did as they were told and didn't challenge the rest of us? Of course not. It was merely role-playing.

As I was drifting off and trying to get the stone-age image out of my head, my phone went. I reached across the bed for it and fuzzily made out the name on the screen. Clive, in person. Couldn't a man be left to suffer in peace? Wearily I took the call.

'Whatever it is, Clive, can't it wait? I'm not feeling too good. Dreadful flu.'

There was an irascible snort from the other end of the phone.

'You're going to feel a good deal worse when you hear this. I've just had a personal call from someone at that property company – the rats story – complaining that we misrepresented the circumstances.'

'Rubbish. We gave them every chance to respond before we went to print. They didn't. The story's solid. We had it lawyered.'

'You better be fucking right.'

'I am.'

I threw the phone down on the bed, irritated at the unnecessary disturbance. Dubious outfits like our property company often went through the motions of complaining when they saw the truth in print. It usually amounted to nothing.

But there was now no chance of getting back to sleep. I dragged myself up and searched for something comfortable to wear. I found a pair of undemanding tracksuit bottoms under the bed and was almost dressed when Adam stuck his head around the door.

'You okay?'

'I'll survive.'

He sat down on the corner of the bed. 'Mum asked me to check on you. She left early.'

'I know. Said she'd be out all day. Seeing people.' I looked up from pulling on my socks to see him studying my face.

'That lip looks awful,' he said.

'It's just a cold sore.'

'You should put something on it.'

'Will do. But about this weekend, your mum and I thought we could all go out for lunch tomorrow. Luigi's, perhaps?'

'Great – if you feel up to it. Okay if I bring Jess?'

'Of course.'

'As long as…'

'As long as what?'

'As long as you and Mum don't argue.'

'We don't argue.'

'Er… last night?'

'That was just your mother's little game.'

'Yeah, sure.'

'It's a big decision. She's got to look at it from every direction.'

'Mainly from your direction, I'd say.'

He looked around the room, avoiding my eyes, and I wondered what he was seeing. Parents' bedrooms had been a place of mystery to me. I'd never been in mine until my father was dying and even then it seemed an intrusion. Adam had always wandered in and out of ours like it was the family den. He turned back to me.

'Dad, are you positive you're okay?'

'It's just a cold.'

'No, I mean…'

'I'm fine, Adam. I'm fine. Can you pass me those trainers?'

He stood up and sighed. It was a fifty-year-old's sigh, like that of a frustrated parent dealing with a stubborn teenager. Come on, Rick, you're making this unnecessarily difficult for yourself. How would it have felt if our roles really were reversed? If I were the son and Adam the father? I could imagine it working rather well, Adam setting boundaries, dealing with my tantrums, doing everything a parent should do. My own father must have done those things, in his own reserved way, but the memories were hazy. The only thing I got from him was learning that I had to look after myself. It was like that instruction in an airline emergency demo. See to your own safety equipment before helping anyone else.

'I'm joining the Labour Party, you know,' Adam said, handing me the shoes.

'I didn't think you were interested in politics.'

'I'm not. Well, that's not quite what I mean. If Mum's going to be an MP, then I–'

'Hang on, she hasn't put in her application yet, let

alone got the nomination.'

'She'll get it, I know, and then I can go campaigning with her. In the Easter holidays – the election won't be before then, will it?'

'Haven't you got exams when you go back? Won't you be revising?'

'I can do both. Anyway, I'm off out now. Oh – can I borrow a bottle of wine for tonight?' The parent who knew best had gone. He was firmly back in the role of dependent teenager.

'Borrow?'

'Well… *have* a bottle then. I got Jess a present – hand-crafted earrings. Have a look if you like, they're in the kitchen. But they were thirty quid and I'm skint now.'

'There's something in the fridge.'

'Thanks, Dad.' And he closed the bedroom door behind him.

I spent the afternoon stretched out on a sofa, watching sport – any sport, whatever was on. There was something soothing about letting it wash over me on-screen, passively watching other people's battles in which I had no part, my own life on hold, trying not to think about family rows or by-elections or even dodgy property companies. Sport and I have a casual relationship. I never made it into any school team, much to my father's disappointment, and I can't claim to fully appreciate the technical skills. But I do like the real-life emotion of it, men and sometimes women trying to beat the shit out of each other, the jubilation or the despondency, the way they take it all so seriously. I flicked between channels for snatches of rugby league, boxing, snooker, and then settled down to a Premier League match. I must have nodded off barely ten minutes in and woke up to a studio panel of sleek ex-footballers discussing a match I had little memory of. It was dark now and the house was empty – I could tell intuitively when Kirsty was there. She was still out. Seeing people.

I hadn't eaten all day. I wandered into the kitchen and put a slice of bread in the toaster. It was all I could manage. My taste buds were dormant.

On the worktop near the toaster sat a fancy paper bag. The earrings for Jess. I pulled out a small box – well, he had invited me to look – and inside was a pair of silver earrings, geometric pendants.

Nice, I thought, although I had no idea whether a very young woman would like them. Hand-crafted silver earrings were rather special for someone who wasn't really a girlfriend, weren't they? But what did I know about that, either?

Next to the bag lay a Labour Party membership card. Kirsty's, of course. I picked it up and turned it over and guessed Adam had done the same. Did she usually carry it in her wallet? Presumably that was what being a card-carrying member meant. Had she got it out to persuade our son to join? Indoctrination. It was tempting to throw it in the bin, carefully cutting it up like an out-of-date credit card. Cut the card, cut Kirsty's political ambitions. Like sticking pins in a voodoo doll. I scanned the paragraph on the back – '...*the strength of our common endeavour... realise our true potential... the many not the few... a spirit of tolerance and respect.*' The rhetoric was self-conscious, self-important, and I wanted to edit it, break it up into shorter sentences, remove the bombast. I remembered how she'd once told me I didn't get politics. Reporting it wasn't the same as doing it, she'd said. Just as well, I now thought, if politics meant reducing everything to a dribble of platitudes.

I took a bite of toast. It was cold. I put on another slice and stood looking out of the kitchen window into the darkening sky. There was no sign of the moon.

**

I'm not a natural saleswoman but I'm learning. There are three of us on the stall near Paragon Arcade, and I don't know either of the others but I'm impressed by their easy ability to talk to strangers. It turns out that Mark, the younger one, is the partner of one of my teachers. She's on maternity leave but coming back soon. What a small world, I tell him. He and the other guy, Steve, they're both regulars, they do this on the last Saturday of every month, important groundwork between elections, reminding people why they should vote Labour when the time comes. Who'd have thought that the time would come so quickly, Steve says.

It gets busier as the afternoon goes on and soon we don't have much time to talk. The anonymity of it all suits me. Swaddled in a heavy coat, woolly hat and fingerless mittens, I'm just someone handing out leaflets and stamping her feet to keep warm, part of the Saturday shopping experience. We have a standard response if Barraclough gets mentioned, which he does, though most people can't remember his actual name. Yes, the news was shocking, but the party acted swiftly and now you'll have the chance to elect someone new to represent you. The cold ends of my fingers tingle when I say that.

Most shoppers give us a wide berth, some even cross the road to avoid us, as if we're about to pressgang them into something they don't want to do. But enough do stop – out of curiosity, genuine interest, who knows? perhaps they pity us for being stupid enough to stand around for hours on such a cold day – and we're kept busy talking to people we don't know and may never see again. I manage to keep the attention of a woman and her mother, both life-long supporters who now aren't sure. Brexit, the party's forgotten about real people, no-one cares. And I try to explain why we do care.

A man stands next to them, drinking from a can and muttering to himself. He drains the can empty and places it unsteadily on our table. Steve asks him to remove it please and the man says move it yourself and swipes it across the table. A trickle of beer runs across a stray leaflet. The man kicks the table leg and turns to leave, swearing and stumbling heavily against my shoulder as he does so, and suddenly politics feels very physical. A dangerous business, Rick said, and I accused him of scaremongering. My shoulder throbs. Mark asks if I'm okay. There's always one like that, he says, an oddball, not necessarily a political assailant. But you still need to be careful. And I'm glad the man's gone, although I'd like to have helped him.

I press on with the mother and daughter – I'm sure they're persuadable – and am aware in my peripheral vision of a group of teenagers watching me. There's a shout of how you doing, miss? I turn to acknowledge them with a smile. One of them is Josh Wenham. Not the one who shouted, but one of the others. He flicks his eyes away from me and I feel a terrible heaviness. I've failed him as a headteacher and here I am moonlighting – it's gone five, it's getting dark. He whispers something to one of his mates and they both look over and smirk. Josh says something else to the boy without taking his eyes off me and they walk away.

The mother and daughter have gone now – at least they took a leaflet with them – and the crowds are thinning out. Mark suggests we go for a drink after we've packed up and that feels sociable, it's what would-be politicians do. But I won't stop long, I say. My husband's not been feeling too good. I shouldn't be late back.

**

It was several hours before Kirsty got home. Adam was at his party and I'd gone to bed but was still awake, thinking through how I could get our lives back under control, hoping there was still a chance she'd do it herself, that she'd come home and tell me that seeing people had clarified things, that she couldn't sacrifice the school and Adam – and me – for this delusion. She was in her study for a while – perhaps she thought I was asleep – and then she came into the bedroom and flopped down next to me, fully dressed. I touched her cheek and she leant over to kiss me, before switching on the bedside lamp to examine my face.

'How are you?'

'Better than this morning.'

'That's a nasty cold sore. You should put something on it.'

'I have. Well?'

'Oh, a really good day. I've talked to loads of people.'

'And?'

'And it's done. I had it ready to go and I've just submitted it.'

That was it then. The end. The beginning, she would say. I paused for only a millisecond.

'Congratulations.'

'Thank you, though there's nothing to congratulate me on yet.' She searched my face again. 'Rick, why did you phone Jim Prodham?'

There was an accusing tone to her voice. What had he told her? All I'd done was point out some commonsense concerns.

'Why shouldn't I phone him? The *Citizen* happens to have an election to cover, you know.'

'He seemed to think you were trying to persuade him I was too busy to stand – as if you wanted to set his mind against me. Can you just keep your distance on this please.'

'You're over-reacting. We discussed the general situation, the Barraclough effect, that sort of thing. I'm your husband. Of course I'm supporting you.'

She stroked my arm and then kissed me once more, a conciliatory kiss, purposeful, devoid of passion.

'I hope so.'

'I've said I will.'

She looked away.

'Tomorrow, though,' I said, 'can we just make it a normal family lunch, with Adam? And Jess.'

'Of course.'

'Promise?'

'I promise.'

I closed my eyes. Saturday had been a write-off.

Luigi's was busy. Sunday lunch was always popular and at one-thirty the place was packed. There were a few couples, but mainly it was families. They spilled out from tables parked close together, children's voices drowned out the background Vivaldi and a couple of toddlers on the loose risked tripping up the waiters. It was many months since we had last been there – on the evening Adam had got his A-level results. But Luigi – if it was Luigi, I was never sure – bustled over to greet us and shook hands as if we were his most loyal customers. He showed us to a small table at the back of the restaurant, under a tourist poster of Palermo. The same poster had been there as long as I could remember.

'This okay?' I asked, as we squeezed into the space. I was pleased with myself for making the effort and not crying off sick. I'd woken up that morning surprised to find I was over the worst of the cold, although my appetite was still dulled by a phlegmy cough – and by Jim Prodham's treachery. That was meant to have been a confidential call.

'Perfect,' Kirsty said, but she was looking over my shoulder and raising her hand to someone. 'Excuse me a moment. I must say hello.'

She'd been unbearably cheerful since firing the starting gun last night. She got up, eased her way out of the tight space and walked over to the table of a young couple with a baby in a high chair. I thought I recognised the woman. They were all smiling and Kirsty was making a fuss of the baby. She was in politician mode already.

'Well, this is cosy,' Jess said, and giggled. I turned

back to her and Adam. The silver earrings peeped out from clouds of auburn curls. They suited her. Adam had good taste after all. In jewellery, that was. I'd never doubted my son's taste in young women.

I looked across the restaurant again. Kirsty was still with the couple. She was now engaged in intense conversation with the man while the woman was spoon-feeding the baby. This was not part of the deal. It was meant to be a lunch with Adam.

'Dad, are you listening? I was telling Jess we've been coming here since we first moved to Hull.' Adam looked around knowingly and grinned. 'It's very Italian.'

'Obviously,' Jess said. She giggled again.

'No, I mean it's *really* Italian. A family business. Sicilian. That guy – the one that shook hands when we came in – I reckon he's the *capo*.'

He looked in Luigi's direction and started to hum an approximation of the theme tune from *The Godfather*. I gave him my most admonishing glare and he ignored it. If only I was an autocratic patriarch, perhaps not Don Corleone, but at least in the style of my father, the undisputed head of the family, whose chair no-one else sat in, whose opinion my mother never publicly disagreed with, whose children never dared to ignore him. It would solve a lot of things. But somehow I couldn't see it working in the Osmond-Dewhirst household.

A waiter loomed into view with a handful of well-thumbed menus. Adam stopped mid-hum and stared with concentration at his empty glass. Jess was still suppressing her giggles as she opened the menu and widened her eyes at the choice in front of her. We were all silent for a moment. I turned around again. Kirsty was on her way back.

'Sorry about that,' she said, as she settled into her seat. 'Rick, you remember Lucy Dawlish, don't you?

From my maths department.'

'I thought I recognised her.'

'She's been on maternity leave. But you'll never guess what. Her partner Mark's on the Labour constituency exec. I only found out yesterday. We were working together on–'

I nudged her foot under the table. Remember, you promised. A normal family lunch. Can't you do it, just for an hour or two? She smiled guiltily. I took that as an apology.

'So Mum, have you put your name in yet?'

'I'm not sure we should discuss this now, Adam,' I said and inclined my head towards Jess, who was immersed in her menu.

'Oh, I don't see a problem,' said Kirsty. 'It's going to be public soon enough. Yes, my application's in. Mark's one of those backing me.'

Adam elbowed Jess. 'My mum's going to be an MP. Isn't that awesome?'

Jess looked up, her eyes wide. She must have been thinking… this family, what on earth had she let herself in for?

I closed my menu. 'So – when's she returning to work then?'

'Sorry?' Kirsty said.

'Lucy. From maternity leave.'

'Oh, next term. And not a moment too soon. It's not easy to find brilliant maths teachers.'

'Jess is going to be a teacher,' Adam said, and he gave her a gentle dig in the ribs. 'Aren't you, Jess?'

Jess blushed. 'Just primary teaching.' Her voice was a whisper. 'I'm starting a B.Ed at Newcastle in September. I've always wanted to teach.'

'That's great. And not so much of the 'just' – primary teaching is so important,' Kirsty said, and she beamed at her. All her attention was now fixed on Jess, to Jess's evident consternation. 'But what are you doing now? I guess it's a gap year.'

Jess gulped. 'I'm working at Aldi, and in a bar a couple of nights a week. Helping my mum, like. And trying to save up before September.'

Kirsty nodded and Jess went on. 'I'm going to have to find a job when I'm at uni, too. I won't manage otherwise.'

Adam's face erupted into a laugh. 'You just get a loan. Simple.' He clicked his fingers. 'It's only money.'

'But you've got to pay it all back, haven't you?' Jess tutted. 'And that's on top of the ginormous loan for tuition fees. I sometimes wonder whether uni's such a good idea.'

Adam opened his mouth to say something else and Kirsty narrowed her eyes at him. They glinted with disapproval. Poor lad, it could be tough having Kirsty for your mother. All he'd done was make a quip about money. I was inclined to agree with him. Why mess up the best time of your life having to work, if you could possibly avoid it?

Kirsty turned back to Jess. 'It's not easy, I know. I struggled too as a student and had to get a job. A long time ago of course, but it was hard.'

Jess raised her eyebrows a fraction and looked incredulous. She was clearly having difficulty imagining this superwoman ever struggling with anything.

'What did you do?'

Kirsty pushed a stray piece of hair back behind her ear.

'Waitressing. Little Chef. Evening shifts. There were grants in those days, but sometimes things didn't work out quite as they should. The tips helped and I'd get a decent plate of scampi and chips at the end of a shift.

Some days that was the only meal I had.'

Another Kirsty gem, one I'd not heard before. Clearing away plates smeared with ketchup, searching for coins left under saucers, hungry but cheerful – always cheerful for the customers. There were things that Kirsty would suddenly come out with, putting another piece into the jigsaw puzzle that her life sometimes seemed to be. Maybe everyone's life was like that. There were things in my life too that I'd never told her. But not many.

'Believe me, it worked out in the end. University was a very good move,' she said. 'Look, Jess, all I can say is, make sure you apply for whatever you can. Newcastle may have some bursaries. Do your research. I'll help. It's not too late. We can go through things together.'

Jess flushed again. 'Thanks. I'll check.' She looked embarrassed, no doubt unsure whether Kirsty actually meant it. But of course she meant it. She would happily spend an hour she didn't have filling in forms with the girl, even though she rarely had much time to spend with her husband.

There was a short break in the conversation while the waiter took our orders and then Kirsty said, 'We thought Adam might want to become a teacher at one point. When he was little, he used to line up all his soft toys and teach them to read.'

'Mum!'

'But then he decided he preferred operating on them instead. Several of them lost their stuffing in what I can only describe as very botched operations. It's a wonder he didn't get reported to the General Medical Council.'

We were all laughing, Adam no doubt relieved that he'd been forgiven for whatever it was he'd done to incur his mother's displeasure. I detected glances between him and Jess, mild astonishment on Jess's part – Adam's mum wasn't so scary after all – and pride on Adam's. He enjoyed showing off his mother.

He poured his wine into Jess's nearly empty glass and replaced it with water. 'I think I had too much last night.' She grinned at him, then quickly looked down at her glass. Good mates? Very best mates, it seemed.

The waiter arrived, precariously balancing four heaving plates. Jess stared at the mountain of gnocchi placed in front of her.

'Just eat what you can,' Kirsty said. 'Buon appetito.'

We ate in silence for a few moments. A tetchy baby was crying persistently at the far end of the restaurant. Kirsty looked around and I followed her gaze. Lucy and her partner had gone. It was another baby. 'She or he needs a nap,' she said and went back to dissecting her rubbery-looking calamari.

'Did I tell you I watched a birth last week?' Adam said.

'You do that as a first year?' Kirsty asked.

'Yeah. Just watching, but it was amazing. Messy of course, I hadn't realised how messy. There's a lot of stuff in there, alongside the baby, that is.'

He waved his fork around, as if somehow to illustrate a point. What point wasn't clear, but our son certainly enjoyed being centre-stage. Just like his mother, he knew how to manipulate an audience.

'Gross. If ever I have a baby, I don't want to be there,' Jess said, and she moved a couple of gnocchi tentatively across her plate. 'Or at least I'll be completely unconscious. And then they can do what they like to me.'

'One of the others fainted. He was dead embarrassed afterwards. Not sure what he'll do when we get to see a post-mortem.'

'Aw, disgusting. I can see why I never fancied doing medicine.'

'Nah, birth, death, and all the bits in between, that's

life,' said Adam with another philosophical sweep of his fork. He'd finished his stuffed chicken breast and was helping Jess with the gnocchi. My appetite had faded completely somewhere around the birth story.

'Dad,' he said, 'what are you going to do now?'

'What am I going to do about what?'

'You know what I mean, with *your* life, when Mum's campaigning, and then when she's an MP.'

'If, rather than when,' said Kirsty, but she seemed to look at me with some curiosity.

We'd managed half an hour away from the subject. But now Adam was back scratching away at the sore. He just couldn't help parading his mother's prospects while also, it seemed, pointing out that I didn't have any. It wasn't a real question. I merely smiled.

He persisted. 'Seriously, what will you do if you can't do your usual job on the paper?'

'There'll be other work to get on with. It's just the politics I'll have to keep off.'

'Yeah, but won't you want to write stuff? Political stuff. You've always got things to say.'

Kirsty's eyes were still locked on me. Wisely she said nothing.

'You know what?' Adam said. 'You should start your own blog.'

'What?'

'A blog. Your thoughts on the election. You could say whatever you wanted.'

'Don't be absurd, Adam. I'm a journalist, not a ranter.' I pushed away my half-finished dish of lasagne. 'Anyone want a dessert?'

'No, but what do you think, Mum? About the blog? Don't you think it's a great idea?'

'I think we'll just get the bill,' said Kirsty, settling the matter for us all.

'What did you make of her?'

We were dawdling back to the car. Adam and Jess were ahead, clowning about and laughing. Adam seemed to be doing his Marlon Brando impression and Jess was shrieking with appreciation.

'I like her,' Kirsty said. 'A bit shy at first, but it must have felt an ordeal, having to sit through lunch with us.'

'Well she certainly came out from under her stone after a couple of glasses.'

'I hope they stick together. She's good for him.'

We were in danger of catching up with Adam and Jess. Kirsty stopped to look in the window of a charity shop.

'You know, I sometimes think Adam doesn't realise how privileged he is,' she said.

'You mean Jess and the loans? He was just joking.'

'But if he could only be more aware of... of what it's like for other people.'

'Oh, give him a break, Kirsty. He's a kid. He can be a pain at times, I grant you. But honestly, he's fine. When I was his age, I was appalling.'

'I have no doubt,' she said and punched me lightly in the chest.

It was starting to rain – soft, indecisive rain. At least it was no longer bitterly cold, just damp and dull. She pulled an umbrella from her bag and tried to put it up to shelter us both. One spoke was bent and the umbrella caved in on itself. She gave up, put it back in her bag and pulled up the hood of her parka instead.

'Come on,' she said. 'We've got to get him to the station. And we'll give Jess a lift home.'

**

Rick is snoring, though if I wake him, he'll deny it. End-of-weekend sex – a pretty significant weekend for me – and he was out like a light. But he does seem to have stopped whinging about the election. I know he's not fully reconciled to me standing, but at least he's gone quiet on the subject. Just as well, because I'm going over and over everything I've got to do and the less sniping from Rick, the better. This is the uncertain pre-campaigning period. There's a lot of pre- at the moment. Pre-selection, pre-election, pre-life-as-I-don't-yet-know-it, all at the same time as running the school. Canvassing support to get on the shortlist, talking to everyone, promoting myself – that's the hardest thing, harder than anything I've had to do before. Persuading a panel of depressed-looking school governors that I was the best person to rescue a sinking school doesn't compare to this. It's all about me. Me, me, me. I'd like to think going into politics is altruistic. But it doesn't feel like it. Vote for me. I'm the greatest. I'll be the best candidate, the best MP you could possibly have. Better than anyone else.

Public life requires so much self-belief, so much self-deception, so much gliding over the cracks. That's the nature of politics, you can't get round it. You have to project an image that isn't necessarily you. It's what put me off when I was younger. I should hate it, the very idea, but now somehow I don't.

Rick will keep me grounded, perhaps that's the good thing about his lack of enthusiasm. If he thinks I'm getting too full of myself, he'll force-feed me a spoonful of Rick-style cynicism and remind me that I'm just Kirsty, Kirsty who sometimes likes to slob out in front of Saturday night telly, who needs to lose a pound or two and who has occasionally been known to dash off to work without having time for a shower. And he'll kick away my soapbox if he thinks I'm posturing too much, and I'll try hard not to be irritated when he does.

He didn't have much to say at lunch. I guess it was the cold, it's still there. But Adam more than made up for him. Oh God, what are we going to do with our son? I love him to bits, but I know we've spoilt him. Everything's been served up to him so easily. And yet I can't put him on a diet of gruel just because that's what I had.

Jess, though, she's the one I can't help thinking about. I must find time to ring her about those grant applications. She shouldn't have to worry about money, none of us should have had to. First in the family to university and all that – she needs encouragement. Adam will help in his own way, but a relationship at their age isn't likely to last for long. Nothing lasts for ever when you're eighteen, though it feels as if it will.

She reminds me of me. Me at that age.

Stop thinking. Block out memories. Mind, body, close down. Oh God, Rick's muttering to himself and turning over. Please don't wake up. He'll want to know what I'm worrying about. Nothing. I've got nothing to worry about.

'You're kidding me. Kirsty Dewhirst–'

'Osmond.'

'Whatever. Your missus, Kirsty *Osmond*, is going for the Labour nomination – that's what you're telling me? Well, you kept fucking quiet about that, didn't you?'

'She only decided on the weekend.'

'Yeah, yeah. But you must have known she was thinking about it.'

Monday morning in Clive's office. He drummed his fingers on the space bar in front of him and the cursor jumped about on the screen irritably. He appeared to be thinking. I could see the cogs randomly going round in his brain, although once they came to a halt, their resting place was always unsurprising.

'Right,' he said, 'I want you off anything – everything – to do with the by-election now. That's now, immediately. You're not running the coverage and you're definitely not writing any fucking editorials. Shona can refer everything to me. I'm deciding what we do – and believe me, that won't be any more than we have to.'

This discussion wasn't going quite as I'd hoped. I knew I'd have to stand back from politics, but surely I could seize the initiative and keep a semblance of control. Instead I was like a recalcitrant teenager being grounded for some act of juvenile defiance. I was powerless and we both knew it.

It had gone wrong from the moment I'd walked into Clive's office. I was suddenly aware that revealing my news to him would make it real in a way it wasn't when it was merely a family confidence shared among the three of us. Oh, and Jess. And Phil. And most of the local Labour Party of course. And whoever else she'd let it slip to. Half the world knew already. But this felt like the point of no return.

Clive swivelled round in his chair to face me.

'What made her want to do it then?'

He picked up an apple from his desk and took a noisy bite. If there was one thing worse than the prospect of my wife going into politics, it was my boss torturing me over it. I ground my fist into the palm of the other hand behind my back. What would it be like to smash Clive to pulp? The splash of blood, the crack of bone, the look in his eyes when he realised I was going to kill him… Fantasising was as far as I got. Hitting people had always seemed an unnecessary flamboyance. I had to learn to box at school and never saw the point of it. There were less dangerous ways of winning. I unfurled my fist.

'I'm surprised you're interested.'

'I'm not.' He took another bite of the apple. 'Just mildly curious as to why anyone would want to go into that snake pit. Your wife's got a good job, hasn't she? Pillar of the community and all that. Why fuck that up just to become Lobby fodder?'

He was right and I was almost tempted to agree with him. Yes, Clive, she's taken leave of her senses, it's a dreadful career move. Perhaps I should have had him there with me that night we debated things round the kitchen table. But my allegiance was now settled, or rather, it had been settled for me.

'You won't be surprised to hear that's not how she sees it,' I said. 'She reckons she can make a difference and do something really worthwhile for North Humberside.'

'Pfft. Well she's fucking things up for both of you. Funny, I always thought your wife was a smart woman.'

I dug my nails into my hand and concentrated on the pain. There had once been an incident. It was at an office party – the first year we were in Hull when the *Citizen* still held Christmas parties. I'd been in the job only a couple of weeks and wasn't too bothered about going to some office shindig. Privately I was still smarting at the exile from London and wasn't convinced that any of my new colleagues was worth spending extra time with. But when I idly mentioned it to Kirsty, she told me not to be so miserable. Of course I should go. As deputy editor, I had to be there, everyone would expect it. And she would go too. She missed our social life in London. She wanted to meet my new colleagues. She'd get something new to wear. We'd have fun. I didn't entirely believe her. She was protesting too much and I was being patronised. But I gave in to keep her happy.

She went shopping the following weekend and bought a dress that I hadn't seen until she walked into the newsroom on the evening of the party, one Friday two weeks before Christmas. It was sparkly black and bravely short. Definitely not her regular kit. She'd come straight from school and must have changed in the ladies. She stood at the door, three inches taller than usual in high, strappy sandals. Her hair was loose, her lips were crimson and her earrings reached almost to her collarbones. Had we been at one of those pretentious media parties we sometimes went to in London, she'd have blended in well. But in the *Citizen* newsroom… even now I wonder what she was thinking of. Half-hearted tinsel was strung around a few computer screens and Christmas cards littered desks, but all of that did little to relieve the dinginess of the place. No-one else had bothered to dress up. Why would you do that just for warm wine and peanuts with your colleagues? That was the collective assumption, I'd discovered late on. Maybe

I'd forgotten to tell her.

I was at the other side of the room, but I caught her eye as she entered and she must have picked up the mild alarm in my face. She glanced around at the blur of sweaters and boots and crumpled shirts. If there was any uncertainty, it disappeared quickly. With just the smallest downward tug at her dress, she smiled at me confidently. It's okay, I can handle this, she was saying, finish your conversation with your colleague. I dragged my eyes away from her and back to an increasingly loud and unsteady Mike Hufford, who was talking at me, rather than to me, completely unaware that he'd lost my attention.

'I mean, the regional press just isn't what it was. When I started out as a rookie journalist – probably you too, Nick–'

'Rick.'

'Well when we started out, Nick, Rick… when we started out, things were different. You learnt through doing it. Now these kids come out of journalism school and flash around their degrees, diplomas, what have you, and they haven't got a bloody clue.'

He swigged from his beer bottle and burped.

'I give the *Citizen* ten years at the most. That'll see me out. Not sure about you, lad.'

I had to extricate myself and go over to her, get her a drink, steer her round the assembled throng. But Kirsty wasn't waiting. She'd walked over to the drinks table and Clive was next to her, pouring her a glass of wine.

'Excuse me, Mike. Catch up later.'

'Okay, Nick, don't mind me.' And he wandered off to find someone else to bore.

I made my way across the newsroom. Clive and Kirsty were now at the side of the drinks table, in the corner next to the photocopier. He was swaying slightly and slowly touching his glass against hers – not exactly a clink since the 'glasses' were plastic, more a physical innuendo. In her heels she was taller than he was and yet she appeared to be pinioned against the wall, trapped between Clive and the copier. He was standing too close, trailing the fingers of his free hand through her hair, across her bare shoulder, her throat. She was trying to pull away, but had nowhere to go. Christ almighty. He leaned over, whispered something in her ear and his hand hovered towards her breast. Then she spotted me and raised her eyebrows in a look that said, thank God, what kept you?

'Everything okay, Kirsty?'

Clive spun round and his mouth fell open. I could smell brandy on his breath and I felt my jaw tensing. In a different place and time, this would have meant pistols at dawn. Even at a booze-fuelled twenty-first century office party, it could have ended in fisticuffs. But there were other ways to manage things.

'Yes, more or less,' she said. 'I was just talking to – sorry, I didn't catch your name.'

'Oh, no need for…' Clive said, avoiding eye contact with either of us. 'I'll just, er…' And he turned to go. I stepped in front of him.

'Don't rush away. In fact, let me introduce you properly. Kirsty, this is Clive Pascoe, the *Citizen*'s managing editor. Clive, this is my wife, Kirsty Osmond.'

'Pleased to meet you,' she said, and she was a headmistress again, about to deliver a disappointing performance review to a junior member of staff.

He cleared his throat. 'Well I'd better get–'

'Kirsty moved here in September,' I said, 'to settle our son in at school and to start a new job. She's a teacher.'

'I see. Well, as I say, I'll–'

'She's just taken on a headship.' I raised my voice

above shrieks of laughter from a group nearby. 'The Phoenix School. She's steering it through to academy status. A big challenge.'

Clive's mouth opened again and remained open. The alcohol in his blood had rendered the world incomprehensible.

'Phoenix?' he said eventually. 'Yes, I'd heard they'd appointed… Well, must circulate. Nice talking to you, Mrs, er, Dewhirst.' And he retreated hastily into the crowd.

'Cunt.'

'Rick!'

'The man's a complete prick.'

She smiled. 'Well I did think about chucking my wine over him, but I assumed he was a colleague and I didn't want to make things embarrassing for you. But your boss… not sure what to say about that.'

She shook her head and I pulled her to me.

'I'm sorry. I guess things like that don't happen in the Phoenix staff room.'

'Not often, no.'

'A bit like being back in Westminster, though?'

Her face creased in disapproval.

'Okay, inappropriate remark, sorry,' I said.

She drew away from me and looked around the room. 'I guess I misjudged things tonight. This dress…'

'Rubbish. It's a great dress. But rather wasted here.'

'Why didn't you warn me about the dress code? I thought party might actually mean party.'

'Sorry. Look, I'll talk to Clive on Monday. When he's sober. Being drunk doesn't excuse what he did. I'm really sorry.'

'For God's sake, Rick, stop apologising. And don't say anything to him. Let's just forget it.' She looked over to where Clive was trying to infiltrate a group of his colleagues. 'He's a lonely man, I'd say.'

'If by lonely you mean screwed up, you're right.'

We left shortly after that and I added the evening's experience to my burgeoning collection of reasons to despise my new boss. But, as Kirsty requested, I said nothing. It took several days for him to look me in the eye. The following year there was no office party and, as far as I knew, he and Kirsty had never crossed each other's paths again. The paper carried occasional news – good and bad – about Phoenix Academy and it had a paragraph on Kirsty herself when she got her OBE. Clive didn't pass on his congratulations. In fact for eight years he never mentioned her to me. As far as he was concerned, I didn't have a wife or a personal life. Not until that morning.

'They'll have an all-women shortlist no doubt,' he was saying. 'Women taking over the fucking world.' He shook his head and threw his apple core in the bin. 'If I was you, I'd lie low for the time being. Keep your mouth shut. Take any leave you've got. Or make yourself useful. Write something we can run. Pretend to be a real hack again. That complaint over the rats story, you've got that to sort to start with.'

He waved his hand in my direction without looking at me. I was a chastened flunkey being dismissed. I got up to leave, but as I put my hand on the door handle, he said, 'I just hope she knows what she's doing. If they can bring down a seasoned politician like Barraclough, what chance does your wife stand if they decide to go for her?'

I slowly turned round to face him.

'My wife happens to have honesty and decency on her side.'

'Yeah well. Just a friendly warning.'

And pure Clive Pascoe. At that moment I loathed him even more than I had at the Christmas party. But

Clive and his twisted logic were no longer my main concern. I needed to talk to Shona. She had looked at me pointedly when she'd got in that morning, but I'd avoided any conversation till I'd spoken to Clive. And now she seemed to have gone out.

'Said she was going to see some councillor,' Dan said. 'Off-diary. Guess she's working on a feature.'

That piece she was determined to do about likely by-election candidates, the piece I'd wanted put on hold… But now… well now, everything was out and I definitely had to speak to her. My wife was a person of interest.

Shona still wasn't back at lunchtime and I decided to go out for some air – the atmosphere in the office was oppressive. I'd take a quick saunter in the wintry sunshine and buy a sandwich in the Old Town. The lift was on the ground floor so I walked down the three flights of concrete steps. A couple of people I knew by sight emerged from the mortgage brokers on the first floor and we nodded at each other. The stairwell was drafty. People rarely stopped to speak.

I had first met Clive – and first walked down those stairs – one similarly bright day more than eight years earlier. I had the sense of escaping from the county jail and I wasn't planning on returning. There had been three of them on the interview panel: Clive, a woman from HR, and the elderly vice-chairman of the board, apparently there to make up the numbers. I had mugged up thoroughly on the region and the *Citizen* and had a fair idea of what they were looking for. I'd been on the other side of the table often enough and understood the underlying matrix that the panel would be working to. I even caught an upside-down glimpse of the question grid the HR woman was busy scribbling on.

She looked up over her glasses and said, 'Can you tell

us a little more about your responsibilities in your present role?'

This was my chance to show them what a favour I was doing them by even turning up for this interview.

'Well, I lead an in-house editorial team – there are ten of us altogether – and I also commission pieces from politicians and academics. I write most of the leading articles and decide on the general editorial direction. So I'm pretty autonomous. Oh, and the budget of course. I–'

I was interrupted by Clive, who snorted and said, 'That's all very well, but what you've got there is a niche political title with a hefty cover price. A long way from the real world of regional newspapers. Hull's not SW1, you know.'

I was beginning to sense something decidedly uncongenial about this small man with thinning dark grey hair hanging lankly on his collar and what appeared to be a perma-scowl on his lips.

'If you come here, you won't be stuck in the Westminster bubble, schmoozing politicians in fancy watering holes. Or writing leaders on the outcome of G20 summits, pontificating on the state of the world.'

'Look, I trained on the biggest paper in the North-East, I've covered Westminster for lots of regional dailies, I was a correspondent on the London *Evening Standard*. I know what makes local papers tick.'

The HR woman coughed and slid my upside-down curriculum vitae towards Clive.

'Yes, we can see your… your extensive experience,' she said. 'I think the managing editor was just testing your… well, just wanting to remind you that this would be quite a… a shift from your present environment.'

I snatched a glance at the grim magnolia walls of the windowless meeting room. That was certainly true.

Clive was making notes and didn't look up. He didn't

speak again while the woman discussed the remuneration bracket and how much notice I was required to give in my present post. I'd done my research and knew there were no internal candidates. I was fairly sure the job was mine. I was also very sure I didn't want it.

But as I trekked back to the station, I knew I had no choice. Kirsty was preoccupied with her new job – she hadn't even had time for a quick coffee the day I was in Hull – and Adam seemed surprisingly happy at his new school. If I wanted to end weekend commuting from London, if family life was to return to something resembling normal, then I had to find a job in the area. And the prospects of any other suitable role seemed remote. I was shafted, my life as a serious journalist over.

The next day, the HR woman rang and offered me the post of deputy editor at *The Humberside Citizen*. I accepted immediately and braced myself for a period of incarceration in a remote and charmless part of England, a sacrifice being made for Kirsty.

I'd promised myself it wouldn't be an indefinite sentence. Although I never mentioned it to her, I set a time limit – five years maximum, and then we'd look elsewhere, Manchester, Birmingham, Newcastle or, better still, go back to London. But it didn't work out like that. Five years passed and Phoenix Academy was still a work-in-progress for Kirsty, while the *Citizen* turned out to be marginally better than I'd expected. I accepted early on that my new boss didn't like me – I was his overqualified deputy with London ways and a high-flying wife, and we'd humiliated him at an office party. But I learnt to manoeuvre around his unpleasantness, picking my battles carefully and ignoring those I had no chance of winning. I even developed a reluctant admiration for the man's indifference to what anyone thought of him. The *Citizen* might not have been cutting-edge journalism and no, this was not where young Rick Dewhirst thought he'd end up, but there was a certain satisfaction in being responsible for producing a paper every day. What's more, I'd lined myself up as Clive's obvious successor early on and it had seemed only a matter of time until I was managing editor.

As for our adopted home, well, Hull remained a tough place, very different from the genteel Yorkshire where I'd grown up, but not without a raw charm. Perhaps we had more in common than I'd imagined, Hull and me. It had quietly insinuated itself in my favour.

And now on a Monday lunchtime I was queuing in an artisanal café that had opened to cater for last year's City of Culture visitors and seemed to have survived their departure. I toyed with the choice of a quinoa salad or a Wensleydale ploughman's and wondered whether it was mild enough to walk towards the Minster and sit outside for ten minutes. My cold was still lurking but I'd ignored it all morning. Perhaps I could venture inside the church – it might be a tad warmer there – and sit and think.

'Rick.'

I turned round. Shona was two behind me in the queue.

'I need to talk to you,' she said.

Five minutes later, we'd found a bench near the church. Chilly, but private.

'You should have said.'

'She was still deciding. I couldn't.'

'Suppose not. I heard last night by the way.'

'So, if you're talking to people, do they think she's…'

'She stands a chance? Come on, of course they do. You must know that. She could turn out to be the frontrunner. I was with Patsy Harvey this morning and it's clear she's worried. She thought she had it in the bag and now she's got big competition. Kirsty's seen as a serious person with a serious job. And people I've talked to reckon that'll go down well with the voters. She's not a career politician, not one of the usual suspects.'

I took off my gloves and unwrapped my ploughman's. Hadn't I said something like that at some point?

'Does Clive know yet?' Shona asked.

'I told him this morning. Let's say he didn't exactly overdo the warm wishes. Of course I'm completely off the election as long as Kirsty's in the running. You're on your own, Shona.'

'Oh, don't worry about me. I can't wait for things to get moving.'

Should I be handing her all my contacts, the ultimate surrender? Over the past few days, there'd been numerous calls from people wanting to talk, share this and that, give me their election predictions, and all I could say was, 'Yes, interesting'. I was set to vaporise, to become a nonentity.

Shona put down her sandwich. 'The thing is, what about you?'

I watched as an excitable crocodile of schoolchildren made its way across Trinity Square and stopped outside the Minster. The children were getting a pep talk from one of the two teachers with them. They quietened down and then started to file in through the main doors under the huge Gothic windows.

'Me?'

'What are you going to do if she gets selected. Where's it leave you?'

'That's more or less what my son asked. He suggested I start my own blog.' I laughed. 'As if.'

'It's not a bad idea, actually. The inside view from the candidate's husband.' She started to pack her sandwich debris back into its paper carrier bag. 'But you must be starting to think about the future, Kirsty getting selected, becoming an MP, and then if Labour get their act together and make it into government… Your life's going to be very different.'

'I guess it is.'

We walked back through the Land of Green Ginger, carefully side-stepping a group of noisy German – or were they Dutch? – teenagers blocking the pavement of the narrow thoroughfare. Hull was still milking its culture city legacy, attracting visitors keen to explore the most exotically named street in England. Green Ginger. The old spice trade was long dead and, cobble stones and ancient public house apart, there wasn't much to see in the street. But the city was learning new tricks, learning to trade on the phantasmagoria in place of its old shipping and fishing industries. The Land of Green Ginger. This would soon be part of Kirsty's constituency. Kirsty Osmond, the MP for Green Ginger.

And Rick Dewhirst, could he learn new tricks too? So far I seemed to be just the Spouse, green and raw and fretting that I didn't know how to deal with this sort of thing. The Spouse? What sort of role was that, for fuck's sake? Women had had generations of practice at subordination. We were still relatively new to it. What did it even mean? Fielding her phone calls? Collecting her dry cleaning? Being wheeled out alongside her, her loyal batman? Was that all I was worth?

I could do better than that. I might have lost the first round, but a new strategy was called for. I'd lived with Kirsty for twenty-four years and knew her foibles intimately. I also had a keen understanding of politics. And that qualified me to be more than a lowly factotum. Forget the dry cleaning. What if I were the puppet master, behind the scenes, pulling the strings, quietly influencing the action, protecting her? Shona and Adam were right, my opinions did count for something. This would require some reinvention, but I owed myself a favour or two.

Part Two

The Project

It was the night before the selection meeting and we were making supper. I was beating the eggs for an omelette while Kirsty was staring into a nearly empty fridge.

'Can you go to the supermarket on your way back tomorrow?' she said. 'We need milk and a few other things. Sorry, I know it's my turn, but I've got too much to do.'

Which went without saying. She was busy and I was biding my time. She'd been out almost every evening for the past ten days, going straight from school to join her loyal cadre of supporters, Team Osmond, meeting people from constituency committees, special interest groups, trade unions, lobbying yet more of the undecideds. Her job was to persuade and charm as many members of the local party as she could. I'd never thought of charm as one of my wife's more notable characteristics. But politics requires some pretence.

'Let's practise your speech again after we've eaten,' I said.

'I'd prefer to go over the questions I might get.'

Her path to here had been smoother than she'd expected. Jim was formally neutral as party chair but they were in daily contact. The initial interview had gone well, she said, rigorous of course, since she was an unknown quantity and wasn't on the party's parliamentary panel. They'd delved into her commitment, her political and professional experience, the reasons she hadn't put her name forward before, the practicalities of standing down as a headteacher and her views on everything from handling Brexit to abolishing private schools' charitable status (that was particularly easy). She had – after some persuasion – accepted my offer of doing practice-interviews and these had paid off. She had won over the interrogation panel and her application had been endorsed by the National Executive. I was beginning to feel proud of my protégée, even though she didn't seem to realise that's what she was.

It was now narrowed down to a shortlist of four: Kirsty, Cllr Patsy Harvey, the foodbank founder Yasmin Farooqi, and a prominent local trade unionist Sonia Devlin. All women of course. And tomorrow evening, constituency party members would meet to make their choice. One member, one vote. All she had to do was face a hall full of socialists and tell them why she was the best person to represent them in this election.

Adam had been aggrieved to discover that his new membership card did not actually allow him to attend the meeting and vote. There was a six-month qualification period.

'You'll still smash it,' he'd said. He was back in Newcastle, but ringing up every day for a progress report.

I was also a new party member. Yes, I had shocked Kirsty – and myself – and joined. A lifetime's practised neutrality down the pan. If she didn't win the nomination, I could always cancel the direct debit. If she did, our project was underway.

We ate quickly. This was the last chance she'd have to rehearse and she seemed nervous about the unpredictability of it all. She had devoured the party's manifesto from the last election ('Do you honestly buy all of this?' I'd asked and she'd said, 'The principles, yes, the practice may need minor adjustments,') and she was thoroughly au fait with all the key policy points and their implications locally. But questions could come in any form, obliquely, trickily. She pulled over an A4 pad from the other end of the kitchen table and handed it to me.

'Let's go through a few things again.'

I leaned back in my chair and scanned the topic headings. I'd helped her draw up the list and we'd been over nearly everything on previous nights, sometimes in bed, with Kirsty endlessly nuancing her position on a subject – 'Yes, I voted Remain, but I respect the outcome… is respect the right word, Rick? is it too restrained?... and our job now is to scrutinise and challenge how the government gets the country there… does that sound right?' – and me occasionally drifting off as her voice mellowed into white noise.

'Any areas you especially want to go over?' I said.

'Just be random. Put yourself in the position of someone who's given up his Thursday night to come and listen to would-be MPs bragging about why they could do the job. Someone who looks at a hopeful like me and sees a professional woman who lives in a big house in a posh part of the city and knows nothing about his life.'

'Don't even think of yourself in those terms. Too negative.'

'It's how lots of people will see me. And I like to have an individual in mind when I work out what I'm going to say. A real person. Someone like my dad – not that he ever joined the party, but if he had…'

Her dad. She hadn't mentioned him for years. How odd that she should do so now, that she should imagine her father as someone upon whom her success depended. That wasn't the relationship I recalled.

I had met Billy Osmond only once, in the nineties, when Kirsty and I had been together a few months. I was surprised when she suggested visiting him – up to then, she'd always been reluctant to talk about her family. All she had told me was that her mother had died from lung cancer while she was at university and her father wasn't well – emphysema, she said. We were having our first weekend away and were heading for the Yorkshire Dales.

Half-way up the M1, she said, 'I'd like to drop in on my dad, if you don't mind. It's a while since I've seen him. We don't have to stop long. Just a flying visit.'

Billy lived in a pebble-dashed semi on a bleak estate on the outskirts of Sheffield. The front garden was mainly concreted over, with a few straggly rosebushes in a border at the side. There were yellowing lace curtains at the windows, a satellite dish on the roof and an air of neglect about the whole place. This, I assumed, was where Kirsty herself had grown up. I'd known all along that our backgrounds were very different and, to be honest, that had always been part of her appeal. Working class felt a little exotic. But as we knocked at the front door and waited, I was suddenly unsure of my role. I'd been in places like this as a journalist often enough, interviewing the occupants but detached from their lives. Now I was here as a participant.

A woman opened the door and said, 'Oh, it's you.' Kirsty had told me her sister Julie lived on the same road as Billy and kept an eye on him. She was an older, heavier version of Kirsty, with a tired face and badly dyed hair pulled tight into a ponytail. She glanced at me for a moment and then, still unsmiling, turned back to Kirsty. 'Suppose you'd better come in.'

Billy was slumped in an armchair by the front window and shared Julie's lack of enthusiasm for their visitors. He nodded at Kirsty as if she'd popped in from round the corner. Then he spotted me and narrowed his eyes.

'Who's this, then?'

The effort of speaking brought on a coughing fit and he pulled a grubby handkerchief from his cardigan pocket and spat into it. He was a thin, pale man with a full head of white hair and milky eyes. I guessed he was not yet sixty. He looked twenty years older.

'It's Rick. My boyfriend.'

'I gathered that. What's he do, then?'

'Rick's a journalist, Dad. We met at Westminster.'

'Very pleased to meet you, Mr Osmond,' I said, and offered my hand.

Billy ignored my outstretched hand and went back to drinking his tea.

'Oh, don't mind him,' Julie said. 'His hearing's not too good these days and he was never much cop with strangers, anyway. Shy really, aren't you, Dad?' And she gently ruffled her father's hair.

Billy made a strange guttural noise – whether a symptom of illness or disapproval, I wasn't sure – then turned up the volume on the TV remote control and immersed himself in the football. I doubted whether he could hear much over his own coughing.

Julie turned her attention to her sister, looking her up and down.

'Well we haven't seen you for a while. Thought you might have forgotten where we live.'

'I've been busy. Sorry. It's not been easy to get away.'

'We do have telephones in Sheffield, you know. And Dad's not well in case you'd forgotten that, too. His chest has got really bad.'

'I'm sorry, Julie, I should've…'

I tried to catch Kirsty's eye, but she looked away. I'd not seen her like this before, admonished, awkward. A side to her I'd never have guessed.

'Yeah, perhaps you should. But at least one of us is around to make sure he eats and gets to his hospital appointments.' Julie lit a cigarette. 'I expect you want a cup of tea now you're here.'

She led us through to the kitchen. Both women were

silent for a few moments, locked in their own separate thoughts, it seemed. There was just the sound of the kettle and the football roar from the other side of a thin wall. After what seemed an age the kettle came to the boil and Julie poured water into three mugs.

'So how's that job of yours that's keeping you so busy then? Never understood what made you want to work with that lot. But I expect it pays well.'

She flicked ash into the sink.

'Not really,' said Kirsty. 'Not for London. But I'm not complaining, the money's okay.'

'I bet it is. Still, don't think it'd be up my street. Honest to God, MPs, what a rabble.'

Julie drew on her cigarette again and looked at the exhaled circle of smoke as if it were a barrier between her and her sister. I wondered how long this flying visit was going to last. I'd given up smoking the previous month after some coercion from Kirsty, and the fug in the kitchen was agonising.

'Anyway, did you get chance to ask her?' Julie said.

'Ask who?'

'About Will moving up to secondary school. I mentioned it a while back. Remember?

'Julie, I told you. Janet's not your MP. You have to write to your own.'

'Like he'd listen! I just thought you might help. The school we look like getting… well, let's just say half the parents don't speak English. I've nothing against them but Will's a sensitive boy and at secondary they come under all sorts of influences, don't they? He needs a decent school. Even if it's a ten-mile bus journey to get there.'

Both sisters seemed to have forgotten my presence. I shifted from one leg to the other, in part wishing I wasn't there, in part fascinated by something way beyond my personal experience. Divided communities, divided families – what brilliant material for a feature this could have made. If only. I let my gaze wander out of the window and settle on a pair of fat robins perched on a sickly-looking shrub, bickering over who had the right to the few remaining berries.

'You can't always judge a school from appearances,' Kirsty was saying. 'Lots of schools with Asian-majority pupils do very well academically. Better often than predominantly white schools.'

'But it's not just about exams, is it?' Julie said. 'Don't get me wrong, I'm not being racist, but you want somewhere your child will fit in. Multi-cultural this and multi-cultural that – it's all very well in London but you don't live round here. And you don't have kids, you wouldn't know. Just wait till you do. As a parent all you want is the best for your children. What's wrong with that?'

The robins flew away and I sneaked a look back at Kirsty. Her face was still and she seemed to be relying on a reserve tank of patience. It would have been different if Julie had not been her sister, if the view had been expressed by someone else. They would have received a passionate tirade on how we all benefit from cultural diversity, how racism damages the offender as well as the victim. Kirsty had a whole armoury of righteous arguments and I'd once seen her slaughter someone in the pub for – to my mind – a much more innocent remark. But an older sister... and in these circumstances... clearly this was different.

'Everyone wants the best for their kids, Julie, but I'm sure Will's going to do perfectly well in the local school and make some great friends, whatever you think. It's hardly something my boss is going to interfere in.'

Oh Kirsty, do you have to sound quite so

patronising, I remember thinking. Julie stubbed out her cigarette in her empty mug and glared at her sister. I had wondered whether she'd been purposefully goading her, but now I decided that wasn't it. She'd been genuinely trying to appeal to some lost notion of sisterhood. It had been a misjudgement and she knew it. The two women lived on different planets and quite honestly I wasn't sure which of them I felt more sympathy for.

'Don't bother,' Julie said. 'If you can't help, you can't. I just thought… I mean, having a sister who works for an MP, I thought you might…'

'It doesn't work like that, Julie. Really, it doesn't.'

'Doesn't it? If you say so.'

Julie collected the mugs and plonked them down next to the sink. The visit appeared to be coming to a natural end. Kirsty went into the lounge to say goodbye to her father and I heard Billy mutter something in response. I waited by the front door and studied the Chinese take-away menu stuck to the wall. Next to it was a framed photograph of two girls in maroon school jumpers, both dark-haired, both unsmiling, the bigger one about ten, the smaller one perhaps six or seven. Two little girls full of promise. I'd never seen pictures of Kirsty as a child before and I barely had time to scrutinise this one, for she was calling 'Bye, Julie' to her sister in the kitchen and was with me in the hall. She looked at the photograph but said nothing. Then she closed the door behind us and glanced at me, her eyes saying that's it, duty done for another year. It occurred to me that Billy might not last another year.

I expected her to explode in frustration once we were in the car, or to deliver a lecture on the need to bring communities together. She didn't. We drove without speaking for half a mile or so and then she said, 'I'm sorry. For taking you there.'

'No need to apologise.' I meant it.

'They're difficult.'

'You haven't met my family yet.'

She ignored the offered tangent.

'It's funny, but Julie and me, we used to get on as kids. Played together all the time – she was just… very protective. My big sister. I remember once when some kids were throwing stones at us and one caught me. A nasty cut.' She touched the tiny scar on her forehead. 'Julie yelled and chased them away.' Her hand returned to the steering wheel. 'But now, well now she resents me. She thinks I've got above myself.'

'You're… you're very different. For sisters, I mean.'

'She had Will in her teens. Suppose we had different interests. To be honest, I couldn't wait to get away. I guess that's obvious.'

'You could say that.'

'But as for my dad, well, he's just plain rude.'

'He's ill.'

'I try to make allowances, but it's not easy. Julie's got a certain way with him and I don't. I should have but I don't.'

'Well, strikes me she simply gets on with it. She's there for him when he needs her. You cleared off – and just swan in if you're passing by.'

A facetious remark, but I was merely trying to lighten the mood. I was still learning to negotiate my girlfriend at that stage and sometimes I miscalculated. But she gave a couple of nods and looked thoughtful.

'True. She's been a better daughter than I have.' She took a deep breath. 'He didn't see the point of me going to university. Said it was wasted on a girl. I should be earning a living and looking for a husband to take me off his hands – that's what he actually said, like I was some nineteenth-century spinster. Instead, I was poncing around reading books and taking drugs and going on demos – his idea of students. When my mum stuck up for me, he shouted her down.'

She looked straight ahead and it was as if she were talking to the windscreen, not to me. In profile, she looked a little like Billy, the curve of the forehead, the tightness of the jaw.

'Your dad was a miner?' I asked.

She'd never said, but I'd always assumed Billy had worked in the pits. Emphysema and South Yorkshire – I'd put two and two together. But I did sometimes wonder why, as a good socialist, she hadn't made more of it.

'For years, yes, he was,' she said. 'But he left, what, ten, twelve years ago, after the strike. He was never one of Scargill's men. If pits were going to close, they were going to close, he said. Didn't see the point in fighting the inevitable. He crossed the picket lines. He… he was a scab.'

Well this was more revealing than most of the things I'd got out of her. She paused to concentrate as we approached a roundabout and I kept quiet.

'He was made redundant, got an okay pay-off and set up a taxi business. Mum gave up her shop job and helped with the admin and things weren't bad for a few years. Surprising that my dad had any business flair, really… But then Mum died and he got ill and that was it.'

I'd interviewed men like Billy when I worked in Newcastle. Ex-miners always made good copy. But it was hard to place this man and this brittle relationship in Kirsty's life. My own youthful discord with my family was unremarkable by comparison.

We'd come to a junction.

'So, now you know my family history,' she said. 'Should we get back on the motorway or stick to minor roads?'

'Minor roads.'

'But I don't want to talk about it anymore. Have you found somewhere to stay tonight?'

I was having difficulty getting a signal on my Nokia so we stopped at a phone box to ring a couple of places from my guide book. The first one had a room and within two hours we were relaxing over whiskies in front of a hearty fire in the bar of the King's Arms. Our room was magnificent, better than we could possibly have expected at such short notice: en-suite with a four-poster and looking out spectacularly across the dales. It was a long way from both Westminster and Sheffield and the weekend was going to be wonderful after all. And so it turned out to be. We walked and drank and made love and I knew I'd never met anyone quite like Kirsty before.

Six months later Billy was dead. If she felt guilty, she never said so.

I put my elbows on the kitchen table and rested my chin in one hand.

'So, let me get this right. You want me to pretend to be your dad and ask why a privileged, university-educated woman like you should represent the poor and down-trodden of North Humberside.'

She winced. 'I'll ignore that. Look, whoever it is, this imaginary person I've got to persuade, they're looking for someone they can believe in, someone who shares their values. I've got a working-class background. And if that comes up, fine, though I'm not going to flaunt it shamelessly.'

'You should flaunt it. It gives you credibility. Someone who's worked hard to get where she is, who understands class politics better than most people.'

'Can we just get on with this, please?'

I knew better than to push the subject – the last thing she needed before the selection meeting was a row. But that political naïvety of hers was going to take some working on.

'So, Ms Osmond, if you're selected, how will you clean up the reputation of politics and politicians after recent events?'

'That's a ridiculous question, Rick. They won't ask that.'

'It's what everyone'll be thinking, believe me.'

'Something else, please.'

'Suit yourself.' I shrugged and looked at my list. My protégée could be unaccommodating at times. 'So… what would you say to persuade an outside employer to set up in North Humberside? How would you sell the constituency?'

'That's better,' she said, with a flicker of condescension. 'Well, North Humberside has enormous untapped potential. We have the space, the infrastructure and, above all, the people…'

And so we went on. Two hours of intensive grilling – on employment locally and nationally, the state of the economy, NHS funding, pensions, housing. Finally I dropped my notepad to the table.

'How about a break? You don't want to exhaust yourself before the actual event. Barraclough's successor's got to come over as full of beans tomorrow.'

In truth it was me who was flagging. Kirsty could no doubt have continued all night. But she opened her mouth as if to say something and then closed it again. What had I said? Barraclough? Was that it? We'd barely mentioned him by name since she'd applied for the nomination. It was as if he were now an extraneous detail that got in the way of what she had to do.

'Well? What is it?'

'I don't know whether I should tell you this, but…' She paused. 'I heard from… well, from someone… that Barraclough's wife has left him. She's filing for divorce, apparently.'

'Really?'

Was that all? Still, a useful titbit. I picked up my phone to make a note to tell Shona to check on it in the morning. Clive of course would say this sort of tittle-tattle was of no interest to the *Citizen*. Shona would beg to differ and I – if I were still allowed to express a view – would back her up. The former's MP's private life was of huge interest – anything to keep the story going while the police continued their investigations. Clearly Mrs B wasn't waiting for the court case. She'd already passed judgment on her husband.

Kirsty looked uncomfortably at my phone.

'It's not really newsworthy, is it?'

'You're joking. Though the only really surprising thing is that she stuck it out for so long. Can *you* imagine being married to Martin Barraclough?'

Kirsty tried to smile. 'Politics destroys marriages,' she said quietly.

'I don't think it's politics that's destroyed that particular one.'

'I shouldn't have told you.' She stood up. 'Anyway, I'll make coffee and then can we get back to a few more questions?'

We managed another half-hour on local issues but her concentration had gone. I put the question list down and kissed her on the forehead.

'Let's call it a night. You have my vote.'

'You don't have one. Not at this stage, anyhow. Just in case you've forgotten.'

I kissed her again, on the mouth. I'd done as much as

I could for now. She'd be fine. No, more than that, she'd be brilliant. I didn't need to be there to imagine her standing at the front of a crowded church hall, blazing with determination, sounding like the MP she was set to become (with my help).

But being a smart politician was about more than rhetoric. I thought about Barraclough again. I also remembered Clive's so-called friendly warning. And his snake pit. Snakes in Parliament, crocodiles lurking outside, ready to bite. There were enemies without and within. We were going to have to deal with the reptiles.

Little more than two weeks ago, I was a headteacher worried about her school's exclusions policy. And now, all being well, I'm about to become Labour's parliamentary candidate for North Humberside. I want it so much. I'm shocked at how much.

We're all here in the church hall for the selection meeting, the four contenders for the nomination, and the place is filling up. We're taken to a side room where we draw lots on who speaks first and then await our turn. Patsy's first, then Sonia, then Yasmin. I'm last. Jim's running through how things will work. Ten minutes each, strictly timed, and afterwards we each answer the same questions from the floor. And then the paper vote and the count. Fair and equal and may the best woman win.

Jim has closed the door and we four women are alone in this small room where boxes of toys are stored for the daytime parent and toddler group. We're each waiting to perform and be judged. My hand is quivering – this is incredibly nerve-wracking – but I press it hard against my thigh and it feels steadier. And so we sit and wait while outside in the main hall the meeting goes through the preliminaries. Patsy asks how things are at the school and Yasmin tells us about a break-in they had at the foodbank – why would anyone bother to break in at a foodbank when all they have to do is walk in and ask? – and Sonia talks about her son's GCSE options. But nobody's heart is in the small talk.

Jim comes in to say they're ready for Patsy. I smile as she picks up her notes, a comradely smile of encouragement, and she looks away. It's not just me who's nervous. She's done this before, been shortlisted for selection in two other constituencies, and perhaps that makes it worse, a serial contender, risking another failure, the stakes higher. I imagine her out there, introducing herself. *For those who don't know me, I've worked in this constituency for twenty-five years and been a party member since I was fifteen.* This is someone I'd happily vote for. Under other circumstances.

Patsy's back in the room, flushed and beaming. And next it's Sonia, a very straight talker and one of the most experienced union activists in the local party. She has a hard core of support and they'll all be here tonight. Then it's Yasmin, a community campaigner who set up that foodbank almost single-handed and seems to have bags of grassroots backing. They're good, these women. Very good. We're spoilt for choice and I'm not sure who'd get my vote. Under other circumstances.

And now it's me and I'm walking into the hall and putting my notes on the table in front of me knowing I won't need them. I look around and feel a surge of exhilaration. I know how to do this. The others might have more direct political experience but this is where I come into my own. I've addressed hundreds of school assemblies, education conferences, too. I'm used to audiences, holding people, sensing the mood. The blood is pounding through my head but beyond it there's a lightness of being, as if I'm flying. I'm a gull soaring over clifftops and on towards the horizon. The world is boundless. All these people, about to listen to me, to absorb my ideas. For ten minutes they're entirely mine.

**

Nine thirty. It had to be over shortly. She'd promised she'd call as soon as she could. I wasn't going to look at social media or news sites. I wanted to hear it first from Kirsty.

My phone rang.

'I've done it.'

A small cloud passed in front of my eyes, from nowhere. But only for a moment. We were in this together.

'Congratulations!'

The atmosphere the other end of the phone sounded raucous. It must have been difficult to find somewhere to call from. She raised her voice.

'I'm so pleased it's over, this part anyway. I've just…' Her voice dipped. The background level of voices and laughter had risen. She let it subside. 'I've just got to talk to the press now.'

'The beginning of our adventure with the media.'

'Our? Anyway I'm going for a quick drink with the team after that. Want to join us?'

'No, I think I'll leave you to it.'

'Please yourself. I won't be late.'

I'd hoped she might want to come straight home to celebrate with me, but no matter. I scrolled through my Twitter feed. The official pronouncement was out from the party. She had secured twelve more votes than the second-placed candidate, Patsy Harvey. The news sites were full of it and friends and supporters were starting to join in. *Labour picks local headteacher for Humberside by-election… Favourite sees off rivals to become Labour by-election candidate… Well done @Kirsty-Osmond – a great candidate #womeninpolitics.* If there was anything less positive – and there would be, there always was – I wasn't going to look for it.

I switched my phone to silent. There were a few missed calls – no doubt people wanting to chat, pass on comments, even find out what the candidate's husband thought – but not that many. I pulled over my laptop and opened a new document. Perhaps this was the moment I'd waited for after all.

**

The pub's busy but we spot a table in the corner. I've promised Rick I won't stay long and I mean it. My head's a swirl of incomplete thoughts and I'm walking on stilts, six feet above the ground, balancing precariously. Mark offers to get a round and I ask for just a small white wine please, the smallest they do. Anything more and I'll lose all hold on reality. Someone recognises me from another table and raises a glass. And then someone else. Is this what it's going to be like now? Fame, of sorts. My chest tightens at the thought.

Tomorrow I'll go into school to confirm things with Louise – she's been tight-lipped ever since I told her I was going for it. In theory this is a sabbatical, but no-one expects me to return. My other life is floating away and I feel no guilt. I turn to Jim and say, I still can't quite believe it. (I'm learning to dissemble already.) We're lucky to have you, he replies. You're a complete breath of fresh air. But it'll be tough, you know. There are going to be people out there who hate your guts. Let's hope most of them are outside the party. He pats my arm and laughs at his own joke. Gerry will keep you on the straight and narrow.

Gerry is to be my election agent, my campaign manager. Some things don't change. Even if the candidates are female, the kingmakers, or rather queenmakers, the Jims, Gerrys, and the rest, are still male. They continue to set the rules and control us, or try to. There's work to do there, sisters. But not tonight.

Mark's back with our drinks and everyone toasts me

and I toast them and thank them for their support and I know there's no turning back now. I'm public property, out there, everybody's. My life will be spread out, for them all to pick over. The tightness in my chest is still there.

Jim raises his pint and says, so we start door-to-door tomorrow. I tell him Adam's keen to help when he gets home from Newcastle. Always good to have young faces in the squad, he says. Rick's thinking about it too, I add. Jim fiddles with a beer mat and says, really? The mood is quiet for a few moments, then someone offers to get another around. Thanks but no, I say. I should go. I need a good night's sleep before it all kicks off.

Above all I need to talk to my husband. It's happened so quickly and I know deep inside he's struggling. He's bound to find it tough standing on the sidelines.

**

A few hours ago my wife, Kirsty Osmond, was selected as Labour's candidate for the Humberside North by-election next month. I'm delighted, naturally – who wouldn't be? Yet I also find myself in very unfamiliar territory.

Over the past three decades, I've covered dozens of national and local elections as an impartial journalist. I've observed scores of candidates and reported on hundreds of manifestos, speeches and interviews.

But this by-election is going to be different.

For the first time ever, my professional impartiality is having to take a back seat. The regular coverage has to be left to others. Instead I'll be recording my own very personal impressions of a campaign in which I have a unique stake.

For this is the inside story from the candidate's husband.

Let's take a step back here and recall what led to this election: the former MP for North Humberside, Martin Barraclough, resigned following accusations of sexual assault. The matter currently sits with the Metropolitan Police. Regardless of the legal outcome, a job vacancy has arisen.

But is it a job that anyone would want?

Every political scandal — whether it's money or sex — leaves its mark on the popular imagination. To many people, Parliament must seem a pretty unsavoury club. At best, politicians are there just for the perks. At worst, they're drunk on power and privilege, egotistical, corrupt. What honest soul would want to apply for membership?

Let me introduce my wife.

Kirsty Osmond has been a teacher most of her working life. For nearly nine years she's been head of one of the tougher schools in one of the UK's tougher cities. She's worked her socks off for thousands of kids and their families here in Hull. She believes in what she's doing and the people she's doing it for. She is what I'd call a humanitarian heavyweight, although she'd hate the phrase. (An aside here: she and I haven't always agreed on politics, or various other things for that matter. Free debate is alive and well in our house and long may it continue.)

But I stand in unqualified awe of what she is now attempting. And I don't just mean winning more votes than anyone else on 26 April. No, it's about much more than nailing the electoral arithmetic. Kirsty is going into this to restore faith in politics. Without that, she'd say, what's the point of this by-election?

That was as far as I'd got when she arrived home – I just needed to find a way of rounding it off. I heard the front door slamming, her shoes being thrown off, and then she was in the sitting room with me, resting her head on my shoulder.

'Sorry if I was short with you on the phone. I think I was still in shock.'

I lifted her head. 'You were bound to be.'

'I don't think I've properly thanked you… for everything. I know this isn't going to be easy for you, the next few weeks, and beyond. Honestly, Rick, I really do appreciate your support.'

Her eyes shone, at odds with the dark ridges under them, as if some cunning make-up artist had tried to turn a young actor into an old character, only half succeeding.

'No need for thanks. It's my job to support you.'

'Your *job?*'

'Yes, my job.' I angled the screen of my laptop towards her. 'It's not quite finished but what do you think?'

She stared to read, her brow furrowed in concentration, but then her lips slowly twisted in what appeared to be amusement.

'What is it? Some sort of *diary*?' She swept her hand through my hair. 'Aren't diaries meant to be private? Why are you even showing me?' She looked at it again. 'Humanitarian heavyweight?'

'Describes you to a tee, I'd say. But no, it's not a diary. I don't do diaries. It's a blog.'

Her hand detached itself from my hair. 'A blog?'

'Remember what Adam suggested? I've decided to share my insights into the by-election with the world. The unique perspective of the candidate's husband.'

'Why would anyone want to read that?'

I tried to smile. I was sure she didn't mean to be so cutting.

She glanced again at the screen. 'You seem to know what's going on in my head better than I do.'

'I'm your husband.'

'You're not me.'

'No, but this is about both of us.'

'Is this some sort of Rick joke?'

'I've never been more serious.'

And Kirsty was missing the point. I felt a stab of disappointment.

She collapsed onto the sofa, shaking her head. 'My God, Rick, I was wondering how you were going to occupy yourself while I… But this… you can't. I mean, it feels all too exposed. As if you're opening our front door and inviting the public in. At home with Rick and Kirsty.' She looked up at me. 'You're mad and this time I mean it.'

'And standing as a candidate in this election isn't already exposing yourself? Come on, neither of us has any privacy now, so we might as well set out our wares in the way we want to see them set out. That way we'll keep some control over the whole thing.'

'You mean you'll keep some control.'

The head-shaking subsided. She was silent for a moment and I saw my advantage.

'Look, the other candidates will be kicking themselves that they haven't thought of this. It's going to shine a light on you as someone who's different, a fresh face, a teacher, a wife, a mother, a real human being who's intent on cleaning up the game of politics.'

'That's bullshit. I'm just someone trying to get elected.'

'And I'm making sure you do. You can't afford to be complacent.'

'Me… complacent?'

'By-elections throw up surprises.'

'You think I don't know that?'

'You've got to establish a head start on your opponents.'

'There are enough people in the party who'll be telling me exactly how to do that. And for starters they won't like this blog idea. It's outside their control. It's not what a candidate's partner does.'

'They won't risk a public row. And if they've got any sense, they'll welcome it as free PR, guaranteed positive. Besides, I'm a professional.'

I tried to plant a kiss on the top of her head but she withdrew, leaning back against the sofa.

'You've got everything worked out, haven't you?'

Well, yes, I hoped I had, though maybe not fully, not yet. I said nothing. A little more generosity on her part would have been appreciated.

'Oh, I don't know,' she said. 'I'll think about it and let you know tomorrow.'

'Kirsty, there's nothing for you to think about. It's

happening. Trust me.'

She stood up. 'Do as you please. I'm going to bed. I've had enough for one night. And this was meant to be my night, in case you've forgotten.'

I listened to her slow tread on the stairs and returned to my laptop. She'd come round as the blog got going and soon she'd be entering into the spirit of it, perhaps even throwing in ideas for future posts. I was a reasonable man. I'd consider whatever she said.

The piece was finished in half an hour, with some judicious editing. In particular, I created a little more space between Barraclough and the reference to corruption. There'd be no lawyering of this piece or any of the others I was to write, but I reckoned it sat just distant enough from any personal accusation. I was talking general truths. And a serious tone seemed right for the first post. The stories, and perhaps the jokes, would come later when we got into the nitty-gritty of campaigning. There should be some jokes in a by-election, shouldn't there?

I stayed up late to create a site, making use of one of those ready-made website builders. It was pretty basic, but I could improve the graphics the following day. I attached my bio.

> *Rick Dewhirst is a newspaper journalist and former editor of a leading political magazine. His blog chronicles developments in the forthcoming Humberside North by-election, in which his wife, Kirsty Osmond, will be standing as the Labour candidate. He writes here in a personal capacity as the candidate's husband. @DewhirstBlog*

Perfect. At two o'clock in the morning I pressed

'publish' and then sent a pre-emptive email to Clive, pointing out that this was an entirely personal initiative carried out in my own time and independently of my work for the *Citizen*. There was nothing in my contract that directly or indirectly forbade it, I added. I was already removed from all political coverage and I was banking on his not caring what I did as long as I kept it at arm's length from the paper. Looking back, that seemed optimistic, but it proved to be accurate. What he would actually say the following day was, 'We should be firing you, but as long as you keep this shite well away from my newspaper, and do what we pay you to do, I don't give a fuck how you waste your spare time.'

But now I closed my laptop, still pumping adrenaline. This was the best I'd felt since Barraclough had resigned. I would set up a dedicated social media account and tweet as soon as the world was awake. And then start thinking about the next post. I was free to write what I wanted and to mould Kirsty's campaign in the way I saw best. She would arrive in Westminster on a crest of high expectations. And I alongside her, establishing myself anew as a serious opinion-former.

Win-win.

I'd made a decision for both of us and overruled her objections – listened to them, of course, but overruled them. This was how things were going to be now. The marital pendulum was being rebalanced. I'd lived in a state of torpor for too long and here I stood at the mouth of a cave of endless possibilities. Dark and uneven the way ahead might be, but she had once said dangerous lives were the only ones worth living. I'd laughed at the hyperbole, but it was true.

I closed my laptop and glanced around the room, my eye settling on the framed photographs on a shelf above a radiator. There was Kirsty at Buckingham Palace holding her OBE, obedient for the camera, but looking seriously uncomfortable in a hat borrowed from a colleague – she'd scoffed at the idea of buying a new one. It was one of those fascinator things – ridiculous word, ridiculous headgear. Next to that was Adam on his first day at school, apprehensive and clutching a toy rabbit. And at the end in a small silver frame were young Kirsty and Rick, kissing on the steps of the Old Marylebone Town Hall. We'd got married without telling my parents or her sister – it was all too complicated, we'd decided – and invited just a few friends. Kirsty wore a long denim dress and her hair was loose, not that different from her current style, except for the recent strands of grey.

Now that was one thing she was going to have to find time for. She'd have to get her hair cut and perhaps coloured, too. It had a will of its own that needed taming – even when she tied it up, wisps escaped. She would have to spruce up for the cameras. Politics was just as much about the superficial as the moral high ground.

I'm not exactly a beginner with the media. I've been interviewed at school quite a few times. And once I was part of a panel on young people's mental health on Radio Four. But this is my first time in a TV studio. And the first time I've talked as a politician. That's the real thing about tonight. My cloak of political neutrality as a teacher is finally off and I'm able to commit myself openly. What freedom.

They sent a taxi for me. I'd said no, it wasn't necessary. But they don't want to risk people not arriving on time, not for a live show, I get that. Gerry's here too – he's going to be holding my hand for all the media engagements, an important part of the agent's job. I daresay I'll get used to it. We spent a few moments going over things in the green room. I've now been shown into make-up where a young woman is casting a professional eye over my reflection in a very big mirror. She says there's time for a full face if I like, and do I have any preferences, eye or lip colour, and I say whatever she think works best, but not to overdo it. She gets to work with her pots and brushes and I begin to resemble a corporate marketing executive. Nothing wrong with that, I suppose. Marketing executives are people. Some of them even become MPs. Your hair's lovely, the make-up lady says, good cut, nice highlights, it doesn't need anything doing to it. She waves a canister of hairspray – that must count as doing nothing – and I shield my eyes and hold my breath so as not to inhale the alcohol fumes. I'm not sure about lovely – my hair feels over-styled, over-coloured, from the salon visit. I wasn't bothered about the grey but Rick insisted, said he'd book the appointment himself if I didn't. Image is everything in politics, he pointed out. As if I didn't know. I expect that'll work its way into one of his ridiculous blog posts.

I'm taken into the studio during a video report and the presenter says we'll be with you straight after this, the interview will be about seven minutes. It's not the regular woman, but a young guy, looks like one of my sixth-formers. The film's finishing now and the red light goes on. It's hot in here and I feel very exposed under the lights, the make-up heavy on my face. The presenter introduces me – Labour's by-election candidate, the first of the five main candidates to feature on the programme this week. He tells the viewers I'm a headteacher – he gives the word a quizzical stress, as if I've accidentally strayed into the wrong interview – the principal of a local academy, and something of a political outsider, perhaps a surprise choice. I suppose that's fair enough, although there will surely come a point when I stop being an outsider. But I remember to smile, at the presenter, not at the description of myself. There's an art to smiling seriously, lips open just a little, head slightly to one side. He asks me what I think the single biggest issue is in this election. The demolition of our public services, I tell him. This election is a chance for the people of North Humberside to deliver a clear message to the Tory government, to say it's enough, we can't go on like this. And he interrupts me to say something about Brexit and taking back control. I'm not sure if it's even a question. I ignore it. I'm not going to be distracted. Take my school, I say. We've had to cut two full-time teaching posts in the last year and we don't have enough help in the classroom for those children with additional needs. Why should our children bear the brunt of the Tories' policies? And it's not just education. You ask anyone here in North

Humberside and they can give you examples of where things have been chopped, squeezed, neglected…

I hope I'm not gabbling. My headmistress's voice fills the studio. Am I too loud? The party arranged two hours of media training and Rick said that sounded superficial, so he got me to do more practice interviews with him. Keep the answers short, don't get ruffled, don't waffle, don't gabble, he said. But show your personality, be human.

It's different when you actually do it. Seven minutes isn't long and there's so much to say. And so many people watching me.

**

The lights in the television studio were surprisingly kind. They bathed her face in just the right amount of warmth and her skin glowed in response. The lines must still have been there, but you hardly noticed them, and the tiny scar above her eye had vanished. There was no doubt that a lick of make-up – at least a lick – had paid off. The new hairstyle helped, too. It was sleeker, layered, the grey merging with an artist's palette of autumn colours. The shape flattered her face and the copper and amber highlights or lowlights – whatever they were – glinted as the camera dwelt appreciatively on its subject. Nice work.

I was in the newsroom, at my desk, watching on my computer screen and listening on headphones. The interview was part of the early evening regional news show, required viewing for me and my colleagues, but the sort of programme that attracted a declining and ageing audience. It was competing with soaps and game shows, football and classy American drama on the pay channels, and no-one under thirty watched television anyway. But Kirsty's by-election opponents would certainly be watching – and making notes in preparation for their own performances. She was the first up, the touchstone against which they'd all measure themselves.

Shona gave me a surreptitious thumbs-up. Clive was back in his office, but I had no doubt he was watching too. Just before the programme had started, we'd had another row – in the middle of the newsroom – about the property company's complaint. It hadn't gone away as I'd expected and was now in the hands of a Leeds firm of solicitors who specialised in business defamation claims.

'We're not paying and we're definitely not going to court,' Clive had said. 'If you and Mike have fucked up – and that's looking increasingly the case – then Messrs Sue, Grabbit and Runne might just go for a nice fat apology on the front page. If we have to eat shit, we eat shit.'

He was over-reacting of course. I was still pretty certain we'd got it right. I'd go over things with Mike and our lawyer again in the morning. But for now I was trying to get it out of my head. I was interested only in Kirsty's TV debut.

'We need a serious programme of investment in our health service, in our inadequate social care, in our police force, our public transport...' she was saying.

Careful, Kirsty, don't rush it. Let the words resonate. On her next breath she seemed to moderate her pace. Telepathy or what?

'...And in building decent homes for everyone. It's people's lives we should be investing in. Not just the privileged few, but everyone's.'

The assertions were not unlike those I had first heard from her twenty-five years ago, assertions that had almost scared me off. She still believed in the same thing: from each according to their ability, to each according to their needs. But did anyone want to hear that anymore? Certainly no-one seemed to believe that politicians were capable of doing anything about it. Politics was nastier than it had ever been and politicians were discredited. And yet someone still had to run the country. More material for the blog. I'd done a couple of posts so far. They were being read. My Twitter followers had shot up. Over fifteen thousand when I last checked.

Kirsty however had had very little to say about the blog since the evening of the selection meeting. 'If you're so set on it, I guess there's nothing I can do to stop you. I've got more serious things to deal with,' she'd said the following morning. There'd been one awkward phone call later in the day from her agent, who'd queried my motives, or more precisely asked what the hell I thought I was doing. No, of course I wouldn't be writing anything to embarrass Kirsty or the party – I was her husband after all. 'Well you need to know there's considerable disquiet about it,' he'd said. 'Not that we're trying to censor you.' Of course not, Gerry. After that, I'd heard no more from him. She'd said he was going to be with her there tonight.

The interview seemed to be progressing smoothly. She eventually allowed the presenter his Brexit question and carefully straddled the party line – respecting 'the will of the people' but ensuring the exit was as painless as possible – before steering her way back to austerity, via a short aside on climate change and the world we should leave our children. She'd certainly mastered the politician's art of saying what she wanted to say, regardless of the question – but she'd had years of practising that on me. And the presenter wasn't much of a sparring partner. He looked about fifteen and must have been unnerved by having a headteacher sitting opposite him. Come on, she's a politician now, you can throw her to the lions. He didn't. She was having an easy initiation, a soft launch. This was the media at their most obliging. It wouldn't last. They'd be going for the jugular, or any other vein they could find, before too long.

She'd been on-screen for nearly seven minutes now. The interview seemed about to draw to a close. The presenter looked down at his notes and said, 'Finally, I'd like to ask you – and this is something we'll be putting to each of the candidates this week – is it significant that the majority of you… that all the candidates from the main parties… is it significant that you're all women?'

Kirsty sat tall in her seat. The novice-presenter was about to be given a piece of her mind.

'Is it significant? No-one bothered to ask the inverse question when elections were seen as a game exclusively for men. But since you do ask, yes it is significant. Very significant.'

Easy, Kirsty, easy. Okay, a stupid question inelegantly put, but he's a beginner. Stay calm.

'Let me tell you that if we had a few more all-female line-ups in elections, we might get rather better representation in the House of Commons. Women's experience, women's judgment and values – we could do with more of all that.'

'Are you saying–'

'I'm saying the male ego has a lot to answer for. In fact, you could argue that if we simply left politics to women, the world might be a better place.'

And she gave a knowing smile. That old joke, casually dropped in. But on live television, under the lights and without a mitigating glass of wine in her hand, it didn't sound very funny. This was surely off-message, even for the now female-friendly Labour Party. The camera went in close on Kirsty, a look of mischief – or was it misplaced triumph? – settling on her face, and then returned to a wide shot, the presenter smiling uneasily, unsure whether or not his interviewee was serious. He seemed relieved to realise they'd run out of time.

'Well on that, er, interesting point, we must leave it. Kirsty Osmond, Labour candidate, thank you. Tomorrow night it'll be the turn of the Conservative candidate, Sarah Clarkson.'

I gave it ten minutes and then phoned her.

'Kirsty, what was that all about? I mean, it was good, very good, till the end, and then, well…'

'Don't say anything. I've just had it from Gerry. I thought maybe a little bit of humour, personality, like you said, but with a serious point underneath…'

She sounded uncharacteristically subdued.

'Jokes are difficult in politics,' I said.

'Oh God, you don't think people will take things out of context, do you?'

'Don't worry too much. Regional news programmes get a fairly small audience.'

I knew that wasn't true. Small audiences were easily multiplied by other platforms. I opened Twitter on my computer screen. It had started already.

Labour candidate calls for women-only elections… Kick men out of politics, says Labour's headmistress candidate… Osmond declares her colours as a man-hater.

That wasn't what she'd said or done and certainly not what she meant, but what did social media care about the facts?

I guess this is what they mean by going viral. A nasty little infection spreading everywhere. It started when I was barely out of the studio and just grew. Gerry dealt with it until it got too much and the press office had to take over. Did I really mean kick men out of Parliament, wipe them out of politics? Was I advocating some form of gender cleansing? Of course not. (Well, not exactly.) I was merely making observations, trying to inject some humour into a trite question, if you like, and things have been taken out of any reasonable context.

But perhaps it was me who got the context wrong. I can see that now. A local TV studio's not the place to be satirical, or philosophical. That's what this is all about, context. I should have given a bland answer. *I'm sure all the candidates are standing on their own merit, but yes of course it's significant. We need more women in Parliament.* The press office issued a clarifying statement and Gerry suggested another bout of media training. Not necessary, I said. I've learnt my lesson. I shall be careful in future.

Yet it's made me think. Things *do* get taken out of context, maliciously, greedily. Social media's always hungry for victims. It's how it works, isn't it? I know that, I've always known it, yet being caught up in it brings it home. If such a stupid little thing can have reverberations like this, then… oh God, everything really does get scrutinised and distorted in the ugliest way imaginable.

So is this a bad idea after all? But no, I'm not even going to start thinking like that. And I refuse to be intimidated by the Twitter monster.

Anyway, interest in what I did or didn't say last night

seems to have waned as today's worn on. A small storm that has blown over. Martin Barraclough's wife chose this afternoon to put out a statement on the death of their marriage. That's kept the scandal-mongers busy. As Rick texted to say, I'm lucky.

I just hope my luck lasts.

But I'm on my way with the team now to an evening of door-to-door canvassing. Forget social media. This is really what it's about if I want to be an MP. Tearing round housing estates, ringing doorbells, introducing myself, explaining, listening, turning a cheek if I have to. I've done it for others. Now it's for me. It's still a hard slog.

Mark is driving and I'm sitting next to him going through messages. The school's passed on a batch of personal emails, mainly from parents or people I don't know, sent to me via the school's admin@ address over the past week. I skim through them, working out which if any I need reply to, which I should pass on to Gerry to deal with, which I can ignore. *Dear Ms Osmond, What are you going to do about jobs… housing… bins… crime?* Someone in the office will do a standard reply to most of them.

And then...

> *Dear Kirsty,*
> *I hope you don't mind me contacting you out of*
> *the blue like this but I've often thought about*
> *you and I've just seen the news that you're*
> *standing for parliament and, well, it's amazing.*
> *Good luck! But I'm also writing because I've got*
> *a project that I'd really like to discuss with you.*
> *If you could call me I'll explain.*
> *All the best,*
> *Marie.*

I read it and my head is numb. Marie. An email address and a mobile number. I force myself to read it again and then close it.

Nearly there, Mark says. We'll split into two groups, same as last night, and continue where we left off. Okay? Okay, I say, and put my phone away. It feels like a brick in my pocket.

We've divvied up the streets and we're ready to go. Adam's meeting us here. It's the second time he's helped out since getting home and I'm bowled over by his enthusiasm. This is great, Mum, real electioneering, he said on the weekend, and then he was off galloping up the steps of another block of flats with a stash of leaflets. He's only just old enough to vote himself. Perhaps I'm guilty of child exploitation getting him to do this. But I can't stop him. Tonight we'll let him go solo. *Hello, I'm from the Labour Party and I wanted to check if you'll be voting for our candidate Kirsty Osmond on April the 26th.* Other team members are around to bail him out if he comes unstuck, which he will, because he knows nothing yet. I remember the first time I did this, the run-up to council elections in Leeds, my last year at university, and someone started on about business rates crippling his chip shop. What did I know about business rates? I tried to say what I thought was the right thing and he told me I hadn't got a clue, which I hadn't. The golden rule, if you don't know, don't pretend. I'll remind Adam of that. Say you'll check and get back to them. And if you don't, well that's why people lose faith in politicians. That and a few other reasons.

Rick should be here soon, too. No doubt he could hold forth on business rates for some considerable time. Not entirely sure that I'd trust him to get the message right, though. I'm pleased he's coming, of course I am, even if I have this niggling feeling that it's just research for that website of his. What is it about that that makes me feel so uncomfortable? I mean, there's nothing *bad* about it, not really bad. It's not like my husband knows something awful that he's suddenly going to reveal about me. Quite the opposite, it's a bit too gushing for my liking. But that's the thing about blogs, they have to entertain. Gerry's still unhappy about it, though perhaps that's more a general wariness of journalists. But the party hierarchy have decided to ignore it and I've heard others say it's great, they don't see the problem. Maybe a supportive and only mildly embarrassing blog distracts from the worst stuff on social media. I've blocked a couple of people after last night. No actual death threats yet, but I daresay they'll come.

Adam's just turned up. He got the bus here and he's wearing that too-thin jacket again. It reminds me of when I used to pick him up from Saturday morning football practice and he was clutching his clobber and shivering and I wanted to hug him to warm him up, but knew I shouldn't, not in front of his mates. He grins. Hi Mum, at your service again. Have you managed to get some uni work done during the day? I ask. Yeah, a bit. I worry that he's spending too much time traipsing around with me when he should be revising, but he insists he's not a schoolkid and he can work out his own timetable. He is still a kid, of course, but I'm chuffed he's here. He's allotted to Mark's group – they're going to take the two remaining tower blocks and then they'll join my group on the roads at the edge of the estate. I watch him listening as Mark flips through sheets on his clipboard and issues instructions and I know he'll eventually be worn down by the tedium and the numbers game that an election always turns into. This is natural Labour territory, although the electoral tectonic plates have been shifting and both the Tories and the far right in their various manifestations have made worrying inroads in recent years. But, as ever, the biggest enemy is apathy. Just being here, showing a face, is what counts.

I ring my first bell. No reply. I count to fifteen – I've worked out that's the optimal gap to leave – and try again. Nothing, although lights are on. I fold my leaflet and put it through the box. The next house is the same, but then a woman peers out from behind a curtain and opens the door. She stares at my rosette and looks uncomfortable. Voting? My husband's out. He decides. I'm not really interested.

A hundred years of female suffrage – and still this.

But I smile and say, well may I just leave this leaflet? I'm looking forward to working hard as your next MP and I'm happy to discuss anything you're concerned about. If you or your husband think of something later, you can ring this number – I point to the contact details on the leaflet – and speak to one of our team. So you'll be taking over from that bloke being done for sexual assault? she says. Disgusting if you ask me. Well I suppose you can't be any worse. She takes the leaflet and I mark her and her husband as possibles.

The next two houses yield nothing, although as I'm leaving the second one, I hear the door opening and turn back to see a leaflet converted into a paper plane whistling through the air. It narrowly misses my ear.

Rick arrives just in time to witness that. Not a bad shot, he says and picks up the leaflet. Okay if I keep this as a souvenir? He gives me a sort of hug and says, can I do the rest of this street with you? I'd like to see the candidate in action. Remember our agreement, I say, no recording anything or making obvious notes. Would I do that? I'm just drinking in the atmosphere. And he takes a pile of leaflets from me. I'll fold these, while you concentrate on the chat. Gerry not around? He wasn't feeling too good, I say, I told him to knock off early. He looks relieved at that. But he's here and I still can't believe it – my husband canvassing with me. Or drinking in the atmosphere, or whatever it is he imagines he's doing.

At one house a man wants a selfie with me. Hang on a mo, while I find my phone, he says. I beam as he poses by my side and holds out his phone at arm's length, and then I remind him of the date of the election, and he says, oh I never bother with voting. You have to laugh, Rick says as we leave.

By the way, he adds, anyone mention the TV interview? No, I say, I don't reckon Twitter holds much sway round here. Welcome to the real world, where people are more worried about jobs and benefits and getting a doctor's appointment.

Aren't you tempted to lay into them sometimes? Rick says, as another front door slams closed on us. Yes, but it won't win me votes.

It's not all like that, of course. There are places where people thank me for calling and offer to put up a poster in the window, and then it's all worth it and I'm sure we'll win and this is going to be the best job in the world. A few people recognise me as the head of their son or daughter's school and ask if it means I'm going to leave. And when I say I'm afraid so, if I get elected, they say that's a shame, can't you do both jobs? and I feel a wave of doubt swell over me and wish I could do this incognito.

A few streets later Adam joins us, the tower blocks completed. He's tired but brimming over with excitement as if it's the most thrilling thing he's ever done, more so even than seeing a baby born. We do the last few houses as a family unit. It feels as if I'm asking people to vote for my husband and son, not just me.

**

By the end of that evening, I was in no rush to repeat the canvassing experience, but I told Kirsty I would. Grim housing estates were okay. I was less keen on pounding pavements in the better-heeled parts of the constituency. Better sticking to places where I wasn't going to bump into someone I knew. Luckily that's the territory where most of the work seemed to be – natural Labour voters who'd fallen by the wayside with Brexit.

It was also going to provide the richest pickings for the blog. Call me a snob, but an evening spent knocking on these particular doors was beginning to engender in me a new sympathy for politicians. At their best (as personified by my wife), they were a much-maligned group and by-elections one of the toughest shows on earth. Between the smiles at the front doors, Kirsty had looked pained but determined, that stoical 'I don't care if it kills me, I'm going to get this done' expression etched on her brow. Great material. Should I also try tackling the TV interview Twitterstorm in my blog? No, clearly unwise, and anyway, it seemed to be subsiding. I kept all such thoughts to myself of course.

There was another thing I kept quiet about. A woman who seemed to put in repeated appearances. I spotted her three times I think, different streets, hovering on the pavement staring at the campaign circus. At one point it looked as if she was going up to Kirsty to speak to her, but she seemed to change her mind and walked off. Kirsty didn't notice. It was most likely nothing. A middle-aged woman, grey hair, anorak, looked harmless enough, not your regular stalker. Probably just curious, nothing better to do with her time. Hardly the highlight of the evening. I decided not to worry Kirsty.

We were now on our way home and Adam hadn't stopped talking since we'd got in the car.

'It's not just the rude ones that get me, but the ones that won't even answer the door,' he said. 'You know they're in. You can hear the TV. Or they peep from behind the curtains and think you haven't seen them. And you play the game and pretend you haven't. Hilarious. Or sometimes they open the door a centimetre – they keep the chain on and say 'no thank you', like you're trying to sell them something.'

'We are. We're tinkers, selling them a promise.'

Only Kirsty would try to turn a by-election into poetry.

'Honest, Mum, I don't know how you put up with some of them. They think they can say what they like to you.'

'Their prerogative, I'm afraid. We're an intrusion. They're making the tea, getting the kids to bed. The last thing they need is some nosey so-and-so with a clipboard banging on their front door and asking if she can count on their vote. But sometimes they do want to talk and then it's all worthwhile.'

But Adam wasn't persuaded.

'Some of them are so ignorant. Going on about foreigners coming over here and taking their jobs and hospital beds, and why hasn't Brexit stopped that? People really are bigoted, you know.'

'Adam!' Kirsty's voice was harsh.

'I know you're not meant to say it, but it's true. Isn't it, Dad?'

From the back seat, he tapped me on the shoulder

for endorsement. I was keeping out of this. But I remembered another conversation long ago, Julie's complaints about her son's school, Kirsty's artificial patience with her sister. Now she turned to Adam, and I caught a glimpse of her face. He was about to be at the receiving end of a Kirsty sermon.

'Adam, you can't do politics if you don't get people. You don't have to love them – great if you can, but that's a special talent. But you do have to learn the knack of putting yourself in their shoes. People have difficult lives. Their own problems can be overwhelming. They're not always nice. They find scapegoats. We have to listen to all that, understand what they're worried about. And, if we can, help them, or at least explain why there's a different way of seeing things. No-one said politics was easy.'

My God, she'd only been at this a week, and already she was playing the politician-philosopher. There was silence from the back of the car, as Adam seemed to process the ideas. He was her pupil. Just as she had once decided that I needed educating politically, now she had turned her attention – no doubt more hopefully – to our son. There seemed to be a new bond between them, a special relationship born of this by-election and from which I was excluded.

I'd felt that exclusion before, a long time ago. Adam's birth had been slow and difficult, and labour had ended in an emergency Caesarean. Afterwards I'd watched Kirsty breastfeeding our scrap of a baby and realised that it wasn't so much that there were now three of us, as that there was now a new pair, plus me. She and the infant Adam were the centre of each other's worlds, as if they were still conjoined, utterly inter-dependent. I was superfluous, outside their private magic circle. It'll be different when a second child comes along, I'd told myself. But that never happened. It would always be just the three of us, or rather the two of them and me.

Inevitably the bond relaxed as Adam grew, and he and I developed our own deep affection and understanding, our private jokes and shared pleasures, father and son. But I'd never forgotten that early sense of mother-son exclusivity. And here it was again. Yet when it came to canvassing, maybe being slightly to the side wasn't such a bad thing.

We were about half-way home when Kirsty's phone rang. Calls now came at all hours. The days when she switched it off and forgot about it were no more. She seemed to hesitate before answering and I half-turned to see her looking at the screen. Then she put the phone to her ear. 'Kirsty Osmond.'

I could just catch a male voice the other end. Kirsty was listening, not saying much, only, 'Yes, it's going well… yes, I know,' and then, 'Thanks for phoning', and the call was over.

'Who was that?' I asked.

'Martin Barraclough.'

'Him? Should he be ringing you?' Adam said. 'I mean, should you even be talking to him?'

'I don't see why not. It was just a private call.'

'What did he want?' I asked. This was something we could most definitely do without.

'Oh, just wishing me luck, you know.'

'No I don't. What did he say?'

'Not much. Be careful and don't take anything for granted. Politics is a rough business – a dirty business, I think were his words. That sort of thing.'

'That's rich coming from him,' I said and made a mental note to tell Shona to check where matters were with the Met investigation. They were taking their time in handing over the file to the Crown Prosecution Service, but perhaps that was no bad thing. It suggested there was much more evidence to be amassed. In the meantime, I didn't want this man messing with my candidate's head.

**

I wish he hadn't rung. Adam was right, it felt wrong speaking to him. The car was so quiet, Adam concentrating on his phone, Rick driving but listening to every word I said. I tried to end it as soon as I could, but I had to be civil and, if truth be told, I felt a tiny bit sorry for him over the marriage business. I'm still not sure why he rang, though. To remind me that I owe him something, that the former MP hasn't gone away yet? To bestow his wisdom and his blessing on me, as if that still counts for anything? Male arrogance, Martin Barraclough always epitomised that. But he said something else. Watch your back, because in politics the attacks come from where you least expect them. Don't trust anyone. I don't know why but I didn't mention that to Rick.

I didn't say anything about the Marie letter, either. I've filed it away to deal with later.

Two blips in an otherwise productive evening. The past twenty-four hours have been tough but I've got through. Abuse on social media and at the front door, awkward phone calls, unexpected emails. If this is as bad as it gets, I reckon I can cope. Hardly enough to derail the whole operation. Tomorrow there's the interview with the *Citizen*. A profile piece. That shouldn't be a problem. But I'll watch how I put things. No more gaffes, Rick says – though I still dispute that's what it was.

Six in the morning. She was walking around the bedroom, phone to her ear, picking up things with her free hand and stuffing them into her bag. At one point she tried, one-handed, to thread an earring into the phone-free ear, but gave up in frustration and went back to the bag operation. I was still in bed, half-eavesdropping on her conversation, half-listening to the early morning news. She was talking to Gerry, discussing the day's schedule. He was feeling better apparently and was coming to the house for the interview she was about to do with the *Citizen*, with Shona.

'If you're here by seven, that should give us enough time to go through the key points. And you can meet Rick.' Gerry said something I couldn't hear and Kirsty looked at me and laughed. 'He'll behave himself.' Another inaudible comment. 'It'll be fine, I'm sure. It's just the local paper.' She turned to me again and mouthed 'sorry'.

The interview was early in the day at Kirsty's request. She'd be too busy later on. Adam would still be in bed. The house would be quiet. I didn't seem to figure in her calculations. Or did I? She ended the call and turned to me. 'I think you'll like him when you meet him properly.' Then she turned her attention to the earrings, this time using both hands.

I wasn't especially looking forward to meeting her agent but it had to be done. I had to get the measure of the man who also claimed to be running her campaign, or at least the practical side of things. But I was still thinking about the call from Barraclough. It had brought a blast of cold air into the car last night, as if the ex-MP had barged his way into a private party, an unwanted guest who stifled conversation and deadened the atmosphere. I was pleased to note she hadn't mentioned it to Gerry. There were some things best kept to ourselves.

Gerry arrived just before seven. He looked pretty much as I'd expected: a man in his sixties, a straight-backed, grey-haired, red-tied stalwart of the party, with heavy-framed glasses but no other distinguishing features. Ex-military perhaps, someone used to campaigns of a different sort. He'd been the agent in a neighbouring constituency in the last general election and had never worked with Barraclough. That seemed a bonus point. I had no doubt he knew what he was doing, a wily man if need be, no-one's fool. Kirsty was in safe hands, his and mine. But as we greeted each other, I detected a degree of caution – just a worried flicker in the eye. 'Odd that we've never met before,' he said. Clearly he was still deciding whether he was shaking the hand of his candidate's husband or of a ferreting journalist. It would do no harm to let him ponder that one. I offered him coffee and left him in the kitchen talking to Kirsty.

At seven-thirty on the dot, the doorbell rang again. Shona.

'Oh, hi.'

She tensed her shoulders. Clearly she hadn't expected to see me. I wasn't sure why. I did live here and it was seven-thirty in the morning. If she'd assumed I'd keep out of the way, she was wrong. Kirsty didn't object to my being there. 'Your blog can't say much about an interview for the *Citizen* without incurring the wrath of Clive,' she'd said, 'so we're pretty safe.'

I took Shona into the sitting room – this woman who was, temporarily at least, not a colleague and a friend but a keen journalist about to interview my wife. 'Kirsty won't be long,' I said. Shona perched on the sofa facing the window and started to flick through her notepad. I opened my laptop and read what I'd started late last night.

Democracy works on the doorstep. In the past day or two I've been putting that to the test, alongside Kirsty on the house-to-house campaign trail. You know the sort of thing: rosetted candidates and their entourage strolling along suburban streets; surprised householders flattered by the attention; minds changed, or at least names ticked off on clipboards.

All the parties do it. It's how you win elections. Hard on the shoe leather, repetitious and unexciting, but otherwise not especially demanding.

But in real life (like so much in politics), that's not how it is. Door-to-door canvassing in a parliamentary by-election is one of the most challenging jobs you can do. And unless you're a true political believer, it can threaten your faith in humanity.

Last night we had abuse hurled at us, front doors slammed in our faces, missiles thrown at us (well, an election leaflet converted into a paper plane — but paper cuts can be nasty). I have no doubt that canvassers from the other parties face the same, perhaps worse. It's a burden the political campaigner learns to bear.

And if it's not abuse, it's apathy. People just

don't want to know. Politics is boring, remote, irrelevant. It's tainted. It's a con. There are more important things to worry about. They don't bother to answer the door when they spot you from behind the curtains, and that can feel worse than being told to sod off. Or they insist on a selfie with you and then blatantly inform you they never bother with voting.

On reflection, I realised I might need to cut some of that, rather a lot of it in fact. It was perceptive, naturally, but I wasn't writing only for observers of politics. Real voters might also read this and maybe the tone was a little supercilious. As Kirsty had said, laying into people wouldn't win her votes.

But you move on to the next place and know you've got to keep going because that's what you do and that's how you're going to win. Kirsty's getting enough positive responses — more than other candidates, I'm sure — to make it all worthwhile: the people who open the door to tell her that yes, they're going to vote for her, and good luck to her; and those who realise they have a small opportunity to influence the way this country is run. They're right. Lots of small opportunities added together make a difference. Voting matters.

Door-to-door takes a certain stoicism, or at least a strong hide. It may be a good apprenticeship for what comes afterwards. Kirsty knows that. Other candidates may be equally tenacious. But I'm unashamedly…

I glanced up as I worked out exactly what it was that I was unashamed about and saw Shona staring at me.

'Rick, I'm sorry to interrupt, but just to be clear, you are going into work, aren't you? You're not staying while…'

'You don't mind, do you?'

'You're joking.' She paused and seemed to realise I was not joking. 'Look, this is my interview and I'd prefer not to have you breathing down my neck.'

I opened my eyes wide. I liked Shona when she got rattled.

'I'm not going to interfere. The interviewee's husband will sit quietly in his own front parlour. Make yourself at home and pretend I'm not here.'

She dropped her notepad onto the coffee table in front of her and folded her arms.

'Well I guess I can't stop you, but I don't like it and it's not going to alter what I ask her.'

With that, she jumped up and began a self-guided tour of the room. She picked up family photographs, examined paintings, inspected titles on the bookshelves and magazines on a side table. I caught her eye once or twice and her look said, 'If you want me to pretend you're not here, that's exactly what I'm doing.' She pulled a fat, leather-bound volume off a shelf. I recognised it as one of mine, *War and Peace,* Lower Fourth Form prize, Waverley College, 1979. She opened it, stared at the inscription for a moment and then ran her finger along the spines of a few other books. I followed her movements, trying to see the room and its contents as she saw them. How middle-class the place must have seemed, how comfortably off its owners were, how different it was from the homes of most of the North Humberside electorate. She'd been here before, to dinner, for drinks. But this was different. She was on duty now and nosiness was a professional privilege. It was her job to observe the candidate's habitat objectively.

The kitchen door opened and Kirsty breezed in, followed by Gerry.

'So sorry to keep you waiting, Shona. It's nice to see you again, though in rather different circumstances.' She was obviously thinking of the supper party a few weeks earlier when we'd lit a log fire and solved Brexit over too many bottles of wine. The following morning I had no idea what the solution was.

'Can we get you a coffee?' She gave me one of her 'would you mind?' looks. Shona raised her eyebrows. Meek Rick, coffee-maker, door-opener, dogsbody. He once was my deputy editor, you know. I went into the kitchen, still irritated by Shona's professional snooping. Should I be offering proletariat-flavoured instant coffee? We didn't seem to have any. I heaped in several spoons of freshly ground Columbian Fairtrade and kept the door ajar to hear the opening salvos.

Shona asked if it was okay if she recorded the interview and kicked off, innocuously enough. Why after years in teaching had Kirsty decided to run for Parliament? Simple. She wanted to fight for the people of North Humberside, just as she had for the students of Phoenix Academy. Well, yes, but... I knew what Shona was thinking. Perhaps something a little less political? Human interest, the woman behind the politician, that's what's needed if this piece is going to get past Clive.

I watched the coffee trickle into the pot, pleased I wasn't conducting the interview. Kirsty could be a tough nut to crack if she chose to be.

'I'd like to find out a little more about your background,' Shona was saying as I returned with the coffee. 'You know, where your real motivation comes from.'

I handed her a mug and sat down again, positioning myself carefully on the periphery of Kirsty's sightline, where I could see her face and that of Gerry standing to the side and polishing his glasses.

Kirsty paused. 'Well, I come from a very ordinary working-class family in Sheffield. Nothing special. I grew up in a council house, one of two girls – my sister, Julie, still lives there – and I went to the local comprehensive. My mum died of cancer while I was at university. When I was younger, she worked part-time in a dress shop.'

'And your dad?'

'He was a miner for many years.'

'That would have been when? The seventies and eighties? The time of the strikes? It must have been tough for your family then.'

'It was tough for everyone.'

'Was your dad prominent in the union?'

A pause.

'He left the NUM in the eighties.'

Shona's mouth slowly opened.

'You mean… he didn't go on strike? So he… crossed the picket line? How did you feel about that?'

Another pause.

'I was at school at the time.'

'But now? As a Labour politician? There was so much hardship among the strikers back then. Do you feel that your father, well… betrayed the cause?'

Kirsty had her teeth firmly clasped together for a moment, her jaw tense, and then she said, 'Look, I can't answer for my father. He died of emphysema in the nineties. But life was hard for lots of mining families. They survived as best they could. I don't feel I can judge people for decisions taken at a very difficult time in their lives.'

'But it looks like you've come a long way from where

you started,' Shona said and she glanced around the room as if to emphasise the point. Her eye seemed to settle on a large abstract in oils above the fireplace – a jagged pattern of greys and greens, just discernibly the portrait of a woman. I'd bought it years ago, without consulting Kirsty. It had cost three grand at a so-called affordable art fair in London and she couldn't believe I'd wasted so much money.

'I was the first in the family to go to university, if that's what you mean. But that's true of many of my generation. I've had advantages that most people in my community didn't have and that they continue not to have. I've always been aware of that. It's something I'll never forget.'

She turned her head and our eyes locked for the briefest of moments. She'd said she wouldn't flaunt her background and I'd repeatedly told her she should. No doubt Gerry had said the same. Whether she had intended to open the can of worms that was her dad's mining career was another matter. We hadn't discussed it beforehand. She must have decided that full disclosure was the best policy in the circumstances, but I felt uneasy.

'I'd like to ask you next about the school,' Shona said. 'Phoenix is a tough place. You've done brilliantly there of course, but how do you feel about deserting it now?'

Deserting it? *Deserting?* Not just leaving the school, but deserting it? I'd made a similar point a while back, though I liked to think I'd phrased it more subtly. Kirsty clenched her fists in her lap.

'The school's in very safe hands,' she said. 'My deputy's a superb acting head, and I'm in regular contact with him throughout the campaign – in fact, I'll be popping in later today.'

'But I understand you're facing challenges. The drugs

culture in the school… parents are concerned. Aren't you letting your political ambitions get in the way of your responsibilities to Phoenix?'

Where had that come from? Surely not the *Citizen*'s education reporter? Lazy Dan couldn't possibly have been talking to parents, could he? If I wasn't mistaken, Shona was looking uncomfortable, as if she had to ask the question but didn't believe its premise. It was a try-on. Bloody journalists. Kirsty's eyes wandered in my direction again. I gave a half-shake of the head. Nothing to do with me, I promise.

She took a deep breath and as she started to speak, there was a tightness in her voice. She would fight to keep her beloved school out of this election.

'Like every school, we have occasional problems. But we work with social services to deal with those problems when they arise. Our priority is always the welfare of our students, all our students.'

She looked at her watch. Her patience had been stretched, but the elastic band hadn't snapped. Nonetheless it was hard to imagine us all sitting around the table at another boozy supper party, setting the world to rights.

'Could we draw this to a close?' Kirsty said. 'I do have to leave shortly.'

'There's just one more area I'd like to touch on. Your recent TV interview and your attitude to male politicians–'

'My remarks were misconstrued, as I think we've made very clear. I was simply looking forward to more women in Parliament, which out of necessity means fewer men.'

'But what are your thoughts on one particular male politician, Martin Barraclough? I assume you know him well.'

Gerry unfolded his arms and seemed about to intervene, but Kirsty ignored him.

'The only thing I can say is that I'll be a very different MP from my predecessor.'

'Have you spoken to him since he resigned?'

'I'm sure you understand that I can't talk about personal conversations.'

'So you have spoken to him.'

'As I say, I can't talk about personal conversations. Now if you don't mind–'

'Just one more point. What are your views on the *Me Too* movement? I'm talking in general, not about Barraclough. I mean, so many prominent men are getting called out for their behaviour now, and so many women have been coming forward to share their stories – is that something you'd encourage?'

This was turning into several more points, a whole bucketful of points. Not bad ones, though. Generous, open-ended questions. A chance to inject something controversial but positive into the piece. It should generate a good quote or two and even Clive would have to recognise it as human interest. But Kirsty was already leaning down and putting her phone into her bag.

'Of course I support *Me Too*. In general – and I stress I mean in general – I'd encourage anyone who has suffered abuse to report the matter to the police. I'm sorry but I must go.'

Is that it? Can't you come up with a bit more than that, Kirsty? Something more heartfelt? More quotable? Shona was giving it one last shot.

'But is it something you feel particularly strongly about? I mean, have you ever had any… personal experience yourself?'

What was Shona thinking? That was a question husbands might ask, but not local newspaper journalists.

Yet Kirsty gave only the briefest of pauses.

'No, I haven't.' And she zipped up her bag.

The door opened. Adam walked into the room, wearing just his boxer shorts and headphones and looking barely awake.

'Where's the coffee pot?'

There was a small twitch at the corner of his mouth as he took in the scene. He folded his wrists across his shorts like a footballer facing a free kick and shrank into himself.

'Sorry, I didn't realise. Sorry, Mum, really sorry.'

He tried to back out of the door but instead banged into it, closing it and imprisoning himself in the room.

'My son, Adam,' Kirsty said, and she smiled at him. She had mentioned the interview to him, but he must have forgotten. From the door, he looked sheepishly at Shona and said, 'Hi'. I gave him an encouraging wink and handed him the empty coffee pot.

Kirsty again looked at her watch and got up from her chair. 'I really must get going now.'

It was over – and a reasonably accomplished, if slightly flat, performance it had been. Perhaps not surprising after the TV interview. She'd remembered some of what I'd told her, but not enough. There were always landmines in an interview like this, and one or two she had stepped straight onto. We had more work to do.

Shona was checking a few facts with Gerry and avoiding my gaze. It was eight-fifteen and I needed to get to the office. Kirsty was standing at the door, eyes on her phone, waiting for Gerry to finish, itching to leave.

**

Bloody *Citizen*, Gerry says as soon as we get in the car. Oh I'm sure it'll be okay, I say, Rick rates Shona. She'll write a decent piece. And I turn to look out of the window. Gerry's annoyed that I didn't tell him about my dad. It never occurred to me it would be an issue, I say, the sins of the father and all that. Gerry huffs and puffs a bit more, everything's a potential issue in politics, he says, you should know that, and then he's quiet. He did ask the other day if I'd like to get my sister over at some point, photos of us canvassing together, that sort of thing. I'd said it wasn't really possible. She was busy, work, family. Thankfully he let the idea drop. I'm slightly ashamed to say I've barely seen Julie since Dad's funeral, though she hasn't made any effort to contact me, either. Christmas cards early on, but that's it. I can only guess how the idea of helping me canvass would have gone down.

But Gerry, he's beginning to read me. Sometimes I need thinking time, a few moments to reflect on what's happened, what's coming up. And really I'm just glad the *Citizen* interview's done. I'd have liked a bit more on policy, on why this country needs a Labour government. It wasn't what I was going to get. Rick had warned me – a personal profile, what makes me tick for God's sake, human interest. As if talking about wanting everyone to have a decent life isn't enough to interest most humans.

But I played the game as well as I could. Perhaps I should have thought things through more, my family, what I might get asked. But it's history. People are voting for me, not my dead forgotten father and his bad decisions.

I suppose the Barraclough questions were inevitable though. I could feel Rick trying to catch my eye when Shona got onto that. Go on, give her a brilliant quote, something the paper can blow up as a headline. Well I wasn't going to. Bringing up sexual assault like that just seemed to trivialise the subject. I said what I had to, no more. Women should report abuse. Tame but okay.

Hardly a screaming headline. The fact is, there are great women who'll continue to make waves on that. It's not one for me to major on.

The school. Now there's something I can't stop worrying about. That was the real nerve Shona touched. My kids. My staff. Have I deserted them? Is that what it is, deserting? But I'm trying not to, not entirely. Carving out time to ring Phil or pop into school is irritating the hell out of Gerry, and yet I must. Louise and some of the other governors are insisting that Josh Wenham is permanently excluded, and there's a limit to my influence from the sidelines. It's just one kid, but there will always be more. If not drugs, something else. And having the press hovering, ready to pounce, doesn't help either. Schools are leaky. If Shona knew, I guess she had to say something, it's her job.

I still like her, I really do. It must be tough as the only woman in the newsroom, at least the only one on hard news and politics. She can't afford to put in a soft interview. If there are issues – things that journalists see as issues, that is – she has to poke away at them. The only woman. My God, in this age, who'd think it? The only black reporter, too. And Clive as her boss – what must that be like? I hope Rick offers a layer of protection. He says he does. And Shona will tell them all to sod off, if she needs to. She's no pushover, I'm pretty sure of that. I hope we can remain friends, even after the election. But every normal relationship gets filtered when you're a politician. Can friends still be friends, even if they're journalists? And husbands – does that change, too?

Right, we're here, Gerry says and returns me to the moment. Just a quick meeting with the troops, and we're on the road again. We pull into the parking area behind the Labour offices and my thoughts slide into the day ahead. It's going to be another long and arduous one.

Being a parliamentary candidate is a complicated business. You face in so many directions at once. Rick and Shona have it easy.

**

Late afternoon, and I was thinking back to all the abysmal assignments I'd ever had as a journalist – ones where I'd struggled to find a story, where the interviewee was monosyllabic, or worse, where I felt out of my depth. Early on, I'd dreaded covering funerals – especially those following a violent or accidental death. Even if the family said they were okay with the press being there, I knew I was an interloper. The first time I was put on coffin duty was for two young brothers who'd drowned off the Northumberland coast. I tucked myself in at the back of the village church and didn't know whether I should join in with the hymns. And how could I describe it all without resorting to cliché? I've been to enough funerals now to know they're always clichéd – from Billy's utilitarian crematorium send-off, with just a handful of mourners and a minister who seemed scarcely to know who Billy was, to my own father's meticulously planned, perfectly executed High Church affair. They're all attended by people who mouth platitudes and wish they weren't there.

What I was doing this afternoon was in some ways easier – at least no-one was dead – but it felt just as funereal. I was writing a formulaic apology to go on the front page of the next edition and to sit very prominently online – an apology to the property company at the centre of our rat-infestation story. The business went by the unlikely name of Safe and Sound Rentals.

Matters had escalated alarmingly since Clive had had that first call from the company, the day after we'd run the story, the weekend I was ill, when I'd assured him there was nothing in it. I still was inclined to believe there wasn't, but things change once expensive solicitors get in on the act. I'd spent several hours the previous day holed up with Mike and our in-house lawyer going through all the details yet again. But to no avail. It seemed that the *Citizen* had lost the battle, although at Clive and the board's behest, there had hardly been one. The paper simply rolled over. And I was there to clear up the mess, to choreograph our climb-down.

'Something to take your mind off your missus's hysterical outburst on TV the other night,' as Clive had put it.

According to their solicitors, Safe and Sound had been working through a backlog of repairs to recently acquired properties and had offered 'superior temporary accommodation' to the tenants affected. In the case of the family in our report, this offer had been refused.

'No way,' Mike had insisted. 'I've checked with the woman and she's positive she didn't get any offer. She's not going to put her kids at risk by staying in a rat-infested hole like that if she had a choice, is she?'

But the company had produced a copy of the letter apparently sent to the woman. They were also adamant they had offered to meet Mike to discuss the situation at the outset and he had declined a meeting.

'Bullshit,' Mike exploded. 'They bloody did nothing of the sort. They're liars and crooks, and so are their lawyers. Bastards, the lot of them.'

He had notes of his phone call to the company, which had resulted in the damning 'declined to comment' pay-off to his story. But there was only the call – unrecorded – and nothing in writing. The lawyer repeatedly clicked his retractable ballpoint as he stared at the letters in front of him. He should have pointed out the need for something in writing before okaying the story. Instead, he had simply let it through without a caveat. Typical that the *Citizen* had managed to hang onto such a second-rate guy.

But astoundingly Clive continued to blame me. I had my eye off the ball, I was obsessed with the by-election, not interested in real news anymore, he said. Had my finely honed editorial instincts really deserted me? Of course not. It was a totally unfounded accusation. We paid lawyers to spot things like this.

I looked again at the ludicrous apology I was now drafting. The phrases stuck in my gullet – *wholly accepts the statement from Safe and Sound Rentals… apologises without reservation for any damage caused to the company's business and reputation…*

I hadn't mentioned any of this to Kirsty. It was another thing I didn't need to worry her with. As the election wore on, I was growing more selective in what I did share with her. I just hoped she'd be too busy to spot our embarrassing surrender when it was published. In any case, she wouldn't be interested in our plight, only in the family, who were still awaiting rehousing, despite a promise from the council. And so the poor are stuffed, she'd say. No doubt that very afternoon she was knocking on the family's door, or that of a family very like them – a family living on the wrong side of the breadline, a family who found existing on either side a struggle, a family who might or might not have received letters, might or might not have read them, might or might not have ignored them, a family who just wanted to survive from day to day. Knocking on their door and asking for their vote.

My job however was merely to finish the correction. Additional cash damages were under negotiation, but Clive was hopeful that these could be kept to a minimum, in view of the generous reparation in words. I doubted it. The company would screw us till the pips squeaked and flew across the newsroom. The *Citizen*, already financially challenged, was sinking further into the mire. The future didn't look rosy.

Just as well I had other things on my personal horizon. I couldn't resist checking the numbers: my most recent post had attracted 34,902 views. And I had over nineteen thousand followers on Twitter. I started drafting my next post.

The Safe and Sound apology was published the following morning, in the same edition as Shona's profile of Kirsty. I wasn't sure which piece was going to annoy Clive more, but as I started to read the profile, it was obvious. He would be delighted with what the *Citizen* had to say about the Labour candidate. In fact, the piece had his grubby finger-marks all over it. I read it with disbelief, then outrage. Fuck, fuck, fuck. What did Shona think she was playing at? I scrolled back to the headline – *A woman on the up* – and started again.

> *Labour's by-election candidate Kirsty Osmond – the woman who this week told a TV audience that men should be kept out of politics – has come a long way from her humble beginnings in a Sheffield council flat.* (Was it a flat? I was pretty sure she'd said a house.) *The daughter of a miner who turned strike-breaker in the 1980s* (that felt distinctly below the belt), *Ms Osmond has left all that behind her and now lives with her husband, a public school-educated* (ouch) *journalist and blogger* (at least they'd got that in), *in a £800,000 five-bedroom Victorian villa in one of Hull's leafiest and most up-market roads.* (Okay, Maple Avenue was a decent place to live, but was it really one of the most up-market? And eight hundred grand? Surely nowhere in Hull was worth that much. We certainly hadn't paid anywhere near

that figure, although that was eight years ago.)

But it got worse. A dozen lines down, there was this.

> *The Labour candidate's sister, single mum Julie Osmond, told the* Citizen: *"I haven't seen her in years. Quite frankly we haven't got that much in common. She always seemed to think we were a bit beneath her."*

'Rick, I'm sorry.'

Shona was standing by my side. She'd come up without my noticing and was chewing her nails, looking at my screen.

'Sorry? Is that it?' I let the contempt bleed out of me. 'I'm guessing this is not entirely your work.'

Shona moved from the nails of one hand to the nails of the other.

'He subbed it. Cut quite a lot. Added other bits. And tweaked the intro.'

'Tweaked? For Christ's sake, Shona. What did you—' I stopped. The usual background rumble in the newsroom had died down. My voice had risen. 'We can't talk here.'

Five minutes later, we were in the artisanal café around the corner. She was ordering coffees — a peace offering, no doubt — and I was sitting hunched over my phone, reading the Kirsty piece for the third time, trying now to assess it as a journalist, not an interested party. There wasn't much that was actually *inaccurate*. House or flat — maybe, but that was minor. And I'd just checked online: a house on our road had recently been sold for £800,000. Most of the piece was factual and there were one or two verbatim quotes from Kirsty herself. Her views and personality just about managed to come through.

But it was that intro – the tone of it, the selection and alignment of facts, the choice of language. And the headline. *A woman on the up*. On the up, on the make. A woman who'd pushed her way into the middle classes, who'd rejected her past. And that quote from Julie – how on earth had they found her? This felt even worse than the TV debacle.

Shona put down two lattes and I opened a packet of demerara. I didn't usually take sugar, but at that moment I craved sweetness.

She took a gulp of her coffee and then fixed her eyes on her cup. 'I know I asked some loaded questions, but I was pissed off with you for being there and I wanted to show I wasn't put off.'

'Yes, I got that.'

'But when I listened back to it, I thought that sense of her working-class roots and her feelings about teaching – I thought all that was good. She came over as a strong woman, a strong candidate. Honestly, Rick, I… I tried to keep a flavour of that.'

Hmm, maybe.

Her voice dipped.

'She was a bit subdued on the *Me Too* thing and obviously she didn't want to be drawn on Barraclough. But it was alright… her message to women that they should report abuse… unexciting maybe, but I could make something of it.'

I wasn't going to let on that I just about believed her. I'd let her sweat a little longer.

'Clive wanted to drop the abuse stuff and have a different intro. He wanted to make more of her dad. And shove in that reference to the house. And to you – I was surprised he risked that.' She looked up at me. 'But then he insisted we find the sister, get something more on her background. He spoke to Julie and came up with that quote.'

'And you let him do all that? It's your by-line. For fuck's sake Shona, you should have kicked up a stink, thrown the office furniture at him.'

'I did. And he overruled me. What could I do?'

'Insisted on taking your name off it?'

'And given him a complete free hand?'

Christ, if she went on like this, I was going to start feeling sorry for her. I looked around. The café was beginning to fill up. There were a few noisy students, an even noisier group of mothers and babies and a couple of solitary laptop workers insulated from the world by their headphones. One man was flicking through the daily papers set out on a side table for customers' perusal. Thankfully the pile didn't seem to include the *Citizen*.

'Well if that's how you and Clive plan to run the election coverage, what can I say? I trust you'll be equally ruthless with the other candidates when it's their turn.'

'That's more or less what Kirsty's agent said. He was on the phone like a shot. Suggested we were on notice.' She paused, apparently struck by a sudden realisation. 'You're not going to write about it in the blog, are you? I mean, you can't, the *Citizen*… it's awkward for you…'

'Not sure yet. There's probably a way.'

She seemed to consider this for a moment and then said, 'What does Kirsty think? Is she… upset?'

'I've not had chance to speak to her. But she won't let this throw her. Just the local paper, she'll say, what can you expect?'

Shona grimaced. I stood up, ready to leave her mulling over that.

'Rick, there's more to this.'

I dropped back into my seat. What now?

'Clive said we should see what other dirt – I'm sorry,

but that's the word he used – what else we could dig up on Kirsty.'

'Jesus Christ.'

'He said he's got contacts in Sheffield, he'd ask them to sniff around a bit, see what more we could unearth. Personal stuff like.'

'But that's laughable. I mean she left the place when she was eighteen. What's he going to do? Check whether she ever bunked off school?'

Laughable, but somehow unsettling.

'You're probably right… I just thought I'd mention it.' She paused. 'He also reckons she's taking campaign advice from Martin Barraclough.'

'What are you talking about?'

'Seems Barraclough's told him he's been discussing the election with her. It's why I asked that question.'

'For Christ's sake, Shona. Let me make this quite clear, since Kirsty didn't. Barraclough called her once, unsolicited. I was with her. The conversation lasted about sixty seconds and she put the phone down on him. If Clive dares to insinuate otherwise…'

'I wouldn't worry about it. It's just Clive. But there is one thing he definitely wants – a story on drugs being openly on sale at Phoenix Academy.'

Another thing to clarify – and one I should have seen coming.

'Look, I'm not telling you this, but as I understand it, there was one incident, which has been dealt with. It could be any school. Why pick on Phoenix? No, no need to answer that.'

'He's asked Dan to write it.'

Dan, the reporter who usually couldn't be bothered to get off his arse to cover a story. I felt as if my hands had been chopped off, my tongue ripped out. This was Clive getting at both of us. That old smouldering resentment – after eight years, it should have burnt itself out. But Kirsty going into politics had reignited it.

'I'll warn her. But if there's going to be any piece, you should write it, not Dan. Make it about the issue in general. Talk to other heads. And refuse to put your name to it if Clive meddles again.'

She put down her coffee cup, her shoulders drooping. She was a slight woman and the chair seemed to envelop her.

'I'm beginning to wonder if Clive rates me.'

'Clive doesn't rate anyone.'

'There've been a few things…'

'Things like what?'

'Oh, just comments and things.'

'What sort of comments?'

'Oh you know. My attitude. Whether I fit in. That sort of thing.'

'Whether you fit in?'

She seemed to shrink further into her chair.

'Whether you fit in?' I said again, louder. The woman at the next table looked over, distracted from feeding her baby, a blob of pale orange gunge dripping from a spoon. Shona narrowed her eyes at me and I lowered my voice.

'Shona, this is harassment. Harassment and discrimination. He's breaking the law.'

'I'm not sure it's that bad.'

'You've got to raise it with the union. For Christ's sake, you're mother of the chapel, aren't you? What's the point of that if you can't even look after yourself?'

'I don't want to make a fuss.' She drew a long breath. 'I want to beat him on his own terms.'

'The managing editor asks whether you *fit in*, and you don't want to make a fuss. He doesn't ask your white male colleagues whether they *fit in*. Does he?'

'Rick, please, I don't need you fighting my battles.'

I shook my head in disbelief.

'Clive is a sexist, racist bastard. We both know that.' I paused. This was delicate, something I'd promised myself I would never tell her. 'What you *don't* know is how hard I had to work to persuade him that he should employ you – as a woman of colour – in the first place.'

'What?'

'I spotted your potential the moment you opened your mouth at your interview. I knew you were just what the *Citizen* needed. And I've championed you–'

'You've what?'

'I've championed you all the way along. You've come too far to just accept–'

'You've *championed* me? I'm not a cause.'

'You know what I mean.'

'I don't think I do.'

Her face was stony. Why were women so deliberately obtuse?

'Oh, come on, I've made sure you've had every chance to shine, in spite of Clive. And I'm obviously not going to let him drive you away now. I won't allow him to win.'

She started slowly to nod and straightened her back.

'You know what? This is all about you, isn't it?'

She was now sitting upright in her chair.

'I get it now. Of course. I'm a project for you, aren't I? Why didn't I see that before? A pet diversity project, to make you look good.'

'Hold on, Shona. Let's not forget I'm the one who should be feeling pissed off this morning – over that Kirsty piece. In case you've forgotten, I've got a lot invested in this by-election and–'

'Ah yes, Kirsty. Do you see all women as projects, Rick? We're all beneficiaries of your patronage and we should all be grateful, is that it?'

She jumped up.

'Well not me. Go f… Go and find someone else to… to champion.'

With that, she gave me one last look, mustering all the scorn she could, and marched out of the cafe. I drained the cold remains of my coffee. This hadn't gone quite as I'd intended. In fact, you could have classified it as a minor fuck-up. Perhaps I hadn't presented things in the best way, but she was obviously over-reacting. Women as projects? The accusation was manifestly unfair.

**

It's been another full-on day. I've done some prep for the first hustings, spoken to umpteen people about upcoming visits by senior Labour figures, including my one-time boss Janet McConnell – I'm looking forward to seeing her again after all this time – and I've dropped in at an old people's day centre and a job-seekers' club. And besides that, more door-to-door work – two long sessions morning and early evening. They went well – more positive responses than we were getting to start with.

So everything feels on a roll. Even Gerry's beginning to calm down after the *Citizen* piece. He rang them first thing to give Clive Pascoe hell. Gutter journalism, completely biased, he said. If they wanted access to their new MP after the election, they needed to think carefully about how they were covering the campaign. He put it on speaker so I could enjoy Clive's responses. Not that I did – two men shouting at each other. All heat and no light. Clive said they had every right to present a rounded picture of candidates and he hoped Gerry wasn't contesting the freedom of the press or threatening the

181

paper. Gerry's eyes were about to pop with rage and I signalled him to end the call. As Mark pointed out afterwards, it's only the local rag and hardly anyone buys it. No-one mentioned Rick.

Gerry also had a go at me about Julie. I'd kept quiet not just about my dad, but about my sister too, he said. Why hadn't I mentioned we were estranged, if that's what it was? And was there anything else I'd forgotten to tell him? It's complicated, I tried to explain, I never dreamt they'd contact her. But I kept thinking about it and this evening I called her. I had an old number and got through and I read out the quote to her. Is that what she'd really told them? She said she didn't mean it like that. A bloke had phoned her, caught her on her way out to work, she didn't realise she was going to be quoted. She sounded really embarrassed and somehow I felt bad. I said it was silly us not talking like this. I should come over and visit some time. After the election, of course.

But now we're heading to the pub – me, Gerry, and the team – for the end-of-day debriefing. We should be going back to the office but just occasionally we decamp to the pub instead and make it more informal. A treat after a hard day. Rick texted to ask what time I'd be home so I suggested he meet me there. He could even have a drink with us if he makes it in time. The sooner he and Gerry get over the thing they seem to have about each other, the better.

**

I was meeting her that evening at The Ferryman near the constituency office. It was a pub I'd been to a few times, a traditional and serious drinking place that for decades had resisted the blandishments of modernisation. Heavy drinkers propped up the bar, elderly couples who'd long since run out of things to say to each other sat at tables and stared into space – did all marriages get to that stage? – and a group of young men jostled each other around a pool table. There were relatively few women in the place.

She was with Gerry and three others – one of them I recognised as Mark, Lucy's partner. He'd been part of the canvassing team the night I'd joined her and it reminded me that I ought to venture out with them again soon. But she hadn't suggested it.

They were sitting around a small table in the corner of the lounge bar, folders, clipboards and leaflets sharing the space with a mess of torn crisp packets and near-empty beer and Coke glasses. She raised her hand to me and I went over to join them. She introduced me to the two I didn't know, and I nodded at Gerry. He'd already started to gather up his papers, as if my arrival was a signal for him to leave.

'Don't rush off because of me,' I said. 'Can I get anyone a drink?'

Mark hesitated and looked at his colleagues. 'Well…'

'Thanks, but we're going,' Gerry said. 'Maybe another time.' His face told me he had no intention of there ever being another time. Understood. The *Citizen* was in the doghouse after that article and Rick Dewhirst was tainted by very clear association. He was not someone you wanted to relax with over a pint if you were the Labour election agent. Fine by me.

I caught Kirsty's eye and pointed at her glass. She shook her head, so I left them to finish their goodbyes and went to get myself a drink. The others had gone when I returned. I sat down next to her and felt the lingering warmth of the seat vacated by Gerry. Kirsty and I had not been out on our own like this – just the two of us, almost a date – for weeks. We hadn't even had chance to talk properly for days. Every morning she was up before I was awake, sometimes out very early for a leaflet drop, catching people before they left home, and every night she sank into bed exhausted. I leant over and touched her cheek.

'How are you?'

'I'm good.'

'I'm sorry about the profile piece.' Hardly my fault of course, but necessary appeasement. 'Clive changed the opening. And got that quote from Julie. Shona feels terrible about it. But overall I reckon you came over okay. There was *some* reasonable stuff in it.'

She couldn't possibly have been fooled by that, but she said, 'Don't worry about it. You warned me it would be like this.' She smiled, a pragmatic sort of smile. 'And I've spoken to Julie. She says it wasn't what she meant. I'll try to get over and see her after the election.'

'Oh?'

'But I'm not going to fret about it anymore. Or the TV interview. Our clarification seemed to put an end to the misinterpretations there. And overall the national coverage hasn't been bad. More interest than we expected and reasonably fair.'

'See, I told you the blog would help. Nearly forty thousand views of the last one. It's taking off.'

She narrowed her eyes at me. 'More likely all the work we're doing on the ground.'

'It's had a couple of mentions in various columns – did you see the one in *The Guardian* this morning? Its honesty seems to be much appreciated. And I've had messages from ex-colleagues congratulating me and encouraging me to keep going.'

'Well, as long as it's keeping you amused.'

It was doing much more than that, but I let the dig go.

'I saw the apology, the housing story...' she said.

I hadn't mentioned my recent little problem at the *Citizen* and didn't want to get into it now.

'Oh, nothing to worry about. What about your day?'

I listened while she talked about the day's canvassing, the doors rapped and the bells rung, relieved for once by her lack of interest in *my* work, and wondered whether anyone here in this pub realised I was sitting with their future MP. Surely she'd be recognised from TV appearances or from her photo on leaflets shoved through letterboxes – some people must glance at those before chucking them away. And yet no-one seemed in the slightest bit interested in us. We were just a middle-aged couple having a drink, talking about nothing in particular.

Of course, I did need to tell her about the school drugs story, but not here, not now. Later, in the car, or when we got home.

'We should probably make a move,' she said eventually.

I finished my beer and stood up to go to the gents.

'Back in a sec.'

Two minutes later I emerged from the toilet and started to trace my way back through a packed pub. The place had filled up in just the time it had taken to drink my half-pint and it was now much rowdier than when I'd arrived.

I didn't register the voice as anything out of the ordinary at first. It was just someone holding forth, part of normal pub banter. But it became louder, more grating, like an irritated wasp trying to find its way through a pane of glass.

'Fucking politicians… all the same… sleazebags, the lot of them.'

I scanned the room and located the owner of the voice. He was a red-faced, large-bellied man sitting two tables away from Kirsty. He was gesticulating towards her, then turning back to his two companions, apparently frustrated by their reluctance to join in.

'Course it's her. Seen her on the telly. She was in the paper, too. Lives in some fucking big house with her posh-boy husband. Dad was a scab back in the day. Jumped up slag, if you ask me.'

Which no-one had. One of the man's friends appeared to be trying to rein him in – 'Give it a rest, Dave' – but with little success.

The pub had gone quiet. I was back at Kirsty's table. She had picked up her two bags and coat. There was a slight tremor in her hand as I took one of the bags from her. She turned to look at the red-faced man and seemed to hold his gaze. He raised his eyebrows at her.

'So? What you got to say for yourself then? Cat got your tongue? Two-faced bitch. You're all the same, you lot. Fucking hypocrites.'

She continued to stare at him and I felt a twinge of panic. Someone called out, 'Language, Dave', and someone else, 'Take no notice, love'. I had to get her out of there, before she told him exactly what she had to say for herself. Although knowing Kirsty, she wouldn't explode – she'd simply explain why he was wrong and why she could make life better for him and his family if he voted for her. The man glowered at her, his face now a virulent shade of crimson.

'Time to go,' I said. 'The car's outside.'

I started to manoeuvre her out and people moved back to allow us space to pass. I was aware of a sea of faces, some staring open-mouthed, a few looking away, embarrassed, pretending not to notice, others whispering, grinning, enjoying the unexpected entertainment.

And then the voice came again.

'Go on, fuck off then. Cunt.'

It lingered in the hushed atmosphere and a still space formed in my head. I dropped her bag, let go her arm and took eight paces over to the man's table – I remember it was exactly eight paces.

'What did you say?' I was calm, totally in charge of the situation, about to put a foul-mouthed tormentor in his place.

His friends looked at me warily. The man took a gulp from a fresh pint that someone had put in front of him. He slowly wiped the back of his hand across his mouth, but missed a glob of froth above his upper lip. He smirked – he was both comical and menacing – and stood up. Somehow he was taller than I'd expected.

'And who d'you think you are, then?'

'Just someone telling you to keep that cesspit mouth of yours clo–'

The thump seemed to come from nowhere, full on the nose, just below the bridge. My eyes watered and a dull ache radiated out, filling my whole head. I wanted to finish my sentence but couldn't remember what I was trying to say. I felt a hand on my sleeve.

'Oh my God, Rick, are you okay?'

There was a warm trickle coming from my right nostril. The man nodded at me with what seemed to be satisfaction and sat down. Was I meant to hit him back? I'd never found myself in a situation like this before and I wasn't sure of the rules of engagement. But I seemed to have missed the moment.

'Here, take this.' She handed me a tissue and I started to dab at the dribble of blood. I was still speechless. 'We should leave,' she said, her face fixed on mine. 'Are you sure you're all right?'

I nodded. 'Just a small nose bleed.'

Someone – it must have been the landlord – came up and said, 'I've called the police. You okay, mate?'

'Yes, I'm fine. It's nothing.'

I dabbed my nose again, pulled the car keys out of my pocket and handed them to her.

'You go. I should stay for the police. I'll see you later.'

'But–'

'Just go.'

**

For Christ's sake, what came over him? I thought I was the one who wasn't going to be able to cope with the poison of an election, at least according to Rick, but the first provocation and he just couldn't help himself. He hadn't even had much to drink. Why do men always have to exacerbate an already difficult situation? Why can't they learn to rise above it? I thought we were going, but then… Of course the abuse was awful and I wanted to say something myself, show the guy we're not all hypocrites, or cowards. But he was too far gone, I could see. He's going to be one of my constituents, I imagine. And he already loathes me. Somehow it's the randomness of it – being at the receiving end of what feels like pure hatred from someone you don't know, someone who's got no reason to hate you, but just seems to… want to hurt you. An ordinary bloke whose kids perhaps went to your school, who might sit next to you on the bus, or come to fix your leaky pipes. There's no rationale and it's probably not personal. You're a politician and he hates you and that's it. I guess you get hardened to it. At least Adam wasn't with us. I don't think I'd have been able to bear that. Thank God he's out with Jess tonight.

Of course I hope Rick's okay. But why couldn't he let it go? Candidate's husband involved in pub brawl. Honest to God, this is the last thing we need. Gerry will raise the roof. Your husband's a bloody liability, he'll say. I know that's what he thinks already, he's said as much. The blog, to start with. And completely ineffectual, he says, when it comes to making sure his newspaper reports this election fairly. I've tried to explain the difficult position Rick's in.

Perhaps I should have stayed, held his hand while he talked to the police, made sure he didn't press charges. I could see why he wanted me to go and he was right, I couldn't be involved, a parliamentary candidate, the election… what if anything else kicked off? But it felt weak clearing off like that. Is this where my courage fails me, where it all starts to unravel?

I can hear a taxi outside the house, its engine running – it must be him.

**

She was standing in the hall waiting for me.

'Thank God you're back. How are you?'

I touched my nose. It was tender, a little swollen.

'Fine. Just a nose bleed, like I said. It cleared up quickly. Nothing broken, from the feel of it.'

'But it's bruised. Are you sure you shouldn't get it looked at?'

'Quite sure.'

She peered at my face for a few seconds more and then said, 'And the police? What's happening there?'

I walked through to the sitting room. She followed me.

'They asked if I wanted to press charges. I said probably not, but I'd think about it.'

I heard her catch her breath.

'Obviously it'd be better if you didn't, if you… just let it go.'

'You mean… pretend it never happened?'

'Yes, that's more or less what I mean.'

'But that's ridiculous. Obviously it happened. Lots of people saw it.'

'I don't think most people realised what it was about, or who we were. It was just rowdy behaviour… a bit of unpleasantness.'

'Unpleasantness? I got hit, you know.'

'I realise that.' She sighed. 'Rick, why on earth did you have to get involved? Couldn't you have just ignored him?'

'What and let him think behaving like that was okay? I thought you might be a tad pleased that I felt so strongly about someone shouting vile abuse at you.'

'I'd have preferred it if you'd exercised some common sense.'

'Common sense? I was defending your honour.'

'Oh for God's sake, Rick, stop acting like some knight in shining armour.' She clenched her hands. 'You may have forgotten but I am in the middle of an election campaign. This kind of thing can't happen.'

'So if we pretend it *didn't* happen, how do I explain this?' I touched the bruising again. 'To my colleagues? To Adam?'

'I'm sure you'll think of something. You walked into a door maybe. Look, I'm sorry your nose got bruised, of course I am, but you've only got yourself to blame. You were a complete idiot to take that man on.'

My nose throbbed, as much at the injustice of her reaction as at the physical injury. She was being deeply ungenerous, yet again. The blog and now this. I was doing my utmost for her, even taking blows on her behalf, and she couldn't bring herself to thank me. Hadn't I warned her that politics could be violent? – although, naturally, I didn't think the violence would be directed at me. I was numbed by her lack of appreciation.

'Okay, I'll try and forget it then,' I said, knowing I wouldn't.

'Good. Why don't we have a drink now?'

She poured two whiskies, handed one to me and sank onto a sofa. I joined her.

'I didn't want to mention this in the pub,' she said, 'but the school had a call from some reporter on the *Citizen* today, wanting to talk about drugs.'

'Ah, I was going to warn you this might happen.'

'Well they got there first. Phil called me. I said he should invite the reporter in. Let him see the school going about its normal business. There's nothing to hide.'

'Are you crazy?'

And I was the one apparently deficient in common sense? Kirsty could be extraordinarily naïve at times.

'But Rick, you've always said—'

'In general, yes, being open works. But, come on, there's an agenda here. Surely you can see that.'

'Oh,' she said, and the penny seemed to drop, plopping into the bottom of a deep well. 'This is about me, isn't it?'

'It's Clive up to his tricks again. It's as if he's got some vendetta against both of us—'

'What, not that party? I mean, that was years ago.'

'It's more than that. I've told you, he's always resented me, and now he's getting at me through you.'

'You're over-dramatising things.'

'I'm not. In fact… according to Shona, he's sniffing around for more personal stuff on you.'

Perhaps I shouldn't have mentioned it – I wasn't convinced there was anything in it – but she needed to be on her guard. And to appreciate how much I was looking out for her.

She sat perfectly still for a moment, her head turned

away from me, and then she said, 'Well let him.'

'I thought that's what you'd say. But I'm going to have it out with him in the morning, the profile, the school, whatever else he thinks he's up to.'

'No, Rick. Don't interfere. The situation is hard enough for you as it is. I'll talk to Gerry. He'll deal with it.'

I put down my glass and turned to her, my arms on her shoulders.

'Speak to Phil first thing. Tell him to say he's too busy at the moment – end of term, something like that. Put them off.'

'He said the reporter had some specific questions.'

'Then offer a written response.'

'Phil's finding this difficult. The media. It's not his thing… Rick, there is something you *could* do. I know I shouldn't be asking, but would you help him… with a statement? In the circumstances, it might be okay…?'

Her voice evaporated into the lightest of question marks. I let go of her shoulders. It most certainly was not okay. Checking the wording of a routine press release or correcting the odd bit of phrasing was one thing. I'd done that often enough. But drafting a defensive statement in its entirety was quite another.

Then again, rules could be bent. And I needed to keep control of this particular situation.

'Give him my number.'

'Thank you.' She touched my hand. 'Phil's under pressure from the governors to clamp down hard. He's out of his depth.' She paused. 'I should be there to lead.'

She leant over and picked up an election leaflet from the coffee table, turning it over. She was looking at her own image, Kirsty Osmond flanked by her supporters, confident, purposeful, an MP-in-waiting.

'Am I doing the right thing?'

'Rather late for second thoughts, isn't it?'

'I know you were a bit iffy about the whole thing to start with.'

'I was just testing your resolve.'

'My resolve?' She dropped the leaflet back onto the table. 'You were right about one thing, though. People can be ruthless.'

'Don't say I didn't warn you. But I'm here to make sure you win. You'll do it. I know you will.'

'Thank you for your vote of confidence.' She laughed and stroked my thigh. 'Come to bed.'

That night we made love for the first time for more than a fortnight, the first time since the start of the campaign. It didn't feel any different, having sex with a parliamentary candidate. Not different, just overdue.

I walked into the kitchen the next morning and she smiled at me. I'd spent some time peering in the mirror at my bruise – overnight it had turned an interesting purple – but she ignored it. She'd made a pot of coffee – a rarity, she usually left too early – and I took that, the smile and the coffee, as her sign that all was well with the world, that any self-doubt had been assuaged by sleep, that much of last night had never happened, just the sex. Periods of abstinence should not be so long in future.

She was on the phone – of course – and about to leave. She already had her coat on, the smarter of her two winter coats, the newish grey one, a belted trench coat that she'd bought in the sales. Her rosette was lying on the worktop next to the coffee pot and she gestured at it with the hand holding the cup. I pinned it on her coat lapel, then stood back to admire the overall effect, while she continued to talk to Gerry about the logistics of the day's campaigning.

This was the day of the McConnell visit. Janet, now Baroness, McConnell – the woman who had, professionally speaking, brought Kirsty and me together in the first place. How many years was it since a bolshie young parliamentary assistant had refused to put me through to her boss and told me I was wasting her time? As it turned out, I hadn't been wasting the time of either of us.

McConnell was now an elder stateswoman of the party and hers was one of a string of visits by Labour's big guns. The cameras would be there, of course, with the main photo opportunity on the waterfront late morning. Kirsty was naturally excited about performing alongside the woman who'd given her her first break and I was looking forward to a long-postponed chat with Janet McConnell and to sharing my views on the progress of the campaign. I would pop out for half an hour or so, join the team, say hello to Janet. First-name terms now.

Kirsty finished her call, fingered the rosette on her coat and said, 'About the pub incident. I mentioned it to Gerry and–'

'Oh, I thought we were pretending it didn't happen.'

'Well obviously I had to tell Gerry. And we think it's probably best if you don't come down to the waterfront today. The bruise… just in case anyone asks questions… or you get caught on camera… people talk you know.'

'What are you going on about? I walked into a door. Remember? Aren't you both being paranoid?'

'It's just that it feels… well… it feels like you've been a bit too much of a focus of late. The blog, the pub, the paper, all of that.'

'Kirsty, are you ashamed of me?'

'Lie low, just for a few days. It's best.'

I slammed down my cup, spilling the coffee. She chose not to notice but squeezed my arm and hurried out of the kitchen, her phone ringing again. The front door closed. Another day began for her, another mountain to climb, never knowing what lay at the summit. And her trusty Sherpa was being left at base camp, an unwanted embarrassment.

This was grossly unjust, beaten up in her defence and now banished, unworthy of being by her side. I had to reassert myself, show her how wrong she was.

Fifteen minutes later, I left the house having made a decision. No more prevarication, I would tackle Clive on his attitude to Kirsty head-on, stop any more sniping, or snooping. Regardless of her plea to me not to, regardless of whether at that moment she actually deserved it, regardless of how awkward it might be for Shona… Shona, I'd almost forgotten about her, would she even be talking to me? Not to worry, she'd come round. No, regardless of all of them, I would thrash things out with Clive. He was threatening my candidate, and me.

Unusually he was already there when I walked into the newsroom. He beckoned me into his office before I'd even taken my coat off. He was making that slow grinding movement with his teeth. Something was up.

He looked across at me.

'Christ, who hit you?'

'No-one. I walked into a door.'

'Pissed, no doubt.'

'No, I just wasn't looking where I was going.'

'Well that says something.'

Punched by a drunk, abandoned by Kirsty and yet again taunted by Clive. I gritted my teeth.

'Look,' he went on, 'I haven't got all day so I'll come straight to the point. We're closing down the print edition in the summer. The *Citizen* will be online-only from June.'

I shouldn't have been shocked. The paper had been limping on for some time and I'd anticipated more cutbacks. I'd already mentally disentangled myself from its prospects, my personal Clive-succession plan had been dumped, my future was heading in more promising directions. But this was quicker and sharper than expected. My mouth felt dry and I fumbled for something to say. Clive didn't wait for any response.

'It's been on the cards for a while. But it was finalised at an emergency board meeting yesterday.'

And he proceeded to outline the financial prognosis they faced: *escalating losses from the print operation… shrinking profitability overall… last straw the Safe and Sound business… heading for a six-figure settlement after all… and the fuckers are rubbing salt in the wound by announcing they're donating fifty per cent of it to a homelessness charity* (strictly speaking, that wasn't part of the financial prognosis, just a supplementary comment by Clive)… *situation becoming increasingly desperate… something has to give… a major restructuring planned.*

I looked through the glass partition into the newsroom. It was the start of just another day and there was a modicum of busy-ness as the early arrivals settled down to work: figures milling, talking, laughing, staring at screens, some even writing. There was the occasional look of frustration as a desk phone was slammed down or the hunching over a notepad as a conversation began in earnest. Twenty people out there were engaged in delivering something that would soon no longer exist, at least not in a form we recognised. Newspapers have always been a transient product, here today, forgotten tomorrow, requiring constant re-invention. Perhaps no-one would miss it. Except those producing it.

'Jobs?' I said, and turned back to Clive. 'What's it mean for jobs?'

There was more teeth-grinding and a look that suggested I was being deliberately obstreperous by raising pernickety details.

'Obviously there are going to be redundancies. We'll be relying mainly on agencies, syndicated features, that sort of thing. The odd unpaid intern. And, well, citizen journalism.'

'Citizen journalism? Jesus Christ.'

The glass partition was poorly sound-proofed and I caught sight of Dan sitting just outside Clive's office, eating a doughnut and looking towards us with some curiosity.

'Keep your voice down,' Clive spat at me. 'Yes, citizen journalism. An online platform for members of the public to contribute their own news and opinions. A new business model for the *Citizen*. Very appropriate, I'd say.'

There was one question that needed asking, even if I knew the answer.

'And how do I fit into this new business model?'

'Ah, well, I was coming to that. The thing is, we can't really justify your post continuing, so… we're going to have to let you go, as they say. Sorry.'

Sorry? It wasn't a word in Clive's lexicon. I'd never heard him apologise for anything before. As far as I could remember, not once, ever. I stared hard at him. I wasn't thinking about the humiliation of losing my job, having to tell Kirsty, fielding her pity… even though I'd already made the psychological break from the *Citizen*, it was still painful. But I wasn't thinking about that. I was simply transfixed by Clive's discomfort. This was Clive on his best behaviour, having to let people go, shifting uneasily in his seat, obliged to say sorry.

'When will I know the terms?' I asked.

'Speak to HR. You'll get a reasonable pay-off. And three months' notice. Generous really, given your editorial negligence over the rats. Not to mention the blog. You're lucky to have held onto your job till now.'

'Am I being sacked?'

'No, you're not catching us out like that. You can forget about dragging this though any tribunal. It's redundancy, same as the others. There'll be emails to everyone next week so keep your mouth closed till then. And after that, consultation and all the business with the union. Pain in the fucking arse.'

'And Shona?'

'No idea why you're so concerned about that woman. Argues too much. An awkward bitch at the best of times.'

My fingers tingled.

'Anyway,' he went on, 'she'll no doubt be taking on management and marching the lemmings up the union hill. Mother of the chapel, isn't she? Up the hill and over the fucking edge.'

Yes, he was now fully recovered from his bout of half-decent behaviour. I shook my head. Shona wouldn't want me to intervene on her behalf. She's not your project, Rick, remember that. She can look after herself apparently.

I stood up. I'd had enough. I couldn't be bothered to tell him to stuff his job, all our jobs, none of us would want anything to do with his cheapskate non-newspaper. I needed to get out, think this through, work out whether it might even be to my advantage. I slammed the door behind me and wandered across the newsroom, trying not to catch my colleagues' eyes. They'd all be going down with the ship, Shona included. But moving on would actually be no bad thing for her. I hoped she made it to shore – if I was permitted to have hopes for her. I scanned the newsroom looking for her. She was out of course, covering Kirsty and the McConnell visit.

And then I remembered. I had arrived that morning determined to tackle Clive on his treatment of Kirsty. I'd been distracted by something as mundane as losing my job. Maybe it was for the best after all. I'd leave the grubby matter of Kirsty's PR battle with *The Humberside Citizen* to Gerry. Quite right, she'd say, you can't micro-manage everything. No, I needed to take a loftier view. I sat down at my desk and logged into my blog.

∗∗

I've been looking forward to this ever since I phoned Janet McConnell the morning after I got the nomination. I hadn't spoken to her for years and she promised she'd come up to Hull as soon as she could. She always knew I'd get to be an MP, she said, just surprised it'd taken me so long to make up my mind.

And so here we are at the waterfront, Janet, me and the team. I've been walking around chatting and shaking a few hands and now we're moving on to the formal part – a mini-speech. We've got a reasonable-sized crowd with us, a manufactured crowd in part – Gerry's seen to that, you always need to get your people there, an enthusiastic backdrop. Adam's among them, to my left, at the front, chatting to everyone, leaflets stuffed in his pockets, ready to hand out to anyone who'll take one. But there are genuine spectators, too – passers-by, people who've popped out of offices and cafés to see what's going on. The television cameras have certainly helped to drum up interest today – we should be on the lunchtime news, regional bulletins at least. And it all seems pleasingly positive, no hecklers, no red-faced men shouting obscenities, no-one throwing punches.

I'm sorry we had to ban Rick, but Gerry is right. It's not worth taking unnecessary risks. Shona's over there with the other reporters, and I smile at her. No hard feelings. I mean that. It's Gerry's job to complain, mine to rise above it and carry on. Not that it didn't hurt, but you can't let it show. And what Rick said last night about Clive still fishing around, looking for personal stuff… But I refuse to be intimidated. If I agonised over every little thing, I'd give up completely.

I'm ready to speak now and Gerry points at a small crate next to Janet. My first actual soapbox. Rick's accused me often enough of holding forth on a metaphorical one so it's satisfying to be climbing onto the real thing. Janet offers me a hand as I step up and someone passes me a microphone. It feels a little stagey to be standing on an upturned crate next to the marina railings as if I just happened to be passing by and have stopped to say a few words to people who just happen to be milling around. Elections are nothing but a series of performances.

I introduce myself – never assume everyone knows who you are, I've learnt that – and tell people I'd like to say something about this election and why I'm standing. I want this country to be a fairer place, a decent place for everyone to live, I say. I want to see more homes built, better social care, more opportunities for our young people. As a party, we want to bring back jobs and investment to parts of the country that have lost out under the Tories. I've churned out versions of this several times now, in the TV studio, to various people I've met in recent days. But the chill air coming across the water gives the message a new edge, even if there are one or two yachts out there whose owners may not be voting for me. I don't need to win every vote, just enough.

Janet leads the applause and helps me down. She pats my arm and says well done, then takes the microphone from me and says she'd like to make a prediction – that this by-election will mark a turning point in Labour's fight to rescue the country from years of austerity. But she hasn't risked climbing onto the soapbox and the crowd is starting to drift away.

**

I'm going to be honest. It's been a tough few days

in By-election Land. If I thought this campaign was going to be a straightforward appeal to the electorate over policies and personalities, and may the best woman win, I was wrong.

I knew we would face apathy and occasional distortions of the truth. But I did think there would be at least a glaze of decency and fairness over the whole business.

Again I was wrong.

This week a newspaper had a go at my wife for her working-class roots. What? you say, but she's a Labour candidate, and doesn't Labour still claim to be the party of the working classes? Well yes, that's what I thought too. But read on.

In its article, the newspaper pointed out that Kirsty Osmond grew up on a council estate, the daughter of a miner. Now she's a headteacher married to a journalist and we own our own comfortable-enough home. In my book, that's called social mobility. The government even set up a commission to promote it. Pretty uncontroversial, I'd say.

But with an attitude worthy of the Victorians, the article implied that people should not attempt to rise above their station. Leave behind your humble beginnings and you're a phoney, a hypocrite even. Born poor, stay poor.

What utter drivel.

Kirsty has never denied her background. Why would she? Let me quote her: "I've had advantages that most people in my community didn't have and that they continue not to have. It's something I'll never forget."

That honesty is Kirsty through and through.

If snide digs are one thing, then open abuse is quite another. And common civility is often the first casualty in political warfare. My wife, like many other female politicians, has already had to block some of the more vituperative contributors on Twitter and the like. As we all know, social media can be very nasty indeed, and there is a limit to how much of that sort of stuff you can bear to see when you check your timeline.

But what if the vitriol turns into something old-fashioned and non-digital that you can't switch off?

Last night my wife and I were having a quiet drink in a pub at the end of a hard day's campaigning, when a man started to hurl abuse at her. I will spare you the details, but his manner was threatening and his language eye-wateringly foul, even to this hardened journalist.

Kirsty tried to ignore the man's offensive behaviour, but I couldn't stand by and let this deeply unpleasant scene continue. No-one else seemed willing to act, so I went up to the man and politely asked him to desist. With no provocation, he punched me.

Disregarding my personal safety may have been a mistake. I reacted instinctively. I was simply defending my wife. The police were called but I have decided not to press charges – I do not wish to load even more work onto our hard-pressed constabulary.

However, I believe my action last night reinforced a very simple point. Abuse – physical or verbal – is not okay in politics.

Throughout all this, of course, my wife has kept going, working hard, persuading people that she will do her best for them, all of them, even the ones who (in my opinion) don't deserve it. She understands the complexities of her future constituents' lives and she wants those lives to be better than many of them currently are.

Today, as part of all this, she was accompanied by Labour peer, Janet McConnell. Together they won over sceptical crowds down at Hull's waterfront. Of course the big cheeses always home in on by-elections and this might have been regarded as merely a set-piece photo opportunity.

But it was much more than that. Baroness McConnell is Kirsty's old mentor, her first political boss before she went into teaching. She is widely respected as that rare beast, an honest politician. Watching both of them, you had a sense of the baton being passed on.

On Tuesday, Kirsty and the other candidates will be setting out their wares at televised hustings. It will be a chance, I hope, for some civilised debate. We will see what it produces. In spite of everything, I remain perversely optimistic.

I'd started it surreptitiously in the newsroom, finished it as soon as I got home and posted it after a couple of read-throughs. This time there'd be no self-censorship. I hadn't got much left to lose with the *Citizen* and didn't care what Clive (or even Shona) thought. I was telling my own story, as much as Kirsty's. And I certainly wasn't going to let her agent suppress the truth.

I'd watched her waterfront performance on my screen at work. The by-election was the second item in the regional news after the opening of the trial of four members of a people trafficking gang. Just occasionally politics could be light relief and today, in contrast to last night, it seemed especially so. Kirsty was shaking hands with people in the crowd, talking and listening, interested in each of them. She could have been one of the more skilful minor royals, although my non-royalist wife would have been horrified if I'd shared that particular insight with her. Admittedly the *couture* wasn't exactly *haute* and the rosette did get in the way, but she was a natural. She knew how to work a crowd. Perhaps that's what came from years of walking through school corridors, stopping to greet random kids, exchanging a few words here, having a real conversation there, letting them know they mattered. Well done on the hockey match, Saffron. Is your mum out of hospital yet, Jake? I'd seen her do it once when I was waiting for her at the school reception. She came out of her office and what should have taken a few seconds – walking fifty feet through a throng of students – took ten minutes. She liked people, in a way that some of us weren't always sure we did, and down there at the waterfront it showed.

I might not have been there but I'd got a sense of it all from TV and I'd added my own enhancements. This was a blog after all, not news. Everything was dripping into it and if the pudding was a little over-egged, so what? The important thing was to keep my profile high, the narrative intimate, the election human, my readers hooked. I'd had no more complaints from Gerry (although perhaps after this one I needed to be prepared). The polls were moving further in Kirsty's direction, the other candidates seemed lacklustre. I could allow myself some latitude.

After posting this latest offering (in my opinion, my best so far), I spent a couple of hours catching up on all the Kirsty coverage, answering personal emails and googling myself. I was doing very nicely there – my blog was taking all the prime spots and the world's other Rick Dewhirsts weren't getting much of a look-in. What's more, I'd just had a request from a feature writer on a national paper, someone I vaguely knew, for a personal interview with me. Yes, me, not Kirsty. Naturally I was considering it. It was all an energising distraction from the other stuff, the Clive business, redundancies and people's lives being fucked up. Not that I was being asked about any of that at home – I hadn't found the right time to tell Kirsty yet.

By now it was gone nine and I was hungry. Kirsty would be another hour or so. I wasn't sure about Adam. I opened the fridge and was about to pull out a plate of cold chicken legs when the front door bell rang – one unnecessarily long ring. I didn't want callers, whether they were trying to sell me something, get me to sign up to a charity donation or bring Jesus into my life. At least it wouldn't be political door-knockers. The Labour banners festooning the windows kept away the other parties, like cloves of garlic warding off vampires. I opened the door, ready to shut it again as soon as I could.

A woman stood there in the light of the outside lamp, a small, thin, grey-haired woman, wearing a well-lived-in anorak, perhaps once pale blue in colour. Had I seen her before? She was on the step, very close to the door, and she looked anxious. Was this going to be some sort of scam – her car had broken down, her phone was dead, could I please help?

'Is Kirsty Osmond in?' she asked. The voice was ordinary, Yorkshire, maybe Leeds or Bradford, but there was a confidence there, as unexpected as the question itself.

'She's out,' I said, relieved that she really was. My hand rested warily on the inside catch of the door. After the pub incident, I was cautious. I wanted this woman off my front door step.

'When will she be back?'

'Later. Can I take a message?'

It crossed my mind that she might actually be genuine. She might have some legitimate reason for calling. Perhaps Kirsty had invited her, told her to pop round any time. It seemed unlikely, even for Kirsty. She knew she had to be security-conscious, she couldn't have people just turning up at her home. But the address wasn't difficult for anyone to find if they put their mind to it. The woman was staring over my shoulder, looking into the hall, as if she didn't believe me and expected Kirsty suddenly to materialise behind me.

She dragged her eyes back to me. 'What?'

'A message. Who should I say called?'

'Tell her it's Marie. An old friend.'

'Friend?'

'From university. We were good friends, she'll

remember me. I'd like to talk to her. It's important.'

'Can I say what it's about?'

'It's personal. Just personal. I sent her an email at the school, but I guess she's been busy.'

The woman fished in her bag and pulled out a chewed ballpoint pen and a small notepad. She scribbled down a name, address, and phone number, ripped out the sheet and folded it. 'Give her that. Hope she can read my writing.' Her hand was trembling slightly. I suspected she was lying about the university connection, but I couldn't be sure. We all had friends we'd grown out of and I could imagine Kirsty saying, what, you didn't even ask her in, offer her a coffee? But I didn't. Just turning up like this wasn't on. I hesitated for a moment before taking the paper from her.

'Okay, I'll pass it on.' I paused. 'Haven't I seen you somewhere before?'

'No, I don't think so.'

She looked away. I hovered, wanting to shut the door, but she made no move to leave. She turned her head to me again.

'I assume you're her husband.' She didn't wait for confirmation and I wasn't inclined to give it. 'I've been reading the blog, you know. Very interesting.'

'Glad you enjoy it.' You couldn't pick your readers, I guessed. 'Look, I'm sorry, but I'm—'

'I've just read the latest one.' She pulled a phone out of her bag and waved it at me as if it were evidence. 'What you had to say about Kirsty's background and that. Social mobility, that's how you put it, didn't you?'

'Yes, but if you don't mind—'

'Kirsty's done very well for herself. I'm pleased for her, I really am.' And once more, she glanced over my shoulder into the house. 'I'm sorry about what happened to you in that pub, though. There are some very nasty types around, aren't there?' Her eyes were again on me, giving my bruise a slow, appraising look. 'Right, I'll be off then. Please don't forget to give her the note.'

She turned to go and passed Adam as he came into the driveway. He must have walked from the bus stop and his shoulders were drooping with tiredness. The woman stopped and looked back at him, but then went on.

He threw his bag down in the hall. 'Who was that? Someone trying to save your soul?'

'They always come in pairs. No, someone for your mother. Said she was an old friend from university.'

'What, just turning up like that? Weird. I'm starving. Anything to eat?'

I followed him through to the kitchen, where he opened the fridge and pulled out the plate of cold chicken legs.

'Okay if I have these?'

'Go ahead.'

He took a bite and then hoisted himself onto the worktop, swinging his legs against the cupboard door under him.

'I've just read your latest stuff. God, I thought you said you walked into a door.' He took another bite. 'Brave, I guess.'

Recognition, of sorts.

'Thank you, Adam.'

'Pity you weren't with us today, though, you'd have loved it, the McConnell visit I mean, it was brilliant,' he said, his mouth still full. 'She said some great things about Mum – proper chemistry between them. Mum says she'll be home soon, by the way.'

I still had Marie's folded note in my hand. It was tempting to throw it in the recycling. Even if the story was true, Kirsty didn't need the distraction of someone demanding help, emotional support, whatever – a leech (albeit one who read political blogs) preying on her goodwill and time.

But I was mildly curious. I unfolded the note and put it on the kitchen table. I'd give it to her when she got back. And I copied the number into my phone. Just in case.

**

I'm exhausted. The day started off so well. Janet was wonderfully supportive, and for the first time I felt part of something so much bigger than me. It was exhilarating. I finished the morning on such a high.

But things went downhill from there. Phil rang just after lunch to say Josh has been permanently excluded. I called Louise straightaway, and she told me – in effect – to mind my own business. I was seething. That child is being dumped God knows where and no-one cares. But in a way she's right about me. The school no longer is my business. It's part of my general concerns, it'll be in my constituency, but it won't be my direct responsibility. Not if the polls are anything to go by. I won't be going back and I can't tell them what to do. Getting something done on exclusions has to be one of my priorities when I get to Parliament… a private members' bill… talk to ministers. It'll be too late to help Josh, though.

And then this evening, that blog post. Gerry saw it first and said I thought he'd agreed to keep quiet about the pub. He did, I said, but he seemed very disconcerted at being asked to stay away today and maybe this is his way of… oh, I don't know, Rick's a law unto himself at times. Gerry looked at his phone again and said well at least he's somehow managed to put a positive spin on that rubbish his paper produced. If he's really got more readers than the *Citizen* has, then maybe it's no bad thing. Perhaps Gerry's right, but I can't help feeling let down by Rick. He promised.

I open the front door, and they're both there, in the kitchen, him and Adam. I'm not going to say anything now, not in front of Adam. Later, perhaps, when we're alone. Rick hands me a piece of paper and says someone came to the house and asked me to give you this.

I open it. An address. A phone number. A name. I can just make it out. Marie. There's a rushing in my ears. I can see Rick talking to me but I don't hear what he's saying. I look again at her name. She's been here, to the house? I swallow and the rushing abates a little.

Anything significant? Rick asks. No, not really, I say, head still echoing. I thought not, he says, and starts to make himself a sandwich.

I walk through to the sitting room and stand alone and think.

I'll call her tomorrow. Maybe I'm over-reacting. Maybe this can still go away.

It was the evening of the hustings. The venue was a banqueting room on the first floor of a large and faux-plush city-centre hotel, a room more commonly used for company away days and sales conferences. It smelt of stale coffee, sharpened by a whiff of disinfectant. I'd been there several times – that very room – covering press conferences and the like, usually during daylight hours, and the smell was always the first thing that struck me. It was there that evening, but fainter, and the light from the chandeliers made the room deceptively welcoming, a place where you could while away an hour or two without anything much happening. The whole establishment was due some serious investment, but the management group was biding its time, and it showed. It could have been any mediocre hotel in any town at any time in the past fifty years, if you ignored the twenty-first century technology now cluttering the place. Oh, the glamour of politics.

The room was organised auditorium-style, with a raised platform at the front and a long table with microphones, two jugs of water and eight glasses placed on it. There were cables taped to the fleur de lys-patterned carpet – the event was to be broadcast live by local radio and cameras were also there from a couple of TV channels. Technicians stood around and someone was checking the sound system.

'One, two, one, two. How's that?'

'It's overmodding. We're getting howlround,' someone else yelled.

We'd arrived early, at Adam's insistence. 'Let Mum

see we're there, supporting her,' he'd said. Officially then I was there in my role as camp follower (although those in the know would understand I was much more than that). And unofficially I was on blog-duty, gleaning ideas to be served up warm in the next post. I was hoping for at least some content this evening, although the venue wasn't the most promising start.

I scanned the room. Kirsty was near the front, in an easy-to-spot tailored red jacket, the new haircut no longer salon-fresh but still good for the cameras. The choice of jacket colour was too obvious, I'd pointed out that morning, but she'd said it was a simple sign – socialist red – to remind the world who she was and what she stood for. A small detail I let go.

She was shaking hands with the Conservative, Sarah Clarkson, and then with the other candidates. There were rosettes everywhere. The place was a rainbow of party colours. She looked up and spotted us across the room and raised her hand in greeting, without stopping her discussion with a young woman wearing a Lib Dem rosette.

'Let's go and say hello,' Adam said.

But she was already finishing her conversation and walking over to us. She kissed each of us on the cheek. It wasn't the kiss of a wife or mother, but of a candidate welcoming two loyal team members.

'Thanks for coming,' she said.

This was really addressed to me, since nothing would have kept Adam away. The bruising had started to fade and I was allowed to show my face again. Perhaps she'd thought I'd sulk and say sorry, I'm busy tonight. But I was on best behaviour and she actually seemed pleased to have me back. She'd not even kicked up too much over the last blog post. All she'd said was, 'Well that was a somewhat edited version of the evening. But I wish you hadn't.' She'd seemed too preoccupied with other things, which was understandable.

'Prepared?' I asked.

'As well as I can be.'

I'd suggested running through things with her late the previous night, but she'd said she was beyond that, she knew what she was doing. Don't get too confident now, Kirsty, I'd thought. This was a mass interrogation. She would be subject to the scrutiny of everyone in the audience. They were all permitted to cross-examine her.

'Good luck, Mum. You'll be great, I know,' Adam said.

'Hmm, maybe. See you when it's all over.' And she headed off.

I looked around. There were lots of faces I recognised – leading lights of the various parties, councillors, pressure group luminaries – but in the mix there must also have been a few real people, coming along to hear the promises and make up their minds. Floating voters – I was one of those once. I did a rough assessment: there were about three hundred seats, and they were already beginning to fill up. Not bad for a chilly March evening. Half a dozen people in some lousy community hall? Wrong there, Clive.

'I'm going to have a word with those two guys there,' Adam said, looking over my shoulder. 'I was door-knocking with them last night. Want to join me?'

'No, I think I'll leave you to it.'

He went and I stood alone in a room full of people I knew. I raised my hand to several of them and exchanged a few pleasantries. The conversations petered out quickly and people moved on. The leader of the Conservative group on the council turned his back on me entirely.

I looked over to the press table at the side and spotted Shona talking to the regional BBC political correspondent. I decided to keep my distance. I was excommunicated from the election press pack tonight and I didn't want to give any bright spark an idea for a gossip item. *Candidate's blogger-husband mooches around at hustings after being kicked off press benches.* Shona glanced across at me, while continuing to talk to the BBC woman. We were communicating in a business-like way in the office, we had to, but not about the election – I'd worked out how to cordon that off – or about her, or Kirsty, or anything that mattered. She'd understand my delicate position tonight and wouldn't embarrass me.

What she didn't understand, of course, was the position at the *Citizen*. She didn't yet know that she was going to lose her job. The news from Clive had slipped into my mind unbidden and unwelcome. My colleagues would be getting their emails in the morning. But that was to worry about later.

I glanced at my watch. Fifteen minutes to go. Kirsty was now with Gerry, in a huddle in the corner of the room, no doubt discussing tactics – nothing, I'm sure, that I hadn't already told her, but he was pouring advice into her ear and she was nodding like a prize fighter at the side of the ring with her trainer. Whether this match would be won on a knockout blow or on points remained to be seen. In my experience, election knockout blows didn't happen very often, not unless someone made a very stupid mistake. Points accumulated through hard slog and occasional luck were what counted.

'Okay, let's find seats.' Adam was back. 'There's a couple there right at the front.'

'No, not the very front row. Feels rather… obvious.'

He raised his hands, palms open, as if querying my meaning. Obvious that I supported her? That I was her husband? That I was a journalist who'd given up all pretence of impartiality? Or simply obvious that I might be making one or two notes? Sometimes you needed to be discreet.

We found two seats in the third row – near enough that she could see us, but not demonstratively at the front. As we settled in, I looked towards the back of the room. Dan Stapleton was leaning against the wall, nonchalantly, as if he'd just dropped in on a whim. What was he doing here? Shona was covering this for the *Citizen* and Dan wouldn't know a political story if it biffed him on the nose. Not that there was going to be any of that tonight.

Adam nudged me. Kirsty and the other candidates were walking onto the platform, seven hopefuls, six of them women. I leant to one side to get a clearer view and in my peripheral vision I saw a figure taking a seat at the end of the row behind us. A thin, grey woman in a faded blue anorak. Marie. She pulled down her hood but kept the anorak firmly zipped up. The room was warm, too warm – most people had taken off their coats and jackets. She sat very still, looking diagonally across the room, towards the centre of the platform where Kirsty now was. I knew where I'd seen her before. On that estate, when we were canvassing.

I turned back towards Kirsty. Her expression was frozen, trance-like. I twisted around again, trying to follow the trajectory of her sightline. She and Marie were locked in a mutual stare. They seemed oblivious to everything else.

The hustings chair – the local radio station's drivetime presenter – was explaining the rules of engagement. I was barely taking it in… going live in five minutes… strict on timings… audience questions as brief as possible… applause encouraged. At that, Adam gave a small cheer, sotto voce.

There was a hush of muted excitement as the

presenter put his finger to his lips to signal quiet. I still had my eyes fixed on Kirsty, but her face had started to thaw. The trance was broken. She filled her glass with water and did the same for the candidate on her left. Whatever had happened in that frozen moment had passed.

I turned to check on Marie.

She'd vanished. The seat at the end of the row was now filled by someone previously standing. She hadn't even waited for proceedings to begin.

'I'm just popping out,' I whispered to Adam. 'A work call – nearly forgot.'

'You can't. Not now.'

'Won't be a sec.'

I stepped carefully over people's feet, slipped out of the door at the back of the room and looked both ways along the corridor. She'd only just gone, she could still be in the hotel. I ran down the stairs. Perhaps she'd decided to sit it out in the bar, sipping a cocktail, waiting for Kirsty to finish. But she didn't look like the sort of woman who sipped cocktails in hotel bars.

I dashed out and looked up and down the street. Nothing. Of course there was nothing. She'd had a minute or two on me and she'd gone.

I breathed in the cold air and regretted my precipitate action. What was I doing, tearing through a hotel, trying to chase some deranged woman who claimed to know my wife but was most likely stalking her? Was I imagining that? And what would I have said if I'd found her? Hey, who really are you and what are you up to? And she'd have said, don't know what you mean, I'm just a friend of Kirsty's. Or she'd have got abusive. And then what? A scene? The police called again?

There was a simpler way – a frank conversation with Kirsty. Later.

I returned to the banqueting room, creeping back along the third row to the empty seat next to Adam.

'You cut it fine,' he whispered.

'Was quick as I could be. Just a short call.'

Kirsty was looking in my direction. I gestured at my phone apologetically. She crinkled her eyebrows in disapproval, glanced down at her notes and then at the chair as he introduced the candidates. They were to speak in alphabetical order. Kirsty would be fourth, the middle of the running order, a good position. The audience would be warmed up but not yet bored. I settled down, now fully attentive.

Sarah Clarkson, the Tory, was first on her feet, talking inevitably about Brexit and how the prime minister had the best interests of the people of Leave-voting North Humberside at heart. Not bad, a perfectly respectable speech, but nothing more – she was there for the ride and she knew it. The sighs around us were heavy and there were heckles from the back of the room, but Sarah pressed on bravely. I found myself fiddling with the pen in my pocket. It was odd not to be making notes on them all, looking for quotes to hone, working out whether a politician was saying anything new or controversial, or at least anything that could be made to sound new or controversial. But my readers weren't interested in the also-rans.

After that came two Independents. Each of them needed both more meat and a serious edit. They weren't so much heckled as ignored. People talked over them. The chair again raised his finger to his lip, gesturing to the audience to quieten down. It had a temporary effect.

And then it was Kirsty's turn. Adam shifted in his seat.

She stood up and slowly looked across the room. She could have been addressing a school assembly of eighteen hundred kids, checking they were all paying attention.

'I know how disappointed many of you must be in politics and politicians at present,' she began. 'I wouldn't be surprised if you feel it's simply not worth voting, when politicians don't do what they promise to do and don't behave as you expect them to. If that's how you feel, I can't blame you. You're right to feel let down. As a teacher and an ordinary voter, I've often felt let down myself.'

The room had gone quiet. This was high risk and people didn't know where it was going. It was my idea of course. Don't avoid the elephant, I'd said. She'd been uncertain. Gerry must have sanctioned it. She paused to milk the moment.

'But now I'm standing before you all as a politician and – I hope – your next MP, and I know you probably see me as 'one of them'. Fair enough. You're right to wonder if you can believe anything any of us say, or trust anything we do.'

She didn't mention Barraclough by name. She didn't need to. The audience caught her drift and there were grins and whispers. A couple of her opponents at the table seemed to be mouthing 'yes' and 'of course'. Sarah Clarkson looked put out. She knew she'd missed a trick in her speech.

Someone behind me shouted, 'There, you've said it. Why should we trust you, then?'

'Please leave your questions till after the opening speeches,' said the chair. 'Ms Osmond, do go on.'

'If I may, in answer to that gentleman, I would say being an MP is a job, like any other, a hard job, but a worthwhile one, and some of us simply want to do it to the best of our ability. I hope you trust me when I say that.'

The man behind muttered something I couldn't catch. Kirsty continued.

'North Humberside is a great place – I chose to come and live here with my family – and you deserve to be represented by someone who believes in you and who's prepared to work hard on your behalf. I've spent eight years here as a headteacher, teaching many of your children or grandchildren. It's been my job to fight for those young people's interests, and I intend to do the same for all of you, if you elect me as your MP.'

Neatly done, Kirsty. And she segued back into her planned speech, talking about the need for real change on so many fronts, jobs, homes, health care, and stressing her determination to listen to people, to prioritise their concerns and to respect their views. Faultless.

She sat down. There was silence. Someone started to clap. And someone else. Adam and I joined in. Then others. And slowly it gathered force. Kirsty looked surprised by the appreciation, although I had no doubt she'd known exactly what she was doing and had carefully calculated the reaction.

'That was brilliant!' Adam said, turning back to me.

It was. She was learning fast, even if she did sometimes dismiss my more astute advice. But – there was a definite 'but' in my head – I detected something I couldn't quite place. She'd hit the points perfectly. She'd deflected heckling to her advantage. And, as ever, it came from the heart. But there was something in her voice that was flat, uncharacteristically so. It had a dull edge to it that I'd not heard before. The frisson of excitement so apparent at the waterfront was missing. No-one else would have noticed, not even Gerry. No-one had known Kirsty as long as I had and was as familiar with the nuances of her speech as I was.

The remaining candidates were running through their

set pieces. Adam was tapping a foot against the floor and fidgeting, but we both clapped dutifully after each speaker. And then it was time for questions. There were several on housing and public transport, a couple on Brexit and immigration, which everyone except the far-right woman sidestepped neatly, causing yet more heckling, and one on opportunities for young people, which Kirsty answered with authority.

A microphone was then passed to a woman sitting immediately in front of me. She'd had her hand up for some time, but the chair had been ignoring the front couple of rows in an attempt to spread the questions around the room. The woman took the mic and waited for her moment.

'Yes, the lady at the front, in the pink jumper. Your question now.'

The woman gave a preparatory cough.

'My name's Tracy Wenham and I want to talk about my son Joshua.'

Kirsty moved slightly in her seat and made a note on the pad in front of her. Then she lifted her head and looked intently at the woman. The chair intervened.

'Can you make sure you ask a question, and briefly please?'

'Yes, I've got a question for Kirsty Osmond.'

There was a touch of annoyance in the woman's voice, as if it was obvious that Kirsty was her target. The other candidates sighed, either with relief or disappointment, and resumed looking at their notes.

The woman went on. 'You talk about young people and how you stick up for them and all that. But your school has just expelled my son. Yeah, he did drugs, but they all do, don't they? He's not fifteen yet. He should be doing his GCSEs next year.'

The chair interrupted again. 'Your question, please.'

'My question is, what am I meant to do? I'm a single parent trying to fight for my child and it's hard. Josh is a clever lad, but where's he going to end up if he's dumped in one of those pupil-referral units?'

The woman's voice had risen in a crescendo of indignation. Everyone was staring in her direction and at the end of our row a man stood up to get a better view. I was so close I could see the small bird tattooed on the back of the woman's neck, I could see her shoulders heaving up and down and could hear her breathing. She was surprisingly articulate. Good copy. The sort of story the press bench had been waiting for. I watched the journalists scribbling and tapping away at laptops. Not much use for the blog, however. One thing Kirsty insisted on – and I always capitulated to keep her happy – was that the school was out of bounds.

Adam was chewing his lip, his eyebrows furrowed in a worried, questioning look. On the platform, the chair looked undecided as to whether this was a legitimate question for the hustings and had his mouth open, on the verge of saying something. But Kirsty beat him to it.

'Mrs Wenham,' she said. 'I'm very sorry about what's happened to your son. I know how difficult this must be for you.'

'Difficult?' the woman shot back. 'You've got no idea.'

Kirsty remained fixed on the woman. 'As you know, the matter is being dealt with by the acting head and the school governors. But I'd be happy to talk to you privately after this meeting.'

'Talk? What good will that do? You're just trying to shut me up.'

The woman was now looking around and addressing her tirade to the whole room. The chair seemed to have given up trying to intervene. This was a story he couldn't afford to cut off. The scribbling and tapping on the press bench intensified.

'So what's Josh going to do? Tell me that,' the woman went on. She was waving the microphone around and some of her words must have been lost to those at the back of the room. 'Kids like my son don't stand a chance... Get rid of them, get rid of trouble. Get them out the school. They're not our problem... Who cares where they end up?'

Kirsty was straining forward over the table, as if making a huge physical effort to engage with the woman. Her concentration had not wavered for a moment.

'I agree with you that too many young people get excluded from school and provision for them is hopeless. We have to do better. None of our young people should be thrown on the scrapheap. You're absolutely right about that.'

The dull edge had slipped from her voice.

'But I don't think it helps your son to discuss this now,' she went on. 'As I say, I'd very much like to talk to you outside this meeting to see what we can do for him.'

'What's the point? You've clearly moved on already. And Josh, well he's not your problem any more, is he? All you're interested in now is getting elected. Well, I'll tell you one thing, you can forget about my vote. You don't deserve it.'

The woman dropped the microphone on the floor – it landed with a clatter that drew gasps from those around her – and then, picking up her bag and using it as battering ram, she pushed her way along the second row, her head shaking in rage.

'Jesus,' Adam whispered. I rested my hand on his arm, reassuringly. This was part of Kirsty's stock-in-trade, dealing with aggrieved parents, although not usually in front of an audience of three hundred voters. The other candidates were looking embarrassed, to their credit. They must have been thanking their lucky stars that they were lawyers or healthworkers or self-employed businesspeople, not headteachers. There but for fortune…

The woman had reached the end of the row and a bulky man, probably hotel security, hovered. He seemed unsure what to do. But the woman was making her own way to the exit at the back of the room, trailed by a gaggle of journalists. Dan had joined them.

I looked back to Kirsty. She had her hands pressed together, prayer-like, resting on her lips. Then she started to make notes. She was already working on the Joshua problem.

Sarah Clarkson leant in to her microphone. 'I'd just like to say that under Labour control, our complacent council has cut spending on drug programmes by' – she paused and flicked through her sheaf of notes, unsuccessfully apparently – 'well, by an unacceptable amount. It's no wonder that the drug problem in schools like Kirsty Osmond's is out of control and that teenagers take advantage of that lack of control, like the boy whose mother we've just heard from.'

Kirsty's face was iron. This was a cheap jibe, political point-scoring of the worst sort. She flashed her eyes at Sarah and then looked out to the audience.

'Funding to local authorities has been destroyed by the Tory government's austerity measures, as Sarah Clarkson very well knows. The council's been shackled. That's what's happening all over the country and it's a scandal.'

I'd rarely seen her looking so angry. Irritated, impatient, yes, but not full-on, unmitigatedly, painfully, furious. It was good, this passion. We should work on it more. I jotted down a note or two and Adam gave me another of his disapproving looks.

'And it's completely wrong to try and exploit personal circumstances about which she knows nothing,' Kirsty said, looking at Sarah again. 'Absolutely nothing.'

Sarah shook her head but wasn't quick enough with any riposte. The chair had decided enough was enough. 'I suggest we move on to another topic now. Yes, the man at the back.'

I wasn't listening any more. I was looking at Kirsty and trying to gauge her mood. The residue of anger was still apparent in the tight corners of her mouth, but her voice was calm as she made her final brief contribution.

And then it was over. The chair thanked the candidates and people started to file out of the hall, slowly, noisily. There was a fair amount of back slapping and laughter. They'd had a good evening out and it had been free. The reporters who had left with Tracy Wenham had now made their way back in and were in front of the speakers' table, waiting for Kirsty, hoping to prise more of the story out of her. Sarah was hanging around hopefully, too, but was generally ignored.

'Will she be long?' Adam asked.

'I shouldn't think so. They're only interested in the drugs story and I'm fairly sure she won't have anything more to say.'

Kirsty was now in the middle of the knot of journalists and Gerry was hovering on the edge, trying to extricate her. He finally succeeded – or, more likely, the journalists realised they were going to get no more – and she and Gerry were alone. Adam and I went over to them.

I kissed her and said, 'Well done. Very persuasive.'

Adam gave her a hug. 'You were fantastic, Mum.'

'Oh, I'm not sure about that. It was just a pity that Joshua Wenham's mother got so upset. She must feel the world's against her.' She shook her head. 'But Sarah Clarkson, for God's sake, that was completely out of order.'

'Well you handled it perfectly,' I said, and meant it.

Gerry looked over at me. 'Good to see you back with us,' he said. 'We've missed you.'

I doubted it. It was the first time we'd acknowledged each other that evening, the first time since our passing encounter in the pub. I'd heard nothing more from him about the blog. Perhaps he'd finally realised I was someone to reckon with. Perhaps I'd exonerated myself by simply turning up at the hustings and dissociating myself from the press for a whole evening. Perhaps Gerry was okay after all. He simply had a job to do.

'But, Kirsty, I wouldn't worry about the drugs story,' he said, turning back to her. 'These things make the news for five minutes and that's it.'

'But it won't be over so quickly for the family,' she said. 'The important thing isn't what gets in the papers, but what happens to Josh.'

The passion had crept back into her voice.

'Look,' she said, 'can we find an hour for me to go and talk to Mrs Wenham? I want to see what we can do for him.'

Gerry sucked in air through his teeth.

'The schedule's tight. It's hardly something we can use as a PR opportunity.'

'There are more important things,' she said.

'Not as far as I'm concerned. But remind me tomorrow.'

No, she's not the easiest parliamentary candidate to manage, Gerry, I could have warned you.

We made our way out of the room, past technicians winding up cables, and down the stairs to the hotel reception. There were a few regular hotel guests milling around, wandering in and out of the bar. No-one gave our group a second glance. But I found myself scrutinising *them*, wondering whether Marie had returned. Was she hanging around waiting for us? I needed to talk to Kirsty as soon as we were by ourselves.

I also had to break the news to her about my redundancy. I had put off telling her so far – I hadn't wanted to worry her before the hustings, or so I'd told myself. Now it felt urgent. The others would know tomorrow and then it would go public.

We said goodnight to Gerry outside the hotel. He turned one way down the street and the three of us walked in the other direction towards the car. We were all quiet, even Adam. I was worn out after an evening of doing nothing, just listening and clapping and making the odd note, punctuated by one pointless dash out of the hotel. Kirsty must have been knackered. We needed to get home and talk, just her and me. And then sleep.

**

I hate hotels. Not all hotels – small holiday places, quaint country inns, they're fine, we've had some good weekend breaks, Rick and me. But no, I mean anonymous city hotels, function rooms, identical bedrooms, lonely bars and dreary restaurants, underpaid staff, nowhere you'd want to stay unless you really have to, hotels full of lost souls.

But it had to be there. It was agreed with the broadcasters, the parties, all the candidates, somewhere big and central and warm, somewhere to draw in a good crowd. And it did. I never imagined she'd turn up, too. I'd phoned her the morning after Rick gave me the note. It was early. I'd had a sleepless night. She picked up quickly and I recognised her voice at once, even after all this time. She sounded flustered, apologised for going to the house, but she guessed I'd not got the message at the school and she needed to speak to me. What about? I asked. And I knew I should have replied earlier, but I'd been busy and the email had festered in a mental too-difficult-to-deal-with-now folder. She had this project, she said, more of a campaign really, she was starting a campaign. What campaign? I asked. She explained. Was I interested in supporting it, giving her some advice on publicity, perhaps telling my own story? She'd heard me talking about young people on the radio once and felt I could help. Now I was standing for Parliament, my name would count. Together we could really help people.

My blood went cold and our long-ago agreement flashed through my mind. A silly teenage thing maybe, a pact we'd called it, but had she forgotten? Never to say a word. We'd promised each other. Permanent silence about something insignificant, something that never happened.

But I didn't mention it. It would have sounded ridiculous coming from me now. So I simply told her I couldn't help, not during the election. She couldn't involve me. It was impossible. She suggested meeting – she was staying in Hull with a friend for a while, she'd seen me out canvassing one night, she'd watched me, actually followed me for a bit, she wanted to say hello, but there were people with me and she didn't like to. Then she'd found my address and plucked up courage and gone round to my house. I told her I was sorry, I really couldn't help.

Eventually she gave up and said she understood. She wouldn't mention my name, she promised, not if it was awkward, she'd leave me out of it, no problem. So perhaps she hadn't forgotten our agreement, I thought. And she wished me luck with the election. I was sure she understood.

But apparently not. Her turning up tonight threw me. She just stared and stared, as if she could make me change my mind. And I was going to have to speak but I was numb and I didn't know if I could do it. And then she left, just got up and walked out, she'd seen enough I suppose, got bored. I looked at my speech notes and there was an iciness in my head, but it began to melt, and when I got to my feet, instinct took over, it was automatic. I barely needed my notes, I just said everything I wanted to say. And there was applause and it was all okay.

**

She was quiet as we drove home, phone calls of course, but between them no conversation, just waves of silence. I allowed her that. She had to process everything that had happened. And I had to think too, about the two matters we needed to discuss. My job. And Marie. I wasn't sure which order to take them in. The good news first or the bad? There was no good news, but at least I knew what I wanted to say about the job.

And so, as we undressed, I casually mentioned the paper's financial plight and, almost as a footnote, my redundancy. Casual was the wrong way to do it. It sounded as if I couldn't bring myself to talk about it.

She slowly stopped pulling down her tights and sat on the bed looking at me, her face crumpling in pity. Kirsty's pity was sometimes too much.

'Oh, Rick, that's terrible. What are you going to do? I'm so sorry.'

'It's not such a big deal really. I mean for the others, yes, but the union will be involved–'

'I should hope so. They're going to have to fight.'

'But for me, well, I've reached the end of the road with the *Citizen*, and no bad thing – the last few weeks have shown me that. The blog's the start of my exit plan. You'll be in Westminster most of the time, and I'll be back in London working too. I'm putting out feelers. I've got three months' notice but I aim to leave sooner.'

'What's your Plan B, though? If I lose the election, what then?'

'That's not going to happen. We're going to win. No Plan B needed.'

I got into bed and she resumed undressing, still going on about me losing my job. There must be things I could go for not so far away, she suggested. Other parts of Yorkshire, I should look there.

I picked up a book but then put it back on the bedside table.

'Who's Marie?'

She was starting to lay out some underwear for the morning, on a chair, with more precision than was needed. She seemed not to hear me.

'She was at the hustings, wasn't she? Is she bothering you?'

'No, she's just someone with a few problems.'

'Problems?'

'Oh, you know, personal problems. She wanted some advice.'

'Why did she turn up at the hustings and then leave? And I'm sure I saw her when we were out canvassing. What's going on?'

She closed her underwear drawer with a sharp shove and turned to look at me.

'Nothing's going on.'

'Is she really a friend from university?'

'Sort of.'

'Meaning?'

'I just knew her.'

'How well? How well did you know her?'

'We hung out together for a while.'

'Hung out?'

'Yes, hung out. Look, can we just change the subject?'

'Did you keep in touch after university?'

'For God's sake, Rick, give over. Stop interrogating me.'

'She sounds a bit unhinged to me, stalking you like this.'

'She's not stalking me. And she's not unhinged.'

'Well troubled, then.'

'There are lots of troubled people.'

'And you can't help them all.'

'I can help some.'

'Not while you're fighting a by-election.'

She shook her head.

'People's problems don't stop just because there's a by-election.'

'Well, as long as she's really not stalking you. You could ask for police protection, you know.'

'Don't be ridiculous. I'm not listening anymore.'

She got into bed, her back to me. I leant on one elbow, stroked her back and tried to kiss her. She wasn't receptive. Was I making something of nothing, developing a new taste for melodrama? I didn't think so. I couldn't have my candidate dangerously distracted by some crazy woman, former acquaintance, friend, whatever she was. If Kirsty wouldn't do anything about it, she'd have to leave it to me. There were ways of dealing with this.

**

On and on and on. He just wouldn't give over, interrogating me about… nothing. A dog with a bone when there's no meat left, none at all, but still it chews. I felt bad about holding things back from him, but it's best. The Marie thing is dealt with. She promised to keep me out of it and I have to trust her. I don't know why I was spooked by her earlier tonight. She just came to see me speak, I guess, but then left. Yet Rick just went on, as if Marie was some sort of psychopath and me her hapless victim.

What we should have talked about more tonight was his job. I tried, but he wouldn't discuss it. Apart from the obvious practical difficulties, it must hurt his pride, Clive shafting him like that. And I can't help feeling it's all because of me. He's already had to step down from what he normally does, and now the management, Clive, whoever, they've decided they can carry on permanently without him. He says there are going to be lots of redundancies, they're all in the same boat, but it feels such a coincidence that this happens as soon as I stand for parliament. The husband of the local MP is clearly going to be an embarrassment to *The Humberside Citizen*. I can see that now.

They're sniffing around the school, too. The paper may be dying but it's like they want to take others down with them. How much will it derail my campaign? Rick's promised to help Phil with a statement – I thought he might refuse. I must remind him.

But the school… I wonder, even now, if I'm doing the right thing deserting my post like this. I prickled at the word when Shona first used it. Deserting. It was harsh. But I can say it now. I'm a deserter. Maybe I should still be there, working from the ground up instead of wanting to transform the whole bloody system top-down, dealing with individual problems, fighting for kids like Joshua Wenham, instead of this… ego trip. We all have egos and mine sometimes needs tethering.

Maybe that's what Rick wants to do. Tether my ego, while pretending to do the opposite. Control my campaign. Manage my life. Write my story for me. But that's Rick. He means no harm. He's only trying to help, in his own perverse way.

I had a vague foreboding of unhappiness when I woke up the next morning. Unhappiness has never been a familiar emotion for me. Irritation, frustration, disappointment, resentment – I could draw up a long list of feelings that have often tortured me, but not what you might call plain unhappiness. Kirsty, of course, had left. I wasn't sure how much sleep she'd had. There'd been a fair amount of thrashing around after we put the light out. And complete resistance to my attempts at affection. Christ knows what she was thinking about. But I was going to sort things out with Marie. I'd decided that last night. That wasn't what I was unhappy about.

No, it was work. I rarely worried about work. Problems, however massive, generally found a way of resolving themselves and I didn't dwell on them. Not like Kirsty. But this was the morning the management emails were going out. Everyone would know pretty soon that their livelihoods were threatened. I was going to be surrounded by a lot of unhappy people and I had no doubt it would be infectious.

By mid-morning the place was quiet, the mood noticeably subdued. There was none of the usual banter, the occasional roars of laughter or shrieks of exasperation. My colleagues were all avoiding Clive and the air of barely suppressed hostility drove him back into his office. Some of them seemed to avoid catching my eye, too.

Shona had called an emergency union meeting for lunchtime. It was in the small meeting room on the floor beneath the newsroom, a room that apparently had once been a refuge for smokers, before they'd been banished from the building entirely. There were tell-tale burn marks on the table and a remembered aroma of fag ash seemed to hit you as you stepped into the room. Now it was combined with the smell of misery.

I arrived late and Shona and one or two of the others glanced at me suspiciously. But I had to be there. I was an NUJ member. I had to be seen to be taking a collaborative stand, even if my semi-managerial position and my early knowledge of the situation set me apart in a no-man's-land, likely to be shot at by both sides. I seemed to be spending a lot of time in no-man's-land.

Fifteen people were crowded into the room, the early arrivals seated at the table, the rest of us leaning against the walls. I looked around, trying to assess individual moods. Everyone knew that the prospects of finding local work in journalism were not good. Those with kids and mortgages would be the most anxious. People were staring at their phones or giving the printed-off email yet another read-through, as if trying to find new meaning in the three terse paragraphs. Mike muttered, 'I've seen this coming for ages,' to no-one in particular, and everyone ignored him.

Shona coughed to signal the start of the meeting.

'I know we're all shocked by the news, by what's being offered and by the way things are being handled.'

There were murmurs of agreement and the room went quiet again as she started to spell out the implications of the email they'd all received. Any jobs on the online *Citizen* would have to be re-applied for. For most of them, it looked like statutory redundancy terms. The management of the *Citizen* was playing games with people's lives. It was chaotic and cruel.

'Are there any questions, any comments?' Shona said. Someone asked why Clive hadn't had the guts to speak to them in person and someone else wanted to know when they could take the whole board round the back and shoot them. There were several cheers at that.

Shona raised her hands for quiet and said, 'I'd like to take an indicative vote simply on whether we accept what's being proposed.'

'Isn't that a bit early?' I said. 'I mean, there are obviously going to be negotiations.'

She shot me the sourest of looks. Okay, you may have done us a favour by turning up, I could see her thinking, but don't make a nuisance of yourself now you're here. We are not your project.

'I repeat, it's just an indicative vote,' she said, 'so I can report back to regional office on what the mood is before negotiations begin. Got it?'

I folded my arms and decided it was in my interests to say nothing more.

'So, can we have the vote then?' she said.

Hands – including mine – went up in a unanimous rejection of the company's proposal.

'Thank you. One more question,' Shona said. 'If it came to it, would you be prepared to fight for your jobs, or for decent redundancy terms, by taking industrial action in some form?'

She looked at me and took an exaggerated breath. 'Again, this is just an indicative vote. Any eventual action would obviously have to be sanctioned by ballot.'

This time the vote was ten to three in favour of action, with two abstentions. I was among the ten and the corners of Shona's mouth curled in disbelief. But I had to show solidarity. Kirsty and her party comrades would expect no less. I had received my terms that morning. Technically I was being offered 'voluntary' redundancy, as an incentive to go quietly, I assumed. I could probably push the exit payment higher with help from an employment lawyer, but if that got out, it wouldn't look good, the husband of a Labour MP trying to boost his pay-off, while the rest of the staff were getting the minimum. So there I was in a grimy room, at a dead-end newspaper, with a bunch of people I had, at best, mixed views of (Shona excepted), showing solidarity. I loathed the word. And picket lines solved nothing. Billy Osmond passed through my mind. If pits – or newspapers – were going to close, they were going to close. There was no point in fighting the inevitable. Management always won in the end. That's the way it was. And this wasn't the nineteen-eighties. Did anyone believe in unions anymore? Industrial action would be folly.

But ultimately it didn't matter. I'd be back working in London well before anyone held up a tacky banner and shouted slogans at Clive as he scurried into the building.

The meeting ended – it had lasted barely half an hour – and on the way out, Shona looked at me. A reconciliation? An apology, even, for her curtness now, her outburst a week ago?

'How's Kirsty?' she asked.

'Fine. A lot on her plate, of course, but fine.'

'Give her my regards then.'

'Look, can we have a chat? D'you fancy a coffee?'

'No. And no.'

And she turned her back on me and caught up with the others.

Three days since the hustings. Less than four weeks to election day. I'm getting there, I'm getting closer. The polls are looking even better and the daily press summary's the best so far. Yesterday one big-name commentator said I was a woman with experience of the real world and I wasn't seeking a free pass to power from the usual coven of political insiders. Gerry thinks we should use that in a leaflet, though I'm not sure how much clout big-name commentators have round here. Rick said it was pretty much what he'd written in one of his blogs and he was flattered by the plagiarism. Give me strength.

But my days are so packed, I don't have time to think about any of that once I get going. Out and about, set-piece appearances, making time to talk to anyone who wants to talk, absorbing it all… I just want to keep working and never stop, never pause to think. Nights can be difficult if I'm too tired to sleep properly and the mind races and I go back over everything… But the days are always fine. They're fraught and hectic, and fraught and hectic I can do. Sometimes I wish I didn't have to sleep and it was all daytime, rushing, talking, listening, smiling, persuading, winning. Busy, busy, busy. And then repeating it all the next day. No night time, no quiet time, no down time. No thinking.

She's gone, like I knew she would be. I haven't seen or heard from her since the hustings, no texts, nothing. She won't bother me again, she promised, and I believe her. I still feel a twinge of guilt that I couldn't help her. But it was impossible. I have an election to win, that's all there is to it.

It's Good Friday and another full day of door-to-door. Rick's joining us again this evening. I suggested it this morning, thought it was about time. He seemed unsure at first, but then said yes, he could do an hour or two. He's gone into work, but he's coming on afterwards. Better than nothing, I guess, and it'll help take his mind off the business with the paper. Shocking that. Minimum terms for most of them – and it's not just Rick as I thought at first, he was right about that. I rang Shona last night to see if there's anything I can do, if a statement of support would help. She sounded embarrassed. After all, we hadn't spoken since that profile piece – she left a message apologising for it and I never replied. But she said a statement would be great if I felt I could. We'll get something drafted over the weekend. Even Gerry thinks it's a good idea. Gives us the moral high ground, not bad PR, though that's a very Gerry-way of positioning things.

It's not something that comes up on the doorstep, the fates of a few journalists. But lots of positive things are coming through. I'm learning, really getting to understand my constituents, my soon-to-be constituents. This job isn't going to be easy, but I've never wanted things easy. Adam's learning too. You're right, Mum, people are complicated, he said the other night, nothing's black and white. That's what he came out with, like it was some big revelation, bless him. Yes, Adam, we're all varying shades of grey. You, Rick, Marie, me, everyone, we're all grey.

**

Another bout of door-knocking. I was beginning to get the hang of it. I could tell when it was worth knocking twice and when it wasn't, and I could predict how people were going to respond the instant they opened the door – stereotypes did exist, Kirsty was wrong about that. And those tiny glimpses of people's existences – the cooking smells and the junk piled in hallways, men in vests, women in slippers, the blare of TV competing with the cacophony of family life or disguising loneliness. It took me back to Billy's house, that Sheffield semi we'd visited back in the nineties – fascinating, if depressing. All those glimpses offered so many prompts for future blogs.

I wouldn't say I enjoyed the door-knocking game, I mean actually *enjoyed* it. It wasn't a way you'd choose to spend an evening if you could avoid it. But it couldn't be avoided. When she'd suggested it again that morning, I'd felt obliged to agree. It wasn't the most convenient evening, but I could manage an hour or so, and it was always useful keeping an eye on things. Everyone else in her team still seemed so enthusiastic. Easter weekend, but they weren't easing up for a moment. They must have engaged in some sort of group brainwashing to keep them going. At least Adam had the evening off to go to a gig with Jess. Kirsty said he'd been doing too much and needed a break.

'Well you have me instead,' I said. 'A poor second, I know, but your lackey to do with as you please.' I bowed and took the leaflets she was offering. Best behaviour tonight.

'Let's get on with it then. You're doing the odd numbers along here.'

And so I did, several roads, odd numbers and even, for nearly two hours. At one point I got snapped in the publicity pictures someone was taking. I didn't object. In fact, I'd see if I could use one of them on my own site. No harm in asking.

'I reckon we're just about done for tonight,' she said. It was nearly eight-thirty – I'd been keeping an eye on my watch. 'Perhaps you should come back to the office with us tonight. As one of the team. Don't know what Gerry will think. I'll have a word with him if you like.'

She had mentioned that she'd definitely be going back for the debrief that evening and it was likely to be a long one. She hadn't raised the possibility of my joining her.

'No. Nice of you to suggest it, but I think I'll go home. I don't want to upset anyone. And… well, I need to work on the blog.'

I hadn't posted for a few days. I'd decided to stand back from everything that had happened at the hustings and let ideas swirl around… the way Kirsty had handled a real personal grievance from the floor… her sense of politicians needing to regain people's trust. I wanted to draw out some deeper truths and glide over any inconvenient moments.

She stroked my arm. 'Thanks for your understanding. I'll see you later. Careful what you write.'

Now, I have to admit here to the tiniest of white lies. I'd already drafted a new post, on my phone at lunchtime. It had some interesting observations on empathy as the key word in electoral politics. *For most people, there's a huge chasm between their lives and those of the candidates seeking their votes. But how many politicians actually get that? How many can stand back from the bigger political picture and genuinely empathise with ordinary voters and their messy, difficult lives? Many claim to. Very few do it instinctively. My wife is one of this very small minority,* I had written, and I had gone on to describe (selectively) the drama of the hustings. I only needed to give the piece a quick read through and post it when I got home. That would take no more than ten minutes.

It gave me plenty of time to speak to Marie.

I'd sent her a text the previous day – I still had her

number in my phone. *We want to talk to you. Our address 9 pm tomorrow tonight. Rick Dewhirst, husband of Kirsty Osmond.* Kirsty wouldn't be back until eleven or so.

Marie had replied with an 'OK'. It was all faintly cloak-and-dagger, but I needed her out of my candidate's life. I could have simply phoned, but I wanted to see her body language and be sure she understood what I was saying. Stalking wasn't an exaggeration and it was no good trying to brush things off as Kirsty had. Politicians attracted crazy people and some of them were dangerous – those were facts of political life. I could have gone to the police, but things there still felt a little delicate after the pub incident. And there was something uncertain about the Marie business that I didn't especially want the police poking their noses into. If Kirsty wasn't prepared to tackle it, if she was willing to be hounded by this woman, I would deal with it. We couldn't afford any lapse in concentration during the final stretch of the election marathon.

My justification then was clear. I just hoped the woman made an appearance.

I turned into Maple Avenue and saw her, a solitary figure caught in the yellow sodium light of the street lamp. She was early. She swung round as she heard the car and stared hard as I drove past her and into the driveway. I turned the engine off and in my mirror saw her crossing the road towards me.

'Kirsty's not with you?' she said as I got out of the car.

'No, she's been delayed. So just me.'

'I see.' She laughed, nervously I thought, and looked at the house. 'I'm looking forward to seeing inside your place, though.'

It struck me then that I most definitely did not want her inside, nosying around, somehow leaving an indelible mark. Why had I even suggested coming here? I'd thought it might be safer than meeting in town where I was bound to bump into someone I knew. This was a miscalculation.

'What I have to say to you can be said out here. It won't take long.'

She was playing with the strap of her bag. 'All right then.'

'I don't know who you really are or what you want from my wife, but I'm telling you now that you have to stop pestering her. Do you understand?'

I looked her straight in the eye. She couldn't fail to be impressed by the authority in my voice. She looked rather sheepish, I thought.

'Pestering? I've not pestered anyone. I just wanted to talk to Kirsty.'

'And now you leave her alone. She's offered you some advice in relation to whatever your problems are, but she's fighting an election and doesn't have time for any more of this. So I'm ordering you to have no further contact with her. No calls. No turning up at meetings. No following her. It's stalking and we will report it to the police if we have to.'

'Stalking? What are you talking about?' She exhaled loudly and folded her arms. 'Well, Mr Rick Dewhirst, all I can say is that it must be great having a husband like you, who goes round *ordering* people to do whatever. And making stupid judgements about them, too.'

I stood my ground, unimpressed by her mock indignation. 'Let me be clear. I'm speaking on behalf of my wife. She asked me to talk to you and request you to desist from any further harassment. And that's what I'm doing.'

She stared hard at me. 'You know what? You're a pompous twat. I should've guessed from that blog of yours.'

Now she was showing her true colours. And I was showing her mine.

'You heard what I said. Do not contact my wife again.'

'And I thought she was someone who could look after herself. She's going to be an MP, isn't she? Can't she handle her own business without getting you to do it for her?'

'I'm simply telling you that if there's any more trouble, we'll report it to the police.'

She stepped towards me – she was only a few inches away – and her eyes were still fixed on me. They were paler and steelier than I remembered from our first encounter.

'Go on, then. I've got nothing to worry about there.'

She was too close. I could smell her sour breath. She sucked in her cheeks as if mustering saliva. She was about to spit at me, I was sure of it. I pushed her away, just a light shove, to get her out of my space. She seemed to lose her balance – her own fault, not mine – she stumbled and fell. A phone, tissues, and worn make-up purse tumbled out of her bag. And a small mirror lay on the gravel, shattered. She got up, rubbing her arm, then bent down to pick up her things, stuffing them back into her bag.

'You shouldn't have done that, you know. Assaulting women, damaging their belongings, that's the sort of thing people do report to the police.' She looked up at me. 'I bet this won't end up in your blog.'

'I've said what I have to say. Just get out of our lives.'

'Your lives are so wonderful, aren't they? God forbid that you actually help someone who might need it.'

Her voice, thin and indignant, resonated across the quiet suburban air. I glanced up at the lit windows of neighbouring houses and wondered whether anyone was observing this pantomime.

'Just go. Go back to wherever you came from.'

She was on her feet again and she pulled up the sleeve of her anorak to examine her arm. There was no mark that I could see, but she touched it gingerly.

'Don't worry, I'm going. But you've made a mistake, you know. A big mistake.'

I waited till she was off the property and then walked to the pavement and watched her retreating along Maple Avenue. When I was satisfied she'd definitely gone, I returned to the drive and picked up the pieces of broken mirror. One long sliver nicked the tip of my finger and a tiny balloon of blood appeared. I went into the house, slammed the front door and found a plaster. In the sitting room, I poured myself a large whisky, opened my laptop, hesitated a moment and then posted the blog.

Part Three

Freedom of the Press

We were now well into by-election month. The first few days had sped by. Easter had come and gone. There was work, such as it was, there was job-hunting, there was Kirsty and the campaign, and there was the blog. I posted more pieces for my ever-growing audience. Ninety thousand followers on Twitter, a lively debate after every post and increasing interest (mainly positive) in sections of the national press. Each of these blocks of my life had previously had its own distinct shade and pattern, but now they all seemed to bleed into each other, like the colours on an overworked palette. I spent as much time as I could on Kirsty-watch. I combed every website, every social media platform, I watched or listened to every news bulletin. I analysed every comment about her (or me) and passed on anything she might have missed. I was fastidious in my research. We were going to win. There'd be no more distractions.

I made up my mind to forget about Marie – job done there, she'd got the message. I certainly didn't tell Kirsty about our meeting. It was pragmatic not to. There'd only have been another row. You did what? What made you even imagine that was a good idea? So I didn't say a thing. I asked her a few days afterwards whether she'd heard anything more from Marie, and she said, 'No. And don't start that again.' End of subject.

I was now trying to be at her side as often as I could, getting along to events, even – God help me – doing more door-knocking. The whole Marie episode, the funny business in the hotel and her reaction afterwards, all of that had prompted deep questions about my wife's emotional resilience. If she'd nearly crumbled once, she might do so again. I wouldn't let it happen. I was there to protect and advise her. I sent her encouraging text messages during the day – she ignored them all – and I checked with Adam on how things had gone when he was with her and I wasn't. Was she bearing up under all the pressure?

'Of course she is,' he said. 'She's doing just great. Why wouldn't she be?'

But Adam was not necessarily a reliable witness. In any case, I couldn't expect him to report back on his mother. There was a confidentiality between them that he would never break.

Yet it was true, Kirsty did seem on top of things. The busier it got, the more on top she was. When I asked, she'd tell me briskly where she'd been, who she'd met, what the day's policy points were, but not much else. If I ventured to ask how she was feeling, all I got was, 'I'm fine.' Conversation was cursory, matter-of-fact. Perhaps that was what happened to any candidate as they got closer to Election Day – emotions were tightly packed away for Victory Night. But at times I seemed to be watching her through a one-way mirror. I could see her, but she didn't see me. She was in her own distant world, oblivious. I'd lie in bed and stare at her back and imagine what she was dreaming.

The closest we got to meaningful discussion was when the *Citizen* eventually ran the article about Phoenix Academy. Shona emailed me a copy shortly before it went to press. No message, just the piece. I read it through and knew straightaway we'd got nothing to worry about.

The story was weak. It didn't say any more than had already been reported and it padded that out with details available on the school's website. It claimed to examine the permissive drugs climate at Phoenix, but did no such thing and reached no conclusion. The opening line – *The academy until recently run by Labour's by-election candidate is this week facing questions over its policy on drugs* – was pure Clive. It hooked you in, but led nowhere. There was a line or two from Joshua's mother, all recycled from her outburst at the hustings, and a couple of old quotes from Kirsty. An anonymous parent expressed the opinion that the school was lax on drugs – an invented comment almost certainly – and Sarah Clarkson repeated her bash at the council. No-one seemed aware of the policy row, the battle between Kirsty and the school governors, over whether kids should be expelled.

Overall, then, it was thin, a shoddy piece with nothing that other media outlets would want to chase. Dan Stapleton's so-called reporting and Clive Pascoe's editing had combined to produce very little. I would have demanded much more if I'd commissioned it. But I was proud of the statement from the school – all my own work. Phil had been on the point of panic when he rang me and I'd sent him a few paragraphs from my home email address. *Phoenix Academy, like many schools, operates in challenging social circumstances. We have a duty of care to all our students, but we will never condone or tolerate law-breaking* – that was the part they chose to use. I wondered if anyone – Clive? Shona? – had recognised my style. Apparently not.

'It's a non-story,' I said, as we got into bed that night. 'If that's the best my colleagues can do, you can sleep easy.'

And so could I. Unsurprisingly, Clive's dirt-digging – that Shona had also warned me about – seemed to have got him nowhere and the *Citizen* had carried no more personal items about Kirsty.

I drew her to me and kissed her, trying to tease my tongue past her lips. She pulled away.

'Not now.' She turned onto her back. 'I reckon Phil did a good job coping with the school story. Oh, and you too.'

An afterthought, a tiny crumb. I'd have to wait till after the election for the appreciation I deserved. I switched off the bedside light.

'So, not long to go then,' I said.

'And you know what? I'm looking forward to being an MP.'

That was the biggest thing she'd shared with me in the past week.

'Just as well, in the circumstances,' I said and took one of her hands, locking her fingers in mine as we lay there side by side. She slowly released them.

'I must sleep. It's another full-on day tomorrow.'

I really am looking forward to being an MP. It might have been a fatuous thing to say last night, but it's true. I just want to get on with the actual job and that can only start the day after Polling Day. What I'm doing now isn't real politics. It's just marketing, selling myself to the electorate. Campaigning is politics with no substance, no power or responsibility – I'm trying to persuade people to vote for me without as yet being able to do anything for them in return. It's a game. Sometimes it's one I feel I'm winning and sometimes it's not.

But at least the Marie business is behind me. Not a peep from her. I can only assume she's left Hull, gone back home. Perhaps in the future, I'll be able to help her. But not now. It was stupid to let it get at me like it did.

Of course, I continue to worry about the school. I'd have preferred it if the *Citizen* article hadn't happened, but Rick is positive it was rubbish and won't go any further and I have to believe him. We still need to sort things out for Josh Wenham, but I saw him and his mother the other day, spent half an hour with them, Gerry outside the room peering in through the glass pane in the door and pointing at his watch, and my mind in two places. Mrs Wenham wasn't entirely placated – why should she be? – but it looks like there could be a solution, a place for Josh at Humber High. Not ideal, but the best we can do.

And so today back to the marketing campaign with no let-up. A local radio breakfast interview, a visit to a biscuit factory, then a meeting hosted by the University Labour Club. More listening, more promising. And we've got a new leaflet with my name writ large, much larger than it need be. I'm the selling point, it seems, more than the party. I'm not entirely comfortable with that, but there's not much I can do about it.

**

I'd arranged to take the last few days off before the election to concentrate on guiding Kirsty through the vital final stages of the campaign. In the meantime, I was counting the weeks till my departure from the *Citizen*. But on that particular Thursday, I was doing a little more than that. I'd proposed a series of features on interesting newcomers to the area – something for one of the juniors to get their teeth into. I hadn't envisaged that this would lead to *me* standing on the side of a football club owner's swimming pool watching his wife doing the backstroke. But Clive had come up with a new ploy to humiliate me and that's exactly where I found myself.

His initial reaction to my feature idea had been very Clive-esque: I was using it to influence the political debate around immigration during the by-election. But when I suggested billionaire Oleg Yakubovich as our first subject, I could see he was tempted. The Russian had recently bought Hull City FC – and an enormous bolthole in the countryside. Even if the paper was soon to shrink to an online parody of itself, it had to continue producing stuff that people wanted to read while it was still in print. And football and money were an enticing combination.

'But you know what?' Clive said, pointing his finger into my face. 'You're going to do it. We need to get something out of the salary we still seem to be paying you.'

This was hardly a task for the deputy editor, but I was

on weak ground arguing. I'd gradually been relieved of most editorial responsibilities and couldn't claim to be over-stretched. I tensed my jaw and said nothing. Clive was enjoying this.

'A nice frothy piece. Lifestyle and sport. No politics – if you can manage that.'

I decided to make the best of an unpromising situation – something I'd grown rather adept at of late. I'd show my colleagues how a feature should be written. And if it meant a few hours away from Clive and Hull on a crisp, sunny day, well I could cope with that. Kirsty would no doubt be circumnavigating yet another depressing housing estate – I was due to join her for the evening canvassing. But the afternoon was for rich Russians and rural escapism.

I drove out of Hull with our photographer Gavin, feeling on quite a high. The cows chewed the cud and unthreatening clouds scuttled across the sky. Spring was here and life in the longer term was looking up. I had some good job leads in London. Unsurprisingly, the candidate's husband was attracting interest. I might even be spoilt for choice. There were other things to think about too. We'd get a flat somewhere not too far from Westminster, two bedrooms so that Adam could come down sometimes, and I'd join Kirsty in the constituency on occasional weekends. She was going to be an MP to watch, a powerhouse on the backbenches. And then if Labour got back into government, up she'd climb. And I'd be with her, steering her all the way to the top. She'd be a minister, a member of the Cabinet, who knew what else? It was time the party had a woman leader, long overdue in fact, and I was psychologically prepared for becoming the PM's spouse. I'd reinvent the role. I'd write a memoir about it, a different take on life in Number 10, inside intel, a bestseller. I'd be in demand everywhere. My old dream of the heavyweight power couple would finally be realised.

Gavin interrupted my thoughts and I slid back down my own greasy pole.

'Bit of a surprise you doing this feature,' he said. 'Thought it'd be a piece for one of the rookies.'

'Yeah, well, we're short-staffed.'

He grinned. 'Worse jobs, though. I gather the wife is quite an eyeful.'

We arrived at the Russian's country home, a Grade I listed Georgian mansion hidden away in many acres, were greeted by Yakubovich himself, a large man with an engaging smile and very white teeth, and proceeded to admire the choice antiques and Hockney watercolours in his drawing room. I had no doubt that he was one of those dubious oligarchs who'd made his roubles through corruption and chaos and laundered them into euros and pounds. But all that was beyond the scope of the *Citizen*. This, it seemed, was to be the journalism of envy – more *Hello!* magazine than *Guardian* or *Sunday Times*. It was a temporary necessity. Soon I'd be reincarnated as the serious journalist I really was.

The interview moved quickly from football to other topics. Oleg – he insisted on first names – told us he found Yorkshire very friendly. Strangers always said that, but this one seemed to mean it and to be genuinely interested in Hull. He even claimed to be partial to its poets and entertained us with a few lines of Marvell and Larkin. Poetry appreciation was most definitely not what Clive would be expecting. I was beginning to enjoy myself.

'But what attracted you here in the first place?' I asked. 'Apart from our great football club – and our poets, of course? The area seems an unusual choice for someone like you.'

'You mean, it's not everyone's cup of tea.' Oleg laughed and then paused to let us appreciate his mastery of the English idiom. 'I like the wide-open spaces. It reminds me of my birthplace, Novosibirsk. In Siberia.'

I ran through ways of working this into the piece. The remote Siberian wastelands of Humberside? Perhaps not. Novosibirsk as a booming provincial city, just like Hull? That was better. My swansong for the *Citizen* – as this would surely be – was going to prove a masterly piece of writing.

Oleg's wife arrived as I was finishing the interview, and he introduced her. 'Tatiana was once a teacher in Moscow. A teacher, like your wife.' He'd no doubt got someone to do a spot of research on me. Interviewees sometimes did that and I was generally flattered.

'Good afternoon, gentlemen,' Tatiana said with a heavy accent and graciously held her hand out to me, like a tsarina. For a moment, I wondered if I was meant to kiss it. She was flawlessly, if emphatically, made up and swankily dressed – that embroidered silk shirt with its top buttons artlessly undone had not been bought in the sort of places where my wife shopped. Her cheekbones were high and polished, her eyebrows sculpted into perfect, assertive arcs. It was a masterpiece of a face, possibly not the one she was born with, but as accomplished in its own way as the Hockneys on the walls. I tried not to catch Gavin's eye. Or to think of what Kirsty would say. I was on an afternoon off in that respect.

After a masterclass in English teatime etiquette – with Tatiana passing around a plate of delicately cut cucumber sandwiches and pouring tea into fine bone china cups – Gavin suggested going outside before the light faded for some shots of the grounds and perhaps the large natural swimming pool. Oleg said, 'Of course,' and his wife clapped her hands and said, 'I will undress. I will pose for you. You will have good photos.' She smiled sweetly, seductively.

Had I misheard? Her accent was *very* heavy. Or maybe 'undress' didn't quite mean what I thought it might mean. There was, after all, undressing and *undressing*. But she'd already hurried off. What sort of piece did this woman imagine I was doing? Gavin seemed preoccupied with checking his camera settings, but his face said, 'Schoolteacher, my arse.' Clive, of course, would love it.

I walked out to the pool, reluctantly, wishing I'd found a way to say no thank you, you don't need to do this, we've got plenty of photos, really. Kirsty's disapproval was bearing down on the scene. Why did you let her do it? What on earth were you thinking of? I looked at Oleg for some clue but got none. He raised his hands, as if to say, 'Nothing to do with me. My wife's got a mind of her own.' I should hope so too, Kirsty would have said, but I'm not sure what she's doing with it.

Ten minutes later, Tatiana re-joined us. She was wearing a demure, one-piece, navy-blue swimming costume. It had broad, functional straps and looked like an item actually designed for swimming. She carried a rubber cap, her glossy hair was scraped back into a ponytail and most of the make-up appeared to have been scrubbed off. She beamed at her husband and he smiled back approvingly. Gavin clicked away as she scooped the ponytail into her swimming cap, dived in and thrashed the water in a determined backstroke. Five minutes later she was climbing out with a heroic look on her face, as if she'd swum the width of the Black Sea. 'Bravo,' said Oleg. She shivered and wrapped herself in a thick towelling gown. Gavin stuck up his thumb to indicate that he was satisfied with what he'd got, and shortly after that we shook hands and left.

'Well, that was rather an anti-climax,' Gavin said as we drove out of the grounds. 'Looks like she just wanted to show off the pool, or her swimming. Not exactly what I thought we were in for, but there you go. Must be quite something for a schoolteacher from Moscow – or whatever she really was – to end up with a place like this.'

I smiled. He was probably right. Social mobility, something of which I approved, something I'd written about in my blog, an idea to develop in a further post. Kirsty and Tatiana, they'd both done it, both moved on in life.

Gavin started to look through his pictures, muttering 'nice, very nice' every now and then. I was working out if it was a story I could tell Kirsty. It would do her good to take her mind somewhere else for two minutes, even have a bit of a laugh, although she wouldn't be at all impressed by the couple's wealth. When I'd mentioned the feature idea to her, she'd said we'd be much better doing a series about real migrants and their lives – people like the woman who cleaned the *Citizen* offices and out of whom, incidentally, I had recently managed to get some conversation. She was thinking of going home to Slovakia because of Brexit. But Kirsty was wrong. Rich Russians who loved Yorkshire, recited poetry and were prepared to don a swimsuit in April were much better material. Naturally I'd doctor my reactions to Tatiana when I described it all to her.

Gavin put the camera down and picked up his phone, stretching back in the passenger seat and scrolling down the screen. My phone was vibrating in my pocket. I'd forgotten it was still on silent. I'd stop to check messages in a moment, before we got on the main road.

'Rick, you better pull over and look at this,' Gavin said.

'What is it?'

'Just look.'

I drew up on the verge and took his phone. I was looking at a photo of Kirsty on a tabloid website – a photo from a few days ago, her big red rosette standing proud on her grey coat. She looked serious but animated, like she always did out on the stump, and pretty too. That didn't always come over in election coverage.

Next to it was a photo of a young woman, her face heavily made-up but part-hidden by a curtain of henna-red hair, her dress strapless and low-cut, a clutch bag in her hand, a very young woman, her youth cheaply disguised, pouting into the camera. The face was familiar. It was Kirsty, Kirsty looking eighteen or nineteen, Kirsty before I knew her, Kirsty as I couldn't ever have imagined her, a photo I'd never seen before.

I scrolled up to the headline.

EXPOSED: POLITICIAN'S CALL-GIRL PAST
Labour's by-election candidate
faces questions after her former life
as a sex worker is revealed

A cow lowed in the field next to us and my mind stood still.

I stared at the words, shifted back to the photos, looking from one Kirsty to the other, then turned open-mouthed to Gavin as if for an explanation. It was Gavin's phone, he must know what it meant. But he was looking down at his knees, avoiding my eyes.

I returned to the phone and started to read through the paragraphs beneath the photos, skimming through them quickly, furiously. I didn't know what I was reading. It could have been written in a foreign language. I got to the end and started again.

After a few moments Gavin said, 'Is there… anything

I…' He didn't finish whatever he was trying to say.

I ignored him and just went on reading, re-reading. After a while, I heard him say, 'Do you want me to drive?'

I still didn't answer. I handed his phone back to him and he turned to look out of the passenger-side window. I picked up my own phone. There were two missed calls from Kirsty and one from Adam.

**

It happened this morning. After the local radio interview, on my way to the factory, in the car with Gerry. A call from a reporter, said he'd got a story, running it later today, online first, then more in print tomorrow, and he'd like my response. I turned my head away from Gerry and said, I'm sorry, I don't understand… can I call you back? And when we got to the factory, I went to the ladies and called the reporter, just to find out… not to say anything. He said there was someone, someone with information, someone I worked with, thirty years ago but memories fresh, facts checked, photos. Perhaps he was bluffing, half a story they couldn't run unless I said something. And I put the phone back in my bag and splashed cold water on my face and checked that my mascara hadn't run and went out and inspected the production line and talked to the shop stewards and the general manager who was worried about exports after Brexit and there were photos and then we said goodbye and Gerry and I got back in the car. And I sat and said nothing as we drove to the next event… I can barely remember what it was… and I turned every thought inside out. I needed to talk to Gerry. Or Rick, he'd know what to do. No, not Rick. Gerry, I had to talk to Gerry first. But I made myself wait, I couldn't be sure, it might be a bluff, wait till this afternoon. And I waited. And then it was too late. It was out. Out of my hands. The party's press office took over, handling things, in control, and there was nothing I could do. And Gerry looked at me and said, you bloody fool.

He's right.

The pounding on the front door and the ringing of the bell started early, before it was light. Insistent, demanding, each attempt seemed to have a different timbre, a different duration, as if eventually there'd be one that hit the right note and persuaded the occupants to open up. Kirsty and I were inside, playing deaf. Occasionally there was a rap on the window or a voice through the letterbox – Ms Osmond… Kirsty… Daily Express here, Daily Mirror, Daily whatever… Hello, anyone at home? – and always a buzz of conversation and laughter outside and the crunch of footsteps on the drive.

Neither of us had slept and at six, as dawn broke, we had given up, crept down to the kitchen and were now sitting there, silently drinking coffee, prisoners in our own castle. I knew what it was like to be on the opposing side of a siege, part of the attacking army, a sentinel for the public's right to know, intent on flushing out the uncooperative captives. I'd done it often enough – waiting for some devious politician to emerge into the glare of photographers' lights and the chorus of reporters' pointless questions. Savvy captives sometimes brought out mugs of tea to show they weren't cowed or to secure more sympathetic treatment. It never worked, but the pictures were good. Now the roles were reversed, and Kirsty and I were cowering inside. I didn't take out tea. I wasn't seeking a truce with the journalists outside. They were my tribe, but for now I loathed them.

The events of the previous evening filled my head and I kept replaying them, starting at various points, configuring them differently, re-imagining the scenes. I returned to the precise moment I'd read the headline on Gavin's phone, except it wasn't a precise moment, more a short hiatus during which the words made no sense. And then, once they cohered to form a meaning, they made even less sense. Whether cock-up or conspiracy, a biographical mix-up or malicious fabrication, it was rubbish. Fake news. Fact and falsehood were confusingly combined. Yes, Kirsty Osmond had studied politics at Leeds University in the nineteen-eighties, but no, she obviously had not worked for an escort agency and had not had sex with clients to fund her student life.

I'd tried to ring her as I sat parked in that narrow country road near Oleg's mansion, aware of Gavin watching me, not knowing what to say. The number was engaged. I texted. *Call me.* I rang again. Still no reply. We swapped seats and Gavin drove us back to Hull, while I kept trying Kirsty. There was Adam's call to return and others coming in, too. I recognised some numbers, colleagues, friends, contacts, and ignored them all, the ones I knew and the ones I didn't. I had to speak to Kirsty first, to tell her of course I didn't believe it. It was ludicrous. We'd go to the Independent Press Standards Organisation. The party would get a good libel lawyer. We'd come too far to be thrown off course by something like this.

We'd got to the office. Gavin stood outside the entrance to the building, pressing his camera bag tightly to his chest. 'I hope everything… I hope things are okay.' I nodded and switched over to the driving seat.

I'd arrived home shortly before seven on that Thursday evening. Surprisingly the media weren't there. Not yet. I checked the back of the house and locked the side gates. The place was eerily quiet. No Kirsty and no Adam. As I opened the front door, I half-hoped to find them there, Adam rocking back on his chair and chortling at the crazy things the tabloids invented – *75% of new jobs go to EU migrants… Freddie Starr ate my hamster… Elvis is alive* – while Kirsty frowned in disapproval. But the house was empty.

There was a folded note among the junk mail on the doormat.

Rick,
I guess you're not picking up phone messages, but please call me.
Shona.

I dropped it back on the mat, closed the blinds in the sitting room and went through to the kitchen. It was all exactly as we'd left it that morning. Three dirty coffee mugs and Adam's cereal bowl sat next to the sink and Kirsty's grey coat lay slung over a chair. At the last moment, she'd decided to change it for a jacket. The weather felt milder, she'd thought. 'Don't kid yourself,' I'd said. 'It's only April.' But she'd laughed and taken the jacket.

Again I tried to phone her, to tell her… or maybe to ask her… Yes, perhaps I did need to *ask* her, a formality, that was all, like an airline official asking if you've packed your bag yourself. Could anyone else have tampered with it, inserted something you don't know about, while your back was innocently turned? I needed to know whether there was anything in it, anything at all, that might have been distorted to become this explosive calumny.

I wandered through the house, restless, wondering. At one point I went to my computer and opened the page for a new blog post. I closed it again. Should I go out to find her, to the Labour offices? I couldn't be sure she was there and I wanted to speak to her alone. She'd have to head home eventually. At seven-thirty she texted.

On my way back. I swapped the overhead light in the sitting room for the two gentler floor lamps and waited.

A key turned in the lock and the door opened. For a few seconds she stood in the hall, leaning against the wall, her arms folded across her waist, an elbow grasped in each hand. Her bags lay at her feet where she'd dropped them. She looked cold.

'Kirsty.'

She glanced across at me and nodded, and I knew. It was just a slight movement of the head, a single nod, and its meaning hit me immediately. Everything in my life, absolutely everything, needed recalibrating.

She walked past me, her jacket grazing my arm, and I followed her into the sitting room. She sat on the hard chair in the corner, her back rounded, her shoulders sagging, her face turned downwards, hidden from me. My eyes rested on the top of her head and the copper highlights in her hair shone incongruously in the warmth of the lamp next to her.

'Is Adam here?'

'He won't answer my calls,' I said.

'Mine neither.'

We were both silent for a moment and then she said, 'It was a long time ago.'

She sat up and looked straight at me. A look of defiance.

'And it wasn't like that.'

**

Nineteen eighty-seven. A different time, a different world, a different me. My first year at university in Leeds and my dad was refusing to support me. He was bringing in a fair amount of money with the taxi business and so I only got a small grant. He was meant to give me the rest.

Parental contribution. But he didn't. My mum was ill. I didn't want to worry her, but I was struggling. I got a job as a waitress. Little Chef – the story I told Jess over gnocchi and calamari, the story I partly told. It was long hours and the tips weren't brilliant. I was tired and I wondered how I was going to manage three years like this.

One day I got talking to someone in my hall. Marie. I'd met her at the beginning of term, similar background to me – dad used to work down the pits, we sort of got on. I told her I was finding it tough, not sure if I could go on like this. And she said she understood, she'd been there too. But then she'd found out about this escort agency. She'd started working for them and the money was good. They were still recruiting people, they seemed keen on students and she could introduce me if I liked. Well, I just laughed in her face. An escort agency? I wasn't that desperate. But she said no, I'd got the wrong idea. It was just like being set up on blind dates, except you got paid. And you didn't have to do anything you didn't want to. She kept going on about it and eventually I thought, well I've got nothing to lose, I'll give it a go.

So I went along. It was a woman I met, very kind, she told me they had lots of lovely clients with money to spend on drinks and dinner and I'd be perfect company, just the sort of beautiful intelligent girl her gentlemen liked to spend an evening with. I was flattered. And excited. This was so much better than Little Chef, a really grown-up thing to do, sophisticated, glamorous. The woman said I should dress up, look gorgeous, clothes, make-up, they'd help with all that. I'd be going to smart hotels – the sort of places I'd not been to before – meeting interesting people. It was risky – I wasn't daft, I knew that. But in a way that was the appeal, the risk-taking. I'd never taken risks before, not real risks, and it was kind of thrilling.

I started the next evening, said I could probably do two or three shifts a week. And the woman said, oh don't call them shifts. You're not a waitress now. This will be so much more rewarding. You're going to enjoy your evenings with us.

The first two times were okay, dinner and talk, lonely men who wanted their egos boosting. I got that, even at eighteen, and I went along with it. A present of perfume from one, a hug and a goodnight kiss from the other. Eyes were on me in hotel bars and restaurants, I was an object of admiration, the world was mine. And I drank more than I was used to. The woman was right, it was enjoyable. Or at least not as awful as I'd thought it might be.

But then the third night, it was a Sunday, at the end of dinner the man suggested we went back to his room for a night cap, a nice way to round off the evening. I wasn't stupid, I knew what he meant, and I didn't want to be difficult, or seem, well, unworldly. I wasn't a virgin, I'd had a boyfriend in Sheffield. So I went. And we had sex, and I told myself that's sometimes what happens at the end of a date and tried to forget I was being paid.

It happened three more times. And each day afterwards, I felt a heaviness inside, a growing sense that this wasn't right, something I couldn't explain to myself and didn't want to. I found it difficult concentrating on my university work. I thought about giving up and leaving Leeds altogether.

One weekend, I'd arranged to go home to see my mum. She was getting weaker. And as she lay in bed, she looked at me and said, are you alright? And I thought, she knows, I don't know how, but she knows. It was me killing her, not the cancer. And that's when I knew it had to end. I went back to Leeds but didn't turn up for the next hotel appointment. Instead I returned to waitressing, working extra shifts. My mother died and for a while I wanted to die, too, but somehow I scraped through my first-year exams, don't know how, but I did. Then my dad's taxi business collapsed and in the second year I got a full grant. I started reading more and handing in essays on time. I made new friends, got involved in the students' union, went on anti-Thatcher protests, grew angry about the poll tax and joined the Socialist Workers Party briefly. But that was just student politics, posturing. At the start of my final year at university, I joined the Labour Party, real politics.

And here I am now. Except I've let them down. Deceived them. At that first selection interview, when they asked me if there was anything… anything in my background that could harm the party's reputation, I said no, nothing. A routine question. I lied. I could have said, well yes, there is something from way back, a small thing, it may not be important, but I should tell you. But I didn't. I lied by omission. A cardinal sin.

That's it. The story. Not much to tell, really. And now I've told my husband, sitting here in our front room. I should have told him years ago. I nearly did, several times, but I didn't know what he'd think and I missed so many chances, and as the years went on, it faded, she didn't fit into the new story of me, that teenage Kirsty who'd gone on a few blind dates and who no-one needed to know about, not even Rick. My new life was public service, politics, teaching, and she just complicated matters. It really was no big deal, I told myself. But I was wrong. Things like that don't go away. They're always there, hidden away but waiting for the right moment to jump out and grab you.

******

She told the story meticulously, as if she didn't want to miss any detail nor dwell on anything that wasn't important, and I sat on the edge of the sofa and let her tell it. The different Kirstys – this woman who was my wife or a parliamentary candidate or an ex-call girl – dissolved into each other and then back into the upright figure on the corner seat, a stranger, sitting in my house, reciting her story. Sometimes she paused and looked at me. Her face was neutral, like a passport photo taken in a do-it-yourself booth. The features were hers, but two-dimensional, drained of life. Then she looked away again and the Kirstys separated themselves out, Kirsty the teenage student, broke and vulnerable, distinct from Kirsty the headteacher-politician. It was a pity they couldn't have met. Kirsty the teacher would have had a lot of useful things to say to her younger self.

And I'd have had things to say to her dad if I'd had the chance. The ex-miner taxi-business owner who never wanted his daughter to go to university and abandoned her when she got there. I struggled with a remembered picture of Billy Osmond – watching football on TV, in his cardigan, not speaking, coughing into his handkerchief – and tried to reconcile it with an imagined picture of a slightly younger Billy Osmond – in a large office, on the phone, fast-talking, chain-smoking, commanding a fleet of taxis. The images sat side by side in my head. It's perhaps a wasted emotion hating people if they're dead, but at that moment I hated Billy.

And Marie. And the men.

And myself? What does a man think when his wife tells a story like this? What do other people think about him? And what does he think of himself?

Well naturally I was sympathetic, and non-judgmental, as I'd be to any woman in these circumstances. I understand the feminist debate over women selling their bodies – choice or exploitation? I too am a feminist, am I not? I didn't condemn her. If she'd told me the story at the beginning, would I have fled? Of course not. I'd have been intrigued, but not repulsed. Wouldn't I?

Yet somehow, in our sitting room that evening, that wasn't the point. Quite simply she hadn't chosen to tell me. If she had, our relationship would have started in another key, the balance of power between us differently weighted, her secret in my keeping. And I definitely would have dissuaded her from going into politics with that on her dark CV. But for twenty-five years she'd kept it from me, as if I couldn't be trusted with such a fragile package. And now I was mired in the lie with her, my reputation sullied alongside hers.

We both needed rescuing.

'It won't be easy,' I said, 'but I'm going to get you through this the best I can.' I paused. 'You know, it sounds to me like you were groomed.'

She jumped up. 'Oh, for Christ's sake, Rick. Of course I wasn't groomed.'

'But the flattery, winning your trust, luring you in like–'

'I knew exactly what I was doing. It's the media again. They've blown it out of all proportion, concocted something out of nothing. I was an escort not a sex worker. There is a difference, you know. The sex was… just something that happened.'

'And for which you were paid. A transaction. Money alters everything. Surely you can see that.'

'I was paid for my time.'

'We can't spin it like that.'

'I don't want to spin anything!'

'Kirst–'

'I did nothing wrong. Morally wrong.'

'Morality doesn't come into it. It's all about perception. I told you politics was rough for women.'

'Should I be congratulating you?'

I stood up, walked over and put my hands on her shoulders. At times her naïvety could be excruciating. 'Kirsty, what on earth made you think you'd get away with it? I mean we all manipulate our personal history a little… but this, well… What is it with politicians?'

She pushed me away and sat down.

'Are you trying to bracket me with Barraclough by any chance?'

'No, but–'

'For God's sake, Rick. You make it sound like I've been caught running a string of brothels. It's hardly the same. I was a stupid kid, the same age as Adam.'

'You need to recognise the jam you're in. A little penitence maybe.'

'Penitence? What are you saying? I'm finished? It's all over?'

I shrugged my shoulders. 'I just think we have to be realistic, that's all.'

She glared at me, breathing hard but saying nothing.

'You should eat something,' I said.

'I'm not hungry.'

'We both have to eat.'

I went into the kitchen and emptied a carton of tomato soup into a saucepan, staring into the pan and willing it to come to the boil. For a moment I couldn't remember where we kept the spoons. But then I found the cutlery drawer and took the bowls of soup through.

She looked up at me. 'There's something else I have to tell you. About Marie.'

I put her soup down on the table next to her and handed her a napkin. She paused as if waiting for me to say something. I balanced my own bowl precariously on my knees.

'Marie?'

'She asked for my support. With a project.'

'She demanded money?' I looked down at the red oily surface in my bowl. Money. This cast an obliging new light on the matter. The woman was an extortionist. She'd got what she could out of Kirsty and then she'd scuttled off to the press for more. She'd been intent on her act of treachery without any instigation from me.

'No, not money, she—'

'You should have told me. We could have gone to the police.'

'Listen, will you. It was nothing to do with money. But it's a long story and I need to take you back a bit first. Marie actually stopped the escort work about the same time as me. And we made a sort of pact—'

'A pact? Jesus.'

'We were teenagers. Just listen. We agreed that we'd never mention a word about the escorting to anyone. We just wanted it behind us, I thought we both did. I trusted her. But we drifted apart – I'd got new friends, new interests – and we didn't keep in touch after we left university. As time went on, the whole thing paled into insignificance for me. Something in the past I'd chosen to forget about. Something that wasn't very important. But not for Marie, it seems. When she turned up last month – I honestly hadn't seen her for nearly thirty years – she had this idea for a campaign to outlaw agencies like the one we were involved with. To stop them from exploiting young people. She's got a daughter now the same age as we were… and she wanted me to help, use my political platform, speak out…'

'Christ, I hope you told her—'

'Of course. I said I really couldn't, not during the

election. And she got that. She promised to keep me out of things.'

This was getting uncomfortably complicated. The woman on my doorstep, the woman I'd, well, exchanged a few words with… a social campaigner? I couldn't quite see it.

'Well… maybe the story didn't come from her then.'

'No-one else, at the agency, the clients, no-one knew my real name. We got paid in cash and I used another name. So it has to be her. But after wishing me luck… why?'

'Money? You know how much some papers pay for that sort of thing?'

'But there wasn't even a hint. Why would she change her mind like that?'

I put the soup bowl down. I was beginning to feel nauseous.

'People are greedy,' I said. A convenient truism.

'But all she seemed interested in was her campaign. I wanted to help her. I was trying to work out whether there was a way I could once I was in Parliament. But this, it doesn't make sense.'

All I had to do was say nothing. She went to the window and stood with her back to me, opening the blind a little to peek out. I guessed she was looking for Adam, waiting for him to come home.

'Close the blind. The media will be here soon.'

She turned, looking startled. She must have known that, Gerry must have told her, the comms people must have given her advice. What *were* they telling her, for fuck's sake? She moved away from the window and looked around the room, at pictures and books, as if the possessions summed up her life, who she was, where she'd got to. At one point her gaze seemed to take in me – was I part of the inventory? – and I turned away, avoiding her scrutiny. I picked up her untouched soup bowl and saw next to it a stray election leaflet. I knew the text by heart. *Kirsty Osmond. Fighting for your jobs, homes, schools and hospitals. Fighting for your future. Vote Osmond. Vote Labour.*

'It can't be over. Can it?' she said.

'Depends how the party play it. After Barraclough, you could say it looks like an own goal.'

She winced.

'There's a meeting in the morning,' she said. 'Gerry, Jim, someone's coming from the national executive, too, I think, and a senior comms person. We, they – I'm not sure how much my view will count – they've got to decide how to position this. There has to be a way through. Doesn't there? I mean, the escorting… I didn't do anything wrong.'

Did she even believe it herself? I was beginning to doubt it.

'Well, you could tell them you're fighting against the double standards that judge women differently, against the hypocrisy of male-dominated politics.'

'For God's sake Rick, you're not writing a blog now.'

But I was, in my head – and not a bad line to develop, although now, in these circumstances, rather optimistic.

'It's me who seems to be the hypocrite,' she said. 'And I should be judged the same as any politician, male or female. Equal rights, equal responsibilities. I made a big thing of being honest and it looks like I fell short. I guess all I can do is apologise.'

'You can give it a go. It was an error of judgement, you can say, a bad oversight.'

'Will it be enough?'

'Who knows?'

There were steps outside, and voices, just a couple to

start with. They'd taken their time, but now they were here and the ringing and rat-a-tat had started. I put a finger to my lip. We'd have to deal with this in the morning, but not now. I took her arm and led her through to the kitchen. It was safer at the back of the house.

My phone buzzed in my pocket. It had done so several times while we'd been talking and I'd ignored it. Now I answered it.

'Adam, finally. We've been trying to get you all evening.'

'Dad? Is it true?'

No greetings, no 'how are you? how's Mum?'

'It's complicated.'

There was a short, low howl from the phone. I caught Kirsty's eye. She was close to me and she'd heard it, too.

'Your mother's here with me. Would you like to speak to her?'

There was no reply.

'Adam, are you at Jess's?'

'Yes.' His voice was small.

'It might be better if you stay there overnight, if you can. The media are here. Ignore any calls from numbers you don't recognise.' I turned away from Kirsty. 'Don't worry, Adam, it'll be all right.'

'Will it?' I didn't know how to reply. He needed me and I could do nothing. 'Anyway I've got to go.'

'Adam–'

He put the phone down and I knew I'd failed him. I turned back to Kirsty. Her mouth was contorted in a silent scream.

Then – not a scream, but a whisper.

'He doesn't want to speak to me.'

'He's confused.'

'Oh, God. What have I done?'

'It's a lot for him to take in.'

'Oh God, oh God.'

She stood there, her face a used rag. I hugged her, and for one short moment she rested her head on my shoulder. Then she unwrapped my arms and sat down on a kitchen stool and started to tap her foot on the floor, hypnotically. I leant against the worktop and watched her, knowing that, once again, I needed to reassess my tactics. My candidate, my wife, was too weak to swim against the tide. Was she about to… drown?

After all, it had happened once before, once when she'd almost drowned.

We'd been married a few years and had just moved to north London. Adam was two and a half and had recently become very clingy, screaming every morning when one of us dropped him off at the nursery. I was wrapped up in my job as a political correspondent on the *Evening Standard*, Kirsty's school was in the middle of an Ofsted inspection and she was fourteen weeks pregnant. She rang me at lunchtime on the second day of the inspection and said, 'I think I'm miscarrying. Can you meet me at A&E?'

I did, and two hours later an ultrasound scan confirmed the loss of the pregnancy. It was her second miscarriage in six months. The first one had been at eight weeks and she'd gone back to work the next day, philosophical about early miscarriages being common, resigned to her bad luck, determined to try again. 'One of those things. Happens to lots of women. I'll get through it.'

This time was different. She didn't spring back. She was quiet, too quiet, but insisted on returning to work the following week. On the second day she came home late and said, 'It's pointless. Everything's pointless.' And she switched on the television, flopped into a chair and sat there all evening, not eating or drinking, the sound from the TV swelling over her, refusing to talk to me, monosyllables, no more.

She took some more time off, reluctantly, agreed to the medication the doctor prescribed, but declined the talking therapy I suggested. In the evening I'd come home to find her in Adam's bedroom, the child asleep, Kirsty standing, just looking at her son in the dim night-light, one hand on the rail of his cot. When I tried to talk to her about the lost baby and the possibility of a further pregnancy once she felt the time was right – a daughter, we both wanted a girl, didn't we? – she'd stop me and say, 'No, not again, I can't.'

For several weeks, I lived with someone who wasn't Kirsty, but then – maybe it was the medication, maybe just time – the darkness passed and she started to emerge from wherever she'd been. Things seemed to return to normal. She threw herself back into work and her career again took precedence. Within three years she was appointed deputy head at another comprehensive. She never mentioned the miscarriage again and wouldn't let me do so. Nor would she discuss having any more children. If I raised it, she changed the subject.

She also returned to her usual worries, about her students, about the state of the world, about Adam, occasionally even about me. I could understand it when she was eaten by anxiety rather than smothered by depression. But anxiety and depression were opposite ends of the same spectrum. There had always been that degree of instability in my wife – I'd been aware of that as soon as she'd thought of running, even though I hadn't been allowed to mention it. I'd tried my best to protect her, but it didn't go away. And it was there that Thursday evening, as we waited for the media to arrive, as she sat on the kitchen stool and repeatedly tapped her foot.

'Kirsty, I'm worried about you. We should make an appointment for you to see the doctor, once you've got through tomorrow.'

'What? What are you talking about?' She stood up. 'I'm going to my study. I've got a few things to do.'

'Don't put the main light on,' I said. 'And don't look at social media.'

**

I'm sitting at my screen staring at a blank email to Adam. I'm desperate to talk to him but it's hard to know what to say. *Dear Adam.* The thought that he doesn't want to speak to me is eating me up. Perhaps all I can say is sorry, sorry for putting you through this. *Dear Adam…*

I write some words and I'm not sure they're the right ones. I press send and know he's not going to reply. The hurt won't go away. But I find myself opening the Electoral Commission site, a distraction maybe, checking the rules, what happens if I withdraw. I know, of course I know, the election continues without me, without a Labour candidate, but I want to see the exact words. *UK Parliamentary by-elections – Guidance for candidates and agents… Completing your nomination papers… The deposit… Appointing your election agent… Withdrawing…* The officialese is unambiguous.

I glance at more messages. Still none from Adam. But I scan some and reply to one from Phil, a query from yesterday about pupil premium. I even spot a text from Julie, saying she doesn't get what all the fuss is about and she'd still like to see me when I've got the time. No gloating, as there could have been, just why the fuss? I reply, 'Thanks', and feel even more guilty.

I open Twitter and close it again quickly.

Rick puts his head round the door. Would I like a tea, something stronger, something to help me sleep? No thanks, nothing. He wants to run through things with me for the meeting in the morning, like we did the night before the selection, the right tone, the right words… misjudgement… hindsight… remorse… all those Rick-words. I refuse. He shakes his head and closes my door again.

There's something going on and I can't work it out. He seems so relaxed about what I've told him. No storms, no eruptions, no telling me I'm a fool, like Gerry did, like I am. I wanted him to shout it out loud. You're an idiot, carrying that around, not seeing that it was bound to come out sooner or later. Couldn't you have kept your head down? But no, your ego wouldn't let you, would it? You had to seek the limelight, didn't you?

There was little of that, just the journalist's reductive way of looking at things. Own goals… double standards… Is it all that simple? Then the doctor, what was that about? Do I need to see a doctor? Pills to get me through things? There isn't time. And I've got to stay clear-headed. Worse has happened before, situations where I've had no agency. There's always a way through things. But now there are so many variables, so many people involved. I just don't know.

It's quiet outside. The media must have given up for the evening. They'll be back in the morning in time for us leaving the house, I guess. Rick's in the bathroom. It sounds as if he's having a shower, rinsing away the day's sludge. Oil and water. Can you really make a marriage out of that, different values, different perspectives, relying on the attraction of opposites, like we have?

I'm going to try and sleep, just for an hour or two. And then it'll start all over again tomorrow.

**

She was due to see Gerry first thing that Friday morning. There were things to go through, she said, before the formal meeting at eleven. She was vague about how it would work, unfocused, detached. Was it some sort of disciplinary meeting or a practical how-do-we-get-ourselves-out-of-this-mess meeting? There'd have to be a full press statement soon, I told her, possibly a press conference.

She put last night's pots in the dishwasher, wiped the surfaces of the worktop and rinsed the sink. Then she went into the sitting room and I followed her through. She picked up cushions and magazines from the floor, rearranged them, straightened pictures, found a couple of other cups for the dishwasher.

'Kirsty, you don't need…'

'I just want to leave the place tidy.'

I was going to drop her at the Labour offices – she'd left her own car there overnight and Gerry had given her a lift home. She put on her coat, her grey coat this time, unpinned the rosette from the lapel and gave me a watery smile. The front door bell rang. There'd been a short lull. Now it was starting again, and the bell was followed by a knock on the window. They were out there in strength, interest in the story fortified by the absence of any firm rebuttal. We'd leave the blinds closed when we departed, to stop snooping. I remembered, when I was a child, the curtains being drawn after my grandmother died. It signalled the need for privacy in grief. Nowadays, it just meant you'd slept in or were late for work and had left in a hurry.

'Right,' I said, 'we go straight to the car. Don't look at the cameras. Don't say anything – 'good morning', if you like, nothing else. And whatever you do, don't have a go at them.'

I was taking charge, this was how it was going to be, and she nodded, like an obedient child, eager to show she'd understood, eager to please.

'Ready?'

'Ready.'

I opened the door and stepped out ahead of her. It was trying to rain. The press pack seemed to have been momentarily caught off its guard. Reporters and photographers were idling on the pavement, on our drive, talking to each other. Perhaps we'd make it to the car unnoticed. But a voice called out 'Kirsty', there was a flash of cameras and microphones were thrust in her direction. In the melee, I spotted Dan shouting her name. She remembered my instructions and ignored them all. I took her arm and steered her to the car, pressing the key to unlock the doors and checking that no-one had blocked our exit from the drive. They hadn't.

I waited for her to fasten her seatbelt. She was fumbling, so I leant over to help her. 'Thanks,' she said and pressed her hands between her knees. There were more flashes at the passenger window as we pulled out of the drive.

'That wasn't too bad, was it?' I said. We were turning from Maple Avenue onto the main road.

'Are they following us?'

'Doesn't look like it. But there may be others waiting for you at the offices. Same routine. Good morning. Nothing more.'

I found a music channel and turned it down low. It was still early, not yet seven, and the streets were relatively empty. Hull looked its usual grey, honest self. A normal day. A Friday. The weekend to look forward to. I pulled up just before the red-painted shop front of the

Labour offices. There were two reporters and a lone photographer standing near the door. As yet, they hadn't noticed us.

I switched off the ignition.

'I guess this is it, then.'

She was staring through the windscreen at the building and seemed not to have heard me. Should I be offering to go in with her, not to the meeting, but just to wait for her? I didn't offer. She'd have said no, no, she was doing this by herself. And I had matters of my own to resolve.

'Look,' I said, 'in the grand scheme of things, the really grand scheme, life and death – when you look at it like that, this counts for nothing. We can go back to how we were before. A quiet life. Losing an election's not the end of the world. Trust me.'

The power fulcrum would definitely be adjusted in our marriage, Kirsty's political ambitions seen off, and me acknowledged as the one who held things together when everything was collapsing, who kept his wits about him while all others were losing theirs. The strong one – with quite a tale to tell. A book, maybe…

She turned to me.

'But it's the shame, isn't it? That's what won't go away.'

I rubbed her arm and she pulled away.

'I wish I could disappear.'

And I couldn't help thinking that there'd been politicians who'd done just that when it had got too much. Disappeared into thin air. Or into the sea. Left their clothes on a beach. To try and escape the inevitable.

The car's heater hummed and we sat in silence.

Then she unfastened her seat belt, and I kissed her goodbye like you'd kiss a child and stroked her hair.

'Kirsty, you need to take care of yourself. You're not

as strong as you think.'

I watched as she walked towards the building, a lonely figure with a deceptively confident gait, ignoring the rain. The reporters spotted her as she approached and the photographer trained her camera on her. She took no notice of them and looked straight ahead as she opened the door, just like I'd told her to do.

The journey from the Labour offices to the *Citizen* took ten minutes. I drove automatically, unaware of the familiar landmarks. Clive had texted the night before and eventually I'd read it. *We won't be expecting you tomorrow.* Shona had also messaged me – a follow-up to the handwritten note I'd ignored. *I'm sorry, I've got to cover it.*

I was going to show them I wasn't cowed. If Clive wasn't expecting me, then I'd definitely be there. And if Shona felt bad about covering it, then that was her problem, not mine. If they both thought I could be written off that easily, they were wrong. I just needed a strategy to get me through the next few days. I wasn't sure what it was yet, but I'd work it out. I had to wait and see how the clowns in the party were going to play it and then respond – on behalf of both Kirsty and myself. Thirteen days to Polling Day and she should have been out on the stump, cajoling and pressing the flesh, reminding people that she was going to fix their messy lives for them. Instead she was about to be stretched on the rack by apparatchiks intent on extracting a humiliating confession over a bad decision half a lifetime ago. That and the small matter of a lie.

I pressed the door keypad and let myself into the sleeping building. The usual blend of disinfectant and damp dog hit my nostrils. In eight years I'd never worked out where the canine smell came from.

I made my way up to the third floor, walked into the empty newsroom and was hit by my solitariness. It was generally good being the first in – I had time to look at the papers, flick through websites, think and plan before anyone else arrived. But now the time and emptiness hung heavily. And it struck me – how had the place received the Kirsty news? Who'd spotted the story first? Did they see it as comedy or tragedy, or neither, just stuff that happened, merely another news story, as good as Barraclough six weeks ago. Better even. Women misbehaving had novelty value.

And what had they said about me?

The morning's papers sat in an unopened bundle near the door, where they'd been dropped off by the early-morning courier. Clive had recently suggested that print editions of the national press were an unnecessary expense. We could manage without them. I'd persuaded him otherwise. Sometimes you needed to see what the news looked like in print, where a story was positioned on the page, how many column inches it occupied. I untied the string and pulled out the tabloid that had broken the Kirsty news. It was as I expected – the photos taking up most of the front page, the 'CALL-GIRL' headline uncompromising, the story continuing, after the first five paragraphs, on pages six and seven. There was more detail here than in the initial online piece, the names of hotels, a photo of Kirsty in her graduation gown, her arms around the shoulders of two male students, their faces blanked out.

There was also a short editorial several pages in. I remembered the never-published piece I'd written on Barraclough. This was punchier, more confident, apparently less worried by the prospect of a legal challenge. It accused Kirsty of deceiving the electorate and pronounced Labour's by-election campaign dead in a ditch. That seemed a reasonable assessment.

I leant back in my chair, looking up at the ceiling. There was a large brown stain up there, an almost perfect circle, which I'd never noticed before. It looked dry and faded. Something must once have leaked from the floor above. I focused blankly on the mark, trying to concentrate. Then I picked up my phone and did what I'd avoided doing last night. I looked at social media.

It was more or less as I'd expected. There were a few posts sticking up for her, pointing out that politicians were only human and condemning the prurience of the popular press. These were in the minority. Of the rest, the least obnoxious were merely self-righteous – *The fall from grace of Ms Squeaky Clean… We deserve better from our politicians (and our headteachers)… Is there no end to politicians' lies and hypocrisy?* Or they tried to be witty – *What is it about Labour politicians and sex?… This isn't a good look for the woman who once wanted to ban men from parliament… So it's not just male politicos who have a secret past #NorthHumbersideByelection @Kirsty_Osmond #MeToo…* The worst attracted all the trolls of the virtual netherworld. Some speculated in flagrant detail on her sexual accomplishments. Others threatened to rape or mutilate her. One or two said she wasn't worth the effort. If Kirsty thought no-one would be bothered by the idea of sex work, not in the twenty-first century, if she imagined no-one would even think it *was* sex work, well, she was wrong. It turned out a lot of people were bothered, hot and bothered. It was open season and she was fair game. I read the stream of vitriol, not with incredulity – there was nothing I hadn't already imagined – but with curiosity. Who were these people, if they were real people? Who actually thought it was a good idea to unload their poisonous thoughts in a public space?

Of course, my name was trending too. I was as big a

hypocrite as she was. The Twittersphere couldn't wait for a new blog post. *Well the next instalment of the inside story from the candidate's husband should be a fascinating read @DewhirstBlog.*

I went to my site and started to skim through the posts. *Kirsty is going into this to restore faith in politics. Without that, she'd say, what's the point of this by-election?... Kirsty has never denied her background...'I've had advantages that most people in my community didn't have and that they continue not to have. It's something I can never forget.' That honesty is Kirsty through and through...*

My candidate had let me down. The project was screwed. For a moment I wanted to shut it down – not keep an archive, not save any of the content or any record of visitors, simply obliterate all of it. @DewhirstBlog, RIP.

I didn't. That would have been a cop-out. No, I'd take them all on.

But not yet. I had to wait to find out which direction things were taking with the Inquisition.

**

Gerry wants to know everything and I tell him everything. Not the everything I told Rick, but the everything that the party need to know. I'll have to tell it again, at the meeting later this morning, with someone from London, someone from the media office, someone else, I don't know who, all those people with the best interests of the party at heart. Because there are much bigger things than me at stake. I'm dispensable, like I once told Phil. And in the end, politics is never about an individual. The greater good, always the greater good – Gerry doesn't need to spell it out. If only we could cancel the election, he says, take time out and start again. If only.

But elections are inexorable, he adds. Once called, they run their course. Lies don't stop them. And that's what you're going to be put through the mangle for, Kirsty. Deception. Everyone who believed in you, you've let us all down. What on earth were you thinking… why didn't you mention it… lay your cards on the table, so we could decide whether it was a problem… why didn't you? why? Stop, Gerry, I know, I know.

At one point Jim comes into the room and shakes his head and says, well this is a right royal mess you've got us into, Kirsty. I was once a breath of fresh air, what the country needed. That's what Jim told me when I got the nomination and vain idiot that I was, I believed him. Now the air is foul and I'm surplus to requirements.

It's stifling in here. When Jim has gone and when Gerry and I have been through everything several times over and there's no more to be said, I tell him I'd like to go out. For a breather, a quick drive, the car's round the back where I left it last night, I can get out without being seen. Is that a good idea, he says, driving when you're so distracted? It's fine, driving always settles me. Well, be careful and don't be late back, we want to start on time. I say thanks, Gerry, thanks for your help, this can't be easy for you, and he shrugs and insists there's nothing to thank him for. But I know he's pleased to be rid of me for a while. I'm hard work to be around, a deadweight, I depress everyone, myself included. Last night, with Rick, I felt so sure. I've done nothing wrong. I can get through this. But now I don't know…

I go out and sit in the car and look at social media. No restraint, I read it all, all there is, and I wonder if everyone else has read this, Adam and Rick, of course they have, and my colleagues, my students, the world's seen it. And I let it wash over me, sicken me and cleanse me, wash away my sins, whatever they are. Then I fasten my seatbelt and switch on the engine. A drive. Out of the city. A few miles, maybe more. Gerry was wrong. I have all time in the world.

**

I had an hour to myself in the newsroom that morning, time enough to absorb all the coverage and start to think through the detailed argument for the blog. Then the door opened and Clive walked in. He gawped at me.

'What are you doing here? Didn't you get my text?'

'I've got work to do. A feature to write.'

Would he order me to leave? But he said nothing more and went into his office, slamming the door behind him, the way he did every morning. I tried to turn my thoughts to Oleg – I'd make at least a pretence of working. I started listening to the recording of the interview, jotting down possible quotes, loosely working out how to sew them into a coherent piece. It was less than twenty-four hours since I'd been with Oleg and Tatiana, charmed and amused by them, free from any concerns other than how to whisk up a smart feature. But now, as I heard Oleg's jokes replayed, the humour fell flat, the lauding of Hull and Yorkshire seemed laboured and insincere, the poetry ridiculous. Instead of Tatiana climbing out of the pool, it was Kirsty I saw, Kirsty wearing not a sensible navy swimsuit but naked.

Others were arriving now. Faces registered surprise and then embarrassment. There were double-takes. Rick in the newsroom? A ghost at the feast. Uneasy nods were exchanged and an unnatural quiet infected the place. People lowered their voices and peered intently at their screens. Everyone knew what everyone else was thinking, but no-one said it. Only Mike came up to me.

'Morning, Rick, how you doing?'

'I'm doing okay, thanks.'

He backed away, muttering, 'Well, better get on.'

People started trooping into Clive's office for the morning meeting. They sat around the table, clipboards and tablets in front of them, or they leant against the wall. Occasionally someone stared through the glass in my direction and hastily looked away when our eyes met. Shona wasn't there. She'd be at the Labour offices, awaiting developments. Clive was doing most of the talking. He was stretched out, feet on the desk, hands locked behind his head. At one point the sound of a group guffaw penetrated the glass screen and I was reminded of the intense journalistic pleasure that a really good scandal could generate. I was on the wrong side of the glass. But I'd show them. Just wait till I produced the next blog post.

In the meantime, I turned back to the text on my screen and willed myself to concentrate on the feature. I'd now got a rough outline, but it was a struggle. Nothing flowed. Oleg and Tatiana deserved better. Being here was a mistake, after all.

I got up and several pairs of eyes followed me from within Clive's office. Out in the stairwell, I rang Kirsty's number. There was no reply. She'd be in meetings, her phone turned off. I sent a message. *Thinking of you.* Then I tried Adam.

'Where are you?'

'Still at Jess's. She's gone to work, but her mum said I could stay. She's being really nice.'

'Pop home, Adam, and I'll join you. I'm at the paper but there's no point in staying much longer. I want to talk.'

'What about the cameras?'

'They'll have gone.'

'And Mum?'

'She'll be at the party offices most of the day. I'll pick you up.'

'It's fine. I'll get the bus.'

'Okay, if you're sure–' but he'd already hung up.

Beneath me, I heard the outside door closing. Quick, light footsteps echoed through the stairwell. I looked down over the handrail and saw the top of Shona's neat head bobbing up the steps.

She glanced up at me as she reached the final flight and hesitated, as if I were barring her way. She looked surprised, uncomfortable, like they all did.

'Anything I should know?' I said.

She screwed up her eyes a little, obviously considering whether the question was genuine, a request for information, or painful sarcasm that required no answer. She appeared to decide it was the former and continued up the steps to stand next to me.

'Internal discussions this morning, but you probably know that. We're promised a statement at one.'

'And?'

'I don't know any more. No-one's saying anything yet.'

'Did you see Kirsty?'

'No, but I gathered she was there.'

She released her bag from her shoulder to the floor.

'How is she?' she asked.

Grudges get blown away in hurricanes. Perhaps she really felt sympathy, for both of us. But her feelings weren't relevant. She had once been a friend. Now she just had a job to do.

'She's… as you'd expect,' I said.

'I don't believe it, in case that helps. Not all of it. Crap journalism, really crap.'

Her lips tightened.

'I sometimes wonder whether what we do is… I

mean… we, all of us, the media, when we report things, difficult things… sometimes I think the freedom of the press has a lot to answer for.'

'Well that's good to know, Shona, but I don't think your insights will make one iota of difference to Kirsty.'

She flinched and the lips tightened again.

'I'm sorry, for what I said, you know, about treating me… treating women… like a project.'

'You're allowed your opinions.'

She put out her hand as if to touch my arm, but seemed to change her mind. The hand remained suspended mid-air for a second or two, like an unfinished sentence. Then she slowly lowered it.

'She's tough, your Kirsty. She'll get through this somehow.'

'Maybe.'

She stared at me for a moment, then picked up her bag and said, 'I should go, I'm late for the meeting.'

She turned towards the newsroom, but stopped just before the door.

'You may have heard, but the Barraclough file has gone to the CPS and they could be announcing something today.'

'Great timing,' I said.

She walked towards Clive's office and I returned to my desk, where I vacantly scanned the Oleg piece before saving it, switching off the computer and packing my bag. Behind the glass, Shona was now doing the talking and Clive was listening. He kept shaking his head. At one point, she glanced over at me and I looked away. There'd be a collective sigh of relief when they spotted me going. I picked up my bag and made my way to the door. Those not in the meeting were on the phone, staring at their screens or quietly talking to each other. There was no-one to say goodbye to.

**

I drive further. The city and the rain are behind me. I'm heading north. The A165. The Bridlington road. And then minor roads for a change. Towards the sea. Much further than I meant to go. Phil lives somewhere near here. We came out for a barbecue one Sunday last summer. His partner, Andrew, is a painter. I'd never met him before. Very different from Phil, handsome, vegetarian, no final-salary pension. He said he liked the light out here, near the coast, especially in winter. They seemed happy, a normal life. What do two people ever have in common? How do we know from the outside? We talked about them all the way back, Andrew so hip and Phil so dull, Rick said. I wouldn't call him hip, I said, and you don't know Phil, so don't make superficial judgements.

I think about Phil a lot. He'll get through this, he's steadier than me. I hope they appoint him to the job permanently, they need a period of stability after this. I tried to do my best for the school, making a difference in lots of small ways, maybe that's the best anyone can do. Oh God, I should be there now, there's so much still to do, but they're better off without me, my colleagues, the kids, especially the kids, what could I say to them? If I'd just kept my head down. But it's too late now.

The sun's breaking through and I wind down the window. The air beats against my face and sweeps my mind clean. I like driving, I have no responsibilities, just a steering wheel, an accelerator, a brake. But I'm coming to a crossroad and I have to decide. The hurt comes back. And then the nothingness again. It's a pattern that repeats itself. Aching then nothing. I've let them all down. It was inevitable. Politicians… we're meant to respect them like they're important, but they're rubbish… year 11, citizenship, which one of them came out with that? Out of the mouth of babes, Phil said. I'm rubbish and the shame stings. Even my son won't speak to me. My baby.

I've stopped in a lay-by to look at my messages and see if there's one from him. There isn't. Lots of messages. But none from Adam.

**

I spotted Adam on the main road just before Maple Avenue, canvas bag across his body, collar turned up against the insistent drizzle, shoulders hunched. He must have walked from the bus stop. I had no idea where Jess lived. We'd offered her a lift home after the Italian restaurant a few weeks ago, but she'd insisted on getting the bus.

I pulled up alongside him and opened the passenger window.

'You look wet. Get in.'

He seemed to hesitate. Maybe he was going to decline. But then he opened the door.

'How was work?' he asked, fastening his seat belt.

'Difficult.'

'Why did you go?'

'I had a feature to write.'

His usually carefully gelled hair had unfurled in the damp and it stuck to his forehead in a limp fringe. He looked like a little boy. I saw that photo of the young Kirsty again. Adam always had her eyes, dark and quick, but there was something else as well, that occasional look of defiance, that determined furrowing of the brow that was often part of her resting, neutral expression. Not that any of that had been there when I'd left her a few hours earlier. No defiance, just defeat.

He caught my gaze and turned his head away from me. We got out of the car without speaking and I looked around territorially, searching for any remaining signs of the morning's intrusion. Footprints crossed the shrub border, daffodils had been trampled and disposable coffee cups littered the drive. I picked them up and spotted a couple more under the hedge. That was what a media scrum amounted to – rubbish strewn around your front garden. I slotted the cups into each other and followed Adam into the house.

'D'you want a coffee?' I closed the front door behind us.

'No. I had a couple with Jess's mum earlier. She's been really nice.'

'You said.'

He sat down heavily on the hard chair in the corner of the sitting room, the same chair that Kirsty had sat on hours before, with her head in her hands as she prepared to tell the story. Now Adam was sitting on it, steadily shaking his head.

'Dad… I just don't get it. How could she?'

'She was young and broke. People do desperate things. They make mistakes.'

'But not like that. Mum never does anything wrong… Dad, she was…' – he seemed to be searching for the right words – '… a sex worker.'

'An escort, not a sex worker.'

'What the fuck, Dad. The same difference. A sex worker.'

The all-encompassing modern term. It sounded matter-of-fact in his mouth. One dull job rather than another. Office worker, shop worker, care worker, sex worker. Routine work with an hourly rate of pay. Was there any point in trying to explain to him Kirsty's convoluted distinction? Hardly. I certainly wasn't going to tell him that I agreed with him, although, if anything, I preferred the term 'prostitute'. There was something dignified about 'prostitute', something ancient, mythological, biblical, with its threat of damnation but always potential redemption.

But that wasn't a thought to share with my son, either. He sat tapping his foot against the floor and repeatedly combing his fringe back with his fingers, willing it to sit back on his head. Nervous energy crackled off him.

'Have you seen Twitter? And Instagram? Have you seen them? Have you seen what people are saying about her? Have you?'

'Yes, Adam, I have.'

'Well? Doesn't it bother you? People saying those things about your wife, my mother? How can you just sit there and…'

His voice throbbed with frustration – frustration directed at me for my complacency, my apparent failure to appreciate the enormity of this. His outrage was exhausting.

'Well, yes, of course it bothers me. And some of it needs reporting to the police.'

'And then the messages I've had from mates. People I know. Messages to me personally. You've not seen those. People think it's hilarious. They think they can say whatever they like. Does she still do it? Am I sure who my dad is? What's it like having a whore for a mum? It's filthy… disgusting.'

'Ignore it, Adam. People write things they'd never say to your face.'

'Ignore it? Ignore? I can't ignore it… I mean, the sort of men… and the dangers, the health risks. STDs, HIV. Jesus Christ, Dad, it's just so stupid, however skint you are. Jess saw it before I did and texted me. She'd been so nervous about meeting Mum the other week. And then this. I didn't know what to say to her. My mum… what was I meant to say?'

His chin dropped to his chest, his words spent, and I felt a flash of irritation at his ego. I wanted to tell him this wasn't about him. But the world is about you when you're eighteen. He couldn't help himself.

'Things aren't looking good for your mother,' I said. 'When I dropped her off at the party offices this morning, she seemed absolutely broken. She's convinced she's lost the election.'

Adam jumped up from his seat with an aggression that startled me.

'Of course she's lost the fucking election. Who's going to vote for her now? Sex worker, former sex worker, who cares?'

'Adam…'

'A liar. An idiot who thought lying was okay. Asking people to trust her, vote for her. All that crappy stuff she came out with about restoring faith in politics.'

'Adam, please.'

'She's a hypocrite, a fraud. And a slut.'

I grabbed his arms and shook him. I'd never laid a finger on him before – neither of us had, of course we hadn't – but now I wanted to hit him, to hurt him. My hand tingled with the anticipation of thrashing him. But I needed him on my side. He had to appreciate how hard I was working to get us all through this, how fragile the situation was. I eased the shaking and looked into his/Kirsty's face. He had made no attempt to brush me off, but stood still, as if to say, come on then, do what you have to do, I no longer care.

I released his arms and took a couple of steps back. There were tears in his eyes.

'She was distraught when you wouldn't speak to her,' I said. 'And this morning she was talking about not wanting to be here.'

'What?'

'Oh, I don't know, that wasn't quite what she said. Disappear. That's how she put it. She wanted to disappear.'

'What… did she mean?'

'I don't know, Adam. I'm worried.'

He sat down and remained still for several moments, his head bent. He needed to think and I let him. Then he looked up and the lines furrowed deeper into his forehead.

'Can't you do something? I'm not forgiving her, but can't you just do something?'

'She's not always been the strongest, your mother. I've tried all the way along to help her. Things have been difficult for a while, you don't know half of it. But the woman who sold the story…'

'What woman?'

Maybe I shouldn't have said anything, but I needed to get the right version of events out there, in case, just in case, anything emerged later.

'A… a former colleague of your mother's, if that's the right word. She turned up a few weeks ago, and–'

'You knew about Mum all the time, then?'

'No, no, I didn't know who the woman was. But she was bothering your mother, demanding money, stalking her. And I–'

'You knew…'

An open mouth, accusing. I had to correct a few facts.

'No, all I knew was that this witch was stalking her. I didn't know why.'

'Why didn't you stop her, go to the police, whatever?'

'That's what I'm trying to explain. I confronted her when she came to the house.'

'Here?'

'Yes, here. I made it very clear to her that she had to leave Kirsty alone, that her behaviour wasn't on. She got very abusive, shouting, spitting, making a complete nuisance of herself. It was shocking. Then she tripped – I mean, she could barely stand up, she was out of her mind on whatever – and she accused me of hitting her. Nonsense, of course, but that's when she got really nasty.'

Adam sat motionless, unblinking. He seemed to be barely breathing.

'And after that she went to the papers?'

'No, no. No, that'd been her plan from the beginning, no doubt about that, though I didn't know at the time. That evening I did the only thing I could do. I gave her an ultimatum – stop the stalking or I go to the police.'

I paused.

'Look, there's no need to mention this to your mother.'

'She doesn't know?'

'Well… no, and we don't want to give her anything more to worry about.'

'No danger of that. I'm not talking to her, am I?'

He got up.

'I'll be in my room.'

His steps trod heavily up the stairs and his door shut with a bang, an instruction to leave him alone.

My phone buzzed. A missed call, while I was talking to Adam. And a text message.

> *I just want to say thank you for the lift*
> *this morning. And sorry again. Tell*
> *Adam I love him. Not long now, K.*

**

It's so fresh out here and the wind's so strong. I pull my woolly hat down tighter and the ends of my scarf flare up against my face. We used to come here when Adam was younger, the three of us, a family, small but perfectly formed, Rick always said. Three, an odd number, four might have been better. But we walked and didn't mind the wind and sometimes we flew a kite. Brilliant Sundays, almost carefree, the nearest I've ever got to not worrying about anything. The kite we had was red and orange with a fluttering tail, and one weekend Adam managed to let go of it and it floated off, up and over the cliff and out to sea, getting smaller and smaller. He sulked all the way home, but I said we'd get another one, though I don't think we did. And then we seemed to stop coming, I can't remember why, I expect I was working too much on weekends and there was never time. Maybe I've always worked too much and now I'm worn out. Drained. It should have been different. You do the thing that feels right at that moment, the thing that should, could, bring about the greatest good. You can debate the pros and cons endlessly, but it makes no difference, in the end it's a gut thing. You take a risk and sometimes you lose. Is that what I am, a failed gambler? Gamblers always lose in the long run, I should have known that. Perhaps if I'd worked out the odds a bit more carefully, I'd be sitting in my office now, catching up on everything, making plans for the new term. Rick said I could go back to that, the quiet life, the same but different. I don't know whether he really believed that, but it doesn't matter, the governors won't have me back. I'm no role model for kids after this. Not even a disgraced MP, a disgraced non-MP who lied and lost a safe seat.

I rang him just now, I don't know what I was going to say, but I rang and he didn't answer, so I sent a text. *Sorry*. I'm sorry for some things but not others, I should have said. He must have been busy at work, or, God, please not writing another blog. Why didn't I stop that at the outset? I told myself it kept him happy, occupied, and it didn't seem to be doing any harm. But it was always ridiculous, making out I was some kind of political saint. And now what will he say? He got that wrong? Rick doesn't easily admit to mistakes.

I should be going back, to face them all, to give them an honest account. The meeting will start precisely on time in ninety minutes, Jim will make sure of that. There'll be a table with them one side – they'll all be men – and me on the other. They'll pummel me into the ground and then when that's done they'll have to decide whether to wash their hands of me, or come up with some compromise, invent some new lie that we all have to tell.

But now I don't know if I can do it, if I can go through all that. Rick doesn't think I can, he thinks I'm too weak, I can't survive this, and I'm beginning to believe him.

**

I looked again at that sparse text from Kirsty. *Not long now*. Not long? Until the meeting? Is that what she meant? The phone buzzed again. Another message. Gerry.

Is Kirsty with you? We want to start soon.

What?

I rang him.

'No, she's not with me. Why should she be? Isn't she

with you?'

'She went out over an hour ago. Said she was going for a quick drive. To clear her head before the meeting. Promised she wouldn't be long. But everyone's here and we thought we could start early.'

I rang her. Engaged. I left a message. *Where are you? Call me.* I started to comb through possibilities. She must have lost track of time. She was distracted, things churning over in her mind, on the edge. Perhaps she'd gone too far, got lost, got stuck in traffic somewhere. Or had an crash, not concentrating, the Mini a write-off. I rang the police to check for accidents. Nothing. Did I want to report a missing person? Being late for a meeting didn't turn her into a missing person. Maybe she just couldn't face it, the judgement of the party's inquisitors, presenting herself to the press and the world. Maybe she'd just… just disappeared.

I skimmed a mental address book. Was there anyone else she might call? She'd been in regular contact with Phil throughout the campaign, trying to lead from a distance, doing two jobs at once, not letting go. And maybe now it was working the other way round, Phil advising her. It was Phil, after all, to whom she'd first confessed her by-election hopes – her colleague, not her husband. That still niggled.

I swiped through my phone contacts and dialled from the landline, leaving my mobile free for Kirsty. Phil would be in school, in his office, working, just like she used to be. He picked up.

'As a matter of fact, she did ring, about half an hour ago.'

'Where was she?'

'I didn't ask. Rick, is everything okay? I mean, I know it's not okay, but…'

'She's due at a meeting and no-one seems to know

where she is.'

'She rang to see how things were, like she does every day. I didn't expect her to, not today, but she did. I tried to ask her… but she didn't want to talk… I guessed she'd been told not to. I just wanted her to know that I'm a friend and whatever trouble…'

His voice trailed off.

There had been a time when I'd wondered… a time when she'd been in the job about a year and she and Phil seemed to have too many late-night phone calls. Work calls, but even so. I watched and listened. Of course nothing came of it and eventually I knew I was wrong, wildly wrong. Phil wasn't interested in women. And even if he had been, he was mind-numbingly dull. But the closeness continued, an unhealthy closeness.

Still, I could forget Phil. He was irrelevant. I tried Gerry again, a now very tetchy Gerry.

'No, she's not back. Where the hell is she? You must have some idea where she'd go. And why's she not answering her phone?'

'She rang the acting head at Phoenix half an hour ago.'

'What's she doing worrying about the bloody school? We need her here – now. There's a little problem to sort, in case you haven't noticed. And quite frankly things don't look good.'

'I can help. With the blog, I mean. I can–'

'Don't you dare, Rick. Just keep out of it. This is about the party's reputation – and damage limitation.'

And about Kirsty, I could have added. My vulnerable wife, a small omission in their crisis management. I put the phone down and fizzled at the injustice of it. Gerry was meant to be her guardian angel and really he didn't give a shit. I was the only one who could steer her through this and I needed to take charge. I paced through the house, went upstairs, my eye on my phone, restless, thinking. Adam's bedroom door was still firmly closed. I hesitated outside, my knuckles clenched, ready to tap a request for entry. Perhaps we could work out something together. But his voice from inside, his phone voice, stopped me and I dropped my hand. 'Imagine how you'd feel if it was *your* mum all over the internet… Oh, Jess, what am I going to do? It's all so fucking shitty.'

The moment wasn't right. Later.

Further along from Adam's room, the door to Kirsty's study was open. I stood on the threshold. It was a good-sized room, dominated by a large window looking out onto the back garden, a light room, buttery yellow in colour. She'd painted the walls herself, over a couple of nights soon after we'd moved in. The rest of the house was white throughout, but she said she wanted somewhere cheerful to work. After a while it had started to look sallow and she said yellow might have been a mistake. But she'd never got round to having it repainted.

I stepped inside. The wall to my left was lined with bookshelves. Opposite, next to the radiator, stood an old grey metal filing cabinet. She'd bought it in a north London junk shop and had rejected my frequent requests to replace it with something that didn't jam every time she tried to open it. In the centre, two tables were arranged at right angles. On one sat her computer, festooned with post-it notes, wires trailing to the overloaded extension lead. On the other table were piled books, files, pens, loose papers – some work-related, others old bank statements or utility bills.

There was also a small dark blue photograph album open on the table. The Adam album. It had been Kirsty's idea to take a photograph of Adam every year on his birthday, and put them all in a single album, one year per page, a measured record of his life. The first one was taken on the day of his birth, as he lay against Kirsty's breast, his hair still damp and matted, his eyes mere slits in a rubbery screwed-up face, his tiny fist almost jammed into his mouth. I turned over the pages and saw Adam transformed from ugly baby to toddler to child to confident teenager. Our son's looks had definitely improved with age. A handsome about-to-be-medical student beamed out of the most recent photograph, amused by his mother's insistence that he adopt the same looking-direct-at-the-camera pose every year.

I put down the album and sat in the swivel chair in front of the computer. I pressed the spacebar and the screen came to life, inviting me to enter a password. We knew each other's passwords, of course. There'd be times, if I was at home and she was working late, when she'd ring and get me to check something, perhaps a document stored on her hard drive. Now I entered the eight digits and felt only the lightest trickle of guilt.

I looked first at the separate Labour Party address she'd been given for the by-election. There was nothing since yesterday lunchtime, before the news broke. She had ceased to exist officially.

I switched to her personal emails. This account was inundated. She'd never been very good at clearing it. I scrolled through. There were lots of exchanges with Phil and some with the chair of governors. Kirsty ended most of her messages by saying she was sorry for not being on hand and they could ring her any time they needed to speak.

But I was really looking for something from Marie. There was nothing. They wouldn't have communicated by email. Blackmailers don't send emails. I went on scrolling up and down, checking I'd missed nothing significant. There was one sent message from late last night – it must have been just before we'd gone to bed. I opened it.

> *Dear Adam*
>
> *I know you can't forgive me. And there can be no excuse for what I've done. I'm ashamed of the deceit and the mess I've created. I've let us all down. I'm sorry.*
>
> *Thank you for all you did to help me with the election. We did some great work on the campaign trail and I'm really proud of you. I'm just sorry for making it end like this.*
>
> *With all my love*
>
> *Mum.*

Making it end like this. I closed it quickly and tried to phone her again. Still no reply. I looked through the rest of her files again for anything, personal notes, clues, signs. There was nothing, just work and more work. Perhaps there'd be something handwritten, a journal maybe, chronicling moments and moods, days of depression or elation. I riffled through the drawers under the desk, through files piled higgledy-piggledy on the shelves. But there wasn't anything and I didn't expect there to be. She always said keeping a diary was a vanity project for people planning on cashing in on their memoirs. You remembered the important things. The rest wasn't worth holding onto.

I returned to her computer and looked at her recent search history. She'd opened one document a couple of times. *UK Parliamentary by-elections – Guidance for candidates and agents.* What guidance could it possibly have offered her at that stage? Didn't she know all this stuff? I skimmed through. *Completing your nomination papers… The deposit… Appointing your election agent… Withdrawing… Death of a party candidate…* I stopped and read two short, legalistic paragraphs.

> *1.107. If the Returning Officer receives proof and is satisfied before the declaration of result that a candidate standing on behalf of a political party (or as a joint candidate standing on behalf of two or more parties) has died, the election is stopped immediately. If the poll is under way or the count is being undertaken, that process stops. There will be a new election.*
>
> *1.108. No new nominations are required: all the existing candidates remain nominated for the new election and retention or return of the deposit is determined by the result at the new election. No new nominations are allowed for the new election, except that a new candidate can be nominated to stand on behalf of the same party (or parties) of the candidate who died.*

Had Gerry suggested she look at this? I could imagine his matter-of-factness. Before the meeting, Kirsty, just make sure you're familiar with the election rules. Our hands are tied. It's up to you now. And the words on the screen were unambiguous in the way that legal documents always are, all caveats listed, no hanging threads. *There will be a new election… a new candidate can be nominated…* The only thing that can halt an election is the death of a party candidate. How convenient that would be for everyone, and Kirsty knew it.

I closed the Electoral Commission website and grabbed my phone. This was now serious, more so than

I'd realised. 999 or 101? Definitely 999. Kirsty was in danger and the fuckers in the party were trying to keep me out of things while they sorted matters to suit themselves.

**

Just a short walk further along the clifftop. April and it's still freezing out here. The wind takes your breath away. I walk head down, a few feet away from the edge. Down there, out of sight, the North Sea's buffeting the rocks, rhythmically, endlessly, but in the distance there's that still point where the grey-blue sea meets the blue-grey sky. I don't know where I'm looking, towards the Netherlands or Denmark? It doesn't matter. A big, mainly white bird swoops over my head and dives down towards the sea. An enormous gull of some sort. Or a gannet or a kestrel or a guillemot. For all I know, it could be an albatross. Isn't that meant to be bad luck? Some poem, I should remember, Rick would know.

Calls, so many calls, I didn't think I'd get a signal out here, but I do. I've switched it to silent but I can feel the vibrations in my pocket, against my hip. I take it out to turn off completely and as I do, there's a name on my screen. Jess. For an instant it means nothing, and then it comes back and I feel bad, I haven't spoken to her since I helped her with those forms, I should have found time to call, at least asked Adam, did she get anywhere with the grant applications? Kirsty Osmond, I say, and there's a small gasp as if she's not expecting me to answer. Oh, she says, it's Jess here, Adam's girlfriend, I hope you don't mind me ringing but I just… I just wanted to say I think you're very brave and the media are disgusting. I don't read the papers but it's all over my feed and it's sick and you should ignore it. There's a pause. She's nervous.

She must have practised what she wanted to say, but now it's all coming out in a rush and it's Jess that's being brave, not me. I remember what you said when you and Adam's dad took us to that restaurant, what you said about things being hard when you were young, but I never dreamt that's what you meant, and I think it's just amazing that you've got where you have. There's a little shudder in her voice and I say that's very kind of you and I try to give her time to catch her breath, but she says, oh no I mean it, I really do. I've never thought about voting, wasn't sure if I ever would, I'm sorry, I don't mean to offend, but I didn't see the point, didn't even know my mum had put my name down. But, well, I'm obviously going to now, aren't I? Honestly, Mrs Osmond – oh, call me Kirsty – honestly, Kirsty, I hope you win and so does my mum. Thank you again, I say. Is Adam with you? No, he's at home, your place, and he's still in a bit of a state to be honest, upset like. I mean he's a lad, he doesn't always get things, but he'll be okay. You're his mum and – she sounds embarrassed – and, well, he loves you, you should call him. I'll do that, I say.

I walk back to the car and tap out a text to Gerry. *I'll be back before 11. Sorry, drove further than I meant to.* Then I see a voice message from Shona and I listen. 'Just ringing to say good luck with everything. And this may sound hypocritical, but I want to apologise on behalf of the media. It's wrong what's happened… Anyway, at least the CPS have come out with the right decision on your predecessor, and I hope that's what he is, I mean that you're the next MP and that… well, as I say, good luck.'

What have the CPS decided? I'm about to look but a text message catches my eye.

From Janet McConnell.

Dear Kirsty, Don't let the buggers get you. Best, Janet.

PS: Great news about Barraclough. Justice will prevail!

**

'Yes, I want to report a missing person, my wife, in fact…'

I was through to the police operator and my pulse was rocketing.

'I have reason to believe she's done, may be about to do, something very stupid… while the balance of her mind… yes… she's a vulnerable person.'

I gave them her name – spelling it out very carefully, as if she wasn't now the most famous missing person in the country – and gave her car reg, and Gerry's details too. The sooner they interrogated him and the whole bloody national executive, too, the better. They'd have someone round to see me shortly, they said.

I slumped into the chair there in her room, my late wife's room. Was this it then? After twenty-five years, alone, a grieving widower? Politics was a filthy business and she'd done the party's dirty work for it, a heroine of sorts in the most wrong-headed way. Soon there'd be police on my doorstep, two officers, a man and a woman no doubt, with the inevitable news. 'I'm very sorry to have to tell you…' And we'd go to the mortuary to identify her, Adam and me – I wouldn't want to let him out of my sight – it would be just a formality, the police would know it was her from the party card in her pocket, but I'd sit in the back of the police car on the way there, next to Adam, praying it would be someone else. But it would be her, still and cold, her broken body under a white sheet, her hair caked with blood, the back of her head hidden, her face unscathed. I'd touch her cheek and then the old half-moon scar above her eye and want to take her home, to have her all to myself. I'd be dried up, unable to shed any tears, but Adam would be crying in small, shocked gulps. I'd put my arm round his shoulder and he'd try to resist me. And he'd say, 'It's my fault, I wouldn't speak to her, I killed her.' And I'd assure him he didn't, that none of us could have known this would happen. And later, after several weeks of police investigation, the coroner would return an open verdict, but no-one would be fooled and the press would continue to speculate. *Disgraced politician's mysterious death.*

'Dad, what are you doing?'

I swivelled round in the chair, the thoughts disintegrating. He was standing in the doorway, accusingly.

'Nothing. I'm just… Adam, I have to talk to you. I don't know how to explain this but–'

'Forget that. Look at the news. It's Mum.'

I turned back to the computer. It wasn't Kirsty, at least not at that moment, but old footage of Barraclough and a news presenter's voice. *'The former Shadow Home Secretary Martin Barraclough is to be charged with rape. The Crown Prosecution Service has announced he's to face four counts of rape and six other counts of sexual assault. Mr Barraclough resigned in February as Labour MP for North Humberside. Meanwhile the Labour candidate in the by-election race to succeed him today faces questioning by the party over newspaper allegations that she worked in the sex industry as a student. Over now live to our reporter in Hull…'*

The reporter stood where I'd dropped Kirsty a few hours earlier.

'Kirsty Osmond, the Labour candidate at the centre of these latest allegations, has now arrived at the Labour party offices here behind me – through a back door, we gather – and a meeting with local and national representatives of the party is about to begin. With just thirteen days to go to the by-election, Labour has a crucial decision to make about whether it continues to back the

candidate who promised to restore trust to politics…'

It seemed I was not a widower, but still the Labour candidate's husband. At least until the meeting was over, when I'd be the ex-Labour candidate's husband.

**

I've made it back. Tight, but I've made it. One small hold-up when I was flagged down by police on the outskirts of Hull. Speeding? I should have been careful, even if time was against me. But no, it wasn't that. They asked if I was Kirsty Osmond – odd, how would they know my name? – and where was I going, and they'd had a report that I was a missing person. That's ridiculous, I said, I'm on my way to a meeting at the Labour Party's offices and if you don't mind I'm in a hurry. And they offered to drive there with me, even odder, but at least it got us there on time. I was embarrassed arriving with a police escort, but I parked in the yard and went in the back entrance, away from the journalists, and I don't think anyone spotted my new celebrity status.

Gerry's here. Where on earth have you been? Just a drive, but like I said, I went further than I meant. I hope I haven't kept everyone waiting. He adjusts his glasses and humphs in that Gerry way and says well let's not mess around anymore, they're in there. I was somehow expecting a courtroom, judge and jury waiting for me, but it doesn't feel like that, it's just a room I know well, a table spread with coffee mugs and phones, someone with a laptop, a pile of newspapers on the floor. Much to my surprise I can breathe. I've been to the edge, almost the edge, and back, and everything looks different when you retrace your steps, facing the opposite direction. I have a story to tell, the formal account, an apology to make, it all seems straightforward now. Jim stands up and moves a chair into place for me and introduces those I don't know, someone from the national executive – a woman, yes a woman – and the comms person from London, another woman, and he says we want first to hear from you, Kirsty, fully, the facts, and then we'll have to ask you to step outside while we have a separate discussion. The comms woman says we need to have a press statement ready by one, a really clear declaration of our position, we've got to close down speculation. Jim says well let's get on with it then, and in a way that's all I've ever wanted to do, get on with it.

**

I spent the next two hours in front of my computer screen, riveted to rolling news, jumping between Sky and the BBC. A statement was expected at one, that's what Shona had said. I didn't want to miss it. Kirsty hadn't returned any of my calls or messages, but she was busy now. I'd go and collect her as soon as it was all over and bring her home – she shouldn't drive, not in the state she'd be in. We'd start our lives afresh. Perhaps I'd put out a statement of my own, on behalf of both of us, with a subtle dig at the party for their hopeless mishandling of the whole situation and a dignified request that the media now respected our privacy, the usual thing people said in these circumstances – well, normally after some family tragedy, but this was not that dissimilar. And then the blog, the first post from the ex-candidate's husband, a finely constructed essay extricating myself from the whole unsavoury mess.

At one-fifteen, the news channel I was watching switched to what looked like a hastily arranged press conference. Jim Prodham was fidgeting with a sheaf of papers in front of him, Kirsty next to him, pale but composed, a woman on the brink of submission. I tried to beam my support into the screen and beyond. A spot of telepathy, that's what was needed. Keep it brief, Kirsty. Bow out gracefully. Leave the rest to me.

Prodham cleared his throat and glanced up from his notes.

'Thank you everyone for coming along.' He paused. 'The past twenty-four hours have seen an extraordinary and vile attack on the Labour candidate in next week's by-election here in North Humberside. We will be referring some of the media coverage to the Independent Press Standards Organisation and to Ofcom. We have also reported a number of incidents of online hate crime to the police.'

Another pause as he consulted his notes.

'I want to make it very clear that the Labour Party – locally and nationally – is continuing to back Kirsty Osmond as its candidate. And I mean fully back her, as someone we are proud of – a woman who had a difficult start in life, who was exploited as a teenager and pressed into something she has since come to profoundly regret, a woman who understands what it is to be desperate, a woman who has come through all of that. Kirsty Osmond is a strong survivor who will make a great job of representing the ordinary men and women of this constituency, and her party is fully behind her. I'll hand over now to Kirsty herself.'

She was… carrying on? I felt vaguely queasy. Jim was nodding at her and she gave him a brisk nod in return, her face tight. She had no notes.

'Thank you, Jim.'

Only three words, but the tone was worryingly confident.

'I want first of all to apologise for failing to reveal some personal details when I was selected as Labour

Party candidate five weeks ago. This was a mistake and I am truly sorry.'

She half-turned to Jim and he nodded again. Then she looked back straight out into her audience, an audience of, what? hundreds of thousands, millions even?

'Thirty years ago, I worked very briefly for an escort agency while I was at university in Leeds. I was eighteen, naïve, and exploited. But I won't avoid the term, I was a sex worker. I was not receiving a full university grant – it was grants not loans in those days – and I had no family support. That is no excuse, I know. It was a very bad decision for me personally and one I have lived to regret. I don't condemn other women – and men – who, for whatever reasons, go into sex work, nor, in some cases, the individuals who seek their services. The exploitative industry behind them is a different matter and one that I hope a future Parliament will take action to control.'

Exploitation? Hadn't that been what I'd said – exploitation, grooming – and she'd said, oh no, she'd known what she was doing? The party might have suggested something similar, but really it was my idea. Nicked and not credited. And the hair-splitting over escort or sex worker, that seemed to have gone too. Everything I'd pointed out to her.

She went on, the maddening beginnings of a smile on her lips, a single-minded, business-like smile.

'The past twenty-four hours have been very difficult for me. But they have not altered my resolve. I have a by-election to win. My aim over the next thirteen days is to ensure we return a Labour MP to represent this constituency and beyond that to fight to improve the lives of ordinary people and to defeat the Tories at the next general election. Thank you.'

She stood up as if she intended to get on with the fighting straightaway. The journalists were interrupting each other with their questions and Prodham was struggling to control them. The programme left them to return to the studio presenter for a reminder of the circumstances of the by-election and the obligatory other-candidates-are-available addendum.

And I was left staring at my screen, as the presenter moved on to the next story. What had happened to the broken woman I had delivered to the Labour offices several hours earlier, a woman unseated on the final lap, on the verge of a breakdown, utterly dependent on me? She had remounted her horse and was riding on, it seemed. And without any consultation with me. Madness. What had they done to her? Had they coerced her? Political grooming, almost as bad as the other sort. And the party's own stance – why hadn't I seen it coming?

Slowly it dawned on me. ...*a woman who understands what it is like to be desperate, a woman who has come through all of that. Kirsty Osmond is a strong survivor...* that was the line I should have taken, what I, the candidate's husband, should have written. Prodham had slathered it on rather thickly, but the basic messaging was good. He'd never struck me as someone with a way with words, though no doubt he was reading notes written for him by some inventive comms hack. This was political expediency with a poetic voice. Silver-tongued and showy. I'd let these Machiavellian schemers in the party beat me to it. The bastards.

I heard Adam running down the stairs, his voice on the phone – 'Mum, it's me, can you talk? I just want to say...' – and then the front door slammed behind him. I had some thinking to do, some adjustments to make.

This is it, then. I've thought that before, but this really is it. The culmination of everything that's happened over the past two months. The ballot boxes have all been emptied and now it's up to the count teams systematically checking the Xs. It looks like a post office sorting room with thousands of messages being delivered from the electorate of North Humberside to the whole country. I love this part of the process, all passion spent, just piles of paper and numbers. Every single vote does count. I wish Jess could see things here and know that her vote's somewhere in those piles.

I've seen quite a lot of her over the last two weeks. She's joined the party, still waiting for her card, but she's come out canvassing with us a few times when she wasn't working. And Adam hasn't missed an evening. There've been some difficult encounters on the doorstep. Some people have strong views, I was ready for that. But there's been warmth, too, and more doors opening than usual. As Adam said, this is 2018 not 1918, what do you expect? I wasn't sure what to expect, that was always the problem. We've talked now, I just had to find time to do that, and we've both forgiven each other, awkwardly but honestly. He's grown up a lot in the past fortnight. And he's quiet at times, he's still thinking, I understand that.

I wanted him with me as my guest at the count tonight, my son, so he could see the process through, experience the finale. But Gerry said it should be Rick, it would look odd if I arrived without my husband. Partners were always there for the declaration. Everyone expected it. So he's here. The candidate's husband. Ready to share my moment of triumph. Not that we've had much to say to each other all night and now he's wandered off to talk to the journalists.

Adam rings. How much longer? he asks. Hard to tell, I say and glance at the big clock on the wall. We've been here more than three hours. Soon, I hope. Adam says he's ready to party through the night, but I tell him it's not over till it's over.

Then Gerry comes up and says the returning officer wants us all together, candidates and agents. He's got the provisional numbers, and mine's big, over twenty-four thousand, bigger than we expected. Gerry gives me a slow-burning smile. He seems lighter, a weight off him, like he's shed a heavy outer skin. But the Green candidate wants a recount, she's only three votes short of keeping her deposit. Fair enough, I'd do the same. It's not over till it's over.

I nearly broke. Two weeks ago. I can see it now for what it was. We're all shaped by events, we wouldn't be human if we didn't react to trauma and loss. The mind bends, there are hairline cracks, it starts to feel as if everything's falling apart. It's happened before, and that was worse, the worst there can be, but I mended then, and I think this has been easier. There's been so much support flooding in, friends, in the party and out, people I don't know telling me how much they get it, women mainly, all those brave women, but some men, too. Phil told me if anyone could get through this, it was me, and the whole school was rooting for me. I'm not sure I quite believe that, but the thought has kept me going. And that morning, out on the cliffs, Jess's call, another thing I can't forget. *I've never thought about voting, wasn't sure if I ever would... But well I'm obviously going to now, aren't I?* It's for others, isn't it? Democratic politics – giving people a say, arriving at decisions in groups, wielding power on behalf of others. You don't do it just for yourself.

I had another call, one I wasn't expecting, the bravest of the lot, the evening after the cliffs, after the press conference. The name flashed up and I didn't want to take it. It was like that call from Barraclough weeks ago, I should have blocked the number. But calls are to be taken, not avoided, I can't turn my back on difficult things. And when I answered it, she started to apologise, over and over. She hadn't dreamt things would turn so bad, it absolutely wasn't what she'd intended. And I asked her what she had intended then. She said she'd come to see me at the hustings just out of interest and when she sensed she was making me uncomfortable she'd left and had no intention of bothering me again. But then that meeting with my husband changed everything. What meeting? I asked, and she seemed surprised that I didn't know. He'd summoned her to the house, apparently, she thought both of us were going to be there, but it was just him. And his manner was aggressive from the start, accusing her of stalking me, threatening to go to the police, and then, she said, he got physical and shoved her. She was really shocked, especially since he said he was acting on my behalf. So after that she no longer felt bound by her promise to me, neither the recent one nor the one thirty years ago. She was already in touch with a journalist about the escort agency campaign and she decided she could now mention my name – it might make the story more interesting for them – and give them a couple of old photos. But when it came out, there was nothing about the campaign, it was all about me. And then everything went a bit crazy – all those moralising twats in the media, as she put it. She was so sorry.

Rick. I confronted him late that night. It was the first time we'd spoken properly since the press conference –

there'd just been one text from him. *Looks like you're pressing on then. Are you sure you can do it?* I'd ignored that. He'd spent twenty-four hours trying to stop me believing in myself. And now we were having this conversation as we were getting into bed, like we'd done so often before. What happened with Marie, I said, you arranged to meet her, why? He tried to change the subject, but I insisted. Just tell me why. And eventually he said, did Adam tell you? No, why would Adam know about that? No, Marie told me herself, she rang me this evening. He was quiet for a moment and I felt cold inside. I was right, she *was* telling the truth. I just couldn't believe what he'd done, interfering, trying to run my life for me. Or had he screwed things up on purpose? And then made me doubt myself? I didn't know what to think, I just wanted him to be open with me. But he got defensive. No need to get excited, he said, all I was trying to do was protect you from that witch, that's all I've ever tried to do, protect you. And I thought, watch the misogyny, Rick, she's behaved far better than you have. The following morning he acted as if nothing had happened and wanted to know if he could rehearse me for media interviews in the final days, and I said no, Rick, I don't want rehearsing.

There've been points over the past two weeks when I've wondered whether it's all over, our marriage, whether it's actually been doomed from the start and it's taken an election to prove it. I'm sure we still love each other, in our own contradictory ways, but I no longer know if that's enough. Perhaps I've always needed more than a lover. God knows what Rick's needed. I fell for him because he was kind and funny and that was more than I'd had from anyone before, but kindness without honesty can be suffocating.

And now? I don't know what I think. Maybe I should have tried to see things more from his point of view, tried to get inside his head. Rick's head? Not an easy place to be, though he'd probably say the same of mine. Maybe I *should* give us another chance. But with some new ground rules – and a little time apart. That shouldn't be difficult to work out once I'm in Westminster. So let me settle in and then we can think things through. I've warned him there are a few things we need to discuss. And meantime we're continuing as normal, pretending everything's fine. Political expediency, his sort of expression. Quite frankly, though, our marriage is not the most important thing on my plate at present. I'm sorry if that sounds unfeeling, but I have to be single-minded.

Gerry's been to check on the recount and he's back now. We're ready to go, he says, the returning officer wants you up there in five minutes. I take a few deep breaths. I have a job to do and everything else in life is secondary. There's a different buzz in the hall, the media folk are scuttling around and the people who've been counting are sitting back, chatting. Rick saunters up and puts an arm round my shoulder. Looks like we've done it then, he says. I never had any doubts.

Oh, yes? I release myself from his arm and walk to the podium.

**

I know I'm here on sufferance. You wanted Adam, not me. Ironically it was Gerry who insisted. Good old Gerry who tried to keep me away from the action whenever he could, now demanding I'm granted my rightful place. No doubt we'll smile for the cameras when the time comes, the happy MP and her husband. But most of tonight you've ignored me. And you know, I've done so much for you, helped to mould your career, created interest and sympathy and beaten the apathy that always dogs an election. Where would you have been without me? I've always been here for you, the patient chief of staff in our uneven marriage, Albert to your Victoria (yes, I know, I know, your republican hackles shoot up at that), controller of our joint destinies, master of the grand scheme. Yet grand schemes drift. Cross-currents come from nowhere and certainties dissolve like sea foam. And now it feels like I'm left washed up on the shore. Jetsam, chucked overboard by Captain Kirsty.

There's a hush in the hall. The returning officer taps his microphone. He's about to speak.

I do hereby give notice that the number of votes recorded for each candidate is as follows... I wait for yours, as you stand perfectly still on the left of the platform... *Kirsty Rose Osmond, the Labour Party candidate. Twenty-four thousand three hundred and thirty-six.*

Impressive. There are cheers and you try to look as though you're surprised. You've increased Barraclough's majority by several thousand. I wonder if he's watching, poor sod. Back at the beginning, you said you felt sorry for him, well almost sorry for him. Perhaps you had a point. On bail till the trial. The beginning of the end of a life.

And my life? Well everything's in abeyance, a temporary state of affairs, I hope. You want to discuss matters, after the election, you said. Funny, it was always me who was keen to get to the bottom of things and you who tried to put me off. Now it's the other way round. And the way you said it, well it did flash through my mind – are you suggesting we're finished? Christ, the ultimate injustice, after all my efforts on your behalf. I just don't get what it is I'm meant to have done. A few missteps, nothing more. No doubt you'll say we're not compatible, never have been. But that's the beauty of our marriage. Who wants to live with a clone of themselves?

There are ways round this, I'm sure of it. I should talk to Adam – if he'll talk to me. Two weeks ago it was you he wasn't talking to, but now it turns out he blames me for what happened. No idea what you've told him, he's been a bit cool of late. Whenever I suggested spending an hour or two together, he said he was busy, out with Mum, the last few days of campaigning, no time. But I'll have to make some attempt soon to get over my side of things.

Shona, too. There's still ground to be made up there. But at least I've said hello to her tonight. She was polite but not very communicative. Someone told me she's got an interview with regional television, for a reporter's job. Good luck to her. She'll eventually realise how much I helped her and I'm sure she'll thank me before she leaves. I must buy her that coffee, perhaps I could even offer her dinner. I always thought we should have got to know each other much better. A few of the others have been paid off early, too. They must have found work somewhere. Clive's going to be producing the final print editions single-handed from the sound of it. Not sure who's left to go on strike. Definitely not me.

The London job offers haven't quite materialised yet. I'm still working on them. And I've been thinking about resuming the blog. The MP's husband, ex-husband, who knows? Perhaps even something entirely incognito. And monetise it somehow. I'm sure I can make it work whichever way. However… the party's lawyers have come on pretty strong. They've suggested there are a number of topics they don't want me touching. Out and out censorship. But they can't suppress free speech. We live in a democracy, don't we? I'll lie low for a while, wait till things calm down.

You've shaken everyone's hands now, the returning officer, your defeated opponents. You exchanged several words with Sarah Clarkson – if only I could lipread. The last time I saw you together, the hotel hustings – remember? – you were ready to crucify her. The game of politics, eh? But there's a lot you've chosen to forget. Including what I did for you. When you have time to reflect, you're going to realise. And yes, you're going to need me when you're at Westminster. You may not know it yet, but you are.

You're at the microphone now, preparing to speak, the new member for North Humberside, wearing that red jacket again, the one I always said was too obvious. Hair, make-up are so-so. You'll do. Breathe deeply, don't gabble, remember what I told you. Smile, above all, smile. Good. Yes, you look the part, wide awake, about to face the world. You're the headteacher on the podium, hundreds of kids in front of you, the triumphant politician, nay-sayers subdued, the dragon-slayer. You take in the whole hall – this is it, winner grabs all – you raise your hands for quiet, the cheers subside. You've done it, haven't you? Turned everything round, pulled off the impossible – or should I say, we've done it, haven't we? Westminster, here we come. You know, we still could make a remarkable team.

Acknowledgements

I'd like to thank all those who helped me turn the germ of an idea into a book, and especially every female politician whom I've interviewed or merely observed from a distance and whose stamina and resilience have astounded me. None of them provided the model for Kirsty, but each of them offered a little bit of inspiration.

More specifically, I'm grateful for the support of my writing buddies, teachers, editors and mentors in reaching the final draft of my first novel. Among those who've helped me on the road to publication are: Tony Chapman (our mutual encouragement of each other's writing continues), Allison van den Hoek and Mariska Martina; Jonathan Gibbs and Sharlene Teo, then at St Mary's University Twickenham, for their critical (at times very critical…) feedback on the first draft; my daughter-in-law Florence Hyde for her insights into the mysterious world of publishing, my son-in-law Paul O'Neill for his design suggestions; my fellow 26 board member Elise Valmorbida for her coaxing and chivvying; my former agent Amy St Johnston then at Aitken Alexander Associates for her perceptive editing help; Maggie Hamand for her initial enthusiasm for my ideas; Sharon Zink for some tough but helpful comments; Cathie Hartigan of the Exeter Novel Prize, together with judge Kate Nash, for pepping me up just when I needed it; and of course my publisher Stuart Debar for his belief in the book and for all his hard work.

Nor should I forget the Society of Authors for all the

supportive new friends I've made through them and for the deft legal advice when it was needed.

I'd also like to thank the City of Hull (if I may thank a place rather than people) for once being my home for three years. I grew to love Hull, although ours was always a subdued romance.

Finally, I must thank my children for letting me borrow their name as my pen name and, above all, my husband Ray Sacks, who for years said to me, 'Why don't you write a novel?' Eventually I ran out of excuses.

SRL Publishing don't just publish books, we also do our best in keeping this world sustainable. In the UK alone, over 77 million books are destroyed each year, unsold and unread, due to overproduction and bigger profit margins.

Our business model is inherently sustainable by only printing what we sell. While this means our cost price is much higher, it means we have minimum waste and zero returns. We made a public promise in 2020 to never overprint our books for the sake of profit.

We give back to our planet by calculating the number of trees used for our products so we can then replace them. We also calculate our carbon emissions and support projects which reduce CO_2. These same projects also support the United Nations Sustainable Development Goals.

The way we operate means we knowingly waive our profit margins for the sake of the environment. Every book sold via the SRL website plants at least one tree.

To find out more, please visit
www.srlpublishing.co.uk/responsibility

www.ingramcontent.com/pod-product-compliance
Lightning Source LLC
Chambersburg PA
CBHW010427170726
48283CB00011B/3095